ATTACK ON THEBES

THE ORION WAR – BOOK 5

BY M. D. COOPER

SPECIAL THANKS

Just in Time (JIT) & Beta Reads

Timothy Van Oosterwyk Bruyn
Lisa L. Richman
Scott Reid
Jim Dean
David Wilson
Marti Panikkar
Mikkel Anderson
Belxjander Serechai
Mannie Killian

Cover Art by Laercio Messias
Editing by Jen McDonnell
Version 1.0.1

TABLE OF CONTENTS

FOREWORD 5
PREVIOUSLY IN THE ORION WAR 8
MAPS 11
DAUGHTER OF AIRTHA 13
THE REMNANT 16
FAREWELL TO SCIPIO 25
MYRIAD CONCERNS 31
AFTERMATH 34
A NEW ASSIGNMENT 38
JUST DESSERTS 48
THE SILSTRAND CLAUSE 54
WINOS AND SLEPTONS 63
THE LONG NIGHT 71
WHEELS WITHIN WHEELS 75
SURVEYING VELA 86
TO KHARDINE 91
THE HUNT 95
UNINTENTIONAL BAIT 102
PRESIDENT SERA 114
NIGHTSHADE 120
SEPTHIA 134
A BIZARRE MEETING 139
THE ROAD HOME 152
THEBES 173
UNEXPECTED GUESTS 179
FALL 198
NOT THE WARM WELCOME... 218
CRASHED 225
THE CAVALRY 230
THREE DAYS 236
REINFORCEMENTS 240
PYRA 251
STEALING A RIDE 255

MARAUDERS..261
GONE TO GROUND..264
DARKEST HOUR...271
ISF FIRST FLEET...278
SAVING HER..285
COMING UP...288
FALLEN..298
THE CARTHAGE..301
THE BOOKS OF AEON 14..309
ABOUT THE AUTHOR...313

FOREWORD

I got to write two words in this book that I've been waiting to write since 2009. I'm certain you'll know them when you see them, and I think you've been waiting to read them as well.

Or maybe you haven't. I've been unintentionally over-subtle in the past. It could be that I've done so again.

In many respects, this book is still the continuation of that singular event that occurred on the bridge of the *Galadrial* when Elena killed Sera's father. That one thing was the catalyst that set in motion every single catastrophe and dire need that's come after.

That's not to say that everything since the president's death wasn't going to happen anyway, but just as the assassination of Archduke Ferdinand set off Earth's first World War, the death of Jeffery Tomlinson has set off the first Galactic War.

As I look over my timeline for all the events that have occurred in the Aeon 14 books—and at those which are yet to come—it's hard to believe that the assassination on the *Galadrial*'s bridge occurred only six months before the beginning of this book.

In fact, everything that occurred in the final chapters of Orion Rising, The Scipio Alliance, and the first three books of the Perilous Alliance Series has happened in the half-year span following Sera's assumption of the Transcend's presidency.

It feels almost surreal. But then again, it's been just over six months since Orion Rising came out, so it's almost as though we're living this in real time—those of us who are writing and reading the books as they come out, at least.

I imagine later readers are bingeing happily on the books, excited to know there is a published resolution down the road.

I bring this up because this book wraps up some threads from previous stories, and pulls a few new ones loose. It also checks in on a few that are dangling about, so be sure to read the "Previously" section below.

Another fun thing that I got to do while writing this book, was to refresh myself on some quantum physics, and chat with some of my physicist consultants about how we're really going to deal with detecting fifth dimensional beings. Suffice to say when the characters talk about branes, wimps, and winos, these are not typos. They're talkin' science!

Parts of this book take place after Collision Course, book 3 of the Perilous Alliance series. That series deals with the fallout of Tanis's sale of her nanotech to S&H Defensive Armaments way back in Destiny Lost. I felt that it was apropos to have that resolution in this book, to tie that together. However, if you wish to have the full story of the mess that made, and how Sera was working to clean it up during the years Tanis was building the New Canaan colony, then I encourage you to read those stories.

For those of you who have been reading the Rika books, the title of this book should ring a bell. If you've not, you may want to read the first three (starting with Rika Outcast) before you dive into Attack on Thebes. You don't have to, but you'll get a bit more flavor as to what is happening in this neck of the woods.

Lastly, it goes without saying, but I'll say it anyway, I had a great time writing this book, and it was awesome to take Tanis to some new places, both locales, and inside of herself.

M. D. Cooper
Danvers, 2018

PREVIOUSLY IN THE ORION WAR…

Attack on Thebes begins to gather some threads together from prior books and we encounter some characters that we've not seen for a while.

While The Scipio Alliance focused very closely on Tanis and her daughters, Attack on Thebes broadens the scope once more to give us a view of what's happening on the larger stage.

At the tail end of Orion Rising, we saw what happened to Adrienne (one of the former president's closest advisors) when he returned to Airtha. His son was killed, and he was captured by Sera…but not the Sera who is allied with Tanis.

Airtha, the AI that was once Sera's mother, has crafted a second daughter. Not a clone, exactly, but another version of her. This second Sera has many of the same attributes, thoughts, and even memories, but she is fiercely loyal to her mother.

When Sera captured Adrienne, his son died in the attack, but his daughter, Kara, got away. Kara ended up being rescued by what is quite possibly *the most* unlikely person: Katrina.

If you have not read the Warlord books, then the last time you saw Katrina was five thousand years ago on the Victoria colony at Kapteyn's Star. However, Katrina had some of her own adventures, and has also made her way to the 90th century.

In this book you'll see more of how that came to pass, and what Katrina and Kara's part to play in this is.

Though the events in Collision Course drew Tanis and the *I2* out of Scipio, this book will start back with Empress Diana and Petra before moving forward to the Silstrand System to deal with the nanotech-related mess there.

Still lying ahead is the retribution Tanis craves for the Trisilieds after they attacked Carthage and killed so many. However, Tanis is now on the hunt for the Caretaker, the mysterious ascended being that left a piece of itself inside Nance, and was also controlling events in Silstrand and beyond…

KEY CHARACTERS REJOINING US

Abby – Wife of Earnest, and former chief engineer aboard the *Intrepid.*

Andrea – Sera's sister who used a back door into Sera's mind to make Sera try to kill Tanis in the Ascella System.

Adrienne – Transend Secretary of State, and close confidant of the former president, Jeffrey Tomlinson.

Cary – Tanis's biological daughter. Has a trait where she can deep-Link with other people, creating a temporary merger of minds.

Corsia – Ship's AI and captain of the *Andromeda*.

Diana – Empress of the Scipian Empire.

Faleena – Tanis's AI daughter, born of a mind merge between Tanis, Angela, and Joe.

Justin – Former Director of the Hand. Was imprisoned for the events surrounding the attempted assassination of Tanis.

Katrina – Former Sirian spy, wife of Markus, and eventual governor of the Victoria colony at Kapteyn's Star—and Warlord of the Midditerra System.

Kara – Daughter of Adrienne, heavily modded with four arms and wings.

Nadine – A Hand agent who had been assigned to assassinate Peter Rhoads and is now aboard the *I2*.

Nance – Former member of *Sabrina*'s crew, now a member of the ISF.

Petra – Regional Director of the Hand's operations in Scipio and nearby territories. Now the Transcend's Ambassador to Scipio.

Priscilla – One of Bob's two avatars.

Rachel – Captain of the *I2*. Formerly captain of the *Enterprise*.

Saanvi – Tanis's adopted daughter, found in a derelict ship that entered the New Canaan System.

Sera of Airtha – A copy of Sera made by Airtha, containing all of Sera's desired traits and memories. President of the Airthan faction of the Transcend.

Smithers – S&H employee Tanis licensed her nanotech to on the PetSil Mining Platform during her first visit to Silstrand.

Terry – Director of the Security Operations Center on the *I2*. A member of Tanis's original SOC team.

Troy – Ship's AI aboard the *Excelsior*. Was on the mission to secure fuel for the *Intrepid* in Estrella de la Muerte and sacrificed himself to save the *Intrepid* in the Battle for Victoria.

MAPS

For more maps, visit www.aeon14.com/maps.

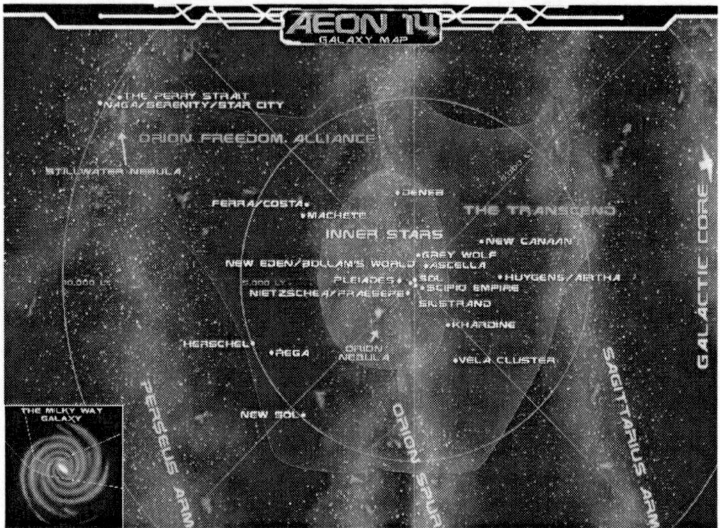

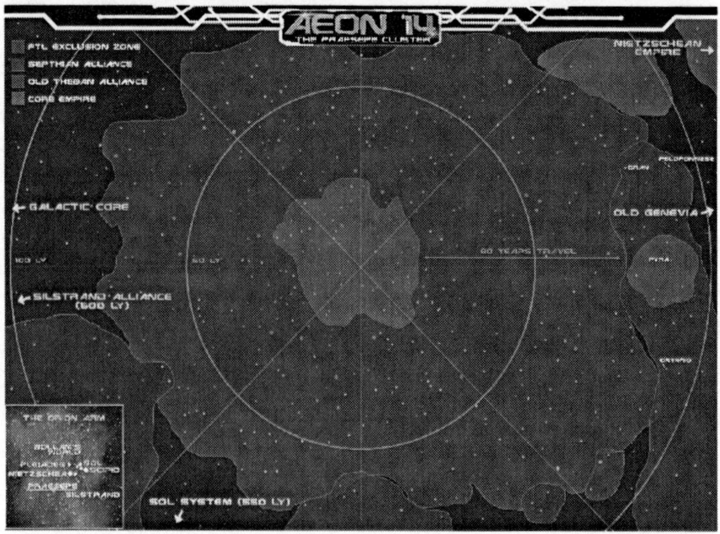

DAUGHTER OF AIRTHA

STELLAR DATE: 08.14.8948 (Adjusted Years)
LOCATION: Airtha Capitol Complex
REGION: Airtha, Huygens System, Transcend Interstellar Alliance

Sera watched Adrienne enter her office, the space so recently occupied by her father, from where the formerly great President Jeffery Tomlinson ineptly ran his great empire.

Adrienne knew he was defeated, knew that Sera controlled him utterly, but still he strode in as though he was the master of all he saw.

She turned away from him, looking out the window at the sweeping arch of Airtha, wrapped around the gleaming white dwarf star. Once, this star-encircling ring had been her mother's body. A prison her father had forced on Justina after she returned from the galaxy's core.

He even stripped her of a name, simply calling her 'Airtha', as though she were just an NSAI whose purpose was nothing more than the management of the structure in which it was installed.

But his efforts to both control his former wife and keep her close had been thwarted.

Mother had ascended.

Airtha was no longer an 'AI', a neural network of physical components constructed out of non-organics. Now she was something more. A being of light that existed in more than the few paltry dimensions that made up the corner of space-time that creatures like Adrienne crawled through.

Granted, Sera also existed in the same narrow sliver of existence, but her mother had given her a glimpse of what lay beyond, the power that existed at her fingertips.

Her mother had gifted her with that vision, and with a piece of herself. Not a shard, but a sliver of self that an AI like Bob might carve off, or like Helen had been.

What she had now was full representation of her mother. Like a thinking memory. She would never be separated from her mother again.

"Surveying your domain?" Adrienne asked as he reached her side. "What little of the Transcend you've managed to claim."

"She's claimed no more than I," Sera shot back, annoyed that Adrienne would open with a critical remark such at that.

Adrienne shrugged. "Perhaps. She has Vela, snatched it out from under you. Admiral Krissy is a formidable opponent on her own."

Sera nodded. "Mother regrets not directing more resources toward Krissy's destruction after the debacle at the Grey Wolf Star. But it was not expected that Finaeus would return and connect Krissy to New Canaan."

"I thought the great Airtha was all-knowing?" Adrienne sneered.

"Do I need to kill more of your children to remind you who is in command here?" Sera asked. "You seem to forget your place with startling regularity."

Adrienne drew himself up to his full height. "My place is beside President Tomlinson. I should never have left it."

"You *are* beside President Tomlinson," Sera replied, giving the man a sidelong look of annoyance.

"I'm beside a shadow of Sera Tomlinson. A puppet created by Airtha. How does it feel to be a puppet, False Sera? Do you have strings?" He waved a hand over her head, a mocking smile on his face.

Sera growled and spun, her hand slamming into Adrienne's throat. Her other hand planting on his forehead, a tendril of nano flowing out of it and connecting to his nerves, lighting them afire.

"Is this false?" she hissed. "Don't think that you can trick me into killing you. I can cause you unending pain without ever doing that."

Adrienne was gasping for air, and she kicked his legs out from under him and let go, dropping the man to the floor.

"You're pathetic, Adrienne."

"And you're unhinged. Unstable," he rasped. "One of these times, you'll do it. You'll kill me, and I'll be free of this prison you've put my mind in."

Sera shrugged. "Perhaps I will. After I'm convinced that you've revealed all your children to me."

The building's NSAI alerted Sera that her guest had arrived, and she turned from the gasping man to greet the newcomer as he approached.

"Ah, General Garza, so glad you arrived safely."

THE REMNANT

STELLAR DATE: 08.15.8948 (Adjusted Years)
LOCATION: Gamma VIII base
REGION: Outer Asteroid Belt, New Canaan System

Cary watched Earnest's eyes grow wide as she walked into his lab in the Gamma VIII base. She still cradled the remnant within her hands, the glowing ball that held the thing that had been inside Nance for so long.

She was accompanied by her father, Saanvi, and two med techs who stood behind the stasis pod that held Nance.

Saanvi had wanted to wake Nance, or to at least try, but their father had insisted that she be put into stasis. His argument was that they didn't know what the thing had done to her. She could be fine, or she could have a trigger nestled within her mind.

There could even be more of the remnant still in her—though Cary didn't think that was the case. She couldn't *feel* any more of it, at least.

"So that's it…a piece of an ascended being," Earnest whispered and gestured toward a table half covered in equipment, standing in the center of the room. "Bring it over here, I want to scan it to see if you need to keep holding it."

"I think she's managed to encapsulate it with magnetically charged membranes," Saanvi offered.

Earnest nodded while not removing his eyes from the sphere in Cary's hands. "Perhaps, perhaps. But if it is a brane, it's a black brane—an M5 at least." He glanced up at Saanvi. "It'd have to be, since this is not a three-dimensional being—though the brane certainly isn't black, is it?"

"All I know is that it hurts my eyes to look at it," Cary said as she leaned on the table. "Though it's funny…it didn't when Saanvi, Faleena, and I were…conjoined."

<*Yeah, it was clear then. I could see it as a…a thing. Now it's just noise.*> Faleena added.

"I feel left out," Saanvi said with a mock pout. "It always just looked like…well, not noise, just a thousand mobius strips, or something."

Earnest slid a porous metal plate under Cary's outstretched hands, and then swung another device over top.

"Spread your hands out a bit more, Cary, so that there's a gap below them."

Cary complied, looking nervously at the device above her hands. "What is that? It looks a bit like a—"

"A gamma-ray gun," Earnest completed for her. "Don't worry, its low power, and very focused. The metal foam below your hands will absorb any residual radiation from the gammas, as well as imaging a 3D representation of the object. It might tell us a bit more about what we're dealing with here."

"What if the brane splits open…? Or whatever they do when they fail." Saanvi had stepped up beside Cary as she spoke and was peering into the orb.

Earnest paused. "Hmm…that could be a problem. Unlikely, but certainly not desirable."

"I'll second that," Joe added. "How do we know it's safe to do this at all? Perhaps you should work on containing it first."

"It *is* contained, Dad," Saanvi said. "Now we need to sort out how to detect them…and contain them without Cary."

"Let's not jump to conclusions, Saanvi." Earnest stroked his chin as he stared at the orb. "For all we know, this is a defensive measure it took to avoid whatever you were going do to it."

"What we were going to do to it?" Cary asked.

Earnest nodded, his eyes still fixed on the orb. "Yes, what were you going to do it?"

<*I wanted to crush it.*> Faleena's tone was sour, and a bit spiteful.

Saanvi pressed a hand to her forehead and nodded slowly "I recall a similar sentiment."

"That's what I was going to do," Cary said. "But then I stopped because I knew that we needed it alive—or whatever. There are probably more of these infesting New Canaan."

Earnest looked up at Cary and Saanvi. "So I'm to assume that you're no longer deep-Linked?"

"Yeah, it didn't seem to be required anymore—the thing stopped fighting, and it's difficult to remain Linked like that for long."

"Well, I'm detecting increased activity in there. You'd better do your thing again, girls. I suspect it's not excited about meeting Mr. Gamma Ray, here, and it may try to break out."

"OK, let's hook up, then." Cary reached out to Faleena and Saanvi, visualizing their minds as spheres of light that she dipped her hands into and then drew toward herself.

Earnest's eyes narrowed. "Are you Linked?"

"We are."

Cary-Saanvi-Faleena watched the writhing mass within the sphere coalesce into a recognizable shape once more. She didn't know what the shape was, no words came to mind to describe it, but she could see its edges, make out filaments.

"You ready?" Earnest asked.

Cary glanced back at her father, who nodded.

"Might as well get it over with," he sighed.

"Do it," Cary-Saanvi-Faleena said.

Earnest activated the gamma ray, which resulted in a very anticlimactic, and almost imperceptible, *click.*

The remnant, however, roiled inside the ball, pushing out in all directions, forcing Cary-Saanvi-Faleena to place more of the black bands around it.

When they had first captured the remnant, they had not understood what they did to contain it. This time was different. Cary-Saanvi-Faleena could see other things all around herself now, extra planes and angles, as though another existence was encroaching on their own.

There were light things and dark things, hot and cold things. The hot things were black, and Cary-Saanvi-Faleena could take them and wrap them around the remnant.

In the other space, the remnant was larger, as tall as her father, but still somehow on the table and cupped in her hands. It seemed to rage, to exude a sense of purpose denied.

"Stop," Cary-Saanvi-Faleena said to the remnant. "Stop, or we *will* crush you this time."

"Do you really think you can?" The remnant seemed to hiss and steam as it spoke.

Cary-Saanvi-Faleena nodded. "We do. We see through you. You're just a shadow, not a real being."

"Real enough," the remnant replied. "You won't be able to hold me forever. I must find the others and expunge them. They no longer serve a purpose."

The more Cary-Saanvi-Faleena watched the remnant, the more she realized that it was little more than a memory, perhaps an ascended AI's version of a non-sentient AI assistant.

But it was smart and had wiles. It had to, for it to have hidden in Nance for so long—and to have escaped the notice of Bob.

How ***could*** *this thing have escaped Bob's notice?* Cary-Saanvi-Faleena wondered to themself. *He is all but ascended himself. If he cannot perceive extradimensional entities such as this remnant, we would be surprised.*

"Cary," her father's voice broke into their thoughts. "What's going on? It looks like the thing is going to explode."

"We're talking to it," Cary-Saanvi-Faleena replied, her voice calm and reassuring—at least she hoped it was. "It is blustering, currently. I *think* it's an NSAI of sorts. It doesn't have many tricks up its sleeve, so it's attempting to use fear. But I think that *it* fears *us*. So much as it can."

"Well, whatever you're doing is working better than the gamma ray. I'm getting excellent data." Earnest had summoned a dozen holodisplays and was frantically working on them as he spoke.

"Is it actionable data?" Joe asked.

Earnest shot Cary-Saanvi-Faleena's father a sharp look. "Joe, I'm learning about an entirely new branch of physics over the course of just a few minutes. I mean…we have theories, but we've never tangibly interacted with these other dimensions…not in real-time like this, at least."

Earnest's voice grew breathless as he spoke. A combination of excitement and worry was clearly audible.

Cary-Saanvi-Faleena realized that she could see Earnest's physical presence in the additional dimensions as well, but not as a tangible thing. More like a shadow.

She turned to see that her father and the medtechs—who looked more than a little concerned—had the same shadows. Nance's stasis pod was a pocket of nothingness in the other dimensions, which was interesting in and of itself.

"Cary-Sa…stars, your names are exhausting to string together." Earnest peered at Cary, then Saanvi. "Mind if I just call you 'CSF'?"

"Not 'FSC'?" Cary said, her voice sounding like her younger sister's.

"Whichever you prefer." Earnest shrugged.

"Call us 'The Triad'."

Earnest laughed, and Joe sighed. "A bit pretentious, don't you think, girls?"

"Well, Dad, we are three. OK, how's about 'Trine'."

"Sure," Earnest nodded. "Now that we have that out of the way, I want to stimulate it again with the gamma ray, but at a different energy level."

"I want to try something, first." Trine-Cary splayed her fingers, and filaments of nano flowed out of them and onto the surface of the brane.

"It has a body," Trine-Saanvi said. "I can see it through Trine-Cary's eyes, though to mine it is still a jumble. But the body we see here and the remnant's *real* body are not the same. It is complete in other parts of space-time, while it's a shadow here. No, that is not right. It is a shadow in others, too. Like it has shed much of itself to be what it is."

<It is a facsimile,> Trine-Faleena said.

"I am no such thing," the remnant retorted. "You cannot understand what you see."

Trine-Cary had deposited enough nano on the surface of the brane that it was visible as silver bands wrapping around the black ones. Then the bands began to glow brightly, and the silver sank into the black.

"How is she doing this?" Trine heard her father ask Earnest.

"I don't know," Earnest replied.

"If *you* don't know, how is it that *she* knows?"

Trine watched Earnest peer into Trine-Cary's eyes. "When you were a baby and you took your first step, did you know how your muscles worked? How your brain sent a signal through your nervous system?"

"Are you saying this is some sort of innate knowledge, a reflex or something?"

"Well, not a reflex, but yes, something that Trine knows how to do naturally."

"Where would Cary—"

"Not Cary." Earnest held up a finger. "When Trine merges, each brings themselves—or at least a part—into the whole. To be honest, what Cary instigates is something I barely understand to begin with. It is like she is able to effect the merger that her mother and Angela have, but at will, and with anyone."

"Not anyone," Trine-Cary said. "I've tried it with others, but only succeeded with Saanvi, and then Faleena."

"Even so, Saanvi is not a blood sister, so whatever bond allows this is not biological. I suspect your inability to deep-Link with others is a mental block, nothing more."

Trine only grunted as she spun the silver bands around the remnant. In three-dimensional space, it seemed only to roil more violently inside the sphere. In *n*-space—a name she decided on for the deeper existence she could now see—it shrieked in pain. Or possibly terror. Trine wasn't certain.

"So you think this ability to see into other dimensions and manipulate matter there comes from Faleena," Joe said after a moment.

Trine wondered about that. It made sense. On previous deep-Links with Saanvi, there had never been any revelations about other dimensions. Nothing had ever looked different.

Could it be because Moms are merging? Trine-Cary thought.

Perhaps. Trine-Faleena replied, her thoughts feeling uneasy. *Does that mean that moms are becoming something more, as well?*

Are we? Or at least you two. Trine-Saanvi sounded as though she didn't know what to think of her place in Trine.

Trine-Cary did not think that was the case. *Seeing more of space-time does not mean that we're becoming anything different—other than having other eyes, at least.*

You didn't say anything about Moms, Trine-Faleena couldn't help but comment.

That's because I don't know what's happening with Moms.

Focus.

Yes, of course.

While Trine had been talking amongst herself, she had also been listening to Joe and Earnest discuss what they were seeing.

"See there," Earnest pointed at one of his holos. "When she twists that band, the thing emits shadow particles, mostly sleptons. I believe I can detect those under a variety of circumstances. They have a very unique signature; we'll just have to figure out how to force it to emit those."

"There," Trine said as the last of the black bands was fully coated in silver. "You now have a control interface for it."

In *n*-space, the remnant had ceased its struggles. It was now wrapped in the silver ribbons that Trine had created. Unlike the representation in three-dimensional space, where the bands wrapped around it and things looked neat, *n*-space showed the ribbons very differently. There, they mostly encircled the remnant, but in some places, they punctured it as well, passing through its body in some dimensions, but not others.

The result was a being that was afraid to move, lest it cut itself apart. And because, for the remnant, thought was movement, it could barely form words.

"Will. Be. Free."

"Keep dreaming," Trine replied, her tone dismissive. Internally, though, she was not so sure.

Can it?

We don't know…if it is NSAI, it is just acting out its programming.

And if this shadow is sentient? Then it has a will.

We must stay to watch it.

So tired…

Cary severed the deep-Link, feeling Saanvi fall away first, then Faleena—though Faleena did not drift far.

"That's…exhausting," Cary said, leaning heavily on the table.

"You've not slept for three days," her father said, at her side in an instant with a gentle hand on her arm. "You need to eat, then sleep."

"Can't," Cary whispered. "What if it breaks free?"

"I have a cot in the corner," Earnest said. "I can have food brought down."

"Sleep." Saanvi nodded in agreement. "I caught shuteye on the trip here, so I can stay up awhile. I'll let you know if we need you."

<*As will I,*> Faleena added.

"OK, just for an hour or so." Cary nodded as her father led her to the cot. "Just a bit."

Cary didn't even remember her head hitting the pillow.

FAREWELL TO SCIPIO

STELLAR DATE: 10.02.8948 (Adjusted Years)
LOCATION: Imperial Palace
REGION: Alexandria, Bosporus System, Scipio Empire

Two months later…

"You know, Diana, you're not half bad."

Tanis nearly spat out her wine, wondering what had come over Sera to say something like that to the Empress. She gave Sera a stern look before seeing, to Tanis's immeasurable relief, that the empress smiled.

"The feeling's mutual, Seraphina. I recall watching you enter my audience room and thinking, 'Now there's a woman who really thinks she's more than she is.'"

Petra sat down on a chair across from the empress. "I imagine Sera and Tanis are certainly more than you expected them to be." She took a small sip of her wine before leaning forward to place it on the low table between them.

Diana's eyes twinkled, and her lips pursed for a moment before she responded. "I was thinking of you, Petra."

Petra's eyes narrowed and her neck and shoulders tensed, but the ambassador held her tongue.

<*Ouch, Diana's still making Petra pay for all our sins,*> Angela commented privately to Tanis.

<*No one ever said she was a kind woman. Makes her just the sort of ally we need, I think.*>

<*Merciless toward her enemies? You know that can backfire, right?*>

Tanis considered Angela's words. If there was one axiom to live by, it was that if a person was cruel to their enemies, they could just as easily be cruel to you. Humans were excellent at rationalizing their behavior when it suited them.

<She's our best option to stall the Hegemony.> Tanis knew it was a weak argument, but she still had hopes for Diana. She'd changed over the past two months, had grown as a person. Tanis liked to think that she and Sera were positive influences on the empress, showing her how one could rule while being empathetic.

<And if our sources are right, a rift may be forming between General Garza and Hegemon Uriel,> Angela added. *<With us backing Scipio, the Hegemony won't be able to stand against them alone.>*

Tanis turned that idea over in her mind as she watched Diana, Petra, and Sera chat idly in Diana's meeting lounge. Would Diana annex the Hegemony entirely? By the empress's own words, she didn't want to expand the boundaries of her empire any further.

But would she feel the same way, once Sol was in her hands?

Tanis hoped the woman would maintain her current stance. Scipio having control of its empire as well as the Hegemony of Worlds was too much. Too much for anyone.

<I see where you're going with that train of thought.> Angela's voice was soft and encouraging. *<You wonder what will happen after this war is over. Where the lines will be redrawn.>*

<I do,> Tanis replied simply. *<Are we going to make things worse in the long run? FTL created the opportunity for wars unlike any others. But even with dark layer travel, it still takes years to get across the Inner Stars. This war is going to seed jump gates all across known space.>*

Tanis felt Angela's agreement fill her mind. *<So long as we can keep a tight lid on how to make jump gates, they can be limited—even destroyed, if needs be. This is a more manageable issue than dark layer FTL.>*

<Or it will allow for someone in the future to create the ultimate tyranny.>

Angela snorted, then began to chuckle.

<*What's so funny?*> Tanis asked, feeling annoyed at her friend.

<*You!*> Angela said after her laughter had died down. <*You're not content with the trouble you have before you, you're borrowing it from future millennia! While we're at it, we should worry about what will happen to human civilization when the Andromeda galaxy collides with the Milky Way!*>

Tanis had a sharp retort ready, but then realized how right Angela was.

<*OK, point taken. I was getting a bit melodramatic, there.*>

<*A bit.*> Angela was still chucking softly. <*Though I'll grant you that we do have to think about who fills the power vacuums that we'll create.*>

<*I really don't want to become the galactic policewoman.*>

<*Me either, I—*>

"You with us, Tanis?" Sera waved a hand in front of Tanis's face.

Tanis looked at Sera, then Petra and Diana—all of whom were directing unblinking stares her way. "Yeah, sorry, was just thinking about what's stacked up ahead of us."

"A great list of deeds, I imagine," Diana said. "The fact that I just have to contend with one enemy—provided *you* get Silstrand and that Rhoads mess under control—is a great relief to me."

Tanis nodded and reached for her wine glass. "I made the mess in Silstrand, I'll fix it."

"And now you have the same nanotech that Tanis gave them, Diana," Sera added. "So there's no need to worry that they have an advantage you don't."

"True." Diana nodded with a smirk on her gleaming black lips. "So long as they keep their stretch of stars from becoming a problem, I don't see a treaty being a problem."

"And the fleet you'd sent to take Gedri?" Sera pressed.

Diana laughed and shook her head. "President Seraphina Tomlinson, do you not trust me?"

Sera cocked an eyebrow. "Trust but verify. I have too many variables to juggle right now to worry about loose ends like this. Like Tanis, I feel partly responsible for the mess in Silstrand. I'd prefer to know that it's taken care of."

"We received confirmation today." Petra's tone carried mild annoyance as her eyes locked on Diana's.

"Petra! You're always spoiling my fun."

"Not everything needs to be a game of wits, Empress."

Petra and Diana stared at one another for a moment before Diana shrugged. "I suppose. I do need to learn not to needle my allies. I'm just not used to having people I can really trust."

<*Do you worry about Petra's allegiance?*> Tanis asked Sera. <*She seems more beholden to the Empress than you.*>

<*Are you referring to her use of 'we' when referring to Scipio?*> Sera asked. <*I certainly marked it—stars. 'Marked it'. I'm starting to talk like Diana. Kill me now.*>

<*Don't worry.*> Angela joined in their conversation. <*Alastar is keeping an eye on Petra. There's nothing wrong with her having a strong loyalty to Scipio. Eventually these political divisions will have to lessen.*>

<*Whoa! Now who's prognosticating about the future?*> Tanis asked.

"We trust you, Diana," Sera said aloud. "By your own admission, you don't want to build a larger empire than what you have. Seeing proof of that is welcome."

Diana's expression grew guarded. "True, but if I do advance into the Hegemony—which I intend to do soon; we won't just sit here and let them build up for a crushing attack against us—I will need to give some consideration to governance of conquered territory."

"I'm in favor of vassal states with as much autonomy as possible," Petra said. "Half of the Hegemony of Worlds is annexed territory as it stands. Many would welcome their autonomy back."

Diana's eyebrows rose as she regarded Petra. "A desire for autonomy does not equate to the ability to effectively self-govern."

"Easy, Di. I did say 'vassal states'."

Diana shrugged. "I suppose you did."

"So, how are you and Tenna getting along?" Tanis asked, seeking a new direction for the conversation.

"Very well," Diana replied. "I'd forgotten how nice it is to share one's mind with an AI. We're thick as thieves, as they say."

<*It's going to be a fun experience,*> Tenna added. <*A lot of responsibility.*>

"You're not running the empire, though," Diana replied with a laugh. "Trust me, when the buck stops at your ass, everything is a lot different."

<*I know I'm not running it, but everyone sure thinks I know everything about everything that is going on everywhere. It's draining!*>

Diana's laughter faded and she nodded soberly. "Welcome to my life."

<*That's a woman of a thousand masks,*> Sera commented to Tanis and Angela. <*I wonder if she even knows who she is half the time.*>

<*I think she does,*> Angela said. <*There's a firm core of self within her. I think that core is a bit of a jerk, but it's there.*>

Sera nearly laughed aloud at Angela's statement, and Tanis smiled, watching Petra say something to Sera as Diana looked on.

There was a strength in Diana, an unalterable belief that her actions were the best way forward for her people, despite short-term pitfalls.

Tanis knew all too well how that felt.

MYRIAD CONCERNS

STELLAR DATE: 10.02.8948 (Adjusted Years)
LOCATION: ISS *I2*, Security Operations Center
REGION: Alexandria, Bosporus System, Scipio Empire

Captain Rachel Espensen let out a long, frustration-laden sigh as she sat in one of the chairs in Terry's office.

"Tanis and Sera are due back on the ship in another day," she said. "Their negotiations with Scipio are over, we're preparing to leave the Bosporus system."

"You say this like I don't understand the implications," Terry replied. "Trust me, this upsets me just as much as it does you."

Rachel pressed the heels of her hands into her eyes. "You're right, Terry. You've been responsible for this ship's safety longer than I've been alive."

"Captain Espensen," Terry rose and took a seat next to Rachel. She reached out and placed a hand on her shoulder. "This ship has survived worse than this. We'll sort it out. We always do."

"You're right." Rachel nodded and squared her shoulders as she gazed out over the *I2*'s Security Operations Center. Though it was far from the bridge, the SOC was one of the ship's many hearts. Always bustling with activity; the work of keeping the massive vessel safe was never over—especially not with all of the Scipian dignitaries touring it.

"But knowing that we brought someone with us from New Canaan who would free Elena—who could fool our sensors…."

"You're worried it's a remnant."

"Aren't you?" Rachel asked. "We can't detect them; Bob doesn't even think *he* can. Any one of us could have one of those…things inside us."

"I'll admit that it does unnerve me. But Earnest has the remnant Tanis's daughters were able to remove from Nance. Once he fully understands it, he'll determine a way to detect them."

Rachel nodded. "At least I know *I* don't have one inside me. From what I read in the reports, Nance knew it was in there all along, she just couldn't say anything about it to anyone."

"Yup." Terry nodded seriously as she cast an appraising eye at Rachel. "Which means you could be lying to me right now."

"Terry!"

"Captain," Terry laughed. "You need to relax. I don't think there's a remnant in you. I think that whoever it's in is someone who can slip about with little notice."

Rachel joined in Terry's laughter. "Well, you're right about that. I can't walk more than ten paces without someone rushing after me with questions, or pinging me over the Link. Or both. Simultaneously. From the same person."

"When was the last time you had a day off, Captain?" Terry's tone was innocent, but her eyes belied concern.

"Stars...." Rachel looked at the room's overhead, thinking back. "Sometime before President Tomlinson—the previous President Tomlinson—dropped in for a visit with his fleet."

"Maybe you should see if you can take a day or two during our next stop."

"It would help if we knew where that was."

Terry shrugged. "Somewhere in the Silstrand Alliance—or the fringe systems between it and Scipio. That crusading fleet of AI-haters is in there somewhere. From what I hear, stopping them is a part of the treaty with Scipio."

Rachel nodded and visualized the region of space surrounding Scipio. On the rimward side was a no-man's land of small, independent systems. Beyond them was the Silstrand

Alliance—a narrow strip of stability in a region known for general lawlessness.

On the far side of the fringe systems were a series of larger alliances and federations, tucked up against the Hegemony of Worlds and stretching to the Praesepe cluster.

"I remember Tanis's stories of Silstrand. Parts of it sound nice."

Terry snorted. "And parts of it sound barely civilized."

"Maybe that's just what I need." Rachel wondered what it would really be like to visit a place where lawlessness ruled. She'd seen them in vids, but her practical experience was much more limited.

"Trust me," Terry replied. "You've not missed much with your sheltered upbringing. Shitty locales are mostly just shitty. Plus, there's the whole part where I have to send a security detail with you and worry that you're going to get killed the whole time."

Rachel laughed and shook her head at Terry. "You worry too much."

"Of course I do. That's my job. Now go fly your starship from your big chair. We'll find whoever let Elena out. I promise."

Rachel didn't have anything encouraging to say, so she simply nodded and walked out of Terry's office, eyeing everyone she passed, wondering if they could have a remnant of an ascended AI in them…making them do things, subverting the mission.

AFTERMATH

STELLAR DATE: 10.08.8948 (Adjusted Years)
LOCATION: Bridge, ISF *I2*
REGION: Outer Silstrand System, Silstrand Alliance

"So much for a spa-day," Rachel said as she stared at the holotanks showing the wreckage of the fleets around Dessen.

Priscilla glanced back at Rachel, the woman's black eyes appearing as endless pools of night on her alabaster skin. "Not a lot of R&R in our future, Captain. I think we may see things like this play out for some time."

"Us crushing enemy fleets like they're nothing?" Rachel asked. "It sounds crazy to say it, but I feel bad for them. It's like shooting fish in a barrel."

Priscilla nodded as she turned to gaze at the holotanks as well. "Yes, that is an apt analogy. If the barrel is made of wood, and we have a nuke."

"I don't think the barrel's material matters if we have a nuke."

"It could be a very, very big barrel…made of some sort of…" Priscilla's voice faded. "Nevermind. That was getting stupid."

Rachel rose and walked to the holotank, watching the S&R crews as they scoured the ships for survivors.

Four fleets were spread out near the dwarf planet Dessen in the Silstrand System. The smallest of which was the ISF fleet, a mere forty ships, though all unscathed thanks to their stasis shields. Next were the ships of the Silstrand Alliance Space Force, of which there were only forty-five still intact. Granted, over one hundred were closing in from all around the Silstrand System. Next were the private military ships of S&H Defensive Armaments. While their ships were smaller in mass, there were over a hundred of them. They had taken heavy damage, but it was also their installation on—or, *in*, rather—the dwarf planet, Dessen, that had been the target.

The last group was the Revolution Fleet. Hundreds of ships, most massing far more than even the Silstrand Alliance vessels, yet it was the fleet that lay in ruin.

The battle had been three against one, and though the one outnumbered the rest, when the *I2* arrived, the outcome had become a foregone conclusion.

In fact, their greatest struggle in the brief, fierce conflagration, had been to keep the S&H Defensive forces from utterly destroying the Revolution Fleet.

"Those poor bastards," Rachel said quietly. "Mind controlled and just plain deluded. They didn't deserve to die horribly just because some crazy man put mind-control mods into all their heads."

That someone could even do such a thing with impunity disgusted Rachel. How had the Inner Stars fallen to such barbarism? How was it possible that a man could amass such a fleet, filled with people who hated AIs so much that they'd die for their cause, and no one had stopped him before he got this far?

"Sure is a mess," a voice said on Rachel's left, and she turned to see Tanis at her side.

"Ma'am," Rachel nodded deferentially. "How did your chat go with that madman's daughter?"

"She didn't support anything he was doing, if that's what you're wondering," Tanis replied. "She's the one who killed him and severed his control over his people."

Rachel backtracked through the battle in her mind. "She got off his flagship three hours before the last enemies were taken out. Did it take some time for people to...regain themselves?"

"Not from what she told us. It seems that there were a lot of true believers who had no need for coercion to hate AIs. I suspect that many of the folks we're picking up out there required no unnatural influences to take up arms."

Rachel shook her head. "What a shame. What are your orders, Admiral? Are we going to be here for a while?"

"Well, given that this system is the seat of the Silstrand Alliance's government, I expect we'll be here for a bit, yes. The Scipian Special Envoy will need to meet with the Silstrand President and ratify a treaty. Diana requires the Transcend as a signatory."

Rachel couldn't hold back a sardonic laugh. "Sounds like the very definition of fun."

"Isn't that the truth."

Rachel glanced at the admiral to see a distant look in the woman's eyes.

"Still," Tanis continued. "No matter who wanted us to do what, we did stop a genocidal purge here. I would have done it just for that. Helping sidestep a war between Scipio and Silstrand is just icing on the cake."

"Sounds like two marks in the win column," Rachel said, pantomiming making the marks.

"It does, doesn't it." Tanis nodded. "You know, I have…interesting memories of this system."

"This is where you got *Sabrina* the weapon upgrades so you could rescue Sera, right?"

Tanis gave a soft laugh. "Yeah, amongst other things. Cheeky and I got up to some crazy stuff on one of their stations."

"You *what*?" Rachel asked loudly, her eyes wide, before lowering her voice. "What did you do with Cheeky?"

"Captain," Tanis admonished. "I did nothing untoward with Cheeky. She and I got in a bit of trouble, is all."

"Now that's a story I'd like to hear, sometime."

"Maybe over drinks some night," Tanis replied. "For now, I'd best go meet with the Silstrand fleet liaison. A Colonel

Grayson. He and I have to pay a visit to Smithers in his hidey hole on Dessen. Or in Dessen…whatever."

Rachel remembered Colonel Grayson. She'd watched him disembark when his ship docked.

"I see that look in your eyes." Tanis wagged a finger in the air. "I'd recommend against pursuing that man. I'm pretty certain he has eyes only for Kylie Rhoads."

"Hmm…" Rachel mused. "I suppose it's not worth it, anyway. We won't be here long."

"Stars willing." Tanis nodded and turned to leave. "Keep me appraised on the cleanup. At some point, Silstrand is going to demand that we turn over all the prisoners, and I want to have a good handle on the situation when that occurs."

"Of course, Admiral," Rachel replied as Tanis strode off the bridge.

The admiral gone, Rachel turned back to the holotank, wondering about all those people who had been swept up by Peter Rhoad's false promises and conscripted in his fleet, only to die here—their cold corpses drifting in the black.

The Inner Stars. What an utter shit-show.

A NEW ASSIGNMENT

STELLAR DATE: 10.09.8948 (Adjusted Years)
LOCATION: Ol' Sam, ISF *I2*
REGION: Outer Silstrand System, Silstrand Alliance

Sera stepped off the maglev to see Nadine waiting for her on a bench tucked under a tree at the edge of the platform. The Hand agent—possibly *former* hand agent—didn't see her right away, and Sera took a moment to observe the woman.

Nadine seemed older than Sera's records showed. Tired and sad. Her report on the events of the last month made for an interesting tale, to say the least. Some of it was nearly impossible to fathom—such as Maverick becoming the president of Gedri.

Maverick! Of all people!

Nadine had been sent to the Silstrand Alliance for one reason: get close to Kylie Rhoads and work out a way to stop her father *before* he massed the fleet which now lay in ruin around the *I2*.

Instead, Nadine had fallen in love with Kylie Rhoads. Not just for the purposes of the mission, but for real. And in doing so, she had delayed meeting her objective.

Again and again.

"President Tomlinson!" Nadine jumped to her feet and almost saluted before simply folding her hands before herself.

"Agent Nadine," Sera said as she approached. "I'm glad that we're able to meet under such serene circumstances."

Nadine glanced around herself at the forest surrounding the maglev station as though she hadn't noticed it before. "It's quite the ship."

Sera nodded. "That's putting it mildly. Walk with me."

Nadine fell in beside Sera as they walked through a shaded path in the woods, neither woman speaking for the span of a minute. Eventually it was Nadine that broke the silence.

"I screwed up. A lot."

Sera blew out a long breath. "Fucking right, you did. Petra sent you in *five years ago*. Five years! You could have had Kylie Rhoads back with dear old dad in six months, tops."

"Never would have worked," Nadine countered, her tone more sad than hostile. "Kylie was estranged from her parents for a decade. She had no interest in seeing them. Just hinting at her family made her shut down emotionally."

"Well, in the end, you had to dump her on a ship and send her to her family unwillingly. Seems like waiting didn't get you anywhere."

Nadine stopped and turned to face Sera, her eyes narrowed. "Things don't work so easily all the time in the field. Human emotional responses are—"

"Nadine." Sera's tone was frank. "Don't give me that. I spent decades in the field. Stars, these are my old stomping grounds. I've flown every route there is in the fringe. I even know half the captains in Gedri. Drank most of those under the table. So don't you give me 'things are different in the field'. You fell in love with Kylie Rhoads. Admit it to me."

Sera watched Nadine work her jaw for a moment. "Yeah, I did. But it's over now. She's done with me, after what I did."

"You misunderstand me," Sera said, stopping and turning toward Nadine. "Love isn't forbidden to us, but we can't let it cloud our vision. I'm not going to say that everyone who died in this battle could have been saved. Who knows what would have happened if you'd somehow gotten Kylie to her father years ago. Maybe he would have put one of his mods in her head, and she'd've been under his control too. But that doesn't change the fact that you let love get in the way of what needed to be done."

Nadine's face had reddened during Sera's lecture, but she didn't respond.

"You have something you want to say to me, Agent Nadine?"

Nadine nodded, perhaps not trusting herself to speak.

"Out with it, then."

"I feel like you're treating me unfairly. Your record is not pristine—I know about Mark, and how you lost the CriEn module. Rumor always was that you were blinded by your love for him."

Sera closed her eyes and nodded, feeling the anger spill out of her like a drain plug had been pulled. "And that wasn't the last time, either. Do you remember Elena? She reported up to Petra before she worked in my office in Airtha."

"I do, I ran a small op with her once on Alexandria."

"Right, I'd forgotten about that." Sera gave a small nod. "Well, would you believe that she's imprisoned on this very ship? She's a double agent for Orion. Killed my father right in front of me."

Nadine's face fell. "I had wondered…. I'll admit, I was scared to ask what happened to your father. He was not universally loved—still, I can't believe Elena would do that. What prompted her to change sides?"

"Stars if I know," Sera replied. "Nothing she says can be trusted. She can rot in her cell, for all I care."

The vehemence with which she spoke surprised even Sera, and she clamped her mouth shut for a moment before giving Nadine an apologetic smile.

"Damn love. Look at what it does to us."

"Think maybe we should try boys?" Nadine asked. "They're simpler."

Sera barked a laugh. "Seriously? How can they be simpler? They never talk. You have to pry everything out of them with a starship-sized grav beam. Besides, remember Mark? Got me exiled."

"Point taken. But when you do get a man to talk, and you pry his thoughts out, it's simple, what it says on the tin. Women're…"

"Onions." Sera nodded.

"Stinky?"

"I was thinking 'layered'."

Nadine's mouth made a soundless 'O', and she nodded.

Sera resumed walking and considered what to say next. Eventually she gave up on trying to find the perfect wording.

"So, do you still want to be an agent?"

"Honestly? *I* don't even know…I've done so much lying. Now that we've begun the unveiling, what does it even mean to be in the Hand anymore?"

"We're still figuring that out," Sera replied. "But mostly it's the opposite of lying. Truthing. We're truthing all over."

"A refreshing change."

"Change, yes. Refreshing, no. You should know this by now. No one really wants the truth. It's scary, messy. It's a big disaster, looming in the future. No one is going to be happy to know that they've been pawns in a bigger game."

"So I take it Empress Diana was not amused?"

"Not even in the slightest. You should have seen what she made Petra wear to the Celebration of the Seven Suns."

"Oh? Petra had always wanted to attend that."

"Not like this, she didn't." Sera passed the image over the Link to Nadine, chuckling as an expression of horror and amazement washed over Nadine's face.

"That's…just a little demeaning," Nadine said at last.

"Yeah, and Petra is still trying to get back into Diana's good graces."

Nadine stopped and faced Sera. "You left her there?"

Sera nodded. "She's the best one for the job. Diana had a change of heart, too—a bit, at least. She apologized to Petra."

"And Petra? She wants this?"

"Remember that whole thing about agents falling in love with assets?"

Sera watched Nadine's face redden. She could tell the woman had something she wanted to get out, but it wasn't the sort of thing you could say to your boss…and president.

"Spit it out, Nadine."

Nadine clenched her jaw, then exhaled. "No, I'm good."

"You sure? This is your one chance."

"OK, fine," Nadine's eyes narrowed. "I fall in love with my asset, and I'm taken to task, chewed out. Petra falls in love with the damned *Empress of Scipio,* and she gets promoted to, what…Ambassador?"

Sera winked at Nadine. "She didn't go off-mission. Took her lumps and moved forward."

"What do you think I did?" Nadine shot back. "I took Kylie out and sent her off with her brother…."

"Which, I'll admit, worked out in the end."

" 'Worked out'!" Nadine was almost screaming. "Have you looked beyond this big fancy ship of yours? A lot of people *died* out there. People who had no choice."

"Now do you get my point?" Sera asked, her eyebrow arched.

Nadine's mouth snapped shut, and she worked her jaw back and forth. Sera simply stared at Nadine until the agent finally said, "So what now? Is this where I get kicked out the airlock?"

"No," Sera said without elaborating, still waiting for Nadine to calm down.

Nadine closed her eyes. "Then what's going to happen?"

"Look, things could have been worse, and we learned about Garza, and about something that Kylie's father saw. Something he called his 'angel'."

"Angel? I didn't hear about that."

Sera turned off the path and led Nadine through the woods for a minute before stopping in a small clearing.

Nadine looked around at the trees, and up at the far side of the habitation cylinder where a lake hung two kilometers over their heads. "Can I just say that I've seen a lot of crazy shit in my life, but never, and I mean *never,* have I seen a warship with a forest."

"It may be a first," Sera agreed. "And there are not a lot of firsts anymore."

Sera dropped a privacy dampener on the ground between them and placed a hand on Nadine's shoulder. "In time, this will become common knowledge. But for now, it doesn't leave your lips or mind. Understood?"

Nadine nodded solemnly.

"I need you to say it, Nadine."

"I'll not tell a soul about what you are about to tell me. Not until it's common knowledge."

"Good," Sera nodded and tried to figure out in which order to explain things. "I'm not going to put an auth token in your mind about this or get carried away with what 'common knowledge' means. You'll know when you can share it."

"You're making me a bit nervous..."

"Yeah," Sera laughed. "You should be."

Sera proceeded to tell Nadine the whole story. Her mother's trip to the core, encountering the Ascended AIs coming back as Airtha. How Helen had been a shard of her mother in her mind. The attack on New Canaan, the clones of Garza that seemed to be everywhere, orchestrating everything, and what they knew of the mysterious entity that called itself 'the Caretaker'.

"Why'd you take us here in the woods? I need to sit down!" Nadine exclaimed when Sera was finished.

"Sorry, you can sit in the grass..."

"No thanks, I finally feel like I got clean for the first time in weeks."

Sera laughed. "You always were a bit of a princess."

"It's why the cover works so well for me." Nadine shrugged. "So, let me get this straight. Airtha is leading a rebellion with some sort of clone of you claiming to *be* you—"

"It probably *is* me," Sera interjected. "Helen was in my head for decades. Finaeus thinks it's entirely possible that she could make another... 'me'."

"That's seriously creepy." Nadine shook her head in disgust. "OK, so there's that. Then there's the core AIs. Orion has Garza running around, cloning himself—which is really unusual behavior for Orion-types. Lastly, we have Ascended AIs pulling our strings like we're all marionettes, and there may or may not be more than one faction of them."

Sera nodded. "Plus all the other stuff, like wars breaking out all across the Orion Arm as the lines get drawn between us and the Orion Freedom Alliance."

Nadine rubbed her eyes and ran her hands through her long blue hair. "This is...Sera...this feels like.... How are we going to deal with all this? Excuse me if I start to hyperventilate."

Sera placed her hands on Nadine's shoulders and locked eyes with her. "We're not without our allies and strengths. Having Scipio on our side counts for a lot. Diana may be a cold, testy bitch, but she can get things done. And what's more, we have New Canaan. They're building more ships like this one. At least fifty. That's the beginnings of a galactic fleet."

"What's the Transcend's relationship with New Canaan?"

"Not as complex as one might think. They're committed to backing us, and Tanis is in it to win it. Even without New

Canaan's resources, having her on our side is easily as big a win as Scipio, maybe bigger."

"New Canaan is just one star system, though. How many resources can they bring to bear?"

"They built a twenty-thousand ship fleet in secret in fifteen years."

"Oh…OK, when you put it that way…. Then why is Tanis out here? Aren't they worried about being attacked again?"

"They worked out how to summon the things from the dark layer," Sera said without elaboration.

"What!? They brought them out? How…?"

"I don't know, and I really don't want to know. I hope they never tell anyone else, either. It was…terrifying."

"And they put them back in?"

"They wouldn't have a star system anymore if they didn't."

Nadine whistled and appeared to be processing everything Sera had told her. "OK, so you don't tell all this to someone that you're canning. But I'm not entirely certain I have any more of this in me. I don't know if I can do subterfuge, secrets, and missions anymore. Not yet, at least."

"Good, because that's not what I have in mind."

"Oh?"

Sera shook her head. "I want you to function as an intelligence officer for Tanis. From the looks of it, she'll be heading to Praesepe. You've spent time there, and your cousin Nerischka is there, too."

"Been a long time since I've seen Nishka. Also, I couldn't help but notice your wording," Nadine said. "I take it you're not coming along?"

"No. I have to get back to Khardine. We were going to get the Inner Stars under control before dealing with Airtha, but with the other 'me' out there, we don't have that luxury any longer. I have to face her head-on."

"Good luck," Nadine chuckled. "You're going to need it."

"Tell me about it." Sera took a step back from Nadine. "So, Agent Nadine. Are you ready to become Major Nadine, officer in the TSF?"

"Major? That's a jump."

"I need people to listen to you when you talk."

Nadine snorted, though it sounded more like a soft squeak. "That'll be a change. So, I don't have to go undercover, lie to anyone, or make promises I know I probably won't be able to keep?"

"Well, I'm not going to make promises *I* can't keep. But none of those things are my intention."

"OK, I'm in. When do we leave?"

"Well, technically, you're staying here. I'm leaving."

"And what about Kylie?" Nadine's voice was strained, as though she had held the question in for too long. "What happens with her…and her nanotech?"

"They've altered it to make it safe. The weaponized aspects were causing problems—would have caused more, too, soon enough. Kylie's signed on to go find her brother and put a stop to this Revolution Fleet business. When she finds them, she has a device called a QuanComm that will instantly reach me at Khardine. Then we send in the cavalry to take out the rest of that fleet."

Nadine nodded. "I guess that's for the best. She needs time away. Do you know if *Grayson* is going with her?"

"The Silstrand Colonel? No, not that I know of. Silstrand has a lot of cleaning up to do. That general…Samuel. He made a right mess in Gedri—worse than it usually is. There's talk of sending a pair of cruisers along with Grayson to clean it up."

"You're going to send just two cruisers to subdue a star system?" Nadine asked. "Seriously?"

"They'll be ISF cruisers. Which means atom beams and stasis shields. They probably only need to send one, but they can cover more ground with two."

"Damn…" Nadine's voice was barely above a whisper. "This is surreal."

"Yeah, just a bit. Oh, crap! Kylie just filed for departure clearance on that tub of hers. You should see her off."

Nadine chewed her lip. "I'm worried about her going out there on her own."

"Don't," Sera replied. "I'm sending Ricket with her."

"Ricket!?" Nadine almost choked. "OK, now I'm *really* worried."

JUST DESSERTS

STELLAR DATE: 10.09.8948 (Adjusted Years)
LOCATION: Dessen
REGION: Outer Silstrand System, Silstrand Alliance

The three ISF pinnaces settled down onto cradles in one of Dessen's docking bays, disgorging Marines before the cradle ramps had even extended.

Once Colonel Smith declared the bay secure, Tanis walked down the ramp to where a very nervous-looking woman waited.

Tanis had a brief memory of the days when she was the person who would make sure a bay was secure before some important person ventured forth.

Even now it still felt surreal.

Colonel Grayson of the SSF was at her side, and when he laid eyes on the woman, he gave her an unkind smile.

"Hello, Shinya, how has your day been?"

The woman took a deep breath and nodded professionally. "We have managed, and we're thankful for both of your fleet's assistance. We are ill prepared to deal with this many wounded."

She gestured to her left, and Tanis looked over to the far side of the bay. Though the Marines had deemed it secure, it was far from empty.

Half the bay was full of wounded men and women, soldiers, and ship's crew, laying on triage cots with automatons and medical personnel moving amongst them like grey wraiths.

"If you need further assistance, we can send it," Tanis said.

Shinya snapped her attention back to Tanis. "Yes, of course. I'm sorry I did not properly introduce myself. I am Shinya, assistant to President Smithers."

"Whatever happened to Ginia?" Tanis asked with a wink. "I liked her. She had spunk."

"Ginia?" Shinya asked.

Tanis nodded. "I met her twenty years ago when I sold S&H the license to use my nanotech."

"*License*?" Shinya asked.

Tanis glanced at Grayson. "She seems to have a lot of questions."

"Shinya, why don't you just take us to Smithers? Is he in his creepy black room?" Grayson asked.

Shinya nodded. "Yes, of course, please come this way."

Colonel Smith nodded to Tanis, and two dozen Marines peeled off and formed up behind Tanis and Grayson.

"Oh…your soldiers can't come along, Smithers said so." Shinya looked more than a little worried as she delivered the message.

Tanis spoke slowly, spacing her words out. "Shinya. Pass this along to Smithers. This can go one of three ways. Option one is the one where I bring my Marines along, and we talk peaceably. Two involves a lot more Marines and an all-out assault on this moon-station. Four is the one where I just blow up Dessen and call it a day."

Shinya nodded and swallowed. "What happened to option number three?"

"I decided to escalate things."

"Um…OK. Smithers said your soldiers can come, too."

Tanis smiled at Shinya and gestured for her to lead the way.

<You have such a way with words,> Angela said, laughing softly as they followed Shinya's hurried steps.

<I practice in the mirror a lot.>

<Liar, you almost never look in mirrors. I know, I live behind your eyes.>

Tanis almost laughed aloud. <*If I wasn't so used to you, that would be really creepy.*>

<*I guess I'll have to try harder.*>

"I want to thank you for bringing me along," Grayson said quietly. "I bear a…special dislike for these people."

"Because of Lana?" Tanis asked.

Grayson nodded, glancing at Tanis. "Surprised you know about her."

"She was in Nadine and Kylie's reports."

Grayson whistled. "You got Kylie to write a report?"

"Well, it was more like a series of images, and then some bullet points. There was a cat, too. Angela thinks her AI put together most of it."

<*Marge is OK,*> Angela said. <*She and I had a long chat, and then I introduced her to Bob.*>

"Bob?" Grayson asked. "That's your big ship-AI, right?"

"Yes."

"Does he not talk often? I got all sorts of orders from someone named Priscilla, but nothing from Bob."

"He does talk, just not to most humans. It's taxing for him."

Grayson frowned. "That doesn't make sense."

"It's not supposed to—not to humans, at least."

Tanis saw Grayson frown and cock his head out of the corner of her eye. "Are you playing with me, Admiral?"

She couldn't help but laugh at the concerned annoyance in his voice. "A touch, but not too much. Bob's a lot to let into your head."

<*Don't sweat it, Grayson. I'll talk to you,*> Angela grinned in their minds. <*I'm **way** more fun than Bob. He's always so serious with his 'I see the future and all things and it's weighty-weighty' schtick he has.*>

"Now I *know* you're messing with me."

Tanis just grinned and shrugged. "Could be."

"Why are all the women in my life so complex?"

Tanis held back a laugh. The colonel seemed wound a bit too tight. Granted, his ex-wife, who she suspected he was still deeply in love with, had just left on her ship to search for her brother's fleet, so she could understand that his state of mind may not be ideal for needling.

"Kylie's not gone forever," Tanis said. "She'll find her brother, and Sera will send in the cavalry. We'll do our best to see that you're a part of that."

"I hope she doesn't find him too soon," Grayson muttered.

"Really? Why not?"

Grayson gave her a predatory grin. "Because scuttlebutt has it that you want to send some ships to Gedri to put Maverick down."

"And scuttlebutt is that you'd be top pick to join in that clean-up job," Tanis replied.

"I don't think I have to tell you how much I'd like to kick that man clear across the galaxy." Grayson's voice had dropped, growing quieter and more menacing. "He's…well, let's just say that I'm all in."

Tanis gave Colonel Grayson a nod. "When I meet with your fleet command, I'll make your command of that mission a requirement."

"Admiral Richards, you have my undying gratitude."

* * * * *

Grayson's description of Smithers' office as a 'creepy black room' was more than apt. At first glance, the floor seemed nonexistent, but Tanis could see that it was a clever holo effect, just like the blazing star on the far side of the room, casting an otherworldly light through the space.

President Smithers stood before the raging pseudo-star, his expression grim as half the Marines filed in behind Tanis.

"Major Richards—or should I say 'Admiral'—fortune has favored you," Smithers said as they approached.

Tanis saw that what had been an old man looking to be at the end of his life was now much younger in appearance, carrying the ageless look of a high-quality rejuvenation treatment.

"And you, it seems. This is a far cry from managing weapons upgrades on the PetSil mining platform," she replied.

Smithers smiled, the expression looking somehow just like it had when his face was creased and worn. "Well, I have you to thank for that—though not entirely. When you sold us your nanotech, you omitted certain things we needed to know."

Tanis shook her head. "I did no such thing. What I sold you was predicated on base technology which you did not possess. Tech that was common knowledge in my time. Either way, I'm sure your lawyers will have told you by now that the contract I signed noted those base technologies, though you may not have recognized them at the time."

"Yes." Smithers bit off the word and then paused, as though the taste of it had stymied him, then continued slowly. "Well, we worked it out. It wasn't easy, but we did."

"And you broke your licensing agreement," Tanis said without elaboration, letting the ball drop on the man before her.

"By making the technology work?" Smithers sputtered. "Preposterous."

"Of course not. But it's how you did it. The viral way you weaponized it. There are clauses in the agreement about how the nanotech can be used, the purposes for which it can be leveraged. What ended up in Kylie Rhoads was not within the scope of that license."

"I—" Smithers began, but Tanis held up a hand to silence him.

"You've caused incredible pain to people, nearly started a war—two, actually. All because you're a greedy little weasel. Now it's time to talk damages."

"Damages?" Smithers whispered.

Tanis nodded. "Yes. You do recall that clause, I made sure it was in there. You caused the loss of an entire star system for Silstrand. I suspect that's going to be more than the entire value of S&H."

Smithers swallowed and looked at Tanis, seeking some sign that she was joking. She was not, and he knew it.

THE SILSTRAND CLAUSE

STELLAR DATE: 10.13.8948 (Adjusted Years)
LOCATION: Government Plaza, Silstrand
REGION: Silstrand System, Silstrand Alliance

"Government Plaza? That's some creativity there," Tanis said as she and Sera—along with a sizable retinue, including the Scipian Special Envoy, a man named Scorsin—climbed the steps leading to a towering stone building where their meetings with the Silstrand government were to be held.

"Yeah," Sera gave a soft laugh. "They're not super creative with names in Silstrand. I mean…when people first settled these stars, they called them 'the Silver Strand', because they're a string of G-class stars surrounded by dimmer M and K ones."

"I recall reading that." Tanis nodded as she reached the top step. "Half the stations seem to incorporate Silstrand, or their original founder—Peter—into their names."

"Or both."

<*I think that Silstrand is a really nice name,*> Angela chimed in. <*I mean…when you stack it up against places like 'Bollam's World' it's practically poetry.*>

Tanis laughed. "Yeah, so that sets the bar low, I guess."

"Maybe you shouldn't be speaking this way about our hosts right on their doorstep," Scorsin said, moving closer to Tanis and Sera.

"Sorry," Tanis replied. "We tend to run fast and loose—you should know that, you spent almost a month going over the treaties with us back in Scipio."

"I have a keen recollection," Scorsin replied.

<*Too bad he had to have his sense of humor surgically removed to facilitate such an excellent memory,*> Sera said privately to Tanis and Angela.

Tanis held back a laugh and cast Sera a scolding look over the Link. <*Stop that. We have to get along with him for just a while longer, then we can get out of here.*>

<*I know you feel responsible for this mess, Tanis,*> Sera said. <*But in all honesty, you're not. Nanotech or no nanotech, this conflict between Scipio and Silstrand would have come about eventually. It's barely worth our time.*>

<*She's right,*> Angela nodded soberly. <*The Silstrand ambassador to Scipio was present when we crafted the treaty. He's sent along his notes in the packet we delivered to their president. This shouldn't be much more than a formality.*>

Tanis nodded absently as she walked through the entrance and into the building's foyer. <*Right, so there's no reason why this won't just get rubber stamped, and we can be on our way.*>

<*Great…*> Sera groaned. <*Both of you…seriously? Now you've gone and cursed it.*>

Inside the building, a delegation of Silstrand dignitaries waited. At their fore was the alliance's president, a tall man named Charles.

Tanis and Sera had already spoken with him several times, once the *I2* had passed within a light minute of the planet, but their prior conversations had been brief, and he seemed to place much more value on a physical meeting.

"Welcome!" President Charles boomed the moment both Tanis and Sera were through the entrance. "Esteemed President Tomlinson! Field Marshal Richards! It is a true honor to meet you. And, of course, Special Envoy Scorsin, you are most welcome in Silstrand."

"And you, President Charles. Thank you for hosting us," Sera said as she approached and offered her hand.

"Yes," Tanis added as she offered her hand. "It's a pleasure to finally see all that Silstrand has to offer."

The president inclined his head gratefully. "Much of which would have been laid waste, if not for your efforts at Dessen. I must admit, we did not expect Peter Rhoads to have amassed such a fleet, let alone to be so bold as to strike us here at the heart of the Alliance."

"We had agents working to stop him—which they did at the end," Sera replied. "Without their efforts, things could have been much worse."

"Yes…your dossier made mention of the fact that you have operatives within the…'Inner Stars', as you call them."

"Are we to retire to a more comfortable location?" Tanis asked. "I've been running around for days; sitting down to discuss these matters would be preferred."

A momentary look of concern flashed across President Charles' face, and he nodded quickly. "Of course, of course. We're to meet in my offices, I'll lead the way."

The president led them up a grand, marble—or a stone similar to marble, at least—staircase to the second floor.

Tanis paid little attention to her surroundings. She had already released a cloud of nano to scout things out, and knew that Major Valerie and the four High Guard accompanying them would be eyeing every nook and cranny.

She was more interested in the people. Alongside several non-military dignitaries of unknown rank and role, was a Silstrand admiral and two generals—one of which was the man named Samuel who had played a large part in the unrest currently tearing Gedri apart.

<*Mind you,*> Angela inserted herself into Tanis's thoughts. <*If he hadn't gone after your nanotech, that Harken woman would have sold it to stars-knows-who. Samuel's decision to send Kylie Rhoads after it was a smart move on his part.*>

<*True enough, but his actions at Freemont—you know, where he attacked Gedri's capital—were…extreme. I can't believe that that Maverick guy is running things in Gedri, now. The universe has no sense of honor.*>

Angela let out a tittering laugh. *<Oh! So you finally recalled where you met him before!>*

<Hey…that night was **really** *hazy. Cheeky released more pheromones than a hundred amped up people. I only remembered him as the 'crazy sex slave trader with the plasma sword'. Not the type of guy I would have thought to become ruler of a star system at some point.>*

Angela nodded in their mind. *<Universe takes all kinds—and has no sense of honor about it, as you said.>*

In front of them, President Charles was going on about how grateful the alliance was for the Transcend's help, interspersing comments about this or that holo of some prior dignitary that they were walking past. Tanis did her best to listen and care, but kept finding her mind wandering.

<Maybe you should have gotten some sleep,> Angela chided. *<If you want, I can run your mouth for you while you nap.>*

<Angela! That sounds seriously disturbing. I can't imagine that would be restful at all.>

Angela broke out into laughter and Tanis realized she had been joking. Maybe.

<I'm fine, I can stim as needed.>

<Tanis, you've had four hours of actual rest in the last week. At a certain point, your brain needs some downtime.>

<After this meeting. I'll sleep on the ride back up to the I2.*>*

<Good.> Angela's tone was resolute. *<Because if you don't, I'll knock you out for a day.>*

<OK, Mom.>

The Silstrand president had reached a pair of double doors at the end of the hall and swept through as they opened to admit the group.

His offices were not over-large, nor too ornate. There were chairs placed artfully around the edges of the space, well-laden bookshelves along the walls, and a quadrangle of sofas in the center.

"Please, sit," President Charles gestured to the chairs. "Would you like refreshments?"

"Yes," Tanis spoke first. "Coffee. And something with carbs. Been a long week."

Tanis sat, nodding at Major Valerie, who took up a position at the door, while the other four High Guard waited outside in the hall.

The Scipian Special Envoy sat on one sofa, and Sera sat next to him. Tanis settled into another couch beside General Samuel, and President Charles sat across from her.

Two of the other men who had accompanied them sat on the fourth couch, while the admiral sat next to the Silstrand president.

"Again, thank you for coming to meet with us," President Charles said. "As I'd mentioned previously, we owe you much, and thank you for your assistance."

Tanis couldn't help but notice that the admiral, as well as a general who stood along the wall, looked less than pleased at their president's effusive thanks.

"It's the least we could do," Sera said, her tone moderated and polite. "Coming here was on our short list, as securing a peace between Silstrand and Scipio is a part of our treaty with Scipio."

At this, President Charles' face clouded. "I read that in the dossier you've provided. I must admit, it's unexpected to have someone who we've only known as a privateer negotiating with the Scipian Empire on our behalf."

"A privateer?" Sera asked.

"Remember? I got *Sabrina* a letter of marque from Silstrand before we found you in Gedri," Tanis said with a wink. "You were the captain of the ship, so your name was on the letter."

"Huh," Sera placed an index finger over her lips as she thought. "You know, I never even looked at that—didn't really expect to be back here."

The admiral, whose name was Manda, from Tanis's briefing, cleared her throat and spoke up. "As interesting as this byplay is, what are your intentions here in Silstrand?"

"Our intentions?" Tanis asked, glancing at Sera, who nodded for her to proceed. "Well, our first intention is to help in any way we can with this treaty. Following that, we'd like to offer a pair of cruisers to help you clean up Gedri—as we'd discussed with your Colonel Grayson. It is also our intention to offer you the same nanotech that we gave to Scipio."

"We already have that nanotech," General Samuel said from where he sat next to Tanis. "Our technicians have extracted it from my daughter, Lana. We—"

"Did you bring her with you?" Tanis interrupted. "Is she here?"

"Yes, she—"

"Good. You need to bring her to the *I2* as soon as this meeting is concluded. I also want all samples you collected, and all research and documentation you have accumulated on the nanotech you extracted from her. If you seized anything from S&H Defensive Armaments, I'll require that, as well."

General Samuel's mouth was working, but no sounds came out.

"What are you saying?" President Charles asked. "You cannot come into our sovereign nation and make demands like this."

"I'm afraid this is non-negotiable," Tanis replied. "Your treaty with Scipio is contingent on it."

President Charles glanced at Scorsin who shrugged. "It's in the fine print, yes. We cannot ratify a treaty with you unless you turn this technology in its entirety over to the ISF."

"The ISF?" Admiral Manda asked.

"Yes, the Intrepid Space Force," Scorsin replied. "That big honking ship I rode in on. So far as I can tell, it is an independent nation within the Transcend."

Admiral Manda turned to Tanis. "Your starship is a sovereign nation?"

Tanis preferred not to reveal New Canaan's existence if possible, and shrugged. "It's more powerful than most nations, why not?"

No one spoke for a few moments, until General Samuel managed to find his voice again. "And *why* do you need to take our nanotech from us?"

"Aside from the fact that it will kill your daughter, Lana, in under two years—that's after it turns her into a violent killing machine—it violates your own laws."

"Kill her?" General Samuel asked.

At the same time, one of the men next to the president, Secretary Jorgens, by the indicator on Tanis's HUD, spoke up. "It violates our laws?"

"The nanotech was weaponized in a fashion that makes it reprogram a host to be a soldier. A violent killer who will eventually be destroyed by the mods. S&H's work was…sloppy. This sort of alteration was illegal in Sol, and it is technically illegal in Silstrand, too. You have laws against using nanotech to irreparably damage a sentient's mind."

"We can fix it," General Samuel said to the president and Admiral Manda. "S&H has the original specs, they—"

"They don't have them anymore," Tanis said calmly. "I have relieved them of the technology. It is scrubbed from their systems. I also own S&H Defensive now, but that is another matter. I'm sure I can transfer ownership to the Silstrand government at some point."

"How is it that you 'own' S&H Defensive?" President Charles was scowling deeply.

<*Not the best start,*> Sera said with a belabored sigh.

<*No, but we have to get all of this out of the way,*> Tanis replied. <*Best to do it now.*>

<Well, carry on. You have some more hopes of theirs to dash, don't you?>

Tanis replied with a silent laugh on the Link before replying to the Silstrand president. "Their contract with me was in the form of a license. It also included damages if they violated their license. It would seem that they never expected to encounter me again, and did not heed the limits of their license. I claimed damages, and they've settled by selling all of their assets to me."

"How did we not hear of this?" Admiral Manda's tone implied more than a little skepticism.

"Things are chaotic out there," Tanis shrugged. "I paid my old friend Smithers a visit and hashed it out with him in person. The ISF owns S&H, including the planet Dessen and all its ships. Granted, I don't really *want* to own it, so I'm sure we can work something out.

"However, this is all contingent on you turning over the nanotech, and Lana. The girl will die if we don't save her."

Tanis cast an eye at General Samuel. "I'm operating under the assumption that you actually care what happens to your daughter—though what I've heard from Kylie Rhoads and her crew tells me that *may* not be the case."

"Kylie Rhoads is a—" Samuel began, but Tanis held up her finger, silencing him once more.

"You gave her a letter of marque which granted her the *Barbaric Queen,* did you not? In honor of your original agreement with her. Which, I might add, she upheld, despite your rash actions in Gedri."

Samuel seemed to shrink down in his seat, and Tanis continued.

"I think what you were going to say is that Kylie Rhoads is a credit to Silstrand. She is now searching out her brother, Paul Rhoads, so that we can deal with him and end the threat the Revolution Fleet presents."

"What do you even need us for?" Admiral Manda asked.

Tanis turned to Scorsin. "Special Envoy?"

Scorsin leant forward and placed his hands on his knees. "You are to expand your influence throughout the fringe systems and bring them to order. We expect all of the systems spinward and coreward of Silstrand to be firmly under your control within five years. Scipio will provide whatever non-military resources you require to achieve this goal."

President Charles sat back, a look of sheer amazement on his face. "Your main condition for peace with Silstrand—aside from the nanotech—is that we annex thirty star systems?"

"Fifty-seven," Scorsin corrected. "Once we get these preliminary matters out of the way, we can dive into those specifics."

"How will that even be possible?" Admiral Manda asked, her eyes wide and face suffused with worry.

Tanis grinned. "Did you notice our shields during the battle?"

Manda's eyes narrowed and a smile formed on her lips. "Now you're talking, Field Marshal. I'll take those shields over nanotech any day."

Sera placed her hands on her knees and smiled at those assembled. "Excellent. Now we have a solid foundation. However, what about those refreshments you mentioned? If I don't get coffee in the next minute, I'm liable to get testy."

WINOS AND SLEPTONS

STELLAR DATE: 10.14.8948 (Adjusted Years)
LOCATION: Gamma VIII base
REGION: Outer Asteroid Belt, New Canaan System

"Stars, I feel like I haven't seen daylight in weeks," Cary complained.

<*Well, I suppose the fact that you actually* ***haven't*** *may play into that,*> Faleena said, winking in Cary's mind. <*You should go for another walk in the base's park.*>

"It's not the same." Cary rubbed her eyes as she sat on the edge of her bed.

<*You can't tell. The simulation is near-perfect. I mean,* **I** *can tell, because you just can't fake starlight to perfection—not that they need to for you orgies.*>

"OK, Faleena. First off, you can't use 'orgies' as shorthand for 'organics'. It's...just don't. As for the starlight, sure, it may *look* perfect, but I still know that I'm down in the middle of a moon with a billion tons of rock over my head."

<*Then go up to the observation dome,*> Faleena offered. <*See Canaan Prime and real starlight for a bit.*>

"You know I can't."

<*You don't need to be within a minute of the remnant at all times,*> Faleena's avatar shook her head at Cary. <***It*** *doesn't know you're that close. If it were going to try something, it would have done so already.*>

"It waited inside Nance for eighteen years. It can play a long game."

<*Technically, the Caretaker's remnant waited for around ten. Before that, it was a shard of Myrrdan that was inside Nance. It was also working hard to get back here—or I suspect it was.*>

"You get my point."

Cary stood up and walked to her wardrobe, which consisted exclusively of uniforms and exercise clothing of ISF issue. She pulled on a pair of compression pants with the space force's logo on the side, followed by a sports bra.

"A run will do me good, get the blood pumping."

She slid her feet into her shoes and bent over to stretch her back and legs out.

<A run is a great idea. At least try to pass through the park; it'll make you feel better.>

Cary finished her stretching, and palmed her quarters' door, ready to start at a slow jog. As the portal slid open, she stepped out and almost walked right into Saanvi, who wore a large grin and was almost bouncing with enthusiasm.

"Cary, Faleena! Good, you're up! Come to the lab, come! We've figured it out."

<'It'?> Faleena asked.

"Yeah, 'it'. How to detect and contain any remnant and shard we find."

"Seriously?" Cary asked. "Just like that?"

"Cary, we've been here for over seven weeks. No, not 'just like that'."

"Right," Cary said as she walked out of her quarters and followed her sister down the hall. "I mean, when I went to bed, you were all banging your collective heads against the wall. Now you've just got it sorted?"

"Well, we *think* we have. We're going to have to let the remnant out to test it."

Cary swallowed. "Uh, kay."

Saanvi glanced back at her. "You knew we'd have to do that eventually. We can't be sure that we can capture and contain a remnant if we don't try it on the one we have."

"What if it fakes it?" Cary asked. "Tricks us into thinking we can capture it."

"Possible," Saanvi said with an exaggerated shrug as they turned the corner down the hall to Earnest's lab. "But Trine will be watching, and maybe we'll be able to see."

"That's weird to hear you refer to 'us' in the third person."

"Language kinda fails to describe what we can do," Saanvi replied as she pushed open the door to Earnest's lab and held it for Cary.

"Damn, it's cold in here," Cary said, rubbing her arms.

"Well yeah, you're dressed for exercising. Why's that?"

Cary rolled her eyes at her sister. "Because I was going to exercise, before you appeared and dragged me here."

Saanvi frowned. "Why didn't you change?"

Cary gave an exasperated groan. "Because you acted like the world would end if I didn't come with you right away, Sahn!"

<*You **were** all bouncy, Saanvi. It seemed very urgent,*> Faleena chimed in.

"Hmm…I guess I did. Oh well, you'll warm up." Saanvi rubbed a hand up and down Cary's arm. "This help?"

"Sahn, cut it out!" Cary jerked her arm away.

Saanvi grinned. "Maybe I *should* have let you get that run in, sister grumpy pants."

"They're running tights, not pants."

"Tights *are* pants," Saanvi countered.

Cary groaned. "We're *not* having this argument again."

Saanvi gave an all-too-chipper chuckle and the two women walked to the table where the remnant floated, the brane Cary had created floating in a magnetic field.

Leads were connected to the silver bands that wrapped around it, and several probes were situated next to the brane, providing real-time data on energy readings coming off the remnant.

Next to the table, their heads together in discussion, were Earnest and two of his top researchers, Harl and Kirsty. His wife Abby was also standing a few meters away, staring intently at the remnant.

Cary had never been entirely comfortable in Abby's presence. The woman felt like a tightly-wound spring that was about to either snap, or break free of what held it and fly about, wreaking havoc.

There were also rumors that their mother and Abby had been at odds a number of times in the past. It made Cary wonder how much the woman really liked them.

"Ah!" Earnest proclaimed when he saw Cary and Saanvi approach. "Just the two transdimensionally powerful beings we've been waiting for."

"We're just one transdimensionally powerful being," Saanvi corrected. "Separately, we're just a couple of girls."

Cary turned her head up and sniffed disdainfully. "I don't know about you, Sahn, but *I'm* a woman."

"Sure, Cary." Saanvi laughed and bumped her hip against Cary's. "You're all woman."

Cary blushed and wished she'd gotten changed all the more.

<Thanks, Sahn. Just what I needed.>

<Sorry, I didn't mean it that way. I just want to get this over with. I could sleep for a month. You get testy when you're tired, I get giddy and say stupid shit.>

"Yes, well, we're ready if you are," Earnest said with a nod to Harl and Kirsty. He walked to the table and touched a boxy device that had seven long prongs sticking out of one end. "It's not named but I'm leaning toward calling this the Slepton Captivator."

"Really?" Harl asked. "That's the name we're going with? I think 'Shadowtron' was way better than that."

"I think people will suspect that 'Shadowtron' is a joke," Earnest replied. "At least 'Slepton Captivator' is better than '*N*-Space Field Stabilizer'."

Abby snorted. "Except that's exactly what it is, *and* what it does."

"Yeah, but it also captures things in the field, so we need that word in the name," Earnest countered.

"Right," Kirsty nodded, speaking for the first time. "And the thing it captures are Sleptons."

"Plus a host of other shadow particles," Harl countered.

Kirsty nodded. "Yeah, but most shadow particles have stupid names. We can't call it the Zino-Wino-Gluino Captivator. Sleptons are the only ones with a good name."

"Do we have to choose before we test it?" Cary asked. "I'm all for a cool name, but if it doesn't work, then it won't matter."

Earnest glanced at Harl and Kirsty. "She has a point."

"OK, but in my notes, I'm calling it a Slepton Captivator," Kirsty groused.

"What we sorted out last night," Saanvi said to Cary as Earnest adjusted the positioning of the device, "is that even in its most dormant state, the remnant emits minute amounts of shadow particles. Barely detectable. But if you pass just the right eV wave through it, it spits out Sleptons like mad—"

"Hence the name," Kirsty interrupted.

"Yeah, hence Kirsty's name," Saanvi nodded. "The seemingly-unnamable thing Earnest has there emits the wave so that the remnant can be detected, and then it can create what we hope is a facsimile of the brane you made to hold the remnant."

"Hope?" Cary asked.

"Well, we've never tested it," Earnest replied. "We have our calculations, but honestly, we've been at this for weeks and we barely know what the hell we're looking at. If we had Bob to help, it would be different…but as it sits…."

Cary nodded. "I understand. Let's do this. If it works, I assume there will be more tests before we can finally call it done?"

Earnest nodded. "Yes. Ideally, we'd like to see if we could draw it out of a human, but...well, that would be a bit too much, I think."

Cary reached out to Saanvi, then Faleena. A part of her wondered if Saanvi joining the deep-Link was necessary anymore, but now was not the time to add that variable to the experiment.

Agreed, Trine-Saanvi thought. *Though I do feel a bit like a fifth wheel sometimes.*

I think you are necessary, Trine-Faleena said. *Something about how we join seems to require you. However, I agree that now is not the time for more changes.*

"We am—are—ready," Trine-Cary said.

"OK, do you think you can let it out without destroying the brane?" Earnest asked.

Trine observed the thing within the brane. It had grown dimmer over the weeks, as though the constant poking and prodding had sapped it of its energy. It also no longer spoke. The most accurate word Trine could think of was 'listless'.

"I believe I can extract it, yes."

"OK then," Earnest said as he pointed at a five-meter-wide platform next to the table. "Stand on that. It has a magnetic shield that's a bit like the brane...but won't kill us to be inside of it. I doubt it can hold the remnant for long, but it should give us time to capture it."

Trine-Cary wondered how many more caveats Earnest could have thrown into his statement. She lifted the brane, pulling the leads off the bands, and then stepped onto the platform. Saanvi joined her; both women had to be within the field to maintain their deep-Link.

Earnest stepped up beside them, and Trine saw a bead of sweat run down the side of his face. *Not the best sign.*

Trine drew a deep breath and nodded to Harl, who activated the field surrounding the pedestal. It snapped into place, the EM field producing a small hum as it shimmered faintly around them, visible only by the air it ionized.

Trine-Cary set her fingertips on the bands and pulled them apart, and then somehow—though she did not quite understand it herself—she split the brane open.

In a flash, the remnant was gone, flying out of the brane and streaking around the sphere.

"It's working," Kirsty crowed as Earnest swept the eV wave around the magnetic sphere.

"Yes, I can see it," Earnest said. "It's much larger…I'm trying to encapsulate it."

Earnest activated the device's emitters, and Trine could see the remnant, which had previously been trying to get out of the magnetic cage, shy away.

"It certainly doesn't like it," Trine-Cary said.

The remnant was drawn toward Earnest's device, and Trine felt her pulses quicken at the thought that they'd finally secured the thing without relying on her abilities.

Then the remnant broke away from the field and smashed into the magnetic sphere. Trine saw the containment field waver, and then the remnant slipped through.

"Kill the field!" Trine-Saanvi shouted, and Cary spun, looking for the Remnant. It was nowhere to be seen.

"Dammit!" Earnest swore. "We were so close!"

"I found it," Trine-Cary said calmly as she walked across the lab, staring into *n*-space as the remnant tried to hide from her. "Earnest, hit Abby with the wave."

Earnest looked at his wife, who appeared more than a little terrified.

"I don't know if this will hurt, Abs."

Abby clenched her teeth. "Just do it."

The moment Earnest directed the device's eV wave at Abby, the holodisplay atop the emitter lit up, showing sleptons coming out of Abby's midsection.

"It's…masquerading as a part of her liver," Harl said. "That must be how it anchors itself to a person."

Earnest walked toward his wife. "Be still, Abby. I don't think this will hurt. I think with a few adjustments…"

"I don't care if it hurts, get it out," Abby whispered hoarsely, her eyes darting to Trine-Cary. "You be ready. I'm not going to spend ten years with one of these things in my—oh shit, it's talking to me! Hurry! *Get it out!*"

Earnest activated the device once more, and Trine could see the remnant writhe as it was pulled from Abby's body, losing its corporeal aspects and flowing from her toward the device.

The entity was drawn into the space between the seven prongs and folded over and over until a sphere snapped into place around the remnant.

"Yes!" Earnest shouted. "Look at that. I made a black brane, and I stuck your remnant ass in it!"

He walked over to the magnetic field emitter where they'd previously held Trine's brane and slid the new one into it.

"And there we have it, safe and sound."

"Check me over again," Abby said. "Make sure it's gone."

Earnest complied, and Trine confirmed, "There is no trace of the remnant within you, Abby."

Earnest turned to Cary, who was now just Cary once more.

"You know what this means?"

"I can finally get some real sleep?"

"Well, yes. Then we can wake Nance."

Cary's eyes darted to Nance, still in her stasis pod, and then to Saanvi. "That would be nice. I'd like to meet Nance again for the first time."

THE LONG NIGHT

STELLAR DATE: 10.25.8948 (Adjusted Years)
LOCATION: ISS *I2*, Forward Lounge
REGION: Orbiting Silstrand, Silstrand System, Silstrand Alliance

Tanis stood in the forward observation lounge, alone with Sera, President Charles, and Admiral Manda.

"I'm sure you hear this a lot," President Charles said, as a servitor brought them the drinks they'd requested. "But this is not like any other warship I've ever seen—or heard of."

"I think it's been mentioned," Tanis replied. "Honestly, it would have been more work to remove things like this lounge than keep them. Plus…it's home, you know?"

Tanis could tell from the look on the president's face that he did not really understand what she meant, despite the fact that he nodded in agreement. Admiral Manda, on the other hand, pressed her lips together and inclined her head.

"I never had anything like this on any of my ships, but I do know what it's like to consider a warship home. It's nice to have sections that are made for form over function. Helps ground you."

"A lot of grounding here in the *Intre—I2*," Sera said, shaking her head. "I still mess the name up sometimes."

Manda glanced at Tanis. "Why *did* you rename your ship, Admiral? Surely you know it's bad luck."

"We wanted a clear division," Tanis replied. "Sure, we fought two major engagements with the *Intrepid*, but those were brief. Flashes in the pan. For two centuries, the *Intrepid* was home. We wanted to always remember it as such, our people's ark. The *I2*, on the other hand. She's a ship made for battle, and when we speak of her, she is that first, and home second."

"Two hundred years…" President Charles mused. "That's a lifetime, just to spend on one ship."

"Not anymore, it's not," Sera replied. "A lifetime, that is. The nanotech that you've received will double—at least—how long you can expect to live."

"That still feels surreal," President Charles said. "It's going to change so much for us."

"Yes, it will." Tanis wondered how well these people would really do with what she had given them. Would they hoard it, keeping it to the rich only? Would they dole it out slowly, or release it to all?

<We can't hold the entire human race's hands.> Angela repeated Tanis's earlier words back to her. *<Sol managed to equalize with this technology—before people created artificial divisions and tore everything apart.>*

<I know, but I still wonder what these people will do.>

<Well, what with the Transcend's longevity techniques, we may just get to watch them and find out.>

Tanis nodded silently as they looked out the window at the space beyond Silstrand's largest moon, a dull blue orb named Kora. The group was observing the moon's L2 point, which had recently been cleared out for what was to come.

"I—" Admiral Manda began to say, and then it happened.

Where there had been nothing but empty space, a ship now drifted in the dark.

"The *Long Night*," Tanis announced, gesturing at the vessel that had just appeared.

"That certainly is something to see," Manda said, her voice filled with sincere awe. "And that ship was just where?"

"Khardine," Tanis replied. "Which is in an undisclosed location. Suffice it to say that it's over three-thousand light years from here. Six years' travel by dark layer FTL."

The *Long Night* was a new design of dreadnought modelled after the AST ships the ISF had fought in Bollam's World. Its hull was five thousand and two hundred meters long, with engines mounted at both ends.

The Silstrand System orbited the galactic core more slowly than Khardine, and the *Long Night*'s engines flared as it boosted to match the velocity of the celestial bodies that surrounded it.

"That's mind-boggling," President Charles replied. "What's the range on these 'jump gates', as you call them?"

"Theoretically, there isn't one," Tanis replied. "Some *very* long jumps have occurred, but if there is no return gate, getting home can take some time."

"I can only imagine," Admiral Manda replied in a soft voice. "Can you…we could eventually go anywhere."

"Remember," Tanis cautioned. "This is not a technology that we're sharing. We will be bringing in mirror tugs to facilitate any jumps that are necessary for your ships. If jump gates get in the wrong hands…"

"I thought the Orion Freedom Alliance already had this technology," Admiral Manda said.

"Well, additional wrong hands," Tanis clarified.

"Like the Hegemony, or the Nietzscheans," Sera offered.

President Charles face paled. "What if they have it? You said that the Nietzscheans are possibly allies of the OFA. Could they not jump here?"

"It's possible," Sera said, nodding slowly. "We'll be helping your people establish interdictor systems. They disrupt the jump-bubble and will make deep insystem arrivals like what the *Long Night* just performed very unlikely."

"That's not terribly comforting," Admiral Manda replied.

Tanis turned and looked at the Silstrand president and his admiral. "Don't forget. This technology did not just spring into existence. It has been a reality for well over a century now. The enemy is just as worried—we believe—about it coming into general use."

Sera leaned against the window. "Regarding the stasis shields, it will take a bit to get them to you, and we won't have enough for all your ships. Even though they *might* be able to jump in here, stasis shield tech is something that none of our enemies have."

"You said you'd be leaving a ship. Will it be the *Long Night*?" President Charles asked.

Tanis shook her head. "No. The '*Night* is just here to deliver the gate. It has other places to be. You'll be getting one of our destroyers. The *Cobalt Flame*."

"A destroyer? Admiral—"

Tanis held up her hand. "A destroyer with stasis shields and ten atom beams. It has firepower equal to half your fleet, and its shields cannot be breached. I'm sure you've watched the vids of the Bollam's World battles. You saw what our ships were able to weather there."

Admiral Manda gave a rueful laugh and looked up at the overhead. "If I recall, *this* ship weathered the relativistic jet from a black hole."

"Exactly." Tanis turned to watch the *Long Night*, as components of a massive jump gate began to lift off a long cargo rail atop the ship.

"I'm eager to see what that will look like when it activates," Admiral Manda said as the ring began to take shape.

"You won't have long to wait," Tanis replied.

She was less interested in the ring than the pinnace which departed the *Long Night*, and began to boost toward the *I2*. That pinnace carried a Shadowtron device and the specifications on how to make more.

Finally, after *centuries*, they would be able to scour the ship for any last trace of Myrrdan and eliminate him. Along with any of the Caretaker's other minions.

That would be a greater victory than any they'd won thus far.

WHEELS WITHIN WHEELS

STELLAR DATE: 10.27.8948 (Adjusted Years)
LOCATION: Ol' Sam, ISF *I2*
REGION: Orbiting Silstrand, Silstrand System, Silstrand Alliance

"You're sure you got this from here?" Sera asked for the third time.

"Yes!" Tanis laughed. "I'm over a hundred years your senior. I can take care of myself."

"Bob?" Sera looked up at the roof of Tanis's cabin. "You'll watch over Tanis?"

<*What am I? Interstellar dust?*> Angela asked.

"You're as bad as Tanis, most of the time," Sera replied. "I can't trust either of you to keep the other out of trouble anymore."

<*I'll keep Tanis and Angela on their path,*> Bob intoned when Sera finished speaking.

"That's not what I asked, Bob." Sera's eyes narrowed as she stared at the cabin's ceiling. " 'On their path' and 'safe' are not the same thing."

A strange sound came into their minds, like a waterfall mixed with rolling thunder.

"Is he…laughing?" Sera asked.

Tanis shrugged. "I guess so. I can't remember the last time I heard Bob laugh like this."

"What gives?" Sera asked the ceiling once more.

<*To think that even* ***I*** *could keep Tanis 'safe'. You place more faith in me than I deserve, Sera Tomlinson.*>

"I always feel like you're one of my childhood teachers when you use both my names like that."

<*Is there some other way I should use both your names?*>

Sera groaned. "Wow. You think you're funny, is that it, Bob?"

"You know," Tanis lowered one eyebrow while raising the other. "I think I'm a very safe person these days. The last dangerous thing I did was rescuing you eighteen years ago, Sera. Since then I've been nothing but circumspect."

"Tanis, you assaulted the Galadrial just half a year ago, with Uriel and a Marine strike team."

"Right! Perfectly safe. I had ISF Marines with me."

Sera groaned. "This is not making me feel better."

Tanis leant over and placed a hand on Sera's arm. "Seriously, Sera. It's *you* I'm worried about. I have the most powerful starship in the galaxy, Finaeus, *and* Bob. Honestly, I think that Finaeus should go with you. You need allies."

"I have Greer; he's loyal, and from his latest QuanComm messages, fiercely determined to make sure there's no repeat of the attack on Keren Station."

"And Krissy seems to be faring well in Vela," Tanis added. "Are you still at least considering moving the capital there?"

"Maybe. I need to visit at some point. Chancellor Alma has not been fully accommodating to Krissy. Understandable, I suppose. She views herself as terribly important, and Krissy, while part of the—" Sera held up her fingers to make air quotes " 'royal family', Alma considers her to be too far from the throne to garner real respect."

"You're going to have to visit a lot of places out there to drum up support."

"Maybe.... Oh! Guess what, Tanis? This came in on the latest burst from Khardine. Guess who escaped from prison…freaking months ago?"

"I hate guessing games, Sera, spit it out."

Sera rolled her eyes. "Always so testy. You should take a page from Bob's book and yuck it up a bit."

"Sera. You're killing me here. I only know one—wait…no! *Andrea*?"

"Hole in one." Sera grimaced, then rocked her head side to side, stretching her neck. "My dearest, least-favorite sister. You'll never guess who broke her out."

"You're right, I won't. Just tell me."

"Justin."

Tanis's eyes widened. "As in Justin, your old boss, the former director of the Hand?"

"One and the same."

<*Allies or enemies?*> Angela asked.

Sera gave an exaggerated shrug. "You got me. If it was Justin on his own, I'd say ally. He's probably less than happy about how he had to fall on his sword for me, but if it were just him, I know we could figure out a way to work together."

"Andrea's a whole different story, though," Tanis said, her voice trailing away as she remembered her last encounter with Sera's sister in the Ascella system.

"Yeah, she's not a fan of yours either, what with the whole 'turning me to kill you' thing that happened."

"So we have to assume that, because Justin freed Andrea, he has a plan for her. A plan that can't be good for us."

Sera began fiddling with her hair, fingers twitching violently as they twisted the long, black locks. Tanis watched, moderately amused as Sera's skin began to change from blue to red. Then it took on the scaled appearance it had when she had masqueraded as a dragon-demon at Diana's costume ball.

"Is that conscious, or is that a new stress response?" Tanis couldn't help but smirk at her friend.

Sera glanced down at herself. "Oh, shit! No, not conscious at all!"

"It's not the first time I've noticed it," Tanis said. "Last time you talked to Elena, you were full-on harbinger of death when you came back."

"I was?" Sera asked.

"Yeah. Maybe you should add a block to stop your skin from taking this form at all."

Sera held up a hand and examined the long claws on the end of her fingers. "Or maybe I'll just make this my default. Think it would help or hinder negotiations with future allies?"

Tanis lowered her face into her hands and shook it. "Sera, how are *you* the President of the most powerful alliance in humanity's history?"

Sera didn't reply, and when Tanis looked up, her friend was just grinning as she clicked her nails together. When their eyes met, Sera asked, "Yeah? Think we're the most powerful?"

<*Of course we are,*> Angela interjected. <*We have us.*>

Sera's skin reverted back to the blue 'uniform' she typically wore. "True, I suppose we do."

Tanis looked at the ceiling. "Bob, I blame you for this. Why did you have to give her this skin?"

<*Humans' natural epidermis is weak and ineffectual,*> Bob replied without pause. <*What I gave Sera—especially now that Finaeus has integrated the flow-armor into it—is far superior. It provides a multitude of tactical advantages, and constant protection. You'd go through fewer hearts if* ***you*** *adopted it as well.*>

"See!" Sera crowed. "My epidermis is superior. Bob agrees."

<*It's true,*> Angela added. <*Sera's fashion proclivities aside, her skin is highly advantageous. If for no other reason than the protective properties, and her chameleon ability.*>

"I can change my appearance," Tanis countered.

<*A bit, but not like her. She can fit in anywhere.*>

<*Humanity's continuing infatuation with clothing is strange to begin with,*> Bob added. <*Sera's desire to turn herself into a mythological creature actually makes more sense to me than the regular clothing people wear.*>

"This is not the way I was expecting this conversation to go." Tanis leaned back and sighed. "OK, Bob, why is it that

Sera turning herself into a demon-dragon thing is more rational than regular clothing?"

<Well, clothing is generally unnecessary for humans, now that you've mastered your environments. Maybe it is needed for completely unmodified humans living on planets, but otherwise it's superfluous. It consumes a lot of resources and general effort, it seems.>

"People like to express themselves through clothing," Tanis replied. "And some people like to hide their bodies."

<Regarding your second point, that no longer makes sense. Everyone has perfect bodies, maintained in whatever form they want. If they feel ashamed of who they are, that shame is likely a representation of something unhealthy in their minds. Military uniforms are useful for showing a common bond. I suppose you organics may need to have other external expressions of commonality, but it doesn't require clothing, per se.

<Which brings me to my first point. Sera's epidermis is far more capable of expressing herself. In fact, I would argue that Sera's desire to turn herself into whatever strikes her fancy, is far healthier than what most humans do, which is try to hide what they are, and blend in.>

"This is not the first time I've heard this argument," Tanis said. "I know that Sera just loves to be whatever she wants to be, and isn't mentally unstable—it makes sense for her. However, a lot of people, even though they can look perfect, don't *feel* perfect. If they were to costume themselves, they would do it to blend in, and it would end up being the same for them as it is now."

<I can't fix every problem organics have, nor should I. I'm simply stating that Sera's behavior is a logical end-result for a well-balanced person who also likes to be visually and tactilely stimulated. No human would argue that things of beauty are inherently wrong, so no one could say that what Sera does with herself is wrong.>

Sera leaned back on the sofa and gave Tanis a smug smile. "Gotta say, Bob. Never thought that you'd back me on this—also never thought of myself as that mentally well-rounded, but I'll take the compliment."

<*You misunderstand me, Sera,*> Bob said. <*I did not mean to imply that you were the pinnacle of mental health. I just said that in this respect, what you do—your free expression of self—is healthier than what most do. The fact that your expression of self is a demonic being, typically associated with vengeance and destruction, contains its own message.*>

"Annnnd my moment of victory is over."

Tanis laughed. "I'll take the win."

<*I'm sorry, Tanis, you still lose. Your value to your people and humanity is tremendous. The advantages that Sera's epidermis provide should—to my mind, at least—outweigh whatever nonsensical hesitations you may have surrounding replacing your organic skin with something more practical.*>

"I think we both lost in this conversation," Sera said, winking at Tanis. "Though it was a nice distraction from what's coming our way."

"Right, and from Andrea and Justin."

"Tanis! I had managed to forget about them for a moment."

Tanis shrugged, her expression unapologetic. "You really can't. You'll need to find them and determine what they're up to."

Sera's lips flattened out and her eyes widened in frustration. "Transcend is a big place, Tanis. Big enough that half of it probably doesn't know my father is dead yet. They could be anywhere, behind the scenes, manipulating things. Justin has contacts *everywhere*. If he's out, he could be subverting agents I had previously considered loyal to me."

"You need to build your own base, then," Tanis replied. "What about the families on Valkris, where Nadine is from?"

"Helping the families on Valkris is a lot like arming my enemies. I mean…they're not enemies now, but what happens when we win this thing? They're not the sort that help maintain the peace."

Tanis leant over and placed a hand on Sera's knee. "Sera, there are two billion stars within the human sphere of expansion. There will never be peace everywhere. Not so long as humans are humans."

"That's a sad way to look at it."

"I don't need everyone to be happy, I just need them to stop trying to kill everyone else that doesn't agree with them."

Sera laughed. "Oh, just that little thing, eh?"

Tanis gave a short laugh and returned Sera's smile. "It's what we're doing, isn't it? Stopping Orion, securing a real peace in the Inner Stars? We'll be done by lunch, right?"

"Don't get carried away, Tanis. It might take 'til breakfast tomorrow."

"OK, I'll make sure I make some time in my schedule for it."

"You do that."

The two sat in silence for a few minutes, Tanis lost in thought, considering her next moves. She assumed Sera was doing the same, since she wore her customary thinking scowl.

"Have you decided where in Praesepe you're going after things wrap up here?" Sera eventually asked.

"Well, I want to find out more about what happened in Genevia—the tech they used in their mech program is just too similar to what Peter Rhoads used to control his people. If there's a lead on the Caretaker there, I want to find it."

"Are you thinking you can use the device Earnest made to take it out?"

"The Shadowtron? Yeah, that's my hope."

Sera laughed. "What a badass name. No idea if it has anything to do with how the thing really works, but badass nonetheless."

"I guess it has something to do with shadow particles."

"And 'tron'?"

"I imagine it must do something with electrons."

"I guess that makes sense, most tech does use electrons. Still a badass name."

Tanis nodded. "Gotta admit that I like how Earnest made it look like a gun, too."

"Sure doesn't hurt. I assume Finaeus is making more?"

"Yeah, he has a team on it. They're also working on a way to enable the ship's internal sensors to run the sweeps shipwide. Would save us a lot of cat and mouse."

"And then you'll finally catch your little mole."

Tanis let a feral smile slip over her lips. "Indeed, we shall. We'll sweep your ship before you go, too."

"Right! Which of your tiny surplus vessels shall become my flagship?"

"Do you want the *Long Night*?" Tanis asked. "Right now, it just has a shakedown crew aboard, but we can get it properly fitted out and crewed up. I bet that half the captains in the fleet would love to get their hands on it."

Sera nodded appreciatively. "With the exception of Rachel."

"Yeah…I don't think I'll be able to pry the *I2* away from her under any circumstances."

"Not unless you make something bigger."

"Maybe not even then. This girl's pretty special."

"Yeah," Sera nodded, looking around Tanis's cabin as though it were the whole ship. "Even in Transcend and Orion space, there are probably only a dozen ships older than this one—if we're counting the date the keel was laid, not service years."

Tanis patted the sofa. "That's right, don't be calling my girl old!"

"So, Praesepe for you, and Khardine for me. And if you find more leads on the Caretaker?"

Tanis honestly had no idea what would follow. "We'll see how fresh and promising they are. Nadine suggested we find her cousin Nerischka. She worked some missions in Genevian space around the end of their war with Nietzschea."

"That's right," Sera nodded. "Made a few 'tweaks' to the upper military echelon. Got rid of the admirals that wanted to keep steamrolling over more nations. If memory serves, Nerischka's in the Azela system, tracking down the source of some weird bio-mods."

"That's what Nadine said, as well." Tanis reached for her coffee cup, only to find that it was empty. "Damn…I don't even remember finishing that."

"Still catching up with sleep, eh?"

"I guess. No rest for the weary, right?"

"That's what I hear," Sera replied. "So you're just going to hunt the Caretaker for a bit around Praesepe? Seems like an unproductive use of your time."

"Well, we have a few leads. But if they don't pan out, we'll cut our losses. I have a desire to knock the teeth out of the Nietzschean Empire, but I also have a date with the king of the Trisilieds. I think that his neck would look great with my boot on it."

"Not ready to forgive and forget yet?"

Tanis's brow lowered. "I think after about 'never' I'll be ready. Don't worry, though, I'm going to exhibit restraint and not raze their capital world to the ground. However, I *will* do something that completely debilitates them. They earned that much."

"How *are* we going to deal with stuff like that?" Sera asked. "Destroyed nations that we leave in our wake. We can't kill everyone, and we can't leave them there to rebuild."

"That's where the allegiances come in."

"If we can build them faster than our half-dozen enemies attack us."

"Oh, is that how few we have?"

Sera shrugged. "Depends on how you divide them up."

<*Anywhere between seventeen and…thirteen hundred,*> Angela supplied with a grin in their minds. <*You should make them start a registry, or something.*>

Tanis summoned a view of the galaxy above the coffee table, then focused in on human space. Closest to her was the Perseus arm, then Orion, and the Sagittarius Arm was up against Sera's knees.

"Last we heard." Tanis pointed at a marker close to Sol. "Jessica and team have moved on from Virginis. She said they formed a solid allegiance there—which I bet pisses off the Hegemony to no end."

Sera leant forward, placing her elbows on her knees and chin on her folded hands. "Yeah, the AST used to run a lot of black ops in Virginis. Getting kicked out by a bunch of AIs must really burn their cookies."

"Which means they're on to Aldebaran."

Sera shifted, rubbing her palms across her face and through her hair. "Stars, good luck with that. I don't even know how they'll get in the system."

"That's why we sent *them*," Tanis replied. "Sure, there are humans on *Sabrina*, but it's almost entirely an AI ship now. If anyone can pull it off, it's them."

"Stars, I hope so. We keep giving them all the shit assignments."

"And they knock it out of the park each time." Tanis gave Sera a reassuring look. "They've got QuanComm blades; if they need us, they'll call."

"What about the delegation to Corona Australis?" Sera asked. "Care to put odds on them?"

Tanis gave a rueful laugh. "They've got better chances than the team at Dorcha. I feel like we should have just sent an ultimatum and then started a war without waiting for a response."

"Don't count Admiral Bartty out yet. He's got some tricks up his sleeves."

"May he have endless sleeves," Tanis said, raising the cup of coffee the servitor had just brought in a toast.

Sera leaned back and looked over the billions of stars that lay between the two women. "I have a feeling we're *all* going to need endless sleeves."

SURVEYING VELA

STELLAR DATE: 11.01.8948 (Adjusted Years)
LOCATION: *Greensward*
REGION: Estrada System, Vela Cluster

"Dammit, she got here first, that bitch," Andrea Tomlinson swore as she glared at the holotank on the *Greensward*'s bridge. "Fucking Chancellor Alma has declared for the Khardine government."

Justin nodded silently as he stared at the feeds displayed in the tank. "Looks like Admiral Krissy showed up with a fleet. I'm surprised to see her operating so openly. The Grey Division really has it out for her."

Andrea glanced at Justin. "I recall hearing something about that, do tell."

"Pretty simple: the Greys were after Finaeus, and Krissy helped him escape."

Andrea considered that for a moment. From what Justin had told her, the Grey Division worked for Airtha…who may or may not be Andrea's mother—a thought both chilling and disturbing.

At present, Andrea considered the Greys to be her greatest threat. Justin—thanks to his centuries as Director of the Hand—had many contacts to leverage, but most of those were in the Inner Stars. Many had allied with Sera—the Khardine Sera, not the Sera who had proclaimed herself President at Airtha.

Within the Transcend, the Greys were the shadow organization behind the scenes. And they worked for Airtha. Dealing with her sister would be a straight-up conflict, that was just how Sera operated. But the Greys would never hit head-on. Their moves would always come from the side.

Just like what Airtha had done by making another Sera.

Just like my sister. Little upstart thinks so much of herself, she can't exist just once. There has to be two of her, and ***both*** *have to be the president, squabbling over the Transcend—which by rights should be mine.*

She realized that Justin was expecting a response, and shrugged. "Well, Admiral Krissy seems to be unconcerned about the Greys now, at least. Showing up with a fleet of ten-thousand ships has all but secured the Vela Cluster for her."

Justin chuckled and shook his head. "Yeah, a fleet of ships—some of which are nearly impervious—have a way of helping out."

"Not funny, Justin," Andrea spat. "If you pulled me out of that mind-prison just to drag me around the Transcend, hiding on this garbage scow…." She left the statement hanging, not sure what else he should have done. A part of her wouldn't mind going back to the beach she had been living on—or had thought she'd been living on.

Stop it, Andrea. That's the conditioning. Fight it.

Justin shook his head. "Only *you* could call a luxury yacht a 'garbage scow'."

"I should be on a fleet's flagship, flying into Airtha to seize the capital!"

Justin raised a hand, gesturing for her to calm down. "We have a fleet, but we can't show it yet. First, we have to get our hands on New Canaan's stasis shield technology. Without it, any assault would just be pissing away our resources."

"Resources we hoped to accumulate with Chancellor Alma on our side."

"Alma and Vela are just one player in the Transcend. There are a hundred sectors just as powerful and wealthy as Vela. Sure, it's larger than most, and strategically located, but alone, it's hardly noteworthy."

Andrea made a frustrated sound and stormed off the bridge, yelling over her shoulder, "Well, let me know when we go somewhere noteworthy. I'll be in my quarters."

* * * * *

For the hundredth time, Justin thought about terminating his allegiance with Andrea.

With extreme prejudice.

The woman's time in the reconditioning prison had caused her to become even more unhinged. Her emotions were always spilling over now, and it had gone far beyond frustrating. The woman's very presence was like having insects crawl all over his skin while a klaxon blared in his ears.

No…that gives insects a bad name.

"I take it that things are not as promising here as we'd hoped?" Roxy asked as she strolled onto the bridge.

Justin glanced at the woman who was his sure right hand—and an amazing fuck on the side. Where Andrea was a raging storm, Roxy was a calm breeze. A deceptively calm breeze.

To look at her small frame, barely over one hundred and fifty centimeters tall, you'd think she could barely heft a rifle; if she were a normal human, that would be true. But Roxy was barely human at all anymore, possessing the minimum organics necessary to feed a brain with the nutrients it required.

Despite that, the package Roxy came in was a delight to behold. Gleaming sapphire skin with azure streaks, and all the right curves and angles made her the pinnacle of desire-inducing beauty.

Justin should know—he'd made Roxy what she was today.

She sauntered toward him, her skin sparkling in the light the holotank cast on the dim bridge, and he reached a hand out to her.

"They beat us here. In the form of Admiral Krissy. Chancellor Alma has sided with Khardine."

"I guess that explains all the shrieking from her imperial bitchiness."

"Yeah, I'm going to have to get a muzzle of some sort for her."

Roxy traced a fingernail down Justin's arm, small sparks of electricity arcing between them when she pulled away. "I could think of something. You know that we have to get her under control…she's not useful like this."

Justin nodded. He'd never planned for Andrea to be anything more than a figurehead; she was intended to be his ticket to rally followers. The problem was that her reputation was legendary, and she had to be full of fire. If he had a sedate, subdued Andrea at his side, everyone would know she was little more than a puppet.

He'd hoped that Andrea would learn to moderate herself, but it hadn't happened. More invasive measures would have to be taken.

"*Could* you think of something? Or *have* you thought of something?" Justin asked Roxy.

Roxy smiled, obsidian fangs peeking over her lips. "Oh, maybe a little from column A, a little from column B."

"Speak clearly, Roxy."

"Well, there's the old-fashioned way, or we can put her back in the reconditioning sims, and alter her personality and convictions just enough to follow you unconditionally."

"That takes too long," Justin replied. "Especially with someone as pig-headed as she is. So much of her personality is tied up in centuries of belief that she's the queen of everything."

"Hmm…" Roxy reached up and ran a finger down her ear—one of her favorite places to be touched and touch. "Well, what if we went the other way? Rather than trying to moderate her, what if we turned her into what she really wants to be: the queen of the universe. Just a *mannered* queen of the universe."

Justin considered that, his lips twisting as he mulled it over. "That could work. She'd be more conniving, though. Right now, she telegraphs everything—which is convenient when it comes to knowing her intentions."

"We could use the thing that *it* gave you."

"The neural lace? I suppose, but that's an extreme option. One that can be detected—it would ruin the fiction that she is her own person."

Roxy nodded. "Understood. Why did you use it on me, then?"

Justin stepped toward Roxy and wrapped her in his arms. "Because you're *not* your own person. You're mine."

TO KHARDINE

STELLAR DATE: 11.02.8948 (Adjusted Years)
LOCATION: ISS *Long Night*
REGION: Silstrand System, Silstrand Alliance

Sera stood on the bridge of the *Long Night*, the holotank before her displaying a view of the ship as it approached the Silstrand jump gate.

She closed her eyes and slowly let out a long breath. *Time to get to work, I suppose.*

A part of Sera wished that she could be the captain of the *Long Night*; just a soldier doing her job, not the one who had to deal with a hundred crises a minute.

<*Thank the stars for Tanis,*> she thought.

<*Sorry?*> Jen asked.

<*Shoot, I've fallen out of the habit of thought segregation. That was just for me.*>

Jen gave a soft laugh. <*Well, we're all thankful for Tanis. Are you worried about her?*>

Sera looked at the looming shape of the *I2* hanging in the distance. <*A bit. Less than I should be? I'm not sure.*> Sera gave a rueful laugh. <*I can't tell my worry about the future in general apart from worry about her, specifically.*>

<*I get that,*> Jen replied. <*Stars, do I get that.*>

<*Well, it's not like I think we're going to lose this war and get our asses kicked, Jen. Don't get all defeatist on me.*>

<*Sorry, that's not the impression I meant to give.*> Jen's voice sounded more upbeat. <*I was getting caught up in your emotions. You're bleeding them across our connection—a lot.*>

Sera grimaced. <*Sorry about that. This feels a lot different than when Helen was in my mind.*>

<It's weird for me, too. Helen had a very non-standard integration. The technicians had to mimic some of the patterns when they interwove my hardware.>

Sera recalled the medtechs telling her that as well. They said that without neurological reconstruction in several areas, they would have to use the existing AI interface points.

When Sera had queried them on what they meant, the explanation was that her connection with Helen had been less buffered than normal. In addition, the locations where the neurological interconnections lay allowed the resident AI to have more access into her mind.

Access that resulted in the bleed-through that Jen often experienced.

For her part, Jen handled the slip-ups with grace and understanding. She was a good person, and brave to take on the added responsibilities of being in Sera's head.

<We'll figure this out eventually,> Sera replied to Jen. *<Still glad you signed on?>*

<Of course! I'm working hand-in-hand—so to speak—with the President of the Transcend! You're the most powerful human in the galaxy.>

Sera snorted. *<OK, Jen, ease up a bit. We all know that's not true.>*

As if on cue, Tanis reached out to her. *<Well, Sera, I'll see you soon. Let's make sure it's not eighteen years this time.>*

<I thought we already said our goodbyes,> Sera shot back. *<If you make me get sniffly in front of my new crew…>*

<If you do, it'll be fine. I'm pretty sure I've cried at least once on the bridge of the Intrepid*, and no one made me walk the plank.>*

<I'll cite that if they try to kick me out an airlock,> Sera said with an audible laugh that got her a few looks from the *Long Night*'s bridge crew.

<*We have the QuanComms. We'll keep in touch. You let me know if you need help. I'll drop a whole civilization in a hot second if your ass is on the line.*>

Sera gave a slight shake of her head. <*No you won't, Tanis. You care too much about…everyone.*>

<*You should see the tongue-lashing I gave a rating this morning. Trust me, he doesn't feel that way.*>

<*Stop trying to cheer me up, Tanis.*>

<*Is it working?*>

<*Yes…and no. Just gonna make me miss you more.*>

Tanis laughed, the sound pure and clear in Sera's mind. <*Don't you go girl-crushing on me, Sera. You know I don't swing that way.*>

<*Oh yeah? Angela told me about how you 'made' Faleena.*>

<*Ang!*> Tanis said in mock anger. <*What did you have to do that for?*>

Angela only laughed in response.

<*It's OK, Tanis. I know you're taken. But I don't miss you in that way anyway—well, I would if you gave it a chance. I bet we could convince Joe—*>

<*Sera!*>

<*Sorry…just trying to take my mind off…everything.*>

Tanis made an exasperated sound. <*You know what I remember?*>

<*What?*>

<*I remember this freighter captain who risked her life to save me, who didn't take no for an answer, and who kicked the asses of an entire pirate base—one in the dark layer, no less—on her own. A woman who, as you tell the story, had already rescued herself by the time I showed up. Always in control, always willing to do whatever needed to be done.*>

Tanis's mental tone was filled with a conviction that Sera couldn't deny. It reminded her of a type of strength she'd forgotten she had.

<If ***she*** *believes in you that much, there's a reason,>* Jen said quietly. *<Sorry, I'm not sure if you left that conversation open to me on purpose.>*

<I did,> Sera replied. *<So long as you're OK with it, I'll leave pretty much everything open to you.>*

<Absolutely.>

Sera was grateful that she'd found Jen. She'd vetted so many AIs who were more than eager to take on the role and responsibilities that came with integrating with the President of the Transcend.

Almost *too* eager.

Jen…Jen had just seemed like she wanted to be friends. Not that she wasn't also well-qualified for the job; all the AIs were, by the time they made it as far as Sera. She'd been told that Bob's vetting process was very involved.

But for all that, Jen just seemed sincere.

"President Tomlinson," Captain Ophelia said from behind her.

Sera turned to see the man standing in front of his command chair, arms clasped behind his back.

"We're ready to go in. Say the word."

Sera nodded. "Just a moment."

<Time to go, Tanis. Remember. If I call, I expect you to come running.>

Tanis laughed again, and Sera relaxed in the warmth coming from her friend. *<You bet I will. Same goes for you, too, Missus President of the Universe.>*

Sera laughed. *<Deal. See you when I see you.>*

<When I see you.>

Sera was ready. Ready to leave the Inner Stars, to take on the responsibilities that awaited her at Khardine. To bring the fight to her mother.

"Captain Ophelia. Take us through."

THE HUNT

STELLAR DATE: 11.02.8948 (Adjusted Years)
LOCATION: ISS *I2*, Bridge
REGION: Orbiting Silstrand, Silstrand System, Silstrand Alliance

<Captain! I need you in Engine.>

Rachel was out of her chair before she even formulated a response.

<Did you find one, Terry?>

<Yes, you said you wanted to be present for the capture.>

"Major Calmin, you have the conn," Rachel called out as she rushed off the bridge.

"Aye, ma'am, I have the conn," she heard Calmin call out as she sped past Tori in the bridge's foyer.

<Good hunting,> Tori said with a wink a second before Calmin sent a query.

<Anything I should be worried about, Captain?>

<Just the hunt, Calmin. Need to keep it quiet.>

She could tell Calmin was suppressing a laugh. *<Ma'am, I don't think racing off the bridge like your pants are on fire is how you keep things quiet.>*

Rachel hiked her skirt up, wishing she *had* worn pants today. *<Very funny, Major.>*

<Aye, ma'am, I thought so. Let me know how it goes.>

<Absolutely.>

She called for an express car to Engine as she slowed her mad dash to a rapid stride down the long administrative concourse to the command deck's maglev station.

When she arrived, the express car was waiting, and Rachel stepped inside. The car started to move, and then shuddered to a stop.

Rachel was about to query the traffic NSAI for status, when the doors opened and Tanis walked in.

"Admiral Richards!" Rachel hadn't been aware Tanis was on the command deck.

"Rachel," Tanis nodded as the maglev train took off from the station. "Hope you don't mind if I hitch a ride. And don't call me that when we're in private. How many times do I have to tell you that?"

"Stars, Tanis, sometimes I think no one has ever disliked their rank more than you."

Tanis laughed as she sat across from Rachel. "I think you'd be surprised. Everyone always thinks they want to get to the top so that no one tells them what to do, but, damn…there's a lot of stuff to figure out when you get there."

"I think I have an inkling of what that's like. I have a lot of respect for you and Captain Andrews."

"Me?" Tanis's eyebrows rose.

"Well, yeah, both of you have captained this ship."

Tanis's lips spread into a wry smile. "I think you'll find that's not true. My butt may have spent a lot of time in that command chair, but I was never captain of this ship."

Rachel made a quick scan of the records. "Would you look at that…for some reason I'd always thought…"

"How's it feel to be the second captain of this girl?" Tanis asked.

"About the same," Rachel grinned. "Like it's the best, hardest job I've ever had."

Tanis winked. "Just wait 'til I promote you."

Rachel's eyes widened, and she felt her eyebrows almost hit her hairline. "Don't you dare, Admiral! No!"

<Stop messing with her,> Angela chimed in. *<She'll chain herself to the keel if we try to give her another command.>*

<I like Rachel where she is,> Bob intoned.

"Uh…wow. Thanks, Bob." Rachel had not expected the AI to back her up. She wasn't sure if that made her feel more confident, or a bit worried that the AI had plans for her.

Tanis, on the other hand, rolled her eyes. "Really, Bob. You don't have a say in who I promote and when."

<*Keep telling yourself that,*> Bob chuckled.

Rachel leant forward and whispered to Tanis. "Did Bob just try to be funny?"

Tanis pursed her lips and nodded. "It's a new thing of his. He's just full of the ha-ha's."

<*Rachel thinks I'm funny. She correctly identified my statement as humorous.*>

"You can recognize an attempt at humor, as well. Doesn't mean it was actually funny," Tanis replied.

<*Ouch.*>

<*Be nice, Tanis,*> Angela appeared as a holoimage on the train and shook a finger at Tanis before disappearing again.

Huh, she looked almost exactly like Tanis. Like she was admonishing herself, Rachel mused.

Tanis looked up and saw that Rachel was staring intently at her.

"Yeah, it's like I'm my own mom or something. Stars, that's a disturbing thought."

"So, what's got you all into the ha-ha's?" Rachel asked Bob, changing the subject.

<*Marge, who resides in Kylie Rhoads, gave me a series of books that I'm reading. They're quite amusing, and I am trying to replicate that humor.*>

"Really? I didn't know you read books, Bob. What are they called?"

<*I do from time to time. This series is called 'Mysteries of Fennington Station'. I understand that it is a type of story referred to as a 'cozy mystery'. People die, so I don't know why it's 'cozy'. I've read all fifty-five books, and the most recent one that Marge stole from the publisher. Now I'm starting over with book 1, 'Whole Latte Death'.*>

"Really? How long does it take you to read a book?" Rachel asked. "A millisecond?"

<*These books are different,*> Angela responded. <*We have to spin off a subroutine and clock it at 99.99MHz. They take about an hour to read.*>

"It makes me feel like there's a bee inside my head when you do that," Tanis complained. "You need to go to the expanse when you read those from now on."

<*You'd enjoy them, Tanis.*> Bob's voice contained a note of humor. <*Especially when the cat finds the je—*>

<*BOB! Spoilers!*> Angela shouted.

<*Sorry.*>

Tanis laughed and shook her head. "OK, I really do have to read these now."

The maglev train slowed as it reached the platform closest to Engine, and the two women disembarked, following the twisted corridors until they reached Terry's location.

The Chief of Security was in a small storage room near one of Engine's machine shops. Rachel noted that they were only a short distance from the MSAR region, where the ship's particle accelerator funneled scooped hydrogen into the matter annihilator that produced energy and antimatter.

Though CriEn technology meant they didn't need to run the annihilator anymore, Rachel preferred to keep it operational as a backup power system.

It was currently undergoing its weekly test run.

"Tanis, Rachel," Terry said as the two women joined her in the storage room.

"All alone in here?" Tanis asked, and Rachel looked around, surprised to see none of the SOC MPs present.

"I figured that there's nothing the three of us can't do," Terry replied. "I have teams nearby, but Finaeus has only made the three Shadowtrons—he has Earnest's original disassembled in his lab."

Rachel approached one of the gun-like devices that sat on a table beside Terry. It reminded her of an ME-33 sniper rifle, but with seven barrels instead of one.

She picked one up. "I still can't believe this is called a 'Shadowtron'. I thought that was a joke when I first heard it."

"Sera loved the name. Said it was 'badass'," Tanis said with a laugh as she picked up one of the weapons.

<I kinda wish I had a Shadowtron,> Angela added.

Terry hefted hers. "I don't care what they're called, so long as they work."

"So, what's the target?" Rachel asked.

Terry passed a data packet to Rachel and Tanis over the Link. "Ensign Kasha. She's a tech who works on the annihilator. Bob says she's in Machine Bay 13.11 working on fabbing some replacement parts for after the test run today."

"Stars," Tanis muttered. "She wasn't even on the list of suspects for people who could have freed Elena. Which means that either the remnant in her is very good, or there's someone else, still."

"We'll know more once we nab her." Terry walked toward the door and looked at the other two. "I'll cover the rear entrance; I assume you want the honors, Tanis?"

"Do you even have to ask?"

"Uh, no, I guess not," Terry laughed.

Two minutes later, they were in position. Terry was just outside the machine bay's rear door, and Rachel outside the main door. Tanis was making her way past the fab units to where Kasha stood at a testing rig that was putting the new components through their paces.

Rachel heard Tanis say something to Kasha, then she heard a scream and a brief scuffle.

A minute later, Ensign Kasha appeared at the far end of a row of fab units, racing toward the door.

Rachel raised her Shadowtron and fired the eV detection wave toward Kasha. Sure enough, the holodisplay on the weapon showed a remnant within the woman. She wasted no time firing the capture field, and saw the remnant begin to flow out of the Ensign.

<*Got it?*> Tanis asked, appearing at the far end of the row, advancing with her Shadowtron held level.

<*I think so, it's coming toward my—*> As Rachel spoke, the wave coming from her Shadowtron flickered, and the remnant broke free from the field.

It streaked past Rachel and down the hall.

<*Shit, it got free!*>

Rachel turned and gave chase, following the remnant via the display on her Shadowtron.

She heard Tanis behind her, but didn't look back as they raced through Engine.

<*It's headed to the MSAR,*> Tanis called out.

<*Trying to cut it off!*> Terry replied.

Rachel rounded a corner and then passed down a long corridor, the remnant a dozen meters away, slowly increasing the gap.

Then Terry appeared at the end of the passageway, firing her weapon. But the remnant was moving too fast, and a second later, it was past Terry and through the doors leading into the MSAR.

The three women burst into the MSAR and raced through the forest that surrounded the annihilator.

<*I lost it,*> Rachel called out.

Terry waved them on from her place in the lead. <*I haven't.*>

The trees began to thin, and they came into the large clearing in the center of the MSAR where the matter annihilator stood on its tower.

<*Shit!*> Tanis swore. <*It's going for the annihilator!*>

<*What will happen if it gets there?*> Rachel asked.

<*It will die,*> Bob supplied.

Rachel spotted the remnant twisting around one of the struts supporting the annihilator and fired at the thing, but it was out of the Shadowtron's effective range.

Terry had stopped running and Rachel caught up to her, Tanis a moment later. Rachel watched through the holodisplay on her weapon as the remnant reached the inlet portal for the annihilator, and passed through the weaker field there before being drawn into the annihilation chamber.

"Damn, it's gone," Tanis said with a heavy sigh.

"I'll count that as a win," Terry said, lowering her weapon.

Rachel realized that Tanis had been staring up at the annihilator without using her weapon's detection wave to see the remnant.

She was about to ask how Tanis could see the thing, when the Admiral shook her head and walked off, leaving Terry and Rachel standing beside one another, wondering if Bob was right.

Had the thing died in the annihilator, or did it escape somehow and evade detection?

"Let's do a sweep to be sure," Rachel said, and Terry nodded.

Neither were surprised when they didn't find anything.

UNINTENTIONAL BAIT

STELLAR DATE: 02.09.8949 (Adjusted Years)
LOCATION: TSS *Regent Mary*, Bridge
REGION: Near Montana, Galas System, Vela Cluster

"Ensign Dyna! What's the ETA on recharge?" Krissy called out as the ship's AI executed a new jinking pattern. The dampening systems were running on reserves, and the rapid maneuvers were beginning to jostle the crew.

"Ma'am! CriEns are *all* offline, main connection got disconnected, backup isn't failing over. Repair team is at the relay, working on it."

Krissy ground her teeth. She'd asked for an ETA, but his answer told her what she needed to know: not soon enough.

She glanced at the main holotank. The three Airthan cruisers were still back there, closing, but holding their fire. They may have caught Krissy's ship, the *Regent Mary,* with its stasis shields offline, but the shield was up now, and even with the CriEn modules offline, the ship could withstand a withering assault.

For about ten minutes or so.

She turned and stalked back to the command seat, settling into it. Captain Nelson should be in it, but he was in the infirmary, having been hit by shrapnel during the enemy's opening salvo.

Krissy blamed herself. Khardine forces hadn't seen any Airthan ships in the Vela Cluster since their arrival, and she'd grown lax.

The *Regent Mary* had been taking in supplies above Montana, shields down and engines cold, when the enemy ships had appeared and opened fire.

"What's the scan data say?" Krissy asked. "Were they stealthed, and we just missed them somehow?"

"No, ma'am," Ensign Donald replied. "They appeared between us and the local star. Even ISF stealth tech would have cast a shadow at that range."

"Are you saying they jumped in?" Krissy asked sharply.

Ensign Donald nodded. "I don't see any other alternative, Admiral Krissy."

Krissy sat back heavily. That meant one of two things: there was a traitor at the Sector Command, or there was a traitor here at Montana. Someone had to have passed the Airthans intel on her location with enough advance notice for them to get the message to vessels that were in a position to jump in.

The Vela Cluster contained thousands of stars, and Krissy's fleet had barely visited ten percent of them—there could be dozens of holdouts harboring Airthans.

I need more ships! Krissy shouted in her mind. She was spreading herself too thin...as evidenced by being in this system with just one ship, and getting caught with her pants down.

Even so, she had a tool that the enemy did not. One that she was all too willing to avail herself of, especially right now.

"Comm. Message to Admiral Orman. Advise him of our situation, and tell him I want his...second division here on the double."

"Yes, ma'am!" the ensign on Comm called out before activating the QuanComm system.

"Let's see you beat this," Krissy muttered aloud, and received a few appreciative nods from members of the bridge crew.

Admiral Orman and his fleet were currently guarding Estrada, the capital of the Vela Cluster. Based on his latest reports, the second division should be close to the system's inner jump gates. With a quick data relay at Khardine and factoring in time to get the ships through the gates, she could expect to see backup within twenty minutes.

So long as the enemy didn't decide to test out the stasis shields on her ship overmuch, they could hold out that long with ease.

"Admiral Orman confirms," Comm announced. "Second division ETA to jump gates is fifteen minutes. Full ship transfer is twenty-seven."

The Estrada System had eleven jump gates. Provided all were currently online, that meant the initial group of ships would be more than enough to subdue the three enemy cruisers.

"Thank you, Comm," Krissy replied, resolving to keep ships closer to gates in the future.

"They're firing on us again!" Ensign Donald cried out from Scan. "Helm's jinking pattern is ninety percent effective."

<*Helm has a name, Ensign,*> Hemdar chastised the man. <*Use it.*>

"Sorry, sir," Ensign Donald replied, reddening as he spoke.

<*Hemdar, be nice to the FGNs, they're not in infinite supply.*>

<*I've only told him privately seven times that I prefer to be called by name,*> Hemdar replied. <*I figured a verbal reminder, so to speak, might serve him better.*>

<*Relax, Hemdar, we've been through worse than this little chase around Montana. Don't let it get to you. Besides, the Airthans will want to take me alive, if they can. Worst-case scenario, we wave a white flag 'til Orman's second division gets here.*>

<*Surrender? Over my burning hull.*>

<*Well, not like we let them board us, or anything. Just let them* **think** *they're going get to board us.*>

A plotted course appeared on the holotank, showing a potential course toward Montana's second moon.

<*They have defensive emplacements on that moon,*> Hemdar spoke over the bridge net as he highlighted a dozen points on the largely barren surface. <*If they fire those, they can drive off the Airthan ships.*>

Krissy drummed her fingers on the command chair's armrest. "Perhaps. *If* the locals aren't the ones who sold us out to begin with—it could be that they might just fire on us."

<*Try the base commander down there,*> Hemdar suggested privately.

<*So bossy,*> Krissy shot back.

Krissy pulled up the records on the Montana system's garrison. Provided no one had abandoned their posts—which had happened in some places—there should be a Major named Kevin in charge.

"Comm, get me the base on that moon. I want to speak with Major Kevin."

<*Why didn't you reach out to him without my prompting?*> Hemdar asked.

Krissy sighed. The reason was simple, but not one she cared to voice. It was because she was afraid. Not afraid of the moon shooting at her, or that the base commander had decided to side with Airtha.

She was more afraid that he would sit it out altogether.

Thrice now, she'd encountered star systems that had declared themselves to be 'independent'. Even the TSF garrisons had joined with the local governments, abandoning their duties and posts.

Somehow that was worse than if they'd sided with Airtha. At least then she could see some amount of honor in their actions. Declaring for nothing was worse than joining with the enemy.

"I have the major!" Comm called out.

"That fast?" Krissy asked in surprise.

The Comm officer glanced back at Krissy. "He called us a moment before I made the connection."

Krissy felt her spirits rise. Maybe she'd get a pleasant surprise. "Put him on."

The vector display shifted to a secondary holo, and the main tank was filled with a broad-shouldered man who wore a deep scowl—which was quickly replaced by surprise.

"Admiral Krissy!"

"Major Kevin, may I assume you are calling to render assistance?"

"Well…I wasn't sure who I was going to be talking to—things are chaotic right now, ma'am."

Krissy cleared her throat. "Major. That was not what I asked. I have three enemy ships on my tail, and the Vela Cluster has declared for Khardine."

It was bluster and they all knew it. Chancellor Alma had declared that the Vela Cluster would side with Khardine. But out here, that meant less than it did at Estrada.

What Krissy really needed were victories against the Airthans. One here would be a huge coup.

Everyone wanted to be on the winning side. Diplomacy was one thing, but decisive action against the enemy would galvanize systems and bring them flocking to Khardine's banner.

"Yes, Admiral, but your ship is damaged, and I have no other support. If I fire on those ships, I can take out one, maybe two. Then they pound my emplacements to dust. I won't throw away my people's lives for nothing."

Concern for his people is better than nothing, Krissy thought.

"We're not out of the fight yet, Major. I just need you to give us cover as we brake around the moon. When we come out the other side, we'll be ready to take them down. I'm not going to leave you high and dry, I promise. If you check my record, you'll see evidence of that."

She could see her words put some steel in Major Kevin's spine. He straightened and gave a firm nod. "I don't need to look up your record, Admiral. I've heard the stories."

Krissy grinned at the major. "Then can I count on you to honor your oath to the TSF?"

He nodded sharply. "Yes you can, ma'am. Is there a priority target, or should we pepper them all and force them into low efficiency jinking patterns?"

"The latter," Krissy replied. "All we need are a few minutes."

"On it, Admiral Krissy. Warming up the guns."

<*See, told you it would be worth a shot,*> Hemdar admonished.

Krissy nodded and didn't reply, she noticed smiles on the faces of the bridge crew. Having that conversation in front of the entire bridge was a risky proposition. If Major Kevin had been a coward, it would have damaged morale.

As it was, spirits were lifted to know that at least this one man and his command were going to stand up for what they claimed to believe in.

"Hemdar, set the course," Krissy said, knowing that Hemdar was already preparing the burn.

<*Aye, Admiral,*> he replied over the bridge net.

The ship pivoted, angling past the moon, and the main engines fired, slowly changing the ship's trajectory. The relative velocity to the moon was just over 0.03*c*, and it began to fall as Hemdar slowly pivoted the ship further.

"The Airthans are braking so they don't overshoot us," Scan announced.

"Good. They *think* that they know what we're doing, and that we don't have the power to fire on their engines while they brake."

The channel to Major Kevin was still open, and he nodded. "Cocky bastards. We're ready, Admiral."

<*I've coordinated our jinking pattern with their targeting NSAI,*> Hemdar added.

I sure hope Angela's fix is still in place here. Krissy resisted the urge to close her eyes. "Fire at will, Major."

Krissy shifted Major Kevin to the secondary holotank and brought up a view of the moon, the three pursuers, and the *Regent Mary* on the main tank.

The Airthan ships were a hair over forty-thousand kilometers behind the *Regent Mary*, and the moon was still one hundred and ten thousand kilometers distant.

Too far for pinpoint precision on jinking ships, but close enough to scare them.

Six rail emplacements on the moon's surface fired, sending uranium slugs streaking through space at over ten-thousand kilometers-per-second.

Just over ten seconds to react gave the Airthans plenty of time to move their ships, but a second salvo was already firing, forcing the enemy vessels to jink in ever more erratic patterns, slowing their ships further and widening the gap between them and the *Regent Mary.*

Krissy wondered what the enemy ships would do. Two of the vessels were Saggitar Class cruisers that could fire rails on nearly any vector. The third was a Cranmore Class destroyer; its only rear-firing weapons system were defensive beams.

If she were the captain of that ship, she would feel very nervous about turning to fire on the moon.

"This is the first time I've ever been happy about a Cranmore's weapon systems," Krissy muttered.

There were a few nods around the bridge, but no one was happy about firing on ships filled with people and AIs who had been comrades just a few months ago.

Sure enough, the destroyer shifted its vector and moved stellar northwest, altering its trajectory to cover the far side of the moon, where the *Regent Mary* would emerge after its loop.

"But they're exposing their flank to the moon," Scan muttered. "Doesn't make any sense."

"Don't forget," Krissy cautioned. "The Airthans have the same information we do about this moon and its stationary emplacements."

"Bastards are pocketing right into a spot our rails can't hit," Major Kevin nodded. "But what they don't know is that when another command in this system…devolved…I picked up a pod of attack drones."

Krissy wanted to deliver a biting comment about not sharing that rather useful information with her before now, but she reminded herself that beggars can't be choosers and nodded to the man.

"Full pod? What model?"

"One hundred and ten, the MK-97s."

Krissy nodded. The 97s were an older model, but that number was more than enough to drive off the destroyer—either that, or the cruisers would have to stop chasing her to aid it.

"Let 'em rip, Major."

"They're in the chutes, deploying in thirty seconds."

Thirty seconds; otherwise known as a lifetime.

Though the *Regent Mary* continued to decelerate on its approach to the moon, the Airthan cruisers were falling further behind. Krissy had to hand it to their captains. Though their jinks were random, their general trajectory was toward the moon's poles.

If the enemy ships continued on this trajectory, they would be positioned on three sides of the moon when the *Regent Mary* passed behind it.

The tactic was solid, and would lead to certain victory—if the *'Mary* was alone.

Droves of civilian ships began to pull out of orbits around the moon, determined to be anywhere but where the four ships were about to begin their fight.

"Comm, keep Orman advised of the civilian vectors. They're pulling out of STC assigned lanes."

"Yes, ma'am, transmitting anticipated enemy positions."

"Orman?" Major Kevin asked, his brows raised. "How is he insystem? We don't see him on scan."

Krissy turned to look at the major on the secondary holotank. "Sorry, Major, you're just going to have to trust me for a little bit longer."

"Yes, Admiral."

Despite her not sharing her plans with him, the Major appeared pleased with her response. She supposed knowing that his base wasn't about to be blown into oblivion was morale boosting.

"Drones are launched," Major Kevin informed the bridge crew. "They have their target."

"I have them on scan," Ensign Dyson confirmed. "The destroyer is altering course."

"Million klick range on those Mark 97's," Major Kevin was grinning now. "They're going to have to run for a while."

With only two targets to focus on, the moon's railguns drove more fire into the Airthan cruisers, who had still not fired back on the moon.

What are they planning? Krissy wondered.

"Major—" she began, when Kevin swore.

"Dammit, that report was never supposed to be circulated!"

Krissy turned to face his holo. "What is it?"

"Our equatorial emplacements can't hit ships above the poles. They're *designed* to, but under testing, the magnetic field strength wasn't enough to bend the shots at acute angles. We've had an order in for upgrades for years, but it's never come. In another minute, they'll only be in range of the two polar emplacements.

"Shit!" Krissy swore. "They'll weather that with ease—or blast 'em to smithereens. What I wouldn't give for grapeshot."

"Ma'am! Grapeshot is against our doctrine," Major Kevin replied.

"Major, if I had grapeshot available, I'd fire every damn gram at these bastards." She turned to Ensign Quan on weapons. "Helm, spin us. Weapons, lay into them with the rails. If they think they're going to hit a dead spot, they've got another think coming. Target the cruiser at the north pole. Major Kevin, concentrate all your fire on that cruiser headed for the south pole. When they're in range, lay on your p-beams."

"Aye, ma'am."

With the dampeners on low power, the ship shuddered as each rail shot tore out of the accelerator, but Krissy didn't care. They just had to hold out for another two minutes.

The *Regent Mary* was within ten-thousand kilometers of the moon now, braking hard from its prior velocity. In thirty seconds, they'd be behind the bulk of the dull grey orb.

But that cover would only last so long.

Based on current vectors, the enemy cruisers would be in a position to fire on the *'Mary* seventy seconds later.

It was going to be tight.

"They're firing on the polar emplacements!" Scan announced.

Krissy watched as the two polar rail emplacements on the moon were smashed to dust by beam fire from the cruisers.

Major Kevin made a small noise of dismay. "Ma'am, I have no further firing options, unless you count close-range SSMs."

"No," Krissy shook her head. "You don't have enough of those missiles to make it past those cruisers' point defense beams and penetrate shields."

The major nodded, and Krissy glanced at the status of the CriEn power hookups. Estimates were at two minutes.

Every eye on the bridge had turned to the main holotank showing the moon with the two cruisers, each approaching over the poles, and the *Regent Mary,* momentarily hidden behind the horizon.

A timer above the display counted down the seconds until the enemy would have firing solutions.

"I hope you have a whole Snark deck up your sleeve, Admiral." Major Kevin's voice wavered, and Krissy turned to nod soberly. "The enemy's gonna wish it was *just* a Snark deck."

The countdown hit zero, and the enemy ships opened fire on the *Regent Mary.* Particle beams blazed trails through space, the lines glowing brightly on both the holo and visuals, excited photons spiraling away as the beams smashed into stray hydrogen atoms in the vacuum of space.

The *Regent Mary* shuddered, and consoles flashed warnings as the backup fusion generators reached critical levels.

That was the problem with stasis; nowhere to bleed the heat. The more the generators worked to keep the shields up, the more heat they trapped within those shields.

Krissy held her breath as the second counter, this one at the bottom of the holo, hit zero.

C'monnnnn, Krissy thought, willing Orman's second division to appear. *What's taking so long?*

One second passed, then two. Krissy drew a deep breath. "Major Kevin, fire every SSM you have."

"Ma'am," the major grunted in acknowledgement.

"I have them, the fleet's here!" Scan cried out.

"Belay that, Major!" Krissy shouted, and held back a whoop of joy as ten ships jumped in, only thirty thousand kilometers above the moon's north pole.

The cruiser above the moon ceased firing on the *Regent Mary* and cut its engines. A signal of surrender if ever there was one.

Seconds later, another ten ships appeared just off the moon's southern pole, one of the newly arrived cruisers narrowly missing a civilian freighter that was boosting away outside of approved lanes.

"Hoooly shit, Admiral," Major Kevin swore and seemed to sag against a console not visible in the holo. "How the hell did you do that?"

Krissy turned to the man and winked. "I'll tell you later, not over comms. Let's just say that it's a tactic the Airthans are going to have a hard time countering."

"Ma'am," Comm called out. "The Airthan ships have signaled their surrender."

Krissy snorted. "I'll bet they have."

On the holo, the ships of Admiral Orman's Second Division continued to jump in, dozens of ships slotting into orbits further out from the moon.

"Tell the Airthan captains I want them on shuttles, making for the '*Mary* in ten minutes. There's a warm spot in our brig waiting for them."

"Aye, ma'am!"

Krissy couldn't help a predatory grin from creeping across her face. An idea was forming in her mind.

PRESIDENT SERA

STELLAR DATE: 02.09.8949 (Adjusted Years)
LOCATION: Fleet Strategy Room, Keren Station
REGION: Khardine System, Transcend Interstellar Alliance

Admiral Greer nodded with approval. "It's a solid plan."

Sera agreed with Greer's assessment. "So long as she doesn't overuse it. Eventually, they'll turn it on her."

"Maybe," Greer agreed. "But with the advantage the QuanComms give us, it's hard to trap our ships. Give us ten minutes, and we can have backup anywhere within a thousand light years."

Sera nodded as she considered Krissy's victory and what it meant. It was one thing to know on paper that they could summon reinforcements anywhere at a moment's notice, but it was another to see it used effectively in practice.

However, it added the risk that they could easily overextend themselves. And there were other concerns, as well.

Even though the tech was hundreds of years old, other than a few skirmishes along the front with the Orion Freedom Alliance, no one had used jump gates in major warfare.

One of the main reasons was because jumping deep into a star system was a dangerous business.

Conventional grav and EM shielding took a few seconds to activate after a jump, which was more than enough time for a stray rock to hole your ship—or for limpet mines to attach to your hull.

But now, stasis shields changed that. Their ability to activate the *instant* a ship exited from a jump negated that concern. Used in combination with the QuanComm system, which provided real-time destination data allowing for precision-placed on-demand reinforcements, the shields made for an advantage that changed the battlespace and invalidated broad swaths of both tactical and strategic doctrine.

"We're going to need to build up more gates," Sera said after a few moments. "And develop strategic supply locations where we mass fleets. Preferably *not* in major systems."

"Agreed. These staging grounds will turn into our greatest weaknesses if the enemy locates them. But it's not a new problem."

Sera nodded absently as she loaded charts of nearby regions and flipped through potential locations for the bases.

"What about SC-91R?" she asked.

Greer's eyes snapped up to lock on Sera's. "What? Are you insane?"

"They'll never, *ever* look for a staging ground there."

Greer nodded emphatically. "Correct, because it would last all of ten hours before it was devoured. Unless…"

Sera nodded slowly. "Unless."

Greer brought up a view of SC-91R on the holotank between them. Officially, SC-91R was a black hole of seven solar masses, nine hundred light years coreward of Khardine.

The official record wasn't entirely wrong.

Once, SC-91R had been a B-class star—a rather unpleasant one—and also the location of a secret dark matter research facility run by the Nakatomi Corporation.

An experiment to test insystem dark layer transitions went awry, and a rift between the dark layer and normal space opened up.

Details were sketchy, but supposition was that the 'things'—known in the Transcend as Exdali, a twist on extra-spatial dark layer entities—had escaped through the rift and devoured the research facility.

Some researchers managed to get out a signal containing some scant details a few seconds before the base went dark. Nakatomi claimed that an accident had destroyed the facility, and provided no further explanation, apparently hoping that the Exdali would fall into the star and be destroyed, hiding all evidence of their colossal mistake.

In some respects, very valuable information *did* come out of the Nakatomi incident at SC-91R. The most useful being that stars do not kill Exdali. Exdali kill stars.

At first, there were oscillations in the star's orbit, combined with fluctuations in its EM output. The observations correlated with one of the star's large gas giants moving insystem—though the rate of change was occurring orders of magnitude too quickly.

Then the star's output began to dim further and further until it exploded from a mass imbalance that no standard model could account for.

A stellar nebula should have formed, expanding out from a white dwarf, or perhaps neutron star, remnant.

But the expanding cloud of gas and dust only survived a few years before it disappeared. There was no sign of any stellar remnant.

Now SC-91R was interdicted, and slowly, a dark smudge between the stars grew year after year, reaching toward other nearby sources of mass.

Admiral Greer glanced at Sera, his expression filled with concern. "True, we saw the ISF close up a small rift…one with only a few Exdali—"

"Few thousand," Sera corrected.

"Doesn't matter, they were tiny. You saw what the survey data shows about SC-91R. Some of the Exdali are of jovian mass. And the core? We don't even know if that's a black hole, some other type of ultra-dense matter, or just one of the damn Exdali!"

"We have to fix it eventually," Sera shrugged.

"Yes, yes we do. After the war. For all we know, taking care of SC-91R could be as large an effort as everything else we're currently undertaking."

Sera nodded. She hadn't expected Greer to oppose her idea so vehemently, but she could tell that this was not the time to push further.

<*I think it's the deep-seated fear people have of the Exdali,*> Jen suggested. <*Up until a few months ago, there was no known way to stop them. Fear was a healthy response; it still might be. We have no idea if that many can be driven back into the dark layer—from what I see here, the exclusion zone is now over five light years across.*>

<*I suppose you're right, Jen,*> Sera replied. <*I'm going to send a missive to Earnest, though. I want his thoughts on this.*>

Aloud, she said, "Your concerns are noted, Admiral. What about STX-B17?"

Greer scrubbed a hand back and forth on his cheek. "You know, Sera, when I backed you for the presidency, I didn't think you were insane. I assume you're aware that STX-B17 is a black hole?"

Sera grinned. "Second-last place they'd look for our staging ground, after SC-91R. Look, there's still a jovian planet out beyond the major magnetic bands. We can set up there."

Sera switched the holotank to show STX-B17's position at the edge of the Orion Arm. "It's centrally located in the Transcend, within ten-minute striking distance of Airtha by jump gate…"

"Are you suggesting what I think you are?" Greer asked.

Sera gave an exaggerated shrug. "If we're going to have a staging ground capable of fueling and supplying a large segment of our fleet, why not make it one that can finish the war in one fell swoop?"

"You'd need a million ships to take Airtha," Greer countered. "Sure, the Transcend has many more than that, but we can't leave every system vulnerable just to mass that one fleet."

"In principle, I agree, Admiral. But remember. We don't have to garrison ships anywhere anymore. We can leave probes and patrol craft in systems, and call for help when needed."

"Don't get carried away, Sera Tomlinson. If we leave too many ships out there with QuanComm blades, the enemy is likely to find out what we're up to. Once they do, it'll only be a matter of time before they find our staging ground. It doesn't take *that* long to send probes to all the likely suspects."

Sera saw Greer's point. Unorthodox tactics were fine, but they were better if the enemy still believed that you were following existing doctrine.

<Look at you, thinking like a military commander,> Jen said with an encouraging smile.

<All that time with Tanis must have rubbed off a bit, or something.>

"I think we're onto something, here." Sera placed her hands on the edge of the holotank. "Draw up a proposal and send it to Krissy. I want her thoughts on this."

Greer nodded slowly. "I'm not entirely sold on this myself, you know."

"I understand, and if you and Krissy recommend against it, I'll reconsider. But we have to figure out a meaningful way to use the advantage QuanComms give us."

"Understood," Greer replied.

Sera pushed off from the holotank and turned to leave the room before stopping and turning to face Greer once more. "Oh, and Admiral Greer?"

"Yes, Sera?"

"We're not going to 'take' Airtha. We're going to 'take it out'. The whole thing—ring, star, everything. Nothing survives."

She didn't miss the momentary expression of worry that crossed Greer's face before he nodded. "Very well. I'll ensure that the strategy reflects that goal."

"Good, now I'm off to discuss the economic implications of feeding resources to Scipio with the secretaries. Wish me luck."

Greer laughed. "Good luck, indeed. I'd rather face SC-91R than deal with that lot."

Sera nodded in agreement. She shared the same sentiment.

NIGHTSHADE

STELLAR DATE: 02.27.8949 (Adjusted Years)
LOCATION: Wells Station
REGION: Azela System, Coreward Edge of Praesepe Cluster

"Watch yourself, Admiral," Nadine cautioned as they walked off the pinnace and onto the bay's deck. "This is not the safest of stations."

"Few places *are* safe, anymore," Tanis replied.

<Lieutenant, keep the reactor warm, not sure how long we'll be, or how hot we'll come in.>

<Hot and ready to be shot. You got it, Admiral.> Lieutenant Markey chuckled at his response.

Flyboys, Tanis thought.

<You married one of those, you know that, right?> Angela chided.

<Oh, I ***know****.>*

"Seems like a strange place for Nerischka to set up shop," Tanis said to Nadine as they walked up the long, gently sloped ramp to the station's passenger decks. "Though I guess it's just the place the stuff she's tracking would pass through."

Nadine shrugged, her blue and purple ombré hair sparkling in the passageway's bright lights, setting off against the figure-hugging white dress she wore.

Tanis was clothed similarly, but her dress was more of a long tunic, red and black, paired with black leggings. When selecting an outfit for this mission, Tanis had realized she so rarely acquired new clothes that most of her wardrobe consisted of items Joe had given her as gifts.

Whenever she was out of uniform—which, admittedly, was rare—her style reflected Joe's tastes more than hers.

<That's because you don't ***have*** *any tastes,>* Angela chided.

<*I do too!*> Tanis shot back. <*My tastes are just simple and understated.*>

Angela snorted. <*When we merge into one person, that's one of the first things I'm changing. I'm going to start dressing us like the goddess we are.*>

<*Wow, Angela, what are you overcompensating for?*>

<*What do you mean?*> Angela sounded genuinely perplexed.

While Tanis continued to speak with Angela, Nadine replied, "Well, it's where the mission seems to have taken her. I'm quite curious to learn what she's found. Sera said that Nerischka thinks this biotech has ties back to Orion."

"Not really their M. O., from what I hear," Tanis replied as they reached the top of the ramp.

The concourse ahead of them was filled with foot traffic, and a few dockcars driving down a designated lane in the center. Nadine wove through the crowds and signaled for a car. A few seconds later, one slowed to a stop, and they climbed in.

"Nightshade," Nadine said, and the car made a sound signaling rejection.

"Destination restricted," the vehicle replied.

Nadine shook her head and sighed. "Well, as close as you can get, then."

The car made an affirmative noise and pulled back into the center of the concourse.

Tanis chuckled as they picked up speed. "Never a good sign, is it."

"You read her mission brief, right?" Nadine asked. "The guy that's moving this biotech is pretty strange. Not surprised that whoever runs this dockcar service doesn't want to go there."

"I've yet to see anything as strange as half the stuff I dealt with back in Sol," Tanis said as she watched the people on the concourse. "Trust me, until you've seen a man whose body is made out of the bodies of other people, you've not seen anything."

Nadine shuddered. "What do you mean…'made out of'?"

Tanis saw John Cardid's monstrous form in her mind; an image hundreds of years in her past, but still not one she'd ever forget.

"Like limbs constructed from the bodies of people…all merged into one body. I really don't want to describe it further. It made the people with spikes driven through their eyes and out the backs of their heads seem perfectly normal."

"Disguuuusting," Nadine breathed with a small scrunch of her nose. "OK, yeah, Nightshade should be a piece of cake for you."

"One thing that wasn't clear in the brief," Tanis said as she pulled it up over her vision. "I thought 'Nightshade' was the guy's name, not the place he…whatevers…at."

"I was a bit fuzzy on that, too. That's why I just asked the car to take us there. From what I can see on the station map, there is a place *called* Nightshade, so I figured why not see if they're one and the same?"

"Seems reasonable," Tanis nodded as she reviewed the station layout further. "Station isn't big enough for them not to be connected."

<*Oh, wow,*> Angela chimed in. <*I went wandering through their nets here and found the security systems for Nightshade. You know, actually working the job while you two chit-chat? Anyway, it's like a cross between a club, and an extreme body mod art studio. All weird biological stuff, too.*>

Tanis saw Nadine give a small shudder. "I hate bio-mods. I know that we all have them, but keeping them under a nice human-shaped package is best. Some people just get…"

"Icky," Tanis filled in.

"Yeah…'icky' is right. As in, 'I don't care *what* your tentacles can do, I'd rather not'."

Tanis was reminded of the informant she used back on the Cho in Sol.

<Sandy Bristol,> Angela supplied.

<Yeah, the one with the pink meter-long tentacles! She was a blast; first and only time I've ever been slipped intel via tentacle.>

The dockcar drove out over a broad atrium, easily a kilometer across. The roadway was suspended high above the deck below, and Tanis could see that it was once a park, the center marked by a dry depression where a lake had been. Now it was filled with small, ramshackle buildings, and chickens. A lot of chickens.

"You bring me to all the nicest places," Tanis said as she peered down.

"Stupid stationers," Nadine shook her head. "This was their best greenspace, and they let it die. Who does that? I'd rather sacrifice lights in my quarters before a station's parks."

Tanis shrugged. "Don't look at me. If I can't fly around with at least fifty square klicks of parkland, I turn into a very grumpy woman."

<Wow!> Angela laughed. *<I can't imagine how bad* ***that*** *would be! I wouldn't have thought increased grumpiness was possible.>*

Nadine covered her mouth to hide a laugh, and Tanis sighed.

"S'OK, I can take a compliment."

<I wish I had a diaphragm so I could groan properly.>

They passed beyond the atrium and turned onto another concourse. The state of repair in this section of the station wasn't bad, but it wasn't great, either.

The car took a few turns and then pulled into a disembarkation lane a few hundred meters from Nightshade.

"Thank you for your matronage," the car announced.

Tanis laughed as she stepped out. " 'Matronage'. My gender feels so satisfied now. What would I have done without that?"

Nadine stepped up beside Tanis. "It's like that a lot on this side of Praesepe. They like to alternate gender honorifics and stuff."

"Why not use gender neutral words like everyone else?"

"I don't know." Nadine shrugged and began walking down the corridor ahead of them. "I'll be sure to query the…well, they don't believe in schools, here. I have no idea what I'd query."

Tanis shook her head as she followed after Nadine, keeping her eyes peeled as they passed clusters of people who appeared to be clean and well-kempt, but also eyed the two women hungrily.

<*I wonder if they're suckers,*> Nadine mused. <*They have that look.*>

<*Never understood that.*> Tanis watched another group pass by, trying to catch sight of their teeth. <*I don't think blood tastes that good…altering your organs to tolerate it, or even live on it, seems…horrible. I mean…no more BLTs or coffee? I don't think life would be worth living.*>

Nadine almost laughed aloud. <*I've only been on your ship for a few weeks, and it didn't take half that time to learn of your love for BLTs. Just be happy you can fight off the crummy nano people have around here. Some suckers mod themselves to infect others so they crave blood after being bitten. Some have nano good enough to biologically alter the people they bite.*>

<*Stars…*> Tanis sighed as she looked around at the people they passed. <*Life must really suck for some of these people.*>

<*With a capital 'S'.*>

<*Again,*> Angela chimed in. <*I can't groan well enough to capture how sad that comment was.*>

A minute later, they reached a wider concourse. The street was several decks high, and in front of them, vertically spanning four decks, was Nightshade.

The entrance was on the lower level, and the pair of women walked through the thin crowds to where a large man and almost rail-thin woman stood before the doors.

The man looked them up and down and glanced at the woman, who nodded for him to open the door.

Tanis was glad she passed muster—she'd worn her nice shoes, after all—and the two stepped through the entrance, finding themselves in a long hall.

On either side of the hall were pillars supporting holos hinting at the sorts of things they'd see within. Tanis sighed as she saw a holo of what looked like a mermaid with flippers instead of arms.

<*Yeah, it's one of those places,*> Angela agreed. <*I hope Nerischka has managed to get into Nightshade's inner circle without becoming a part of his collection.*>

<*It's usually one of the fastest ways, though,*> Tanis replied. <*Show maximum commitment.*>

< *'Maximum commitment' in places like this is often fatal.*>

Tanis nodded slowly. She knew *that* all too well.

Sound and light suddenly flooded into the corridor as a man and a woman pushed open the doors at the far end.

They were laughing and half draped over one another, entwined in a way that made it hard to tell where one ended and the other began.

This was made more difficult by the additional appendages both possessed. Tanis wondered if the meter-long thing in the middle of the man's face could best be described as a tentacle, trunk, or maybe a flaccid penis.

She realized the woman had two of them coming off her face, as well, and decided that she'd prefer to think of them as tentacles.

<*The second one is coming out of her mouth,*> Angela clarified.

Tanis tore her eyes from the pair…either they were talking by exchanging chemical signatures on their extra limbs, or they were having sex. Either way, looking felt like intruding.

Nadine stepped through the doors first, and Tanis followed. She'd already had a view of what to expect, having flushed her nanocloud through when the couple exited, but seeing the sights all around her was something to behold.

The room was a well-lit, open space, filling all four levels. Displays were scattered across the main floor and on the walls above, where catwalks encircled the open space, allowing the 'artwork' to be viewed up close.

The artwork, of course, consisted entirely of humans with extreme bio-mods. Directly in front of them was a woman who was standing vertically in a tank of water, with her head protruding from the top. From the neck up, she looked relatively normal, though bald; from the neck down, her skin seemed leathery, more like an octopus's hide, and things resembling sea anemones grew out of her body in various places.

As Tanis watched, a fish swam close to one of the anemones and was caught in its mouth. The woman moaned in pleasure, and Tanis resisted the urge to shake her head. She and Nadine were, after all, masquerading as patrons—or matrons—of the establishment, and sights like this shouldn't disturb them.

<*Crap, I think I see her,*> Nadine said from beside Tanis. <*Looks like she's…relatively unaltered.*>

Tanis followed Nadine's gaze, which was directed at the bar. Instead of the usual polished surface, the bar consisted of people. At first, Tanis thought it consisted of alternating men and women, but there were a few combos in the mix that made it hard to tell if a pattern was present.

<OK, I've seen a lot of stuff—good stuff, bad stuff—but I can't imagine enjoying a drink while that's going on in front of me. Is Nerischka one of those?>

<Stars, no, thank the gods. I would never be able to look at her at family reunions if she was—not without laughing and cringing at the same time. She's one of the bartenders.>

Tanis breathed a sigh of relief. Mostly because she was certain that the people who made up the bar were all physically bonded to one another.

It really didn't bear thinking about.

Nadine led Tanis to a display near the bar, and Tanis appeared to focus her attention on it, though she was actually reading a recent supply report. She had it over her vision, front and center, to block out what was going on.

They didn't have long to wait before a woman walked out from behind the bar—on legs, thank the stars—and approached Tanis and Nadine.

Her general form was hominid, but from there it diverged rapidly from the norm, appearing to be made of a flexible, veined granite. Coral grew out of it in artful patterns, running along her limbs and creating whorls around her breasts and abdomen. Her head was covered in a crown of coral, and when she spoke, Tanis saw that even her tongue had small bits growing from it.

"What could I possibly get for you fine ladies?" the woman—who Tanis assumed was Nerischka—said in a voice that sounded half like grating stone, and half like a bubbling fountain.

<I have to admit…I'm impressed by this one. That is living coral. It's growing out of her body in open air—can't be easy to do.>

<Yeah, but can you imagine how hard it must be to sleep?> Tanis asked. *<You'd have to do it standing up. Actually…I think you'd have to do everything standing up.>*

"What is your special?" Nadine asked. "We're in a hurry, need to meet a friend very soon."

Nerischka's face took on a sad expression. At least that's what Tanis assumed; her facial movement was restricted by the coral tracing her cheekbones.

"I'm sorry, we're out of the Ambrosia Red. I can offer you our house vintage, though—it's very close."

Nadine shook her head. "No, I need the Ambrosia Red. Nothing else will do. Top shelf."

Nerischka nodded, her eyes darting to her left for a second. "I will have to double-check our supplies in the back. You don't need to wait for me here, I'll find you."

"Thanks, we'll sate our curiosity," Nadine replied, before turning back to look at the display they were standing in front of.

<She can't get away easily. Nightshade is around here somewhere,> Nadine said. *<She needs us to meet her around the back.>*

<I gathered that,> Tanis replied. *<She seemed reluctant to leave; I noticed you had to invoke Sera.>*

<Well, the brief said she'd been working Nightshade for over a year. I can't imagine what being like **that** *for a year would entail. She probably doesn't want to screw it all up and waste the effort.>*

Tanis and Nadine wandered the floor for another ten minutes looking-without-looking at the various displays. Once the prescribed time had passed, they broke into an argument, and Tanis stormed out, followed by Nadine.

<She's staring at your ass,> Angela snickered. *<I think Nadine finds you attractive.>*

<Ang! She's just playing the part.>

<Of course! What was I thinking?>

Once outside Nightshade, they took a circuitous route around to the shipping and receiving entrance at the back of the establishment.

The pair ducked into a dark corner behind a stack of empty crates and proceeded to pull off their clothing. Underneath, both wore flow armor, and Nadine shivered as it spread over her hands and across her face.

<I practiced with this back on the ship, but I still feel like I'm going to suffocate and die when it goes over my mouth.>

<Yeah, not my favorite, either, but worth the trade-off.>

With their clothes tucked under a pallet, Tanis triggered the flow armor's stealth systems and led the way across the shipping corridor. She approached a smaller door beside the larger freight entrance at the rear of Nightshade.

Angela giggled and whispered in their minds, *<Open sesame.>*

<Did you just ***giggle****?>* Tanis asked.

<It seemed funny to me.>

<I think what Bob has is catching.>

The door popped open, and the two women slipped inside, moving in the direction Nerischka had indicated. They followed one hall, then another, and finally came to a room where a door was ajar, revealing racks filled with bottles.

The pair slipped in, gently closing the door behind them.

Tanis's nano cloud revealed Nerischka standing in a back corner, pretending to be reviewing a few bottles.

"Nishka," Nadine said quietly as they approached.

For her part, Nerischka didn't even flinch as a disembodied voice spoke next to her.

"Did you kill the surveillance in the room?" she asked.

"Of course," Nadine replied. "Not our first op."

Nerischka nodded, still looking at the bottles ahead of her. "Who's your friend?"

"I'm Tanis Richards."

That grabbed Nerischka's attention, and her head turned toward the sound of Tanis's voice. "*The* Tanis Richards?"

"Maybe. I imagine there must be other people with the same name."

"What are you doing here?" Nerischka hissed, regaining some of her calm. "I'm just days away from finding out who Nightshade is working with. This tech is crazy advanced stuff, it rivals some of what we have in the Transcend."

"And he's using it just for his kink-fest in there?" Tanis asked.

"No, that's just him skimming off the top. The real bulk of what passes through his hands is going elsewhere, but I don't know where, yet."

"Doesn't matter," Nadine replied. "You're getting pulled. We're going to Praesepe and old Genevia to look for clues about who might be spreading the Genevian Discipline tech."

Nerischka nodded slowly. "That sure brings back memories. Not good ones, mind you. The man you're going to want to seek out is General Mill. He has his finger on the pulse of what's left of Genevia, and is in possession of a number of bases spread around Septhia and into the gulf between Praesepe and Nietzschea. I don't need to go, though. I can just give you everything I have. I've worked too long here—I mean, look at what I've done to get in this deep with Nightshade."

"Nishka," Nadine said in a soft voice. "It's the unveiling. We're coming out of the shadows."

"What? How?"

"It's a ridiculously long story. Why couldn't I get you on the Link when we approached?"

Nerischka gestured at her body as though that answered all questions, which Tanis supposed it did. "I had to strip down my tech for this job. With how much Nightshade messes with our bodies, I couldn't have anything that gave me away. He removes our wireless transmitters, and our nano—what he lets us have—is shit."

"Damn, Nishka, you shouldn't let yourself become so vulnerable."

The coral-covered woman shook her head slowly. "Look what he's doing here, Nadine. This is just the tip of the iceberg. Nightshade has facilitated the transfer of enough bio-mods to turn millions, maybe even billions, of people into...into whatevers."

"There are certainly military uses for tech like this," Tanis said. "That's the only reason I can see Orion shipping this stuff into the Inner Stars—well, I suppose they could use it as a mandate to cleanse systems, as well."

"See? Either way, it has to be stopped. I recently got intel that Nightshade has been in contact with someone called 'Angel' about where to deliver the next shipment. Angel seems to be higher on the food chain, and I need to find out where it goes."

"Angel? Do you only have a name?" Tanis asked, her pulse quickening.

<*A lot of people who call themselves 'Angel',*> Angela cautioned.

<*Too coincidental,*> Tanis replied.

Nerischka shook her head. "I have heard two names, but the other one was only used once. It was 'Caretaker'."

<*OK...so you were right.*>

"Caretaker," Tanis breathed. "And your assessment is that Angel and the Caretaker are different people?"

Nerischka turned her head toward the sound of Tanis's voice. "You sound like you've heard of the Caretaker before."

"It's one of the reasons we're going to Genevia. We have reason to believe the Caretaker was involved in their recent war."

Nerischka nodded slowly. "It makes sense. I think this biotech might be moving through Nietzschean space—much of which was formerly Genevia."

<*She needs to stay here, work this end of things,*> Angela said.

<*I know,*> Tanis replied. <*But she's too vulnerable. She'll need help.*>

"OK, Nerischka. Nadine can fill you in later, but we do need to find this Angel. That target is more important than the source or destination of the bio-tech—though I imagine the objectives are aligned.

"Nadine. I'm going to need to continue on to the Praesepe Cluster, but Nerischka's in too deep on her own. If Angel is an ascended AI, or even just a human with a remnant—"

"A what?" Nerischka asked.

Tanis nodded, though she realized no one could see her movement. "We're up against ascended AIs and things called remnants, which they can leave inside of other people. They can completely take someone over, and there's nothing you can do about it."

"It's true," Nadine added. "Things are getting crazy."

"OK, then I need to get you what I know about Mill and the Marauders, plus the situation on the ground in Praesepe," Nerischka replied. "I dumped all the intel that I couldn't fit up here—" she paused to tap her head, "in the records of a defunct financial auditing firm. If you search for Lucas Knight Industries, you'll find it in their 8937 financials."

<*I'm in,*> Angela informed Tanis a few seconds later. <*Oh, wow, that's a treasure trove!*>

"OK, we have it," Tanis replied. "Nadine. Angela has already signaled for the *Aegeus* to send in another pinnace. It'll have supplies for whatever you need, and a med suite that can put Nerischka here back together when the time comes. I'll ensure that there's a Shadowtron aboard. I think you're going to need it."

Nadine nodded, and Nerischka shook her head. "I feel a headache coming on. Nadine, I need to get back out there, but come back during third shift; I can get away for thirty minutes, and we can figure out what's next from there."

"OK, I can't tell you how glad I am to see you, Nishka. I'd hug you, but I'm afraid something would break off."

Nerischka laughed. "Wouldn't be the first time."

The stone-skinned, coral covered woman left, and the pair of stealthed women slipped out a few minutes later. Back behind the crates where their clothing was stashed, Nadine let out a long sigh.

"OK…that was sad and weird."

"I can imagine," Tanis replied. "Do you think she's OK…mentally? Working into a place like that has to mess with your head."

Nadine glanced toward Nightshade. "Stars…she's tough, and she seems together. I worry how she was going to get out of that place on her own, though."

Tanis nodded and clasped Nadine's shoulder. "Sera told me how you feel about operating in the field. I understand how taxing that can be. If you're not ready for this, say the word."

Nadine was holding her dress, and she looked down at her hands for a moment, twisting the fabric between them. "I don't want to lie and betray anymore…I can't wear that kind of mask again." She looked up at Tanis. "But this is different. Nishka's family, and from the looks of it, she really needs me."

Tanis glanced back at Nightshade. "Yeah, I think you're right. Remember, if you *are* going up against a remnant, they're sneaky. The Shadowtron isn't a sure bet. If things go sideways, get out and call for help."

"Understood, Tanis. We'll get to the bottom of this."

SEPTHIA

STELLAR DATE: 06.25.8949 (Adjusted Years)
LOCATION: ISS *I2*
REGION: Edge of the Lisbon System, Septhian Alliance

The non-space of the jump transition lasted for only a second before stars snapped into place again around the *I2*.

"Scan, confirm location," Rachel called out.

"Stellar cartography confirms that we are on the edge of the Lisbon System, seventy AU from the local star."

Rachel nodded. "Very good. Nice jump, Helm."

The pair of ensigns on Helm both responded, acknowledging the compliment as they adjusted the ship's vector to match local space.

The main holotank displayed the forward elements of the ISF escort fleet arraying themselves around the *I2*. Every ship was on its assigned trajectory, taking up the flying cross formation.

Correction, the *Derringer* was off a hair. She'd have to keep an eye on Captain Mel; the woman was becoming rather cavalier.

"Captain," Tanis gave Rachel a crisp nod followed by a quick smile as she approached the holotank. "Another day, another star system."

"Well, hopefully we'll stay put for a bit, now."

Rachel watched the Admiral's brow furrow before Tanis replied. "I certainly hope so, Captain. It's been months of chasing leads around the edges of the Nietzschean Empire, while Septhia hemmed and hawed about letting us enter their space."

"Plus the detour in the Azela System," Rachel added.

Tanis caught her eye and sighed. "And what a detour that has turned out to be for those two. With luck, we'll hear something from them soon."

Scan showed the Septhian ships still to be several hours from the rendezvous, and Rachel busied herself with a variety of tasks, while the admiral continued to scowl at the holodisplay.

She was speaking with the head of the Comm team when a voice called out from the bridge's entrance.

"So! The Septhian prime minister has finally pulled his head out of his ass and agreed to see us, has he?" Brandt asked as she approached the holotank.

"Brandt!" Tanis exclaimed and clasped the Marine Commandant's hand. "I was starting to wonder if you'd ever catch up to us."

Brandt nodded. "Caught the QuanComm update a minute before we were about to jump to Killgrave. Managed to get our vector altered in time to make it here—thank stars. Been waiting here for two days, hoping your invite was good enough for the whole family."

"I take it they didn't get grouchy at you for lurking out here?" Tanis asked.

Brandt gestured to the holodisplay, and Rachel noted thirty Septhian cruisers on an intercept course for the ISF's formation.

"I can't tell if that's grouchy, or just a cautious hello. Things are pretty tense in Septhia, from what I've heard."

"Less than in Scipio?" Rachel asked. "How were things there, by the way?"

Brandt let out a sound of dismay. "Is that a trick question? Out here, Septhia is worried about being steamrolled by the Nietzscheans, and Scipio is preparing to steamroll the Hegemony—provided Diana can put an end to the assassination attempts. It's starting to take a toll on her."

Rachel could only imagine what dealing with two coups and half a dozen—at least—assassination attempts would do to a person's morale.

"She'll be OK." Tanis turned back to the holotank and stared at the approaching Septhian Armed Forces cruisers. "I'm not worried about Diana. She's got a rock to lean on."

Rachel wondered what Tanis meant, but Brandt groaned and rolled her eyes. "Petra. Rock. Nice one, Field Marshal."

"On this bridge, I'm an Admiral," Tanis corrected the commandant.

"Not when you make lame jokes, you're not."

Sometimes the way Brandt spoke to Tanis amazed Rachel. Tanis was more familiar and approachable than many officers, but she was still *the* Admiral. Granted, Brandt had been working on building the ISF with Tanis since before the *Intrepid* had passed through Sol's heliopause.

That was a long time to build up comradery.

It also helped that Brandt was a small, thoroughly ferocious force of nature that everyone—including Tanis—was a bit leery of.

Tanis only frowned and darted her eyes toward Brandt.

"Captain, Admiral, we have a message from the SAF fleet. Text only," the Comm officer announced.

"Let's have it, Lieutenant," Tanis replied.

The comm officer put the message up on the bridge net, and Tanis sighed. "Looks like they don't want to come here—that's a first. Care to join me for a little jaunt, Commandant?"

"Of course I'm joining you," Brandt replied.

Tanis turned to Rachel and nodded. "Stay sharp, Captain. You have FleetConn in my absence."

"Aye, Admiral. I have FleetConn."

Tanis smiled and followed Brandt off the bridge as Rachel returned to her command chair.

<Major Grange?> she called down to the fleet CIC.

<Yes, Captain Espensen.>

<Admiral Richards is leaving the I2 *with Commandant Brandt to pay a visit to the Septhians. I have FleetConn in her absence. When her pinnace leaves the ship, I want two stealthed cruisers to follow. Full Marine complement.>*

<Aye, Captain Espensen.>

Rachel eyed the approaching Septhian vessels, considering their strengths and weaknesses. Against the ISF fleet, they were barely worth mentioning. But with Tanis aboard their ships? That was a horse of a different color.

Time passed slowly as Tanis's pinnace left the *I2* with the two stealthed cruisers shadowing it. The admiral hadn't commented on the extra precautions, so Rachel assumed she didn't object.

Tanis often left people room to execute the way they thought best. If there was a fundamental problem with a plan, she'd speak up, but otherwise she often left well enough alone.

The Admiral's pinnace slowed and held position beyond the formation of ISF ships surrounding the *I2*—though not beyond weapons range.

The SAF ships continued to slow, until they were moving at only a thousand kilometers per hour relative to the ISF ships, one fleet slowly drifting past the other with a hundred thousand kilometers between them.

At that point, the Admiral's pinnace began to move away from the ISF fleet, closing the gap between it and the SAF ships.

Rachel couldn't help but worry that something terrible was going to happen to Tanis. It was irrational, the Septhians had no reason to act aggressively. They knew the ISF was coming and had granted the fleet permission to come to the Lisbon System.

Stars, their Prime Minister was on one of those ships.

Still, she felt better as the two stealthed cruisers eased out to follow the admiral's pinnace.

<*I can feel your anxiety from here,*> Priscilla said, speaking to Rachel from her plinth in the foyer beyond the bridge. <*Relax, the admiral knows what she's doing.*>

<*She sure likes to put herself out there. After what happened at Scipio, I'd prefer she didn't do this sort of thing.*>

Priscilla laughed in Rachel's mind. <*Do you think you can stop her? If so, let the rest of us know how. She's always been like this. Only while Cary was young, were we able to rest easy.*>

It was Rachel's turn to laugh. <*Well, there you have it. We just need to keep Tanis pregnant. I'll be sure to talk to Admiral Evans about that.*>

<*I can just see her racing around the Inner Stars, forging alliances and popping out babies.*>

Rachel had to stop herself from laughing aloud at the thought. <*Priscilla!*>

"The admiral's ship is matching *v* with one of the SAF ships," Scan announced. "It's the *Everlasting*."

"Thank you," Rachel replied as she watched the pinnace approach the SAF vessel.

Good luck, Admiral.

A BIZARRE MEETING

STELLAR DATE: 06.25.8949 (Adjusted Years)
LOCATION: SAS *Everlasting*
REGION: Edge of the Lisbon System, Septhian Alliance

Tanis stepped off the pinnace with Brandt at her side and a fireteam of ISF Marines at her back. The bay they found themselves in was small, with perhaps only space for another ship the size of the ISF pinnace.

The instant the Marines set foot on the deck, they spread out around the bay, covering corners, ready for anything. They moved with smooth precision, and Tanis wondered how aggressive their deployment and posture appeared to the Septhians.

Another four Marines formed up behind Tanis and Brandt, ready to operate as an escort once they left the bay.

Of course, with their hosts absent, they weren't leaving yet.

Brandt sighed and drummed her fingers on her thigh before whistling a little tune. Tanis connected to the vessel's public shipnet, about to reach out to whoever was listening, when the interior bay doors finally opened.

The exit stood empty for a moment, before a tall woman with long black hair entered, flanked by a pair of guards.

She walked toward the ISF delegation with a smile on her face that appeared genuine, but it didn't seem to match her strident steps.

"Admiral Richards," the woman said, extending her hand as she neared. "It is a pleasure to meet you. And Commandant Brandt, I was not expecting you to be present, how exciting!"

Tanis shook the woman's slender hand, hiding a smile at the woman's exuberance as Brandt replied.

"Uh, sure. I thought it would be nice to get out, stretch my legs, and see the locals."

"Yes, of course," the woman replied, nodding her head emphatically, while looking a touch confused.

"It's very nice to meet you, as well…" Tanis began.

<*She seems unwell,*> Angela commented. <*You should ask her if she's OK.*>

<*Me? Why don't you?*> Tanis asked.

<*OK, su—*>

<*Ang!*>

"Sorry," the woman replied with a nervous smile. "My name is Oris, sorry, I don't know how I got all this out of order."

<*If you don't ask her, I will,*> Angela warned Tanis, just as Brandt spoke up.

"Oris, very nice to meet you, are you alright? You seem out of sorts," the commandant's brows pinched as she spoke.

"Well, the PM *just* showed me the little holo you sent. The one explaining where you and your ship—which looks *a lot* different now—have been for the last two decades. I must say that it's…hard to believe."

Tanis nodded and gave Oris a reassuring smile. "I've been in your shoes, but trust me, it's real. We've spent most of the past two decades in the Transcend."

"How is it—sorry. My questions are not important. Follow me, and I'll escort you to the PM."

Oris turned, and Tanis followed with Brandt at her side. The Marines walked down the ramp after her, and the two SAF soldiers followed behind.

"So, was there any part of our explanation that was particularly distressing to you or the Prime Minister?" Tanis asked, interested in any information that would aid in the upcoming meeting.

"Well, the fact that the volume of explored space is vastly larger than we had ever thought was something rather surprising. And not just a little bit…but *a lot*!"

<She really likes to emphasize 'a lot'. I wonder if this verbal tic is hers alone, or if Septhia is just weird.>

<Very little will be 'weird' after seeing Nightshade,> Tanis replied to Angela before addressing Oris. "I can relate. In the space of a few months, I went from the belief that humanity had not gone more than a few *hundred* light years from Sol, to thousands, to tens of thousands."

"Yes, I'd forgotten that. Your ship predates FTL…when you left Sol, you had to fly for decades to the next star."

"Or centuries," Brandt added.

"I can't imagine," Oris said breathily as she gestured for them to enter a lift.

Only two of the Marines along with one of the SAF soldiers could fit in the lift with them. When they reached the next level, Tanis waited for the other Marines to arrive.

"I'm sure they can catch up," Oris said, her tone attempting to convey reassurance.

"Of course they can," Brandt said with a small smile. "They're Marines. But it'll be easier if we wait."

"Um…OK," Oris replied.

<This woman ***cannot*** *be this scatterbrained,>* Angela said to Tanis and Brandt. *<It has to be an act to disarm us.>*

<Or she's a dear, fragile thing, and our news has disturbed her so,> Brandt replied, raising the pitch of her voice and drawing out her words.

<Stop it, Brandt,> Tanis replied. *<I don't want their PM to watch me laughing at their aide on the feeds.>*

<Think he's watching us?> the commandant asked.

<Of course he is. Why else make us traipse through his ship? He's measuring us up.>

<Should have made him come to us,> Angela groused.

The lift doors opened, and the Marines and other SAF soldier stepped out.

"Ah, there we are," Oris said with a smile. "Let's be on our way now. Just down this corridor."

<I'm perfectly fine meeting here,> Tanis replied. *<We get to observe them as much as they observe us.>*

They followed Oris down the corridor, took a right, then a left, and reached a single door on the right side of the passageway.

"Your guards will have to wait outside," Oris said as she rapped on the door.

Brandt scowled but nodded to the Marines, who took up positions on either side of the hall.

"Come," a voice said from within, and the door slid aside to reveal a table sitting under a pergola, with rolling hills stretching into the distance. It was a decently constructed holoview, though Tanis could spot the artificial irregularities.

Seated at the table was a man who Tanis recognized as the Septhian Prime Minister, and a uniformed woman with five stars on her collar.

<Just the two of them,> Angela commented. *<I guess there will be less banter, at least.>*

"Prime Minister Harmin," Tanis said as she entered the room and held out her hand. "I love the view. Is this from one of your worlds here in Lisbon?"

The PM stood and walked around the table to greet Tanis, while the Septhian admiral approached from the other side.

"It is, Admiral Richards. It's from T'Riva, our capital world."

"Very lovely," Tanis replied as she turned to shake the woman's hand.

"Admiral Vera," the woman introduced herself with a curt nod.

"Very nice to meet you," Tanis replied.

Brandt exchanged greetings as well, and then the group, including Oris, sat at the table as servitors approached with a selection of drinks.

<*You're so smooth when you want to be, Tanis,*> Brandt commented. <*I feel like you should have flowers in your hair or something.*>

<*Shut up, Brandt,*> Tanis shot back with a mental scowl.

The PM spoke as soon as they'd settled. "I'd ask you how your journey was, but I don't even know how you travelled here so quickly. The information you provided put the Transcend's borders thousands of light years coreward of the Praesepe Cluster."

Oris chimed in with an over-wide smile. "Either way, I imagine it was pleasant enough. Your ship is large enough to carry every amenity."

"It's not a home away from home," Tanis inclined her head. "It's just plain home."

"I suppose it would be," Prime Minister Harmin replied. "If the stories are to be believed, you've spent some time on that ship."

"We certainly have, Prime Minister," Tanis agreed.

"Please, you may call me 'Harmin', no need to dwell on so much formality when it's just the five of us."

<*My kinda guy,*> Brandt said privately.

"I imagine you're wondering *why* we've come to Septhia," Tanis said, ready to get to the meat of the conversation.

Harmin chuckled. "I'll admit, the thought has crossed my mind. I don't really follow why you sent us the information on the *Transcend,* as you put it. Though I suppose it does explain how your ship managed to get FTL capabilities, and where it went—though the fact that the FGT is still alive and well is a bit of a shock."

"Maybe even more so than your arrival from the distant past," Admiral Vera added.

"Not just the FGT," Tanis clarified. "The Transcend Interstellar Alliance, and the Orion Freedom Alliance. Two massive powers that have been vying for control for some time."

"It's interesting, to be sure," Harmin said, stroking his short beard. "But, if I may be so blunt, how does it affect us? We're a small alliance of stars, just making do in our little corner of space. We have no quarrel with this Transcend or Orion."

"You do, however, have a quarrel with the Nietzscheans." Brandt leant forward and raised her eyebrows. "Or maybe they have a quarrel with you—hard to say which. Nietzschea seems to have a bone to pick with everyone."

"Then you know why we're not looking for more trouble right now," Harmin replied. "We're building alliances around the Praesepe Cluster—and within—working to build up a defense against the Nietzscheans."

"Who do you think is supplying the Nietzscheans?" Tanis asked.

"Honestly?" Harmin gave an exaggerated shrug. "Our money is on the Trisilieds. Being in the Pleiades gives them access to vast resources."

"We're investigating how they're moving supplies between the two empires with such ease," Vera added.

"As far as *we* can tell, the Nietzscheans and Trisilieds aren't working together at all," Tanis said amicably.

Vera scowled at Tanis, the expression on her face carrying no small amount of disdain. "Pardon my skepticism, but what intelligence network are you using to gather that information?"

"They're called The Hand," Tanis replied. "Remember those massive empires beyond the Inner Stars that don't really matter to you? Well, they have agents everywhere. Either way, the main reason why the Trisilieds aren't supplying the

Nietzscheans is because Orion is funneling resources into both of them. Along with the Hegemony."

Tanis let the words fall and picked up the glass of wine a servitor had set down, taking a sip and watching Harmin and Vera, who were clearly chatting with one another over the Link.

<*This is not going the way I expected. I don't understand why they're being so defensive,*> Angela commented.

Tanis wondered as well, then realization dawned on her.

"Prime Minister Harmin, you don't, by any chance, think that we've come here to seek a place to settle, do you?"

Harmin's eyes darted toward Tanis's and narrowed. "The thought had crossed my mind. I hate to speak so bluntly, but it's far more likely that you've been running from system to system with the Hegemony on your tail, than spending time in some fanciful empire beyond the edges of human expansion."

"Huh." Tanis sat back and shook her head. "I don't know why, but I never expected anyone to have that reaction. Though now that you say it, I can see why you'd suspect our motives."

"Look at it from our viewpoint," Admiral Vera raised her hands in a gesture of frustration. "Last we saw you, you were fleeing the AST ships after blowing up a planet in Bollam's World."

"I think it's worth noting that the AST blew up the planet. The Bollers had clearly posted warnings about not messing with the thing." Tanis gave a slight smile at her wit, but the PM and his admiral did not join in.

<*I'm with them, it was a bit weak,*> Angela commented.

Tanis ignored Angela and continued, "Right, well, I'm sure you have some analysts who can take a look at the fleet we have, and tell you that these are not the same ships that we had at Bollam's World. We have a colony world with our own shipyards, and ample resources flowing in from starmines. We don't need anything from you other than a little bit of intel and safe passage."

"Intel?" Harmin asked.

"Yes," Tanis replied. "The current location of General Mill, leader of the Marauders. I need to find out what he knows about the origins of Genevia's mech program."

Harmin and Vera looked at one another for several long moments before the PM turned back to Tanis and frowned.

"So you don't want to trade with us?"

"Well, I'll trade for what I just requested. Information on General Mill's whereabouts—I know that his mercenary group works for you almost exclusively—and then permission to take my fleet to him."

Tanis had expected the conversation to immediately turn to allying against the Nietzscheans, but they hadn't even brought it up. It was strange, but then, everything about the Septhians had been strange thus far. Now she didn't know if she *wanted* Septhia as an ally.

"What do we get for this?" Harmin asked.

<*This is the weirdest negotiation I've ever been in,*> Tanis said to Angela and Brandt. <*They clearly want things from us, but they don't seem to want to trade…or to just come out and ask for it….*>

Angela made a soft sound of disinterest. <*Maybe they're scared.*>

<*I think they're stupid.*> Brandt gave a short laugh. <*Maybe there's something wrong with the air on their worlds.*>

Tanis wondered about that. Fear made people act strangely. "Well, what do you want?" she asked plainly.

"Your picotech," Admiral Vera replied without hesitation.

"No," Tanis shot back.

"Well then, your shield tech."

"Also no."

Harmin placed his hands on the table. "Admiral Richards. We are gearing up for a war with Nietzschea. If you don't have something meaningful to offer us to help in that effort, then you'll have to forgive us, but we need to be going."

"So you *do* want something I can offer," Tanis replied. "I imagine that you need ships. Chances are that you're starved for resources right now. What with Nietzschea building up their military, people are hoarding or gouging for everything."

"You won't give us your shield tech…but you'll give us ships instead?" Vera's face was the very definition of disbelief.

"Well, we don't have a proper allegiance, and I don't think we can form one, because you don't believe I'm telling the truth. If you did, then we could work something out. However, I have a way that we can work toward that."

"Oh?" Harmin asked.

Tanis nodded. "See, I know that the Trisilieds and the Hegemony are working with the Orion Guard, on account of the fact that they attacked our system not long ago. Luckily, I didn't have to completely destroy their fleets."

"It must have been a small force, for you to have survived." Vera still looked as though she didn't believe a word Tanis was saying.

"Well, it was small when compared to the entirety of their armed forces, yes. The enemy hit us with roughly two hundred thousand ships."

Vera's mouth dropped open, then snapped shut, while Harmin's stayed agape.

"Are you mocking us?" Vera asked.

"Stars," Tanis glanced at Brandt. "Empress Diana was significantly easier to deal with than these two."

"Diana of Scipio?" Harmin asked, disbelief warring with wonder on his face.

"The same," Tanis replied. "We're supporting her in her war against the Hegemony. Now, I have a few ways I could *prove* to you that I'm not lying. I *could* take you to New Canaan, but I won't. I suppose we could go to some location in the Transcend, like Khardine or Vela, but I don't think I'll do that, either…your lack of openness is not encouraging. What I'll do instead is show you that I am not here with my hand out.

"I'll offer you one hundred Trisilieds cruisers in exchange for the information I want, and permission to travel through Septhia at will."

"One hundred cruisers?" Harmin asked. "How? Where?"

"Pull up your Scan feeds, they should be jumping in now."

On one side of the table, the holoview of rolling hills disappeared, now showing the ISF fleet. In the center of the display lay the *I2*, framed by the twenty ships on patrol.

For a minute, nothing happened, then a point of light appeared beyond the ISF ships, and the holodisplay focused in on that location, enlarging it to fill the space next to the table.

"Shit, that's a Trisilieds cruiser!" Vera exclaimed.

<*Real quick on the uptake,*> Angela commented.

"I hope this isn't some trick." Oris's voice wavered with uncertainty.

Another cruiser appeared, followed by another. The pace quickened, with as many as five appearing at a time, then slackened once more until a hundred new ships were spread in a loose formation beyond the ISF fleet.

"What are your intentions with these ships?" Harmin asked.

Tanis couldn't help a long look at the holographic sky above them before she responded. "You're *really* not used to things going your way, are you? Those ships are for you. A gesture of my goodwill. Vera?" Tanis asked. "I'm sure you're talking with your CIC. Tell me about the ships."

"Well…there's almost no EM coming off them, main drives are offline, no shields. There appear to be a hundred tugs…all making for your other fleet."

"Do you believe me now, that I don't need a planet, or a place to settle in Septhia? Which is ludicrous, anyway. Why would I settle so close to Nietzschea?"

Harmin's lips drew into a thin line, and his brows pinched together. "It seems that I've misjudged you, Admiral Richards. Your general assessment of our situation is as you've described. We've worked hard to build ourselves up in preparation for a Nietzschean assault…but by making ourselves the strongest, we've become their primary target in the region."

"We're low on almost every raw material, our mining operations are running constantly, and our shipyards are producing vessels as fast as we can," Oris interjected. "But it's like you said. Our neighbors are all doing the same. Many key resources are skyrocketing in price."

"What about the Praesepe Cluster, itself?" Tanis asked. "Those stars must be rich in raw resources and volatiles."

Harmin nodded. "They are, but FTL is not possible within the mean tidal radius of the cluster. Reaching the core is an eighty-year trip. Each way."

"I can see how that would be a problem," Brandt laughed.

Tanis considered her options. "I wouldn't want to spend an Intrepid Class gate on it, but I could see setting up a smaller gate to get in and out of the cluster's core."

"A gate?" Admiral Vera asked.

"Those ships out there?" Tanis gestured at the holodisplay. "They were about four thousand light years from here before they arrived."

"Four thousand?" Harmin almost choked. "That takes a decade to traverse!"

"Not with jump gates, it doesn't," Tanis replied. "And don't ask. You're not getting that tech, either. If we *do* grant you assistance that employs the use of gates, we'll loan tugs, like those you saw bringing the ships in."

"So *that's* what they were for," Harmin said with a pensive nod. "Even if you can use jump gates to get into Praesepe's core, you may not find a warm welcome there. The people who live in the cluster *like* being isolationists. They won't be keen on visitors who can just appear for a visit."

"What I wouldn't give to see the looks on their faces when your ships jump in." Oris laughed as she spoke, and Vera shot her a dark look.

Tanis held up a hand. "Let's not get ahead of ourselves. Besides, I doubt we need to go to what I've seen noted as the 'Core Empire' on local charts. A venture there would assume they have the ability to provide raw resources at a rate which you would find worthwhile."

"It would give them a safe place to mine and manufacture, though. Easier to fuel the war effort that way," Brandt noted.

"Could you not aid us directly?" Harmin asked. "You say that the Orion group is feeding the Nietzscheans. Why don't you do the same for us?"

Tanis fixed Harmin with a cold stare. "Ten minutes ago, you were behaving as though you wanted to shoo me off your doorstep."

"I'm truly sorry for that." Harmin's tone did carry a note of sincerity. "We let our fears drive our actions. Septhia is all that stands between Praesepe and Nietzschea. If they take the cluster, you know they'll just keep marching coreward."

"We're preparing for bigger fights than this one," Tanis replied. "I need some people to stand for themselves. I had thought Septhia was one of those places."

"Please!" Harmin almost shouted. "We're months, a year at most, from being in a fight for our lives."

<OK, Tanis, you made him grovel. Now give the poor man a lifeline.>

"Are you willing to become formal allies of the Transcend?" Tanis asked. "We'll aid in your defense against Nietzschea. I promise."

Harmin slouched back into his chair. "What are your terms?"

"Would you believe we have a standard agreement?"

THE ROAD HOME

STELLAR DATE: 08.11.8949 (Adjusted Years)
LOCATION: ***Voyager***
REGION: Germine System, Within the Transcend borders

"There it is," Katrina said, unable to keep the slight rasp from her voice. Her body was getting old again, impossibly old. It may be time to avail herself of rejuvination.

Though rejuv was having more and more diminishing returns each time.

"How will we use it?" Kara asked from beside Katrina. "Freighters like this don't have mirrors—or at least, we're not supposed to."

Katrina glanced at the woman—if that was the right word—next to her and grinned. "I've a few tricks up my sleeve. Sneaking about the galaxy is my job. So long as the coordinates you have are correct, we'll be having breakfast on the *Intrepid* tomorrow."

"The *I2*, you mean," Kara corrected her.

"Yes…interesting name, that."

Katrina glowered at the holodisplay, willing events to unfold faster, but rushing things would not lead to a favorable outcome. Patience was key. She had waited half a millennium for this; she could wait a few hours longer.

She widened the view on the holo, taking in the inner five AU of the Germine System. It was a well-populated star system, sporting two terraformed worlds, several megastructures, and, most importantly, jump gates. Nine, to be exact.

The wild jump from Airtha, executed during their escape with Kara, had landed them far from any system with gates. It had taken almost a year to reach Germine, and during that time, much had changed.

The Transcend had fractured, many systems declaring for Airtha, many others for Khardine. Most, however, seemed prepared to wait it out—or at least see which of the two Seras was stronger before choosing a side.

Germine was one such system, though they had gone further. They had declared independence from the Transcend, a move possible because of the immense wealth and strategic placement of the system.

Also, they're probably holding out for the best deal, Katrina mused.

She wondered if the Transcend would survive this civil war. It was too large to begin with. Many of the worlds in the alliance served in name only.

While President Tomlinson had maintained a strong core, the freedoms he allowed meant that the Alliance's fringes were far more autonomous than in the Orion Freedom Alliance. There, Praetor Kirkland ruled with an iron fist and ensured compliance with his strictures through swift and decisive use of his Orion Guard.

As far as Katrina was concerned, it was all a shit-show. Tanis and New Canaan offered the only real safe haven, a haven Katrina craved.

For a long time, she had worried that the *Intrepid* would not survive its arrival in the future. So much had changed from what they were used to. But after watching the feeds from the Battle of Bollam's World, Katrina had been reassured that Tanis would not let the colony ship fall to anyone.

It had been a bittersweet experience. Just the knowledge that the *Intrepid* had survived Kapteyn's Streamer, finally arriving in the future, had lifted Katrina's spirits greatly.

The moment she learned that she'd arrived in Bollam's World a mere three days after the *Intrepid* jumped out ranked as one of the worst of her life.

And Katrina had experienced many terrible moments.

However, her study of the battle had revealed one important clue. Tanis had allied herself with a freighter captain who operated in and around the Silstrand Alliance.

Katrina's travels over the past five hundred years had taken her far and wide. Even so far as the Transcend. Few would have known that captain's true identity, but Katrina did.

The Tomlinson resemblance was unmistakable.

And so, Katrina had spent the last twenty years travelling to Airtha, the one place she knew she could find a lead, only to be too late once more.

Kara was her silver lining. Someone who not only had *been* to New Canaan, but who had seen Tanis and Sera with her own eyes.

Katrina didn't believe in a god—if some entity had directed the events in her life, it would have a lot to answer for—but finding Kara was something of a miracle, enough to make her wonder.

"Katrina?" Kara said loudly.

"What? No need to yell, girl."

Katrina wondered what was going on behind the featureless oval that was Kara's head. Did the girl have a mouth to speak with? Her ethereal voice emitted from a sound-strip on her neck, and she never ate; instead taking in nutrition through a port in her abdomen.

Katrina suspected that Kara had no face at all, that the helmet was her head, cushioning her brain in a ballistic gel, making her a more effective killer.

Kara had said as much—about being a killer, at least. Her most important goal in life was to protect her father and destroy anyone who threatened him.

"I had asked why it was strange that they named it the *I2*."

"Oh, that." Katrina nodded slowly as she wound her thoughts back to that point. "Well, it just seems odd to me.

They really liked the *Intrepid*…it was their home. Now they've changed it into something else."

"Does that upset you?" Kara asked.

"No…we all change. I guess it means that the future wasn't what they hoped it would be, either."

"Is it ever?" Kara asked.

Katrina shrugged. "No, not really."

She turned her attention back to the holo display and the nine jump gates. The gates were all in orbit around Farska, a moon in orbit of the system's largest gas giant. Most of the commerce in the Germine system centered around the gas giant, so it made sense for the gates to be nearby, as well.

That was useful for Katrina. It meant her ships could make a close approach without any trouble. It would only be over the final hundred thousand kilometers that they'd be in violation of the local STC's flight paths.

Katrina's other ship was further ahead, almost at the edge of the no-fly zone surrounding the gates. That vessel, the *Kjeeran,* was empty, though automatons simulated human activity within the ship, should someone scan it closely.

Her entire company, all that remained of her once-sizable military that had escaped the Midditerra System all those centuries ago were now the crew on her last ship. The *Voyager*.

<*It's in the pipe,*> Troy said. <*I've cut the tightbeam to the* Kjeeran. *Too much traffic; someone was going to catch its bleed-off.*>

"Well, it's not like we need the ship to do a good job. The whole point is for it to make a mess."

<*Vicky has confirmed that she can alter Gate 7 when we approach. She wants to come with us, though.*>

Katrina groaned. "How's she going to do that? She's a gate control AI. She can't just leap across space to our ship."

<*Well, we're going to have to figure something out, she said she won't do it otherwise. Something about being 'truly free'.*>

More AI nonsense, Katrina thought to herself.

"Well, did she propose any means to do this? Or shall we just invent teleportation over the next hour?"

<*She can get one of us to her core for extraction, and then operate the gate on remote,*> Troy replied.

"I'll do it," Kara volunteered.

"You?" Katrina asked, looking the jet black, four-armed, winged woman up and down. "You blend in about as well as a missile."

"They're unaligned, I can claim to be a special envoy on a secret mission from my father. Then I kill whoever is escorting me, get to this Vicky's core, and free her."

"Getting shot at the whole way back to the *Voyager*," Katrina added.

<*Well, someone is going to have to do it,*> Troy replied. <*Kara here is a killing machine of epic proportions. She only ever wears armor, so no one will be shocked to see her in it.*>

"OK, mister smarty-AI," Katrina countered. "What's her reason for going aboard the gate control platform? We need something better than 'Dad sent me'."

<*Easy, she needs to provide special coordinates for her ship.*>

Katrina scrubbed her face with her palms. "They're not declared for Airtha *or* Khardine. How do we convince them to do something for Kara here?"

"Easy," Kara replied. "Greed. We offer a payoff to whoever runs the platform. The very fact that Germine hasn't aligned with either side tells us that they're in it for the money."

Katrina considered that. It was likely true, but it didn't mean that whoever ran the gate control platform felt the same way.

"It's a lot of variables to deal with in one hour," Katrina said. "We need more time."

<*Then we'd best stop the* Kjeeran *from finishing its suicide run,*> Troy advised.

"OK, yeah. Put it in a stable orbit and see if you can get Vicky to validate our way in with Kara, or suggest a better one."

Katrina looked at Kara, wishing once again that she could see the girl's facial expressions. "You sure you're up for it? You've never had to do something like this while not under your father's aegis."

Kara nodded resolutely. "I know. But I can do it. He told me to get to Sera, that only she can save him."

"Kara, that man controlled your mind your entire life. He made you serve him as a slave."

What irony for **me** *to be saying those words.*

Kara made a warbling sound that Katrina had learned was her variation on a laugh. "He's my mother, too. Did you know that? Father's a natural chimera hermaphrodite able to spontaneously gestate. I know it sounds insane, but as much as I hate my father, I love my mother. How messed up does that make me?"

Katrina shrugged. "I once used a dressing machine to tear all my skin off and replace it with armor. I was in agony for weeks and got addicted to the pain. We're all messed up in one way or another.

Kara nodded, then cocked her head to the side. "You're right, that *is* nuts."

Katrina patted the strange young woman on the shoulder. "It does explain why your Father-Mother spells his name like that."

* * * * *

Kara drew in a deep breath, calming her nerves as she drifted through the umbilical connecting the *Voyager* to the gate control platform—which bore the uninspired name, 'GCP1'.

Katrina had coached her on what to say and how to react to any challenges. The old woman was listening on the Link, ready to offer help as needed.

The AI, Troy, was there as well, likely ready to dole out sarcasm-laden advice. Kara wasn't sure if she liked him or not. Not that it mattered; she didn't like most people.

At the umbilical's end, Kara cycled the airlock open and floated in. As it matched pressure, the lock also brought the gravity up to GCP1's standard 0.7*g*.

While she waited, Kara wondered at her luck of meeting Katrina during her desperate escape from Airtha. The one person in the entire star system who was able to help had been there at the right time. Not only that, but Katrina had also possessed the means to make a speedy escape.

Luck was not something Kara believed in, but there was an undeniable serendipity to the events.

And what a strange old woman she was. To think that for five hundred years, Katrina had waited for the *Intrepid* to return. Hiding in dark corners and skulking about the Inner Stars, eventually passing into Orion space, and later the Transcend.

What a tale that must be. Aaron would have loved to hear it….

Kara pushed the thoughts of her dead brother from her mind as her clawed feet settled firmly on the deck. The airlock's door cycled open, and she looked out on the corridor beyond.

It was a narrow space, with grey bulkheads and a grey deck. An equally grey man stood waiting for her, his colorless uniform bearing no markings of any sort. On either side of him were two soldiers in matte black armor.

Kara smiled—or would have, if she still possessed the ability to do so.

It had been Aaron's idea to remove their faces and replace them with featureless ovals. He had done it so that they could be more effective in their defense of Father. But now Aaron was dead, and Kara was no longer under her father's aegis. She wondered for a moment what it would be like to have a face again.

What visage would she choose?

The man cleared his throat as Kara stepped into the corridor, her folded wings scraping the overhead. "Kara, daughter of Adrienne. Welcome to Germine and the GCP1. I understand you wish to use our jump gate for 'Special Transcend Business'."

Kara nodded, gazing down at the man. "I do. I have the coordinates, but I need to enter them myself with a record lockout in place."

"You wish to obscure your destination from the Germine government?" the man asked, his eyebrows raised halfway to his hairline. "That is highly irregular."

"Not for a cabinet member's envoy," Kara replied.

The man worked his mouth for a moment while nodding slowly. Kara imagined that even with two soldiers at one's side, a two-hundred-centimeter tall black demon looming over you was more than a little intimidating.

After all, what was the point of turning oneself into such a creature if you couldn't scare the crap out of officious little weasels?

The man finally replied, his voice tinged with disdain. "You surely know that Germine is no longer officially affiliated with the Airtha government, nor are we aligned with Khardine. Germine is a free system; your father's position means little here."

Kara kept both sets of hands folded in front of her, but made a point of slowly scratching her claws along her armored skin.

"I understand that…"

"Stationmaster Nuermin."

At least I've started at the top.

"Well, I'm sure that you'd still like for Germine to have favorable relations with Airtha. President Sera is an accommodating woman, but she is also resolute in her desire to destroy the usurper at Khardine."

To his credit, Nuermin did not back down. Instead he countered, "You are referring to the usurper who also claims to be President Sera? Hopefully you can understand why we're not interested in joining in what is clearly some sort of strange family squabble."

Honestly, Kara didn't blame the man or the populace of the Germine System. Staying out of the early stages of a civil war seemed like a smart play. Let the two sides show more of their hands before declaring allegiances.

Nevertheless, pacificity would not benefit her here, and she bore no particular love nor obligation to the people of Germine.

"Yet you agreed to let us dock and meet with me," Kara replied.

"I would not be so rude as to dismiss you out of hand—though the ship you're on did make me think twice...."

"A necessary subterfuge."

"I suppose. I don't need to know specifics of your mission."

<Stars, he's taking forever to get to the part where he asks you for money,> Katrina spoke for the first time. *<Make him an offer before he loses his nerve or something.>*

Kara agreed. She didn't want to spend forever trading pleasantries with this man.

"Stationmaster Nuermin. What will it take to use the gate? I assume that if there is a maintenance and upkeep cost associated with a jump, we could compensate the people of Germine for that?"

Kara had made her fair share of shady deals on her father's behalf. She was under no illusions that the 'people of Germine' would ever see a single credit.

"Well." Nuermin tilted his head, as though her words had only just now opened up a new avenue of thought. "I suppose we could determine the cost to the people, were I to allow you the use of a gate. However, we cannot remove destination information from our systems. There is no maintenance cost associated with that. It's simply against policy."

"I understand," Kara said. It didn't really matter. The AI, Vicky, would be configuring the jump gate and destroying all targeting data in GCP1's systems. "Do you have a number?"

Nuermin hemmed and hawed for almost a minute, behaving as though he'd never done this before. Kara glanced at the guards and could make out one of them rolling her eyes behind her faceshield.

"I suppose we could arrange a jump for seventeen million credits."

Kara nearly choked and was amazed that the stationmaster had managed to state the number with a straight face.

<*What a highwayman! And people call me a pirate,*> Katrina snorted. <*We can cover it, though. Not that it will come to that. Of course, don't take his first offer.*>

<*This is not my first deal of this sort, Katrina,*> Kara replied tonelessly.

<*OK, no need to get upset about it. Just making sure.*>

Kara gave the stationmaster a shake of her head. "I understand the economics of gate travel well enough to know that there is no scenario under which a jump costs more than ten million credits."

Nuermin nodded, a commiserating expression on his face. "Yes, that is normally the case, but with the troubles that abound, antimatter prices have gone up. Supply and demand, you know. A lot of demand right now. Not to mention demand for gate travel. Our queues are stacked for days, and I assume you want a speedy transit…"

He left the word hanging, and Kara nodded.

"I suspected as much. Well, in that case, I hope you understand that I cannot saddle so many people with this disruption for less than sixteen million."

Kara and the increasingly detestable stationmaster haggled for a few more minutes before settling on fifteen million, with a full refueling for the *Voyager* thrown in.

Once they agreed on price, Kara insisted that they do the transfer over a secure terminal, recording the transaction with system banking NSAI to ensure everything was above board.

This threw Nuermin for a loop, but eventually agreed to it.

<He's going to ask for a separate transaction just for himself,> Katrina muttered. *<Slimy bastard.>*

<Doesn't his greed favor us?> Kara asked. *<If he were an honest man, we would not be able to pull this off.>*

<Perhaps. We would at least be able to get you close to Vicky, though, which is really all we need to do.>

Kara decided that was true. *<Very well, when should I terminate this man and fetch Vicky?>*

<I'm bringing Vicky in on our chat,> Troy said. *<She can coordinate with you directly.>*

<Hi, Kara, I hear you're my ticket out of here.> Vicky's tone was brusque, yet somewhat melodic.

<I am, as you are ours,> Kara replied.

<You'll need to get Nuermin past this corridor,> Vicky marked a corridor on the map of GCP1 they shared over the Link. *<I'm just past there, about thirty meters.>*

<How do I get him to go that far? From what I see, there's a secure hard-terminal much closer. From the route he's taking, I believe he is planning to use that one.>

<Not for long,> Vicky chuckled. *<I'm about to invalidate its tokens.>*

<*Good,*> Kara replied, not sure if the AI wanted to be thanked for its efforts.

Stationmaster Nuermin stopped in his tracks a moment later and groaned. "Damn, we're going to have to use another terminal. Follow me."

He turned down a side passage and began leading Kara in the desired direction. She followed silently, paying more attention to the guards behind her than the man in front—a useful advantage of always wearing a helmet.

The guard on her left—the woman who had previously rolled her eyes at Nuermin—seemed bored. She was clearly watching personal holo, or engaged in a Link conversation. The other guard was a thin man who moved with the grace of a cat as he prowled along behind Kara. She felt a modicum of respect for him, as he paid close attention to his surroundings, his eyes darting to Kara if she so much as twitched a wing.

He would go down first.

Five minutes later, they crossed the demarcation Vicky had made on the map, and reached the room with the secure terminal.

Nuermin led the way into the sterile chamber, which only possessed four chairs along one wall and the terminal in the center.

Both parties were to hard-Link into the terminal and register special encrypted tokens for use in the transaction. Kara, of course, had no intention of doing that.

As Nuermin walked to the far side of the terminal, Kara readied herself to strike the guards, both of whom had entered and now stood behind her on either side.

I imagine they get a nice cut. Kara grimaced at the thought.

<*Resetting Link transmitters in that part of the station. You'll have thirty seconds before these three can reconnect,*> Vicky advised.

<*What about the terminal?*> Kara asked as she readied herself to strike.

<*I can't lock that out. You'll need to make sure they don't use it to call for help…and…GO!*>

Thanks for the countdown….

Kara snapped her wings wide, filling the room with their inky blackness, and kicked back at the wary man, clamping her clawed foot around his calf and pulling him forward.

She thought he'd fall, but instead, he hopped forward and crashed into her back, then drove a fist into her armored side.

With only one leg on the floor, Kara slipped and spun around, smacking a wing into Nuermin and knocking him away from the terminal.

Both of the guards faced her, the bored woman suddenly alert and swinging her pulse rifle up at Kara's head, while the man staggered backward, still unslinging his weapon.

Kara whipped a wing in front of herself as the woman fired. The carbon-fiber, polymer coated construction of her wing blocked the woman's pulse blast, and Kara slashed at her with the clawed tip of her wing, trying to hook the weapon and pull it away.

Meanwhile, the man had leveled his weapon and fired a pulse shot that Kara also blocked with a wing. The man lowered his weapon for a moment, his eyes registering dismay, and Kara lunged forward, one of her left arms grabbing his rifle, while another clamped around his neck, lifting him into the air.

So much for Sharp Eyes being the biggest threat.

She threw him at the woman and spun once more, whipping a wingtip at Neurmin, who was struggling to his feet. The blow sliced his face open from ear to chin, and he fell back with a shriek.

Kara turned her focus back to guards. She had succeeded in relieving the man of his rifle, but it was biolocked, so she tossed it aside.

<*Twelve seconds left,*> Vicky warned.

<*Quiet!*> Kara shot back and slammed a fist into the man's faceshield, the blow cracking the hard plas.

He yelled something unintelligible, and Kara wanted to smile. Having titanium alloy knuckles driven by her augmented limbs was more than his helmet could withstand.

She hit him again, and this time her fist drove through his faceshield, smashing into the flesh and bone beneath.

Kara continued to drive her lower left fist into the man's face while she grabbed the woman by the throat with one hand and grasped the underside of her helmet with the other two.

A sharp twist was all it took to break the helmet's locking mechanism, and then the woman's neck.

"You should have spent prior bribe money on better armor," she whispered as she turned to Nuermin.

<*Four seconds.*>

The grey man was blubbering as he crawled back across the grey floor on the far side of the terminal. Kara slammed her wingtips down into the deck plate, surging through the air to land on his fragile body—the force of her impact shattering his left hip and ribs.

Kara flexed both feet, snapping the stationmaster's pelvic bone and sinking her claws into his chest, feeling his heart muscles contract around her talons.

Nuermin drew in a sharp breath, about to scream, when two of Kara's fists smashed his face. Then she rained another two blows into his head, leaving it a shattered ruin.

<*Link is back online…and shit, Kara,*> Vicky made a coughing sound.

Kara turned to the two guards and confirmed that both were dead. She clamped a foot around the woman's helmet and leapt into the air, smashing the helmet and head within back against the deck.

<*What was that for?*> Katrina asked.

Kara returned to Nuermin, tore a strip of his pants off, and began to clean her hands. <*Just in case the armor had any transmitters—which it still may. I need to move.*>

<*Right,*> Vicky said and updated the map with the best route to her node. <*You're a bit brutal, Kara.*>

<*I hadn't noticed,*> Kara replied as she picked up the two pulse rifles, depositing nano on them to work at the biolocks. Then she slung the straps for each over her shoulders and held them behind her back with her lower arms.

Kara had felt empty while dispatching the guards and the stationmaster. Normally, striking down her enemies felt…better. She wondered if it was because her father's aegis was gone, or if it was because Aaron was not there with her.

Perhaps it was both.

A stray thought wandered into Kara's mind as she peered out into the corridor, ensuring the coast was clear. *Katrina was able to reattach my arm with her medbay on the Voyager. I wonder if the people at New Canaan can fix me….*

She didn't know exactly what needed fixing, but it felt like something was broken inside of her. Surely the people with the most advanced technology in the galaxy would know how to repair what was broken.

She crept through the passageways, pausing and ducking around corners twice when Vicky told her to—not a simple task, with her height and wings.

Ten minutes later, she was at the entrance to Vicky's node chamber.

<*OK, when I let you in, silent alarms are going to go off all over. You'll have thirty seconds to get me into a transport case—which is to the left of my pillar.*>

<*What happens after thirty seconds? And why is it always thirty with you?*> Kara asked.

<*Well, in this case it's an estimate as to how long it will take for the closest patrol to arrive. I can jam the turrets, but I can't jam the guards. You may have as few as ten seconds, if you keep stalling.*>

<*Open it.*> Kara wanted to tell Vicky that getting intel on what she was about to face wasn't stalling, but that would just eat up more valuable time.

The door slid open, revealing a small room with a gleaming Titanium-Au cylinder in the center. Kara spotted an AI case on a rack to the left, and grabbed it as the panel slide open on the cylinder. Within rested the tetrahedron-shaped AI core.

<*You ready?*> Kara asked.

<*Yeah, we don't have all day.*>

Kara snapped her wings wide in frustration, and grabbed the core, forcing herself to be gentle—as much as she didn't want to—and then set it in the case.

Once she closed the lid, Vicky's presence rejoined her. <*OK, let's go. I'll highlight the route to the closest escape pod.*>

<*The gate?*> Kara asked.

<*It's already aligning,*> Troy announced. <*I'm separating from the station. Get in that pod, and we'll pick you up.*>

Kara nodded silently as she peered back into the corridor. No one was present, and she turned right, rushing down the corridor with both pulse rifles held in front of her, all pretense at subterfuge long gone.

A pair of guards rounded a corner ahead, and Kara fired on them, knocking one back. The other ducked behind the corner and tossed a grenade her way.

Kara didn't even flinch. She snapped a wing out and swept the grenade further down the hall to her rear, continuing her mad dash.

She came around the corner and slammed a shoulder into the guard, then kicked him out into the intersection as the grenade exploded blasting flames down the passageway.

<*Efficient,*> Vicky commented.

Kara didn't reply as she resumed her run through the station.

<*The* Kjeeran *is on collision course for the platform,*> Troy announced. <*Impact is in seven minutes.*>

<*Understood,*> Vicky said, and suddenly an audible alarm sounded.

<*I thought you said it would be silent?*> Kara asked.

<*The one for my chamber being breached is. This is the general evac alarm.*>

Kara shook her head in frustration, cursing aloud. "What the fuck, Vicky! That wasn't the plan."

<*I'm not a monster! We have to give everyone time to get to escape pods before the* Kjeeran *hits the station.*>

"Just hope there are pods left for us," Kara grunted as she picked up the pace.

One advantage of the general evac being sounded was that no one cared about fighting the large winged woman racing through the station.

They were, however, prepared to fight her for a place on the escape pods.

Kara rounded the final corner to find droves of people crowding into escape pods, and four soldiers with kinetic slug throwers watching over them.

She skidded to a halt as soon as she saw the soldiers and scampered back the way she'd come as kinetic rounds tore through the air around her.

One ripped a hole in her wing, and another cracked the armor on her leg before she was back in cover.

<Vicky! Why didn't you warn me, don't you have internal feeds!?>

<Sorry, duking it out with Gert. He **should** *be ejecting his AI core from the station, but the damn fool is trying to lock down all the gates first.>*

<You can't do that and keep an eye out twenty paces ahead of me?> Kara asked.

<No, Kara, I can't! I have limited bandwidth in this case. Now, please! Shut up and let me do my thing, while you go swing your appendages at organics.>

The statement stopped Kara cold. *Is that all people think I'm good for?* It was what her Father had used her for the most. A joke came to mind about people who were so stupid they weren't good for much more than being walking meat-suits for AIs.

Was she even that? Or was she nothing more than a weapon for others to wield?

<Kara! What are you doing?> Vicky wailed in her mind. *<The pods…fuck! They're all gone!>*

Kara snapped to and peered around the corner. Sure enough, all the pods *were* gone.

"Shit! I just stood there for a second!"

<Kara, it's been a minute! This is going to be ground zero for an antimatter explosion in four minutes!>

Kara nodded, considering her options. *<Katrina? How close can you get to the station?>*

<Close as we have to,> Katrina replied. *<But we can't match* v *with it. No time.>*

<Understood.> Kara drew a deep breath, and disabled her external oxygen ports. *<Vicky. Get ready to blow one of the evac pod doors open.>*

Vicky didn't respond, and Kara hoped the AI understood what to do.

She took off at a full run toward the first evac pod's chute, bracing for an impact that—thankfully—never came. When she was a meter from the door, it blew open, and Kara tucked her wings in tight as the explosive decompression shot her down the pod's launch tube.

She slammed into the tube's walls and screamed silently when one of her wings caught on something and snapped.

Then they were out of the chute, and the guns fell away from her hands, and she clutched Vicky's case with all four arms, watching as GCP1 began to shrink behind them.

Kara turned, looking for the *Voyager,* and spotted it, a pinprick of light noted on her HUD.

<*Coming in fast, starboard airlock is open,*> Troy announced.

<*Got it,*> Kara replied, suddenly feeling weak and dizzy.

Something's wrong, she thought as her body began to feel cold. She looked herself over, checking for injuries, and saw red gouts of blood drifting away from her leg.

<*Damn…that's more than cracked armor,*> she said, trying to gauge the time until the *Voyager* reached her. Was it a minute, two? The numbers on her HUD kept shifting, dancing about in little circles.

<*Say again?*> Katrina asked. <*Are you injured, Kara?*>

Katrina's words started to sound strange to Kara, like they were bendy. Then more warbling voices that were indistinct gibbering nonsense.

<*She's bleeding out,*> Vicky replied. <*Not just her leg, her back, too. Shit! Hurry!*>

Kara saw the red glare of engines, and felt a grav beam tug at her, jerking her body around like it was a rag doll.

Hold the case, Kara, hold the case. Don't let go. Do it for Father.

Then the darkness of space was replaced by the clean, white interior of an airlock, and Kara flexed her fingers to be sure it was still there.

Got it. Daddy will be proud.

*****

Katrina struggled to pull Kara's listless form into the ship, hollering for someone to help. Carl was at her side a moment later, sliding a grav board under Kara's body and lifting it into the air.

"Quick, medbay!" Katrina shouted, and they pushed Kara to the ladder shaft and then up to the next level.

"She's in shock," Carl called out as Kara began to shiver and convulse. "We should get her in stasis, deal with it later."

Katrina nodded and tried to get Vicky's case out of Kara's grasp.

"Noooo," Kara moaned. "Gotta keep it for Father."

"Your father's here," Katrina said, stroking Kara's arm as Carl got the stasis pod ready. "He needs the case. I'll take it to him."

"Suuure?" Kara's synthetic voice warbled with what sounded like fear.

"Yes, I'm sure. And you'll be safe, too."

Kara's grasp on the case lessened, and Katrina was able to lift it free.

<*Thanks, Kara,*> Vicky said, her voice filled with sincere gratitude. <*Sorry I was such a bitch to you.*>

Katrina maneuvered the grav board to the edge of the stasis pod where Carl waited. He grabbed her feet, and Katrina folded Kara's wings around her before sliding an arm below the woman's shoulders.

As quickly and carefully as they could, they got her into the pod. Katrina was about to close the lid, when Kara's arm shot up and grabbed her wrist.

"I want to see Father." Kara's voice rasped and wavered.

"You will," Katrina whispered. "Everything will be fine."

"No…" Kara's voice fell. "Not fine. Me. I want to be me again."

Katrina folded Kara's arm back down and stroked it for a moment. "You and me both."

"Kat!" Carl whispered hoarsely. "Get to the bridge. I got this."

Katrina coughed. "Yeah, OK." She grabbed Vicky's case and rushed up the ladders to the bridge, settling into one of the seats as the glowing shape of Gate 5 grew in front of them.

<*Nice of you to join me up here.*> Troy said. <*Twenty seconds to the gate.*>

"Good," Katrina said as she placed Vicky's case on the seat beside her and wrapped a strap around it.

<*I feel so safe,*> Vicky said, her voice dripping with sarcasm.

<*You shouldn't,*> Troy replied. <*The* Kjeeran *is going to hit GCP1 three seconds before we reach the gate. They fired on it and blew off one of the cargo pods—which ended up speeding its acceleration.*>

<*Awww, crap. That must have been Gert! I had those weapons offline!*>

Katrina shared Vicky's general sentiment and pulled up their rear view on one of the holoscreens, keeping one eye on it, and the other on the gate.

"We should have enough time, it's a short jump…"

Ahead, the gate's mirrors focused the negative energy into a roiling ball at its center as Troy deployed the *Voyager*'s mirror.

Behind them, the gate control platform crumpled as the *Kjeeran* plowed into it. Then it and the station were swallowed up by a blinding flash of light.

Alarms sounded, and half the cockpit's consoles lit up as the antimatter explosion bathed the *Voyager* in gamma rays.

Katrina gritted her teeth and gripped the armrests on her chair as the ship bucked and shuddered, its shields and dampeners barely able to compensate for the energy slamming into it.

A second later, the *Voyager*'s mirror touched the roiling ball of energy, and space-time disappeared.

THEBES

STELLAR DATE: 08.13.8949 (Adjusted Years)
LOCATION: ISS *Aegeus*, Bridge
REGION: Albany System, Thebes, Septhian Alliance

"And here we are, the Albany System, regional capital of the province of Thebes," Oris announced as the *Aegeus* dropped out of the dark layer and into normal space.

<*We have maps, now,*> Angela commented to Tanis and Rachel. <*Not sure why Oris thinks she's a maglev announcer.*>

Tanis didn't know and wished she had left Oris back on the *I2* in the Lisbon system. With no more Intrepid Class jump gates available to deploy, Tanis had been hesitant to bring the ship this close to Nietzschean space.

Instead, they'd spread the ISF First Fleet throughout systems in Septhia, searching for the current location of General Mill.

Tanis decided not to acknowledge Oris's statement and turned to the Comm officer. "Let me know if there's anything about Marauder ships in the system. We can't keep hopping around forever. Eventually we've gotta find these mercenaries."

"I wish you'd tell me what you hope to learn from General Mill about the Genevian mech program," Oris said. "I might be able to use it to help you search them out."

<*How would* **that** *help?*> Angela wondered privately. <*Seems like she's just fishing for intel—badly, too.*>

"They work for you." Tanis gave Oris a look signifying lessening patience. "How is it that you don't know where they are?"

"Well, they move around a lot." Oris shrugged as she turned to look at the bridge's holotank. "They have operations in a number of systems. But you know how it is, interstellar comms are only as good as the routes courier ships take to relay messages."

"If we don't find them here, perhaps we should widen the net," Captain Sheeran suggested. "Go from pairs of cruisers to single ships visiting each system,"

"Yes, we may have to do just that." Tanis considered where they could send their escort, the *Derringer,* next.

"If the Marauders have moved on from Albany, then we should go to the Hercules System," Oris advised, providing one possible answer to Tanis's unvoiced question. "They have a training facility there—recently established. They may know where the general is, currently."

"Ma'am!" the Comm officer called out a moment later. "I've stripped the beacon. STC has record of an MSS *Foehammer.* It entered the system a week ago and was headed for the planet Hudson in the inner system. No record on this nav beacon of it leaving the Albany System after that."

"General Mill's flagship," Oris said with a grin.

"Finally!" Tanis grinned at Captain Sheeran. "We can have our chat with this General Mill and learn what we need to know."

Sheeran shared Tanis's smile, then turned to his bridge crew. "Comm, pass the tokens we were given by the PM to the system STC and set a course for Hudson. See if you can find anything out about where the *Foehammer* might be berthed."

Tanis wondered where this lead might take her, if it was a lead at all. Following the Caretaker backward through its various actions may not guide them to any place other than where the entity had been in the past. Perhaps she should turn her focus solely toward stopping Nietzschea. Once she found additional allies. There was still something about the Septhians that didn't sit right with her.

<*Either way, Nietzschea must be stopped,*> Angela said, her tone almost weary. <*Despite your early reservations about Prime Minister Harmin, he does seem dedicated to that goal.*>

<*Sort of. Praesepe wants to build walls. They've been bolstering defenses, when they should have been rapidly expanding their fleets. Despite the fact that they're mercs, these Marauders seem to have the right idea. Be mobile, strike the enemy when and where they least expect it.*>

<*Sure, then maybe we can put this Mill in charge of the right resources to get the job done. If his actual tactics are as good as his ability to hide in his own backyard, he'll be quite the asset.*>

Tanis couldn't argue with that logic. Hopefully Mill lived up to the reputation.

"Admiral?" the comm officer asked. "I got a response from a local STC NSAI just a few light seconds out. It says that it never received authorization codes to match ours. We're being denied entrance to the system."

Tanis blew out a long breath and turned to Oris. "Well, time for you to do your job. We need to be insystem yesterday. Please work with Comm to sort this out."

Oris nodded, walked over to the Comm station, and bent her head toward the display.

Tanis made a sound of exasperation in her mind. <*Maybe we should just drop a jump gate, fly to the heart of the Nietzschean empire, blow up their capital, and then start our search from there.*>

Angela gave a mental nod of agreement. <*Well, I've wandered into the STC NSAI's beacon, you know, very cordially—*>

<*Right.*>

<*And the* Foehammer *is docked at a station called Judine. It's in high orbit around Hudson, so there's that much good news, at least.*>

Tanis pulled up the data they had on the world. It was a smaller terrestrial world, right around Mars's size and mass. It was interesting that the ship wasn't around the regional capital world of Pyra, but then she saw why.

"Whoa! The Nietzscheans attacked this system just last year."

"Yes," Oris nodded from where she stood next to the comm station. "They were repelled by a combination of local forces, the Marauders, and our SAF fifth fleet."

"I see," Tanis said aloud, while commenting to Angela, *<That would have been nice to know. If I'd realized that the Nietzscheans were already making advances into Septhia, I might have been more forgiving.>*

<Those Marauders sure seem to be popping up a lot. I'm reading news feeds about how they took out a despotic empire anti-spinward of here, called the Politica. It was using a lot of Genevian mechs, too.>

<That's very interesting.> Tanis nodded as she looked over the feeds Angela had pointed out. *<Looks like Oris was right about the training facility in the Hercules System, though. The Marauders are setting up shop on a planet called 'Iapetus'.>*

<I guess if the General isn't on his ship, that will be our next stop.>

Tanis reached back, pulling at her ponytail. *<It's been nearly a year since we left Scipio. I really did not want to spend this much time before dealing with the Trisilieds.>*

Tanis could sense that Angela wanted to say something, but was considering her words.

<Spit it out, Angela.>

<I know we have a bone to pick with the Trisilieds; they killed a lot of people at New Canaan. But they're not actively expanding their borders. The Nietzscheans are a larger threat to this region of the Inner Stars. I don't think we should just bolster the Nietzschean's enemies, I think we should take them out entirely. Ourselves. I bet if we do, the Trisilieds will reconsider aggressive action—especially with Scipio attacking the Hegemony. At the very least, they'll be less likely to aid the Hegemony.>

Tanis chewed on Angela's advice. She knew that the Nietzscheans were a clear and present danger, but every time she thought about not taking the fight to the Trisilieds….

<*I sent Ouri to her grave,*> Tanis replied quietly. <*I put her down on Carthage with barely any protection.*>

<*This is going to sound cruel, and maybe it is, but you send a lot of people to their graves, Tanis. And you didn't leave Ouri hanging alone. Brandt was nearby, and she had an entire fleet of submarine nuke launchers, and a whole planet's defensive capabilities.*>

Tanis swallowed. She didn't need Angela to remind her of her failings, of the mountain of bodies that was piled up behind her. But in this case, perhaps Angela was right. She *had* given Ouri everything she could…and the Trisilieds soldiers had killed her. For that, they would die.

<*Sometimes…sometimes it's all I can think about, the faces of those I've killed, and those I've failed to protect. Parents burying their children—or worse, never knowing what happened.*>

<*What could you have done differently?*> Angela asked. <*You've never acted out of self-interest. You've* ***always*** *made the decisions needed to protect those who are under your charge.*>

<*Don't you ever think about just leaving?*> Tanis asked. <*Get a jump-capable ship, and head to the far side of the galaxy? Leave this mess behind us.*>

Tanis could feel Angela's comforting presence grow in her mind. <*What of Joe and our daughters? What of the children of our friends who would be left at risk?*>

<*Why do you think I'm still here? Trying to track down this stars-be-damned Caretaker so that I can put an end to its meddling? Find out what it knows about the Core AIs. Find out how we can destroy them.*>

<*Then you'd better buck up, Tanis, because we have a long road ahead. Honestly? What we've been through so far is just the beginning. But don't worry. No matter what happens, I'll always be with you, backing your play.*>

Tanis drew a slow, steadying breath. *<Thanks, Ang. You really have a way of depressing the shit out of me and building me up at the same time.>*

<It's a skill.>

"Admiral Richards?" Comm called out. "We have managed to get permission to take one cruiser in, but they won't allow both passage. I imagine if we get in touch with something other than this f—stupid NSAI, we can get an exception made."

"How far away is the closest sentient?" Tanis asked.

"Nine light hours, round trip."

"So we could be looking at days before we get approval for both ships." Tanis straightened her back and looked to Captain Sheeran. "Captain, take us in at whatever max speed they allow in this place. I'll let Mel on the *Derringer* know that she's to wait for us out here."

"Aye, Admiral. Setting a course."

Tanis glanced at Oris, who was still talking with the NSAI at the Comm station. She considered saying something to the woman, but decided not to.

There was a BLT with her name on it in the officer's mess, and more conversation with Oris was bound to sour her stomach.

<Getting so testy in your old age,> Angela laughed as they walked off the bridge.

Tanis snorted. *<Pretty sure that's your mind bleeding into mine.>*

<Hmm…maybe. Getting hard to tell.>

UNEXPECTED GUESTS

STELLAR DATE: 08.13.8949 (Adjusted Years)
LOCATION: ISS *Andromeda*
REGION: Edge of the New Canaan system

<*What is it?*> Joe asked, rubbing his eyes and pushing himself to a seated position. <*Are the girls OK?*>

<*Sorry, sir,*> Major Blanca, the Andromeda's XO, apologized. <*Your daughters are fine. I'm alerting you about a ship that's just appeared at the edge of the interdiction field.*>

Joe resisted the urge to give the major a snippy comeback. Ore haulers from the Grey Wolf Star were jumping in every day, along with couriers from Khardine. For all their hopes at secrecy, New Canaan was practically a bustling hub.

Then the second part of her statement hit him. An interdicted jump. That meant the ship was not jumping on a predetermined schedule, and had been caught in the system's defenses.

<*Go on, Major.*> Joe sat up, swinging his legs over the edge of the bed.

The long search for the remnants had worn him and his daughters down, but now they were taking the entities to a special detainment center outside of Canaan Prime's heliosphere.

That arduous task was almost complete. Whatever this was couldn't be a patch on extracting extra-dimensional entities from human hosts.

<*Well,*> Major Blanca began. <*You're never going to believe this, but it's the* Voyager*, sir.*>

The major's voice was filled with excitement, but Joe couldn't determine why. *Voyager,* he mused. The name was familiar.

<Major Blanca, sorry to be obtuse, but I'm still in dreamland here. Can you refresh my memory?>

<Sorry, sir. It's just so hard to believe. Voyager, *as in the escape ship left behind in the Gamma base at Kapteyn's Star.>*

The memories flowed into Joe's mind like water pouring down his back. *Voyager*. The ship Tanis insisted they leave at Kapteyn's Star, 'Just in case Katrina has a change of heart'.

<Blanca…> Joe almost didn't want to ask. *<Is it her?>*

<Yes, sir! We have an initial transmission. She's a bit worse for wear, but it's Katrina.>

"Hoooolееееe shit!" Joe whispered as he flung his blankets aside and grabbed the uniform he'd draped over his chair the night before. *<Direct that ship to meet us. I'll be up on the double.>*

<On it, Admiral,> Major Blanca replied.

OK…so maybe this **is** *on par with capturing remnants.*

Joe dressed quickly while pulling up the scan data. The *Voyager* was just over a light minute from the *Andromeda*. Based on their current speed, it would take Katrina's ship half a day to arrive, but that would give him plenty of time to catch up with her—even with the communications lag.

He looked at the optical pickups that were tracking the *Voyager*, marveling at how it barely looked the same. Scuffed and scratched, mismatched hull plating across its port side, and a dozen cargo pods attached amidships.

"What have you been up to, Katrina?" he whispered.

<I hope she didn't draw it out too much,> Corsia said, a warm presence in his mind. *<Blanca was so excited, I let her share the news.>*

Joe laughed. *<It was fine. Just shocking. I keep expecting to be woken and told that the remnants are free, taking over the crew.>*

<Don't worry, I'd blow the ship before that happened,> Corsia replied.

<Stars, Corsia, there are a few contingencies before that one.>

Corsia only laughed, and Joe shook his head. Motherhood had softened the once hard-as-steel AI a lot. Somewhere along the line, she had developed a strange sense of humor.

As he was walking to the *Andromeda*'s bridge, Joe pulled up the latest transmission from the approaching vessel. His breath caught in his throat at the sight of Katrina.

She looks so old, what's happened to her? And how did she find us here and now, arriving by jump gate, no less?

"New Canaan, and Carthage," Katrina laughed and shook her head. "I appreciate the irony. Troy's altering vector, we'll get there as fast as we can. Got a lot to catch up on."

Yeah, a lifetime from the looks of it.

Then the name Katrina had spoken sank into Joe's mind. "Troy?" he whispered aloud before sending a message to the approaching ship.

<Voyager, *this is Admiral Joseph Evans. Stars, it's the best thing ever to hear your voice, Katrina, but did you say 'Troy'?*>

<*It can't be…*> Corsia's mental tone was a whisper.

He sent the message off as he stepped onto the bridge, nodding to Major Blanca as she grinned like a fool. His brow furrowed as he wondered why she was so happy, but then it dawned on him.

"Blanca! I can't believe I forgot! Katrina is your great aunt."

Blanca nodded vigorously. "Great-great, actually, but who cares? Can you believe she's alive?"

"With Troy, no less." Joe nodded in response, feeling a bit silly as he and the major bobbed their heads at one another, but not caring in the least.

With all the struggle the last year had seen, he'd take any good news he could get. As far as he was concerned, Katrina and Troy arriving now was like a message from the ancient gods.

"But it can't be *that* Troy," Major Blanca said, twisting the long white braid that hung down her back. "He…he died at the Battle for Victoria. Three RMs hit the *Excelsior.* We all saw it."

Joe shrugged. "Did you ever expect to see Katrina again?"

"Well…no, sir."

"Then let's hold onto hope a bit longer. Troy is one of our greatest heroes. Having him back…."

His voice trailed off, and Blanca nodded silently.

Joe saw that the three ensigns on bridge duty were staring at him and the major. "OK, you, keep on task. No bets on whether or not the Old Man can shed a tear."

The ensigns spun about, and Blanca laughed. "It's already up to a hundred cred—no, two hundred. Damn, that pool's growing fast."

"I need plausible deniability here, Blanca," Joe chuckled. "Don't ruin that for me."

"Oh, I was talking about the price of a piece of art at auction I'm following, sir. No idea what *you're* talking about."

Joe nodded. "Good, I hope you win."

Blanca snorted. "Odds—I mean bids—are too rich for my blood."

<*She's lying,*> Corsia said, a wink in their minds.

They had only a minute longer to wait until Katrina's response came back, and Joe put it on the main holotank.

Seeing Katrina at life-size was both less and more shocking. She still held herself erect, her eyes sharp and her measured smile giving her the same wry look he remembered so well.

But her face bore creases telling of many long years, and her hair was silver—not an affectation, either. Most of all, the difference was in her voice. It sounded tired and thin, though there was a joy in it.

"*Admiral* Joe now, is it? I seem to remember a cocksure young commander glued to Colonel Tanis's side. Well, now that I think back, I suppose you were a colonel or something yourself before you left. I forget some of those specifics.

"And yes, it is *that* Troy with me. Would you believe he was just hanging out down on Anne's surface, taking a break while we did all the work?"

"I remember it a bit differently," Troy's voice came from the holo, as dry and sardonic-sounding as ever.

"Troy…" Joe whispered, shaking his head.

"You're one tough hombre," Corsia added. "I recall you getting blown up."

Troy laughed. "I got better."

"You are some hard sonsabitches to find," Katrina said with a coarse laugh. "Sorry, you're going to have to pardon my language. I've fallen in with some less-than-savory types over the years. I've become a bit more colorful as a result."

"And by a bit, she means *a lot*," Troy interjected audibly.

"We have a lot to talk about, but why don't we wait 'til we're just a few light seconds away. My mind wanders too much with this much lag to have a meaningful conversation."

"Otherwise known as her senior moments," Troy added. "Is the *I2* here? Bob?"

Joe opened the channel and sent a response. "I look forward to chatting more when you get closer, Katrina. Troy, I can't tell you how glad I am to see you. You know we held a funeral for you? Anyway, Tanis and the *I2*—interested to know where you've heard *that* name—are not here. Bob, of course is with them. Couldn't pry him from that ship with a black hole. At present, they're in the Silstrand System. We can chat more about all that when you arrive."

He closed the transmission and met Blanca's eyes, which were brimming with tears.

"Good thing they weren't betting about me," Blanca said with a small laugh.

"Gotta get some steel in your spine, there, Major. Let me know if anything changes. I need to put on some clothes that smell better, and get some grub. I'll be back before an hour is out."

*****

A half-dozen other issues cropped up before Joe got back to the command deck, and when he did, the *Voyager* was within a few light seconds. He reached out, making a direct, though delayed, Link connection to Katrina, glad to feel her amber presence touch his mind.

<*Joseph Evans,*> Katrina said in greeting. <*So you're in charge now, are you?*>

<*I do a bit here and there,*> Joe replied. <*Jason's the governor, though. He hid in the woods for almost twenty years, but we finally convinced him to take the reins.*>

A rueful laugh came over the Link. <*I don't blame him. You recall that I took over at The Kap for a bit. Then they wanted more structure and a bigger government. Named themselves the Kapteyn's Primacy—though I suppose you remember that. Most of it went down before you left.*>

<*I do,*> Joe replied. <*A few months before the* Intrepid *shipped out. Without you, I might add. How—*>

<*Well, Admiral Evans, that is quite the tale. I'll tell you the whole thing sometime, but only if you have a spare year. The fact that you're surprised is what's surprising. What do you think I'd do after the* Intrepid *disappeared? Just shrug and walk slowly toward my grave?*>

Joe had considered that over the years. He had always imagined Katrina being saddened when the *Intrepid* failed to check in, when it should have reached New Eden. <*I thought a lot of things, but I didn't think you'd come find us—***especially** *not out here.*>

<*Well, young man, I had half a millennium to track you down.*>

<*A what?*> Joe almost choked.

<*I came out of the Streamer before you. Eighty-sixth century, as a matter of fact. Was a…a bit of a rough time at first.*>

Joe whistled in appreciation. <*I can imagine. I hear that things were none too stable back then.*>

<*Not so much better now, what with the trouble you've stirred up.*>

<*We're just trying to find a place to settle down,*> Joe replied. <*Turns out everyone wants a little piece of us first.*>

Katrina laughed again, her voice sounding clearer than it had at first—even though it was just her mental voice he was hearing. <*Oh, I know all about that. I've come from the Huygens System. Picked up a little something at Airtha.*>

<*You **what**?*> The conversation was going nothing like Joe had expected. Granted, he had not been sure *what* to expect—certainly not that Katrina was traipsing about the Transcend.

<*I've gotten around, Joe,*> Katrina replied. <*I know more than a little about what's going on. Like what Airtha really is—*>

<*A nearly-ascended AI who is the former wife of President Tomlinson, and Sera Tomlinson's mother?*>

Katrina made a small sound of amusement. <*Well, I didn't know that she was President Sera's mother. Which one?*>

<*Both, from what we know.*>

<*Damn, you're always in the thick of it. Anyway, you'll want to update your intel. Airtha is ascended. No 'almost' about it.*>

Joe thought he'd be ready for additional bombshells, but that one caught him by surprise. <*How?*>

<*We saw her when rescuing Adrienne's daughter, Kara. I have optical feeds of the landing pad on High Airtha. Saw Adrienne being captured and brought before what sure looked like an ascended being—though I suppose it **could** have all been a charade.*>

Joe let out a low whistle. <*And you have his daughter? Kara?*>

<*Nice girl, a little manic. I suspect she has no small amount of psychological damage from what her father did to her.*>

<*I'm not surprised,*> Joe replied. <*Those two kids of Adrienne's were a little disturbing.*>

<*He had done something to them—to all his kids. At least that's what Kara has told me. We took to calling it his 'Aegis'. We can talk more about that later.*>

Joe sat back in the command chair and looked at the arrival time on the holo. Just a few more hours. <*Sure. I imagine we'll have more than a little to discuss.*>

<*Yes, and the thing we need to talk most about is what the Ascended AIs have in mind for Tanis.*>

This time Joe did choke.

<***What!?***>

* * * * *

"I don't know what is more surprising," Joe said as Katrina stepped out of the *Voyager*'s airlock. "Seeing you still alive and kicking, or seeing this ship."

<*And what about me?*> Troy asked.

"Depends, Troy. Got a hot tub in there?"

<*Does a jacuzzi count?*>

"I never quite figured out the difference, so I guess it just may."

By then, Katrina was before him, and he extended a hand, which she swatted away.

"Joe, if you weren't Tanis's husband, I'd kiss you. At least give an old woman a hug."

"Of course, Katrina." Joe wrapped her in a warm embrace, surprised at the strength in her limbs. "Got more kick in you than I would have thought."

"I put on a bit of a show for the others," Katrina whispered in Joe's ear. "Plus, we used stasis a lot on the longer trips. I'm not quite as ancient as I play at."

Katrina pulled back and cast her eyes on Earnest, who had managed to extract himself from his studies of the remnants to join them.

"Earnest, the great architect. It is truly a pleasure to see you once more. And stasis shields! What's a woman gotta do to get one of those for her ship?"

Earnest embraced Katrina as well, laughing as he did so. "*Your* ship? I distinctly remember requesting this vessel for *my* research base back at The Kap."

"Oh? Is that how you want to play this? Well, Earnest, finders-keepers."

"I suppose you can have it," Earnest shrugged. "I can just grow another."

"Grow? Starships?" Katrina asked. "Will wonders never cease."

"Katrina," Joe captured her attention once more. "I'd like you to meet my daughters, Cary, Saanvi, and Faleena."

Katrina turned to the two young women and cocked her head, "You know, it's not kind to play tricks on your elders."

<*Hi, I'm Faleena,*> Joe's youngest introduced herself first.

"Ahhhhh," Katrina glanced at Joe. "So…you, Tanis, and Angela finally made it official, did you?"

"That's a very progressive attitude for a Sirian," Joe shot back, laughing as he spoke.

He'd forgotten how much fun he and Katrina used to have, often chatting amongst themselves while Tanis and Markus were making their plans. Katrina could do a mean Tanis impression that had him in stitches more than once.

It was good to have her back.

Katrina stepped forward to embrace Cary and Saanvi, and Joe's attention was drawn to a man and woman who appeared at the ship's airlock, pushing a stasis pod on an a-grav pad.

"Katrina, we have Kara for their doctors."

<Our medbay can heal her, but we're low on supplies that you likely have in abundance. I imagine your facilities will be able to take much better care of her,> Troy explained.

"I never saw Adrienne's children in person," Joe said as he approached the pod. "Those are some amazing alterations."

He nodded to a pair of medical techs who had been waiting nearby, and they took the stasis pod, one of Katrina's crew trailing after.

"Carl took a bit of a fancy to Kara," Katrina said as she watched him go. "Not that I blame him—she's a brave, brave woman—wait…Blanca!"

Major Blanca had just stepped into the docking bay, and rushed past Joe to sweep Katrina up in her arms.

"Auntie! I just can't believe it!"

<This is going to take forever,> Troy groused.

Half an hour later—after Katrina had introduced her twenty crewmembers, and a few other members of the *Andromeda*'s crew had filtered through the docking bay to greet the former Victorian governor—Joe declared it time for the assemblage to move to the mess hall so the dockworkers could begin their work, assessing repairs to the *Voyager*.

"What exactly are you going to do to my ship?" Katrina eyed Earnest suspiciously.

<If we're going to be pedantic—which I'm always in favor of—I'm pretty sure you gave **me** *the* Voyager *back at Bollam's World,>* Troy replied. *<And I'm going to let Earnest do whatever his heart desires.>*

"Back at Bollam's World?" Katrina stammered. "That was just while I resc—" she stopped for a moment. "Nevermind. Do what you want."

Joe wondered at what Katrina had been going to say, but could see that the memory brought her pain, and didn't press for details.

He led the way to the mess hall, while the off-duty ISF personnel intermingled with Katrina's crew, learning where and when they were from and gleaning snippets of their adventures over the years.

"I'm glad you finally found a home," Katrina said as they entered the mess hall and found seats at the end of a long table.

Joe sat across from Katrina, his girls on one side, and Earnest on the other. Blanca sat beside Katrina, and several of her crew settled nearby, as well.

"We have," Joe said, his voice laden with the weight of many memories. "It hasn't been all peace and prosperity, though."

Katrina nodded. "The picotech, I assume. You tipped your hand at Bollam's World."

"If we hadn't, we wouldn't have won the engagement. Then our technology—and the *Intrepid*—would have fallen to the AST…er, Hegemony. Whatever."

"They keep flopping back and forth between those names," Katrina nodded. "Half their populace doesn't know what to call themselves anymore."

Idle chatter continued for a few minutes, while the humans placed orders over the Link, and servitors began to bring them food.

"Ah…civilization," Katrina sighed. "You have no idea some of the backward places I've been to."

"Katrina, you said something before, about ascended AI," Joe changed the subject. "And what they have planned for Tanis. I really need to know what you were talking about."

Katrina's eyes narrowed. "And what do you know about ascended AI?"

"Well, I've met one," Nance said from a few seats down. Joe hadn't noticed her arrival, but Nance had been very quiet in the weeks since she'd been taken out of stasis.

"You have?" Katrina's eyes locked on Nance. "In person?"

Nance nodded. "Named the Caretaker, back on Ikoden."

Joe watched Katrina stiffen as she peered at Nance.

"You must isolate her," Katrina said, glancing at Joe. "She's likely under its control."

"Not anymore," Cary said. "Trine drew the remnant out of her. We have it contained."

"Trine?" Katrina looked up and down the table. "Is she here?"

"We are Trine," Cary said in the eerie voice she used when she deep-Linked with her sisters. "And…wait. There is something in you, too. Like the remnant, but different."

Joe's gaze snapped to Katrina. "Katrina. Did you bring a remnant here?"

"I don't even know what that is," Katrina replied. "Well, I suppose I can guess. Is that what you call it when an ascended AI leaves a sliver of itself behind in a human?"

Trine-Cary nodded. "It is, and I can see something like it in you…. Hold still, and I'll remove it."

Katrina pulled back, a look of horror on her face. "No! How can you even do that?"

Joe raised a hand toward his daughters, and they relaxed a hair. He could tell by the expression on their faces that they didn't trust Katrina, and he suddenly wondered whether he should.

A lot can change in five hundred years.

"You'd best explain yourself, Katrina," he said in calm, even tones. "Quickly."

Katrina nodded, her eyes narrowing, sharpening the creases that ran onto her temples. "OK, but then you need to explain how your daughters can see things inside my body."

Joe nodded, waiting for Katrina to continue.

"It happened a long time ago. I met an entity that called itself Xavia. It got me out of a pretty tough bind. I didn't even know it left a part of itself in me until later when it began to guide me."

"Guide, or control?" Joe asked.

"Guide. Xavia is in opposition to the Caretaker. She has splintered off from the AIs who want to keep humanity in a perpetual state of disharmony."

"They also want to keep humans from ascending," Nance chimed in. "I caught that sentiment very strongly from the remnant when we were in Star City. I don't *think* the remnant managed to share knowledge of that place with anyone else, though."

"Star City?" Katrina asked. "What is that?"

"A tale for another time," Joe replied. "So, this Xavia, how do you know she only guides?"

"I think she's telling the truth," Trine-Saanvi interjected. "The mass and composition of this remnant are different, and it's not tangled up in her mind, like Nance's was—or like the others we've extracted, for that matter."

"How do you know that? Others?" Katrina asked. "What *are* you?"

"They're my daughters," Joe said, unable to keep the defensive tone from his voice.

Katrina looked back at Joe, and her eyes widened. "What an interesting byproduct."

Joe felt his blood pressure rise. Katrina's riddles were starting to get under his skin. "What are you talking about?"

<I should tell you alone, first. Then you can decide if and how you disseminate this information.>

<Very well.>

Joe stood and grabbed his sandwich. "Katrina, if you'll follow me."

She rose and nodded politely to the table. "Thank you for your hospitality. I look forward to chatting more with all of you soon."

Katrina walked around the table, and Joe led her out of the mess and down the hall to an empty office. Once inside, he closed the door and deployed privacy measures.

"OK, Katrina, spill it."

Katrina didn't speak for a moment, her eyes boring into his as though she were trying to determine if he was worthy.

"Katrina…"

"The AIs made Tanis." She dropped the words into the space between them like a bomb, and Joe took an involuntary step back.

"I can tell by the expression on your face that it makes some sense to you. Do you remember how Bob kept questioning Tanis's 'luck' as he called it? She told me about it one night, out of frustration."

Joe nodded. "She hated it, said that if her life was lucky, she couldn't imagine what it would be like to be cursed."

"Well, the ascended AIs had a hand in that."

"Fuck, Katrina, just spit it out, already. Don't make me drag every word out of you."

Katrina clenched her jaw, and a look of frustration filled her eyes. "This isn't easy for me, you know. I had to sit on this knowledge for *centuries*. Then I miss you by days at Bollam's World, and Tanis goes off and starts a galactic war!"

"She didn't start it," Joe replied. "But she's going to finish it."

Katrina opened her mouth to reply, then closed it and shook her head. "OK, fine. Here's what I know. Some of it I've been told, some of it, I've guessed at. You ready?"

"Hell yes."

"Back when the Sentience Wars ended, everyone thought the ascended AIs had been destroyed. Some thought they *might* have escaped, but no one had the resources to go hunting for them."

Joe nodded. "Right."

"Don't interrupt, Joe. You want me to tell this, let me tell it."

Joe drew in a deep breath and gestured for her to continue.

"OK, well, sounds like you already know they didn't all die. They also didn't all agree on what to do with humanity. Some of them just buggered off for the galactic core, getting a head start on their post-stellar civilization, or whatever they get up to out there. Others decided that guiding and managing humanity was their calling. Like children caring for aging parents.

"Anyway, most of the Ascended AIs want to keep humanity mostly as it is. Sure, they'll allow some advancement, L2s like Tanis and the like, but they're not keen on humans transcending their mortal coils, so to speak. Stars, most of the ascended AIs aren't even interested in any other *AIs* joining their ranks, let alone humans.

"From what I've managed to gather, there were a lot of ideas tossed around as to how to keep humanity in check, while still allowing them to expand through the stars. I don't know why the AIs want us to expand. They could have stopped us, yet they facilitated a faster expansion by helping us develop dark layer FTL."

Joe wanted to ask more about that, but nodded silently instead.

"And so we have ended up with this mess. The Inner Stars in constant turmoil, the Transcend trying to keep them in check. Then the core AIs send Justina back as Airtha to drive a wedge in the existing divide between Tomlinson and Kirkland—which fractures the Transcend, just when it was close to bringing real peace to the Inner Stars.

"I still don't know if the AIs anticipated jump gates or not. That one may have come as a surprise to even them. It's why they clued Finaeus in on Airtha—I think. He may have figured that one out on his own. From what I can tell, Finaeus is a real pain in the ascended AIs' ass."

"Seems like a general trait for him," Joe said with a laugh, though it faded quickly. "Get on to the part where they made Tanis."

"Easy, now. OK, I don't know if the AIs have a crystal ball, or if they just have a lot of contingencies. Maybe both. Either way, they deliberately sent you through the Streamer to disrupt things before the Transcend and Orion Guard ironed out their differences—or maybe just wiped one another out."

Joe nodded. This aligned with what Tanis had discerned as well, after her discoveries in Silstrand.

"OK, about Tanis. You know that she was one of the first L2 humans to get an AI, right?"

Joe nodded. "Right, her AI, Darla."

"That was all orchestrated by the Caretaker. He wanted her to be on the ship when he sent it forward in time through the Streamer. Only, things didn't work out the way he wanted."

Joe cocked his head. This is what he wanted to know more about.

"Remember what I said about the ascended AIs not wanting new kids on the block? Well, they weren't keen on Bob. Still aren't. They tried to take the *Intrepid* out, but then Tanis got on *that* ship, where she ended up thwarting them at every turn. See, they wanted to make her into a military commander that would kick off the next major dark age when she jumped forward—a role she's diving right into, so far as I can tell."

Joe clenched his jaw, and Katrina saw him do it.

"Look, Joe, it'll make sense. Bear with me."

"OK, I'm bearing."

"Good. The fly in the ointment is Bob—well, Airtha too. They didn't expect her to ascend; at least, I doubt they did. Anyway, about Bob. He started to figure things out. A lot of things. The ascended AIs fed him misinformation a few times, but by and large, he ferreted his way through it all and probably has a pretty good picture about what's going on by now."

Katrina paused, her eyes meeting Joe's. "So Bob altered the AIs' weapon."

"Tanis," Joe said quietly.

"More importantly, Tanis *and* Angela. I know that for most people, Tanis is a curiosity. Sort of a 'why hasn't she gone insane, yet' enigma. Xavia believes that Bob has been subtly altering Tanis to make her more powerful than a non-ascended being would otherwise be. Which is what's so interesting about your daughters. Well, specifically Cary and Faleena. Though the fact that your daughter can do what she can with Saanvi is very curious."

Joe couldn't stop his eyes from narrowing. The way that Katrina spoke of his daughters like they were an experiment bothered him even more than the thought of Bob altering Tanis and Angela.

Katrina carried on, either not noticing, or not caring about Joe's clouded expression. "Anyway, it makes me wonder if Bob intends for Cary and Faleena to be a backup in case something happens to Tanis."

Joe leant back against the room's desk and turned his head, slowing his breathing and willing himself to calm down. Katrina stopped, finally realizing that she'd best be silent for a bit.

After a moment, Joe spoke. "These are some…incredible? incredulous? preposterous? accusations you're throwing around."

"Some of this is supposition. Some is evidenced by what I've seen or been told. Obviously, the core AIs and the Caretaker—which may be more than one entity, I'm not certain—are the enemy, and not exactly sharing their plans with us."

Katrina took a step forward and met Joe's eyes. "But I do know for sure that Xavia is endeavoring to see the Caretaker fail. She does not believe that humanity must be kept in check with war and destruction. However, she does not want Tanis to ignite the stars into an all-out war. She believes there is a way to establish a peace for humanity."

"And what is that?" Joe asked.

"I don't know, not exactly, anyway. It *does* involve Tanis, but Xavia doesn't know Bob's intentions. Bob has been manipulating you and Tanis for years, Joe. He's been manipulating everyone on the *Intrepid,* and now this colony!"

"Why do you think he's been 'manipulating' us?" Joe asked. "Perhaps we know exactly what's going on."

Katrina snorted. "Right, sure. Tell me another one, Joe."

"We do know that Bob doesn't share everything with us. He confessed long ago that he can predict the future with great accuracy, however, he has also admitted there are things he's gotten wrong—probably because the other AIs fed him lies at some point that he thought were true, and it altered his algorithms. Either way, we don't *want* to have some AI telling us the future. Does he alter things by knowing? Of course he does, it would be impossible not to—at least so long as he's with us. But he's remained with us because he wants to help keep us safe. Plain and simple."

"So you trust Bob with your lives?" Katrina asked.

"Absolutely."

Katrina raised an eyebrow. "Even if he's fundamentally altering Tanis?"

"I've known Tanis for a long time," Joe replied. "I know she and Angela are merging, becoming something more. *If* Bob is involved, perhaps he's helping that process go smoothly. I imagine I owe him a debt of thanks. It's probably his alterations that have kept the two of them from going insane."

Katrina took a step forward and stared into Joe's eyes. "What has made you such a believer in Bob's altruism?"

"Centuries of mutual trust. Why do you believe Xavia so much?"

"Because I'd be a despotic empress without her."

Joe nodded slowly. "So you say. But I don't think I can believe you, so long as her remnant resides within you."

He turned to the door as it slid open and nodded solemnly.

"Trine. Take it out of her."

FALL

STELLAR DATE: 08.17.8949 (Adjusted Years)
LOCATION: ISS *Aegeus* approaching Pyra
REGION: Albany System, Thebes, Septhian Alliance

Judine Station turned out to be just another leg in the journey. Before they'd arrived, General Mill's ship departed for Pyra, deeper in the system.

Luckily, Tanis had managed to make contact with the general's ship; they had a meeting set up for shortly after the *Aegeus* arrived at Pyra.

The locals—Thebans, as they were known—were not excited about having a warship of unknown provenance travelling through their system. Only a short year ago, they had been a sovereign alliance, but after being attacked by Nietzschea, they had joined the Septhian Alliance for protection and stability.

The Thebans were still working out how to cooperate with the Septhians. As a Septhian herself, Oris's assurances that the *Aegeus* was an allied ship were falling on deaf ears.

Oris had sent dispatches back to Lisbon to see why the authorizations for the ISF fleet had not reached Albany, but at best, those confirmations were over a month away.

Tanis could reach out to the *I2* over the QuanComm network and get new authorizations, but with the way the Thebans were acting, she doubted they'd trust anything that didn't come through proper channels.

<*Crazy how you can talk to Sera or Joe in real-time, but you can't get an issue like this resolved inside a month,*> Angela commented, apparently in sync with Tanis's thoughts.

<*Well, our goal is to meet with Mill, and now we will. Just a few more hours, and we'll find out who started the discipline program in Genevia. I'm also keenly interested to find out if Garza was involved.*

I can see Orion playing both sides, providing the mech-tech to Genevia, while feeding the Nietzscheans resources>

<*Or it could have been someone else entirely,*> Angela suggested. <*There are over a hundred empires the size of Nietzschea in the Inner Stars. Secret alliances likely abound.*>

Tanis nodded as she stepped off the lift and walked down the corridor to the flight deck where her pinnace waited.

"Afternoon, Admiral," Brandt drawled as Tanis walked into the bay. The commandant was bent over a crate, a tray of food before her while four Marines stood nearby.

Tanis saluted the Marines, and nodded for them to board the pinnace. "Finishing your lunch, Commandant?"

"Yeah, I hate to eat and fly. Not sure why, just feels weird to me, it's a new thing. I think I'm getting senile or something in my old age."

"You realize we're *flying* right now, Brandt."

"Yeah…well, it's different on a cruiser. I'd die if I didn't eat on ships; I almost never set foot on dirt anymore."

Tanis snorted a laugh. "Well, there'll be food on the station too, so don't gorge too much."

Brandt finished her sandwich. "All set. Let's get this show on the road."

They boarded the pinnace and took seats in the forward cabin.

<*Take us out, Lieutenant Mick,*> Tanis instructed the pilot.

<*Aye, ma'am, I have clearance from Aegeus flight control. Bay doors are opening now.*>

<*Very good, Lieutenant,*> Tanis replied.

<*Good luck out there, Admiral, Commandant,*> Captain Sheeran said as the pinnace rose off the deck. <*Call if you need anything—change of clothes, a new pillow, platoon of Marines.*>

<*Don't worry,*> Tanis replied. <*It's not like we're going to see a repeat of Scipio. I'm not even going downworld.*>

The captain made a choking sound. <*Please, ma'am, don't say things like that.*>

Tanis could hear Angela attempting to perfect her groan and decided to ignore the AI. <*Sorry, Sheeran, though after what you pulled off at Scipio, I don't feel like I have to worry.*>

<*Stars, Admiral, I think I had kittens at Scipio. Seriously, be careful. Don't run off and attack the enemy on your own. Remember, lots and lots of Marines up here.*>

<*And they haven't gotten to shoot at live targets in a while,*> Brandt added. <*Makes 'em all twitchy.*>

<*That's part of what I'm worried about,*> Sheeran replied.

Tanis laughed, and Angela replied on her behalf. <*Don't worry, Captain. I'll make sure we don't go flying any aerojets or anything.*>

<*Somehow I only feel marginally reassured,*> Captain Sheeran replied. <*Good luck, though, Admiral.*>

<*Thanks, Captain,*> Tanis replied. <*We'll keep you advised as we proceed.*>

<*Understood.*>

The pinnace drifted out of the bay and cleared the *Aegeus* before boosting toward the station. Tanis watched idly as the pinnace filtered into the traffic around the planet, closing on Appalachia Station, where they'd meet General Mill.

Brandt whistled as she looked out of a window. "Stars, this place got *pummeled*."

"Which, the station, or the planet?"

"Both. Though I was talking about the planet. There's a big stretch of seacoast that's just black. I guess that's where their capital used to be. Most of their leadership got taken out when the Niets hit. Explains why they joined up with Septhia after that."

"The Niets?" Tanis asked.

"Yeah, the Nietzscheans, Niets.... Haven't you noticed that's what the locals all call them?" Brandt asked.

"No," Tanis shook her head. "I guess I've not been in touch with the folks."

"Too much time as special-famous-visiting-dignitary-Tanis." Brandt shook her head and squinted at Tanis as though evaluating the name's fit. "I wonder if we can make an acronym for that."

Tanis couldn't help but laugh at Brandt. The woman was imperturbable about pretty much everything.

<Need something that has more vowels for that to work,> Angela said, her tone both pensive and sardonic. *<How about, Famous-Aristocratic-Dignitary-Elite-Tanis. FADET.>*

"Dunno," Brandt mused, a hand tucked behind her neck, fingering her short locks as she thought. "Doesn't have the right ring to it. However…Dignitary-Aristocratic-Famous-Tanis is perfect."

<DAFT?> Angela barked a laugh. *<I love it!>*

"Stars, what did I do to deserve you two?"

"Not sure, must have been pretty awesome. You're lucky to have us." Brandt reached out and punched Tanis in the arm. "Ow! Damn. I forgot you hadn't gotten a real left arm yet."

Tanis held up her left hand and changed it from flesh tone to silver, then back. "It's just so damn handy…"

<Stars, I wish I was an organic so I could groan properly. I feel like I've said that a lot lately.>

"I got your back," Brandt said, and let out an exaggerated groan. "That do?"

<Yes, you've expressed my sentiment accurately.>

Tanis slid her lightwand out of her left arm and activated the monofilament dicarbyne blade, watching as it shot out of the hilt before the electron flow activated.

"That seems longer than it used to be," Brandt commented. "Are you compensating?"

"Funny. I was just demonstrating the benefits of a non-standard limb."

<I'm pretty sure you're not supposed to fiddle with electron-swords on the pinnace,> Angela cautioned. *<It probably wreaks havoc with the instruments.>*

Tanis sighed and switched off the light-wand and slid it back into her arm, straightening her jacket. "Here I am, trying to lighten up, and I get chastised. There's no winning with you."

"Lighten up. I see what you did there. It's not like every Marine doesn't have one of those, Tanis." Brandt shrugged and pulled hers out of her boot. "I just don't need to tuck it into my body. Anyone who tries to get this thing away from me can pry it from my cold, dead hands."

"Where do you think I got my first one?" Tanis asked. "They weren't standard issue in my branch. The CO of the 242nd Marines gave me this one as a gift."

"Ender?" Brandt asked. "He was a good guy, I served under him way back, you know."

Tanis snorted. "Of course I know. Who do you think recommended you to me before we left Sol?"

"Shit, Tanis, two centuries and there's still new stuff to learn."

<On final approach,> Mick called back. *<We're in Bay 13A. Station maps show that as only a klick from your meeting with the general.>*

Tanis pulled up the map and saw that the meeting with General Mill was not to be on his berthed ship, but rather in local recruitment office run by the Marauders. "Wonder if he doesn't trust us, or if it's just where he is right now."

"We'll find out soon enough," Brandt replied as she rose from her seat.

Outside the windows, they could see the dull grey bulkheads of the station surround the pinnace, and Tanis rose as they settled into their cradle.

<Welcome to Appalachia Station, Admiral, Commandant.>

<Thanks for the smooth ride, Lieutenant,> Tanis replied.

<You call, Vac-Cav answers.>

Brandt shook her head. " 'Vac-Cav'. These guys are always so clever."

The four Marines were already down the ramp, eyeing everyone in the bay—which held a dozen other passenger ships—with suspicion.

As she stepped onto the deck, Tanis spotted a woman weaving her way through the crowd with two soldiers at her back.

"Marauder insignia," Brandt commented. "Looks like a captain."

The woman approached and offered her hand. "Admiral Richards, I'm Captain Ayer with the Marauders."

Tanis clasped the captain's hand. "Very nice to meet you, Captain Ayer. This is Commandant Brandt."

Brandt shook Ayer's hand. "Also known as her personal security guard. The admiral gets in a lot of trouble."

"Uh, yes, of course," Ayer nodded. "Normally you wouldn't be allowed on station carrying arms, but with a Marauder escort, I can bring you and two of your soldiers to the general without the need to leave your weapons behind."

Tanis nodded, and Brandt signaled two of the Marines, corporals Johnny and Anne, to join them.

<Not sure about these Marauders. Can't tell a Marine from a soldier,> Brandt muttered over the Link.

<I hate to burst your bubble,> Angela interjected. *<But 'marine' means 'soldier of the sea'. In the original Latin, the word for sea is 'mare'. You don't sail many seas, so I suspect that 'marine' is actually less accurate than 'soldier'.>*

<Angela?> Brandt asked.

<Yeah?>

<If you had a physical body, I'd fight you right now.>

<You'd lose.>

Brandt barked a laugh, and Tanis tried to ignore their banter as she spoke with Captain Ayer.

"Folks seem a bit on edge here in the Albany System."

Ayer nodded as they wove through the dockworkers. "A bit. Having your worlds almost get crushed by a Nietzschean invasion will do that. Not to mention that they'd been trying to avoid absorption by Septhia for decades."

"I heard about that," Tanis replied. "I understand from what I saw on the feeds that your Marauders aren't looked at too fondly for how things went last year, either."

Ayer nodded slowly. "There's some tension. Less here at Pyra. They saw us pull out all the stops to drive the Niets back."

Despite Ayer's words, Tanis could tell that more than a few locals were casting the Marauders—and Tanis's party—unkind looks.

They walked in silence for a few minutes, passing onto a broad concourse that led through the station. Ayer passed by a maglev platform without boarding, and Tanis guessed it was because the locals wouldn't want to stand cheek by jowl with a bunch of soldiers.

Eventually, Ayer spoke up. "I have to admit, Admiral Richards, I'm curious what brings you here. It's hard to believe that you're *the* Tanis Richards, but the nets are ablaze with speculation about your ship. It bears a striking resemblance to ones seen at Bollam's World twenty years ago."

"I'm looking for someone," Tanis replied without addressing all Ayer's questions. "Someone that was operating in Genevia at the beginning of the war with Nietzschea. There aren't a lot of people still around from back then, and I don't have time to perform a vast search across the stars. General Mill was around then and may know about my quarry."

Captain Ayer frowned. "That's not why I thought you'd be here at all. There's scuttlebutt that you've come to help us with our fight against the Niets."

"I've come to help the Septhians help themselves. Though I suppose that will extend to the Thebans and your organization."

Tanis watched Ayer's lip twitch, as though she were considering what to say and stopping herself. Finally, she spoke.

"Well, maybe you'll reconsider after you talk to the general."

The rest of the walk was made in silence. Five minutes later, they arrived at an establishment, tucked between a bar and a clothing store, with the Marauder logo above its entrance.

Once inside, Captain Ayer led them past several desks where men and women were talking to candidates, before passing into a short hall.

Off to one side was a break room with a few tables and a chiller plastered with plasnotes. On the other was an open door that lead into a conference room.

Brandt nodded to the two marines to wait in the hall as Captain Ayer led them into the room.

At the end of the table—which was half covered in plaswork and holos of nearby star systems—sat a tall man with broad shoulders and greying hair.

"General Mill, Admiral Tanis Richards, and Commandant Brandt of the ISF," Ayer said before walking around to the far side of the table, where she stood waiting for the handshakes to be completed.

"Please, have a seat," General Mill gestured to the chairs around the table once the greetings were over with. "Pardon the mess. I just got out of a meeting with a local security agency that would like to join up with the Marauders. We were evaluating deployment options."

Tanis sat and nodded to the star systems hovering around the table. "The Septhians give you a lot of leeway in their alliance."

General Mill nodded. "That they do. We've been instrumental in bolstering them against the Niets. Without the Marauders, you'd be sitting in Nietzschea right now."

"So I've heard."

General Mill folded his hands on the table. "Let me cut to the chase, Admiral Richards—or perhaps, allow you to. Captain Ayer informed me that you are not here to help us in any way, but instead you are hunting someone who was a part of the creation of the mech program in Genevia."

"That is correct," Tanis replied. "Specifically, responsible for the system I understand was referred to as 'Discipline'."

"And why should I take time out of my day to chat with you about Genevia's past sins?"

Tanis drew in a long breath, eyeing the general. Yet another man in Septhia who seemed more antagonistic than was warranted. Perhaps it was some symptom of what they'd been through, fighting the Niets for so many years.

"Well, there's the cruisers I gifted to the SAF. I imagine they'll be mutually beneficial. It's caused the Septhian High Command to become quite grateful to me."

"It may help, it may not," General Mill shrugged. "I've survived this long by looking out for my people first and foremost. I'll gladly accept help, but I'm not going to bank on it."

"I studied some of the accounts of the Genevian war with Nietzschea," Tanis replied, nodding slowly. "I can see why you feel that way. Your leadership made some rather unfortunate blunders. I'm somewhat surprised you lost the war, to be honest."

"Well, hindsight, and all that," General Mill muttered. "I'm sure you think you would have done better."

Tanis shrugged. "I wouldn't have fled the Parsons System, that's for sure. That was a critical system for Genevia. Yet they held onto others that had almost no strategic value, shifting resources from Parsons to those."

General Mill coughed and shook his head. "You've a keen eye, Admiral Richards. I share your sentiment, if it helps. Perhaps I'm just so…jaded about the whole thing that I can't fathom what a path to victory would have looked like."

"Let's not dwell on that, then," Tanis suggested. "What I want to know is who came up with the idea to make mechs from convicts, and how Genevia got their discipline tech. May I access the table's holo?"

"By all means," General Mill gestured and swept away his holos.

Tanis put up two images. The first was of General Garza of the Orion Guard, and the second was of the Caretaker, as Nance remembered seeing her.

"What is *that*?" Captain Ayer asked.

"You didn't study the briefing packet I sent ahead?" Tanis asked.

The general and captain shook their heads. "We didn't receive it. Undersecretary Oris didn't have any specifics in her original missive."

"For fucks sakes." Brandt smacked her palm against her forehead. "This explanation takes *forever*."

Tanis nodded in agreement. "OK, I'm going to give you the quick version and provide the details for you to study later. First off, there's a big bad empire known as the Orion Freedom Alliance. They operate out of a system called New Sol, about a thousand light years or so past the Orion Nebula. The man you see, General Garza, is from there. He's been flitting about in the Inner Stars for the last…well…I have no idea how long, making a general mess of things."

"Pardon? The Inner Stars?" General Mill asked.

Tanis added a display of the Orion Arm of the galaxy. "Everything along the arm for about three thousand light years from Sol are the Inner Stars. They represent about a tenth of human space."

"Well, shit," Ayer muttered. "That's an eye opener."

"It gets better," Brandt chuckled.

"Right." Tanis nodded, carrying on as quickly as she could. "So, Garza wants to make a mess. He's backing the Trisilieds, and the Hegemony—and *maybe* the Niets. I've allied with a group called the Transcend, and we're backing Scipio and a few others on the far side of Sol.

"Garza is doing his damnedest to seed dissent and ruin shit everywhere so that when everyone is worn out, the Orion Guard can just sweep in and take over. He may or may not also be working against his own leadership. Jury is still out on that."

"OK, and the glowing thing?" Mill asked.

"That's the Caretaker. It's an ascended AI—possibly from as far back as the Sentience Wars in Sol. It's been responsible for half of the major wars in the last five thousand years, maybe more. Its goal is to get the Transcend and Orion Guard to fight on the battlefield of the Inner Stars and trash the place."

Captain Ayer had paled considerably. "Why in the stars does it want to do that?"

Brandt snorted. "Because it and the other ascended AIs are butt-hurt that the unification group kicked their asses back in Sol."

Tanis laughed. "You have a way with words, Brandt. These AIs also seem to think that they should keep humans in some sort of median state for eternity or something. Honestly, their motives are just supposition at present. That's why I'm trying to track the Caretaker down."

"And you think this…glowing AI person was responsible for what happened in Genevia?"

Tanis shrugged. "The mind control tech that was used in Genevia bears a striking resemblance to what we've seen elsewhere, and that was connected to the Caretaker. Or one of his ilk, at least."

"Well, I'll tell you one thing for sure," General Mill said with a soft laugh as he gestured at the image of the Caretaker. "If I saw anything like that, I think I'd remember. I can't imagine it staying hushed if anyone else had, either."

"Understandable." Tanis removed the image of the Caretaker. "And General Garza? He doesn't stand out as much, but he's been active in the Hegemony, Trisilieds, Scipio, and Silstrand."

"He gets around." Mill sat back and stroked his jaw. "That's a lot of travel for one man."

"Jump gates and clones," Brandt replied.

"Jump what?" General Mill asked, at the same time Ayer shook her head and said, "I hate clones."

"Jump gates allow for near-instantaneous travel on a galactic scale," Tanis replied. "They're on the downlow right now."

General Mill shook his head as he stared at Garza. "Well, I don't remember him, but that doesn't mean he wasn't around. I do, however, recall a consultant that was present at the beginning of the mech program. She was a strange old lady."

"Lady?" Tanis asked. "Do you have any records?"

Mill frowned and nodded. "Think so, checking. Aha! Here we are. She was at the first demonstrations."

An image of a woman appeared above the table, floating serenely next to Garza's.

"Fuck," Brandt whispered. "That's…"

"Katrina," Tanis said, swallowing a lump that had formed in her throat before turning to General Mill. "What are you playing at, General?"

Mill looked genuinely surprised at the vehemence in Tanis's voice. "I'm not playing at anything. She was there. I heard talk that it was her tech that was instrumental in making the Discipline system work without causing irreparable damage to the mechs."

"Are you certain? Really certain? That's Katrina, governor of the Victoria colony at Kapteyn's Star. From five thousand years ago."

Captain Ayer whistled. "She looks good for five-thousand. I mean, not great, but—"

Mill shot Ayer a stern look, and the captain pursed her lips and shook her head.

"Sorry, all this has me a bit out of sorts. Is it classified?"

"No," Tanis sighed as she stared at Katrina's face. "Truth is one of our best allies at this point."

"That's an encouraging—and unorthodox—viewpoint," Mill said.

Tanis opened her mouth to reply when Captain Sheeran called in from the *Aegeus*. *<Admiral! A fleet has jumped into the system! They're only five light minutes away! Get back to the—>*

The Link connection to the ship went dead and an audible alarm began to sound.

"We're under attack!" General Mill shouted as he rose from the table.

"Two cruisers," Ayer said as she leapt over the table. "Firing on the station!"

Brandt was already at the door, where Corporal Johnny stood staring down the hall. He glanced into the room.

"I assume we're leaving, ma'ams?" he asked.

Tanis nodded, and Brandt shook her head. "Bright lad."

They moved out into the hall, and Tanis wished she had access to tactical feeds from station scan. A moment later, she had them filling her mind.

<*Not asking permission from these people,*> Angela said without apology.

<*Not judging,*> Tanis replied as she took in the feeds.

Just as Captain Ayer had said, two cruisers were attacking Appalachia Station, while another three were firing on other nearby ships.

"Those are SAF vessels," Tanis said as they moved down the hall to the concourse outside the Marauder recruitment center.

"Former Theban," Mill replied as he drew a sidearm and looked out into the concourse where people were running past.

One of the ISF Marines passed a pulse pistol to Tanis, and she checked its charge before peering past the general.

"Fuckers are firing at their own damn station," General Mill swore. "Admiral, you won't make it back to your pinnace in time. Tell it to get back to your cruiser. I have a shuttle in a bay close by."

Tanis nodded to Brandt. "Tell Mick to get his ass back to the *Aegeus*."

"Already on it. Let's not wait around on my account. Where's your shuttle, General?"

Mill passed them a location on the map and directed his soldiers out onto the concourse. Captain Ayer gestured for three of the office workers who were still present to join them.

"You want to live? Come with us."

"But my family!" a man called out.

"Tell them to get to an evac ship or escape pod. This station isn't going to last," Mill hollered as he gestured for everyone to get out of the offices.

As if to emphasize his statement, the deck beneath their feet shuddered, and a load groan echoed down the concourse.

<*Air pressure just dropped,*> Angela announced. <*Station's getting holed!*>

"Go! Go!" Mill yelled, and the group took off, pushing through the crowds that were running the opposite direction until they came to a side passage. The Marauder soldiers stayed in the lead, and the ISF Marines brought up the rear as they raced down the narrow corridor.

Tanis considered sending out nano, but with the station's atmosphere starting to whip past them, she knew there was no way the probes could provide any meaningful information.

<*What is it about us and stations getting shot up while you're aboard?*> Brandt asked.

<*I'm a trouble magnet, haven't you noticed?*> Tanis replied as they rounded a corner and came into a wider concourse once more.

Ahead, the Marauder soldiers stopped at a wide staircase leading down through the decks and waited for the group to catch up. Mill nodded to the pair, and they rushed down the stairs, checked the broad landing, and proceeded to the next level.

They passed through a dozen decks that way, once again finding themselves amongst thickening crowds. One of the Marauder recruiters rushed off at one point, and Mill swore about idiots getting themselves killed. He seemed to consider going after the man for a moment, but then thought better of it.

As the group progressed, the station began to shake more and more around them. At one point the a-grav cut out entirely, and a young man ahead got pushed over the edge of a staircase, only to fall three decks when the gravity came back on.

Tanis swore and checked the map. Just one more deck to go, and they'd be at the private dock where Mill's shuttle waited. A minute later, they reached the desired level, and the Marauder soldiers turned down another side passage.

Mill was about to follow, when weapons fire streaked down the passage; a rail shot that tore clear through one of the lightly armored Marauders and a recruiter behind him, spraying blood and bone across the bulkheads.

The other soldier fell back and took cover around the corner, returning fire.

"The fuck!" Mill shouted. "The alternative route will cost us five minutes."

The air was relatively still. Either there were no holes down here, or a-grav shields had finally been deployed to hold in atmosphere. Tanis decided to send out a few probes to scout down the passageway. At the end, she saw a pair of women with railguns laughing as they fired at passersby in the far corridor.

"Hold this." She tossed her gun to Brandt, and quickly stripped off her clothing.

"Uh…what?" Mill asked as Tanis revealed the matte black flow armor she wore beneath her uniform.

"Getting to be another habit," Brandt shook her head. "We have Johnny and Anne here for that."

"Their armor takes longer to get off," Tanis said as the flow armor crept up over her face. "See you in a minute."

She activated the stealth system and leapt up onto the exposed conduit run at the top of the passageway. There wasn't enough room for Tanis to rise to her hands and knees, but with all the noise and chaos, she wasn't worried about making sound as she scampered along the pipes.

It was only thirty meters to the end of the corridor, and when she arrived, the two women were still laughing hysterically as they fired their railguns at everyone in sight.

Tanis drew the two blades out of her forearms and slid off the conduits, holding both blades vertically as she dropped.

One blade struck true, sliding between the collarbone and neck of the woman on the right. Tanis's other target had moved at the last moment to shoot at a small child that ran by.

Tanis kicked at the shooter's knee before she could fire, and twisted the blade inside the other woman.

The rail shot went wide, and the child made it safely past. Tanis wasted no time pulling the blade out of the first woman and slicing the head off the other.

<*We're clear,*> she sent back.

Johnny and Anne were the first ones down the narrow passage, moving to cover Tanis as the others approached.

Brandt tossed Tanis's gun back to her. "You forgot this."

"What about my clothes?"

"I'm not your maid." Brandt grinned as the group began to move down the next corridor.

"Just ahead," Mill called back. "Nice moves, by the way, Admiral."

"Tanis," she replied while sidestepping a man who was trying to gather up all the donuts he could from a toppled cart.

"Station's going to go down," Ayer shouted at him as they ran past. "Idiot."

<*A thousand Niet ships have jumped in,*> Angela advised, more than a little concern in her voice. <*They've closed to within a hundred thousand klicks.*>

"Mill, when we get aboard your shuttle, we have to get to our ship. Your shields can't handle that firepower!" Tanis called out over the din surrounding them. Mill nodded, but she couldn't tell if it was to her, or the remaining Marauder soldier as they turned into a docking bay.

Inside lay four ships, all mobbed with people. A ship on the right bore the Marauder crest, and Mill shouldered the crowds aside as he moved toward the shuttle. The craft's door was still closed, and Tanis could see a woman waving through the cockpit window as they approached.

The two ISF Marines fired low intensity pulse shots into the mob to disperse them, but the shots barely made a dent. They upped the power, and the crowds started to fall back. Ten seconds later, the group reached the shuttle's door, and the Marines and remaining Marauder soldier took up positions as the door slid open.

Ayer stepped in first, followed by the remaining recruiter from the office. The Marauder captain turned and gestured for Tanis and Brandt to follow as the crowds surged in close. General Mill stepped up next and turned to cover the troops.

"Get in! Fast!" the pilot yelled, then screamed as weapons fire tore through the crowds from across the bay, cutting the civilians down in droves. The Marines piled in, hauling the Marauder after them, and Brandt pulled the door shut.

"Go! Go! Go!" Brandt shouted, and the pilot wasted no time lifting off the cradle and boosting out of the station.

Tanis clenched her teeth, filled with sorrow and rage as she watched a group of soldiers wearing SAF uniforms work their way across the bay, killing everyone in their path. Stray shots pinged off the shuttle's hull, but no warnings sounded, and Tanis pulled her gaze from the window to see Captain Ayer standing over General Mill, tears streaming down her face.

The old soldier lay on the shuttle's deck, a small hole in his forehead. From Tanis's position, it looked like that was the extent of the wound.

The brains and blood sprayed across the bulkhead next to Ayer told a different story.

Tanis turned away and moved into the cockpit, where the ashen pilot sat, threading the dozens of ships and pods pouring out of Appalachia Station.

"Get to my ship," Tanis directed, but the pilot shook her head.

"I have to get back to the *Foehammer*!"

"The *Foehammer*'s shields can't hold up against a thousand Nietzschean cruisers!" Tanis shouted at the woman. "Get to the *Aegeus*!"

The woman shook her head, and Tanis slid into the seat beside her. She touched the console and deposited a passel of nano.

<*On it,*> Angela said, and the console in front of the pilot shut down.

"What the hell?" the woman yelled, looking over to see Tanis initialize holo controls and direct the ship around the station toward the *Aegeus*.

The pilot reached for Tanis, but a fist shot out from Tanis's periphery, hitting the pilot in the head.

"Thanks, Brandt," Tanis grunted.

"Any time."

There was a scuffle in the back, and Tanis heard Brandt say, "Easy, now," and then a pulse pistol fired.

She assumed all was well and poured on as much speed as the shuttle had, arcing around the station to see the *Aegeus*, engines glowing brightly and stasis shields flaring as fire rained down on it from the five Theban cruisers.

The *Aegeus* returned fire on one of the ships, its atom beams cutting through the enemy vessel, tearing it apart.

Tanis felt a grim smile form on her lips as she continued her approach. Then her board lit up with a message from one of the Theban cruisers, and Tanis toggled it.

"Surrender, Admiral Richards."

"Shit, that's Oris," Brandt said from behind Tanis.

<*That little bitch!*> Angela swore. <*I have a tightbeam to the* Aegeus.>

Tanis was about to reply, when enemy fire stopped splashing against the *Aegeus*'s shields and instead began to cut through the ISF cruiser.

<Admiral!> Captain Sheeran's voice came across the tightbeam. *<We've got…we've been sabotaged! There's something in the system! I've lost contact with Humu!>*

Tanis caught sight of dozens of missiles streaking out from the Theban cruisers toward the *Aegeus.*

<Get out of here!> Sheeran cried out a moment before the *Aegeus* disappeared in a nuclear fireball.

The shockwave tore through the vacuum of space, colliding with Appalachia Station and buckling its torrid ring. Tanis dove the shuttle below molten debris as the pieces of the *Aegeus* streaked through space all around them. Above them, the looming form of the station began to fracture, breaking apart piece-by-piece.

"Strap in!" Tanis called back as she dove under the disintegrating station, joining in with the swarm of ships and escape pods heading for the planet below. Then something struck the ship, and one of the engines failed.

<Strap in yourself, Tanis. I'll bring us in,> Angela yelled as the shuttle began to vibrate violently around them.

NOT THE WARM WELCOME…

STELLAR DATE: 08.17.8949 (Adjusted Years)
LOCATION: ISS *Andromeda*
REGION: Edge of the New Canaan system

Katrina turned and saw Cary standing in the room's entrance with her sister, Saanvi, behind her. Both women wore sober expressions, and Cary stretched out her hand.

"What are you doing?" Katrina asked, backing away. "Joe? What is this?"

"I want to hear your impressions when it's just you in there," Joe replied. "We've had no end of misery from ascended AIs lurking in our populace. Our trust comes with a cost. This is it."

Katrina opened her mouth to speak, but her breath caught as silver filaments streaked out of Cary's hands and into her body.

Her own internal nano defenses seemed unable to stop them, and Katrina felt something change. It was indescribable, and she couldn't discern if the feeling was good or bad.

Then a white light began to form between Cary's hands, and, a moment later, she held a glowing orb.

"It's done." Cary said in her strange voice. "I'll take it to the lab."

"Wait!" Katrina called out, reaching for Cary. She was stopped short by Joe grabbing her wrist.

"How do you feel, Katrina?"

"Like you becoming an admiral has turned you into a raging asshole!" Katrina shot back. "You had no right—"

"This isn't about rights." Joe cut her off. "We're in a fight for our survival. One interpretation of what has occurred today is that you secreted an enemy onto our base. I'll give you the benefit of the doubt that it was unintentional, but I'm disinclined to trust ascended AIs at present. From what you've said, they seem to be responsible for just about everything that's gone wrong since humanity reached the stars."

Katrina felt drained—whatever Cary had done to remove Xavia's memory had left her barely able to stand. "Don't hurt her. Please. She's a gift from Xavia."

"We won't, so long as you don't tell us to."

"What?" Katrina's knew Joe's words should make sense, but they just didn't line up. "Why would *I* tell you to hurt Xavia's memory?"

"Well, if you were under duress, you may change your mind about your feelings toward her."

"Joe!" Katrina wanted to bang his head into the wall and see if she could knock some sense into him. "What's it going to take to convince you that she wasn't manipulating me?"

Joe sighed. "I don't know, yet. Come, let's go to the lab and see what Xavia's memory has to say for herself."

"What? Just like that, we're all friendly again? You just tore a part of me out of myself."

Joe took a step toward Katrina a finger in her face. "No, I took a foreign entity who has the ability to control all of your words and deeds out of your body. How can I trust you with that thing in there? For all I know, you're so conditioned at this point that you have no idea who you even are anymore."

"Joe..." Katrina began to speak, but he turned and walked away. She followed him out of the room to see a squad of ISF Marines waiting.

Somehow that felt worse than anything else. Like Joe had betrayed her. Some of these Marines could be friends, or even family, and now they saw her being treated like a criminal by one of their leaders.

<Your own daughter said Xavia's memory wasn't entangled in my mind,> Katrina said to Joe as the Marines fell in around them.

<*At that moment,*> Joe replied. <*I'm not going to debate this with you, Katrina. Maybe if you had announced that Xavia's 'memory'—as you put it—was in you from the outset, things would have been different. But she didn't know we could see her, and she thought to hide from us.*>

<*Why does she have to declare herself? What did she do wrong?*>

Joe glanced over his shoulder. <*Declaring people crossing into a nation is not an unfamiliar concept. Smuggling people across borders is usually frowned upon.*>

Katrina didn't reply; her teeth were clenched so hard she thought they might break. To have struggled so long to stay alive, only to be treated as a criminal upon her arrival.... Part of her wished she'd never come back. To think of all she had sacrificed to get this information to New Canaan, only to have it end up a catastrophe.

But Xavia had told me that I must.

A sliver of doubt crept into Katrina's mind, accompanied by an unwelcome memory of how she had controlled people like puppets back in the Midditerra System. A mind-control technology that had eventually worked its way across the stars to destroy countless lives in a dozen conflicts.

Could I have been under her spell?

Katrina shook her head, knowing that her own doubt was evidence that she was not under Xavia's sway.

<*Troy.*> She wanted to reach the AI and advise him on the situation.

<*Troy is not available to speak with you right now,*> Corsia responded instead of her old friend.

<*Corsia? Why not?*>

<*Troy and I are chatting right now. Your crew and ship are under quarantine while we scan everything.*>

<*Scan it for what?*> Katrina asked.

<*More remnants of ascended AIs.*>

Katrina almost missed a step. <*You can do that? How?*>

<Sorry, Katrina,> Corsia's mental tone carried what felt like genuine compassion. *<I can't tell you that.>*

A feeling of sadness welled up in Katrina. This was not at all how she had envisioned her reunion going. It was supposed to be joyous. In her imaginings, Tanis had thanked her for revealing that Bob had ulterior motives…they had taken steps to avert the war that was brewing.

Now Joe was ruining everything with his rampant paranoia.

Katrina didn't speak further to Joe or Corsia as they walked through the base's corridors. After five minutes, they reached the doors to Earnest's lab, also under guard by ISF Marines.

The guards opened the door, and Joe led her into the room.

It was a cavernous space—as Katrina had expected—much of it shrouded in darkness. To her right was an illuminated area, where Earnest stood beside Cary and Saanvi, along with another man and woman.

At the edge of the space, a dozen tall columns stood, each containing a white orb wrapped in silver bands. Katrina was shocked to see so many captured remnants.

How do they do that?

Then Cary moved, and Katrina saw another orb on the table in the center of the space. "Is that her? Is she OK?" Katrina asked as she rushed past Joe.

"Yes, yes, Katrina," Earnest said without taking his eyes off Xavia's memory. "Safe and sound. So far as we can tell, being trapped in the brane doesn't do these Scubs any harm."

" 'Scubs'?" Katrina asked, and the woman next to Earnest nodded.

"We were calling them 'Self-Contained Sentient Sub-Entity Shards' but that was a mouthful, and SCSSES sounds too much like 'skuzzes', so we ended up with 'Scubs'," the woman explained.

"Uh…thanks for the etymology lesson," Katrina muttered.

"She says she's sorry," Cary said, still speaking in the strangely ethereal voice. "She knew we wouldn't trust her, but she didn't know we could see her. She's not happy that the Caretaker's Scubs are here."

"Is there any more we can learn from them?" Joe asked.

Cary and Saanvi both shook their heads, and Saanvi replied, speaking in the same unnatural voice as Cary. "Doubtful. Most of what they say are lies and misinformation, anyway."

"Then perhaps we should terminate them," Joe replied. "So far as we know, Scubs aren't actually sentient beings."

Earnest held up a hand and wobbled it back and forth. "Eeehhh, that's debatable. They're smarter than the average human, and there is much to learn about their abilities."

"Regarding the intelligence, you could say the same about an NSAI," Joe replied. "The question at hand is whether or not Scubs are sentient."

"They might be," Cary said. "If they are, do we need a trial before we execute it?"

Joe ran a hand through his hair. "Yeah, we would. Not that it would escape conviction. Murder and attempted murder are hard raps to beat."

"I can wall them off," Cary said, and suddenly the orbs in the pillars were completely occluded by black spheres. "Hmm…that has made Xavia happy."

"What do you mean?" Katrina asked. "Why is she happy?"

"This will become tedious very quickly," Saanvi said. "I will speak for Xavia's remnant. It is more than a memory, Katrina. This is a being, not a recording. If it has led you to believe that, then it has been lying to you."

Katrina chewed on her lip. Xavia's memory had never claimed to be anything in particular, it just helped out from time to time. But Katrina had also never considered it to be a sentient being—if it was at all. There did not appear to be a consensus as yet.

"Ask her…ask her if she lied to me," Katrina said to Cary.

"I do not need to relay it, she has enough of a foothold in this portion of space-time to detect the vibrations you make in the air," Cary replied.

"I have never lied to you, Katrina. That is not my way," Saanvi said, channeling Xavia's words.

"Then what is your way?" Joe asked.

"I seek to foster peace between humans and AIs," Saanvi said.

Joe glanced at Katrina, and then turned back to the orb. "How do you plan to foster this peace? Through conformity of thought? Removal of all potential harm?"

"I said foster," came the reply. "It is not possible to force peace."

"Well, that much we agree on," Earnest muttered.

"What was your purpose in coming here?" Joe asked.

Saanvi did not speak for a few seconds, and Joe cocked his head in question.

"She's not saying anything." Saanvi shrugged.

Katrina took a step forward. "Xavia?"

"I wanted to get you here to keep you safe, Katrina. And I needed you to share with Joe the information about Bob, Tanis, and Angela. Together, we must all stop them from starting a war that will consume everything."

"She's already working on that," Joe replied. "Her goal is to take the head off the snake as quickly as possible."

"How will she do that?" Katrina asked.

"By making the strongest alliance. Tanis plans to establish an accord between humans and AIs, the Transcend, Inner Stars, Orion. Us all." Cary replied.

Katrina snorted. "And how long will that hold for? A century? A millennium? She'll have to enforce it."

"It'll be a lot easier after the core AIs are dead." Joe crossed his arms and stared at Xavia's sphere. "How does that strike you, Scub? If we kill the Caretaker, and all your kind."

"She laughed," Saanvi said, then smiled. "If that is your goal, then I shall freely assist you."

CRASHED

STELLAR DATE: 08.17.8949 (Adjusted Years)
LOCATION: Jersey City, Pyra
REGION: Albany System, Thebes, Septhian Alliance

Tanis pushed the impact foam away and leant over to check the Marauder pilot.

She was dead, a spar was driven through her torso, sticking through her chair and into the rear cabin.

"Brandt!" Tanis called out as she pulled herself out of the cockpit. "You'd better be alive, you old battle-ax."

"Gonna outlive you, crazy woman." A muffled voice came from the back.

"Ma'am," Johnny reached into the cockpit and grabbed Tanis's arm. As he helped her up, Tanis caught sight of Anne's broken body and clenched her teeth.

Well, now the Niets have made it personal.

She blinked at the thought, wondering whether it came from her or Angela.

Ahead, Brandt was helping Ayer out of her seat. Tanis stopped to kneel beside Anne.

"Your parents would be proud of you," she whispered, knowing that there was no family left to tell of Anne's sacrifice. Everyone close to the Marine had died in the attack on Carthage last year.

She triggered the Marine's tech scrub, then rose and grabbed the woman's weapon before following Johnny to the door. He slid it partway open before it jammed.

With a cry of rage, the Marine kicked it open the rest of the way and peered out into the darkness outside.

It took Tanis's eyes a moment to adjust before she could make out a darkened city street. She'd tried to avoid any buildings when they came down. From the gouge in the street behind the shuttle, it looked as though that much had been a success.

Johnny exited the shuttle, followed by Brandt. Tanis looked back at Ayer, who was shaking the Marauder soldier. "Don't you die on me, Ben. We've got a lot of terrain to cover, and my leg's fucked up. I need your stupid ass as a crutch."

Tanis could see that Ben was already dead; his chest was still, and there was blood running down his side.

"He's gone, Ayer," Tanis said, reaching for the captain. "Look, he got shot back on the station."

"Get the fuck off me!" Ayer screamed at Tanis. "Look what you did! You got the General killed. It's all over."

Tanis grabbed Captain Ayer's shoulder and spun her away from the dead Marauders. "You want to stay here and mourn your people, I understand that. Stay. But do it *quietly*."

Ayer just blinked at Tanis and then turned back to looking at the general.

"We gotta move," Brandt said, leaning into the shuttle. "Dropships are raining down like…rain. We need to find some sort of local garrison. Hold out 'til the *Derringer* gets here."

Tanis rolled her eyes as she stepped out and looked up at the sky. Above them, hundreds of red streaks glowed against the darkness; beyond hung the glowing smudge of what remained of Appalachia Station.

And the *Aegeus.*

<*Did you get any sort of call out to the* Derringer?> Tanis asked Angela.

<I called. Who knows if it made it anywhere. That was a coordinated attack, and Oris…>

Tanis nodded. Not only was Oris a traitor—mostly likely for the Nietzscheans—but the only way she could have subverted the *Aegeus*'s ship AI would be with help. The sort of help that didn't come from people with Nietzschea's level of technology.

<*Oris was either from Orion, or she had a remnant in her.*>

<*We need to carry Shadowtrons with us at all times,*> Angela replied.

<*No argument here.*>

Johnny took up a position at the front of the shuttle and called back. <*Civvies are starting to come out. We need to move.*>

Tanis looked around and saw lights on in the buildings nearby, and people standing in windows and doorways. A sound came from behind, and she saw Ayer step out of the shuttle.

"Damn Jersey City. I can't believe I'm going to die here."

"I'm not dying," Tanis said. "Keep your head down, and you won't, either."

<*Jersey City, OK,*> Angela said to Tanis. <*I have the map, and our position. Damn, this city is half-trashed. Ah hah! There's a small civilian spaceport on the north side of the city. Other than finding a hole to hide in, it's our best bet to get out of here.*>

Tanis nodded as she looked up the best route to the spaceport, sending it to Brandt and Johnny. Then she turned back to Ayer.

"Captain. I'm sorry about Mill. I really am. I just lost hundreds of my people, as well. But I'm not going to leave you here to wallow in sorrow. You can mourn later. Right now, stay sharp so we can give 'em hell later."

Ayer drew a deep breath and closed her eyes for a moment. "Where to?" she asked, and Tanis added her to the combat net.

<*Munis Spaceport.*>

The Marauder nodded and lifted her rifle, holding it across her chest. <*OK, I'm ready.*>

At first the small group made good time through the streets of Jersey City, but it didn't take long for the roads to become crowded with fleeing people—some on foot, some in ground cars, all trying to get out into the surrounding countryside.

Then the Nietzschean dropships started to touch down, and the group's progress slowed further as they kept to the shadows, checking corners and scurrying through open spaces as quickly as possible.

Several hours later, they were holed up in a sublevel of an exotic food store, waiting out a squad of Niets who were working their way down the street, rounding up any citizens.

Ayer stood near a small window, watching the boots of Niets move past. She was still favoring her one leg a bit, but it seemed to be better than when they'd left the shuttle.

Tanis was tempted to tell the captain to stand back. She was being sloppy in her grief, almost acting as though she wanted to die. Yet Tanis worried that if she ordered Ayer to move, the woman might start yelling again.

Instead, Tanis deployed a small passel of nano to create a film on the glass and dampen any motion or EM.

"They'll be setting up AA emplacements on some of the tallest high rises," Ayer whispered after a moment. "At least, they did last year. Niets aren't known for changing up their tactics."

"They ever infiltrated an enemy military like this before?" Brandt asked.

"Well…no, I guess not."

"Less chatter," Tanis said. "I can only mask so much."

The group fell into silence for the next twenty minutes while they waited for the Nietzscheans to move on. Then they waited another five minutes before exiting the sublevel and returning to the streets.

They leapfrogged from building to building this way, all through the night, until dawn came and it was no longer safe to move.

Brandt led the group down into a utility tunnel that ran between two buildings. Partway down, they came to a small storage room with a door on the far side that connected to another passage.

"Three ways out." Tanis nodded with approval. "Works for me."

Ayer didn't speak as she leaned against a wall and slid to the ground. Johnny sat on a table, resting his rifle on his knees.

"How long 'til the *Derringer* gets here, do you think?" he asked.

Tanis had a countdown running on her HUD with several times listed, each accounting for different scenarios.

"Best time would be seven days," Tanis replied. "But I wouldn't count on that. They're going to have to go slow to avoid detection with that many Niet ships out there. It depends on whether or not all of the SAF and Theban ships sided with the traitors. If the Niets drop more than ten-thousand ships, then the *Derringer* will wait for the *I2*. In which case we could be looking at weeks. Maybe a month."

Johnny almost choked. "A month, Admiral?"

"That's an extreme case. *Derringer* will already be on the QuanComm. By now, they'll have seen the attack. Whether they wait or not, Rachel and the *I2* won't be far behind."

Johnny didn't look much happier, and Brandt placed a hand on his shoulder. "Don't worry, Corporal. You get to spend quality time with me. What more could you ask for?"

THE CAVALRY

STELLAR DATE: 08.18.8949 (Adjusted Years)
LOCATION: ISS *I2*, Command Deck
REGION: Edge of the Lisbon System, Septhian Alliance

Bob's presence in her mind startled Rachel out of a deep sleep. She rolled off the couch in her office and landed on her side, her face pressed against the floor.

<Bob! What?> she asked, scrambling to her feet.

Bob's only response was to show her an image of the *Aegeus* exploding next to a space station that was torn apart in the resulting blast.

"Shit! Fuck!" she swore, rushing out of her office and onto the bridge without even checking to see if she was dressed. "Status!"

Major Jessie rose out of the command chair, her eyes wide. "We just got it…we don't know anything yet."

Her voice was hoarse, and her eyes were fixed on a replaying image of the Aegeus's shields failing, the enemy missiles impacting, and then the nuclear fireball expanding through the cold vacuum of space, buckling the toroid on the nearby station like it was made of paper.

The attackers were former Theban ships with SAF idents, but there were also Nietzschean ships appearing deep inside the system.

"This is all we got in from the *Derringer,* so far," Comm called out. "Oh, they just messaged that the Admiral was not aboard the *Aegeus* when it was destroyed. She was on the station…"

Rachel drew in a steadying breath. The station had been destroyed as well, but that had been a much slower event. Tanis could have gotten off. *Would* have gotten off.

"Signal every ship in the First Fleet to get to Pyra," Rachel ordered. "Tell all ships to form up on the *Derringer*'s position, and pass this data on to Khardine."

She paced back and forth on the bridge, chafing at the knowledge that without a jump gate, the *I2* was a month from the Albany System.

"And, Comm," Rachel called out. "Tell Khardine we need a gate delivered. *Now.*"

"How did they..." Major Jessie whispered as she replayed the attack on the *Aegeus*. "There were only five of them. No way they got through the stasis shields."

<It could only have been sabotage,> Priscilla said. *<And there was only one person on that ship that it could be.>*

Rachel clenched her jaw. "Oris."

Rather than wear a hole in the deck while waiting for a gate to be delivered, Rachel left the bridge for the CIC. She nodded solemnly to Priscilla on her plinth in the foyer as she walked past.

<Buck up, Captain,> Priscilla said with a wan smile. *<This is Tanis Richards we're dealing with. The universe isn't done with her yet.>*

<I sure hope not.>

Rachel wondered about Priscilla's statement. If there was one thing she'd learned about Bob's avatars, it was that they were often windows into his mind.

If Priscilla thought Tanis was alive, that meant that Bob also believed it.

The thought put a spring in her step—or at least helped her straighten her spine as she walked into the CIC and approached Major Grange, who stood at the room's main holotable.

"Major Grange." Rachel nodded. "What do you have?"

"I'm waiting on updates over the QuanComm, but here's what I have for now. As you know, New Canaan just shipped another thousand Trisilieds vessels to Septhia, which means they're all but out of the serviceable hulls that were surrendered. All that remains are two thousand functional Orion ships, and ten thousand ISF ships."

"Which is the bare minimum fleet size for New Canaan," Rachel replied.

That was something Tanis had carved in stone. New Canaan was not to overextend itself, offering aid to others. It was still one of the top targets in the galaxy, and any attack elsewhere could be a feint meant to weaken the home fleet.

"What about Diana?" Rachel asked.

"Latest word from Scipio is that they've taken their forward elements and engaged the Hegemony. They have maybe a hundred ships they could send us, *if* they're still near the jump gates."

"What about Khardine and Vela?" Rachel asked. "They should have ten thousand ships they can send."

Grange nodded. "They do, but they just started 'Operation Possum'. They have ships everywhere, many in dark layer transition. Krissy will need to halt the op and recall her bait ships before sending help."

Rachel nodded slowly. "And Khardine?"

"Greer just launched a number of raids against the Dresine Combine. Right now, Khardine is at minimum strength."

"Dammit!" Rachel swore. "I assume they'll try to form up some sort of support for us?"

"Yes, we're still waiting on updates. Stars…how did this timing line up so badly…" Major Grange's voice trailed off and he leant against the holotable.

"We don't need to match their strength. Even with ten-thousand ships, we could take out those Nietzscheans," Rachel countered.

"Perhaps," Grange replied. "But if we come in too hard, they'll simply destroy the planet Admiral Richards is stranded on."

Rachel swallowed. Grange was right. This was going to take some delicate maneuvering.

* * * * *

It took over three days for a gate to be delivered to the Lisbon system. Including initial light lag before the *Derringer* even saw the event, over ninety-two hours had passed since Tanis had come under attack.

The *Derringer* had sent so much data that the ship had disentangled all but one QuanComm blade. Now the updates following the first data burst contained only the message, 'no change'.

Time for some change, Rachel thought as she watched the jump gate come to life.

"Take us in," she ordered helm.

The *I2* surged toward the gate, touched the negative energy at its center, and then the stars around the ship disappeared for an instant before coming back in new positions.

"Confirming…" Scan announced. "Jump on target, we are at the edge of the Albany System!"

Rachel strode toward the main holotank and looked over the initial scan data as it poured in. Only seven other ships were in position near the *Derringer*. Three were members of the ISF First Fleet, and two were dreadnoughts from Khardine. Not much, but a start.

Though when she saw what lay within the Albany System, she felt the blood drain from her face.

That's over seventy thousand enemy ships.

<*Captain Mel,*> Rachel called the captain of the *Derringer.* <*What's your status?*>

<*Captain Rachel,*> Mel replied. <*Glad you've made it. We've been soaking up every transmission those bastards have made. They have not, I repeat,* **not** *captured the Admiral. However, they're searching for her like there's no tomorrow.*>

<*Do they have any leads?*> Rachel asked.

<*Over a thousand civilian pods and ships dropped down on the planet when the Niets showed up and destroyed the station. The enemy lost track of the Admiral in the chaos and debris.*>

Rachel breathed a sigh of relief. That was good news—or it meant Tanis had died…

No! I'm not going to think that.

<*Mel, send over everything you've grabbed. I'm going to have the fleet analysts recomb through it to be sure.*>

<*Aye…Captain?*>

<*What is it, Mel?*>

<*I just about died, just sitting out here. If we send in stealthed ships….*>

Rachel understood what Mel was getting at. <*You'll be in the vanguard, Mel.*>

<*Thanks.*>

"Major Jessie," Rachel called out to her XO. "I'm going down to see Grange in the CIC. You have the conn."

"Aye, Captain Rachel, I have the conn."

When Rachel arrived in the CIC, Grange was looking grim as he stood at his table. He was surveying the situation in the Albany system and shaking his head.

"That's a lot of ships," he muttered.

Rachel nodded. "Admiral Evans's strategy is sound…it's just going to take *forever* to be ready."

Grange locked eyes with Rachel. "It's his wife…wives—you know what I mean—down there. From what I see, all of the admirals agree this is our best shot."

"It's just going to take so long to get them in position," Rachel said, trying not to sound like she was whining—except she really wanted to whine.

Grange was nodding silently when one of the fleet analysts called out from his station.

"Captain, Major! We were combing over the data the *Derringer* sent, and Bob found something!"

<*I helped,*> Bob amended.

"It was in data stripped from an outer relay," the analyst said while nodding effusively. "Part of the buffers were corrupted, but we managed to piece them back together. There's a message. From Angela."

Rachel felt a weight fall from her shoulders, and was surprised at how much more easily she drew her next breath.

<*They got on a Marauder shuttle,*> Bob said. <*Headed for the surface. A final trajectory update from Angela puts them on course for a place called Jersey City.*>

"Stars…" Grange sighed. "Suddenly I'm starving, I haven't been able to eat more than a bite in days."

Rachel gave a soft laugh, but felt no mirth. "Well, we know she was alive and where she was headed. Now we just have to get there."

She held back the reminder that the intel was four days old.

It was something, at least.

THREE DAYS

STELLAR DATE: 08.24.8949 (Adjusted Years)
LOCATION: ISS *I2*, Bridge
REGION: Edge of the Albany System, Thebes, Septhian Alliance

Over the last three days, nearly a thousand ships had arrived at the edge of the Albany System: Scipian cruisers and dreadnoughts, a host of TSF ships from various locations around the Transcend, three hundred vessels from New Canaan, and even a small detachment from Silstrand.

From the messages flooding in, Rachel knew that Sera was beside herself with worry, though the President knew she couldn't jump to the system and put herself at risk as well.

That didn't stop her from sending a message to Rachel that was half encouragement, half stern warning that Tanis had better be OK.

Joe, on the other hand, had sounded almost deadly calm in his last communication—at least that's how Rachel read the text.

He was ready, just waiting on the signal.

Rachel watched as the fleet elements settled into position, ready to begin the burn toward Pyra—and their conflict with the seventy thousand Nietzschean ships waiting insystem.

She opened her mouth to issue the command, only to have scan call out "Contact! A Nietzschean fleet, half a light second to starboard!"

Rachel felt her throat constrict, but then saw the number of ships that appeared.

"Is this some sort of joke?" she whispered.

Seven ships appeared on the main tank. Three Nietzschean cruisers, though one looked almost as large as a dreadnought, two destroyers…and a pair of Marauder vessels.

Even stranger, all ships were broadcasting Marauder IFF signals.

"Hail them, tightbeam on the dreadnought," Rachel ordered.

"I have a response," Comm replied a few seconds later. "Putting it on the main tank."

Rachel rose from her chair and approached the tank, altering its configuration to ensure that whoever she spoke with would only see her, and not the rest of the *I2*'s bridge.

A woman appeared in the holotank—a woman unlike anyone Rachel had ever seen before. She was tall, and from the neck up, appeared perfectly normal. Her face was plain, but pleasant-looking, and was framed by long blonde hair that fell over her shoulders.

But that was not what had caught Rachel by surprise. Though the woman appeared to wear powered armor, it was plain to see that her limbs were nonorganic, especially her right arm, which was effectively nothing but a large, multi-mode rifle.

Even stranger, everyone behind her was also just as much machine as human—some, more.

<*They're mechs,*> Bob supplied. <*Genevian mechs.*>

Rachel nodded slowly. She knew about the mechs, studied them before coming to Septhia. However, seeing them, knowing there was a whole culture—civilization?—of these machine warriors was something else entirely.

The mech-woman spoke first. "Hi, there, I'm Rika, Captain of M Company, Marauders 9th Battalion. I assume the fact you're floating way out here means you're not on speaking terms with the Niets?"

Captain Rika's words kicked Rachel's mind back into action, and she gave a curt nod before replying.

"Nice to meet another friendly face. I'm Captain Rachel, commander of the ISF First Fleet. You're correct in your assessment. We're not fans of the Nietzscheans being here at all."

Rika smiled, an expression that animated her face and transformed it from pleasant to vibrant. "Well, then. You're our kinda people. What are you doing here, though?"

Rachel wondered what to tell this mech-woman. The fact that she was in possession of five Nietzschean ships offered new tactical options.

<Tell her what we plan,> Bob instructed, his tone almost jubilant. *<She will help. Chances of a successful rescue increase dramatically with Rika.>*

Rachel wanted to ask him what made him so happy, but only replied, *<Don't have to tell me twice, then.>*

"Well, Captain Rika, we're readying an assault to go in and rescue our leader, Admiral Richards. As chance may have it, she was meeting with your General Mill when the Nietzscheans attacked."

An expression of appreciation came over Rika's face. "I'm all for kicking Nietzschean ass and saving General Mill. But you do realize that there's a shit-ton of Niets down there? You're gonna need a bigger fleet."

"We have very good shields," Rachel said, wondering how to broach her idea to this newcomer. "But you know what works better than that? Not getting shot at…at all."

A smile came over Rika's face, and she lifted her right arm, resting the weapon's barrel on her shoulder. "I think I might have a way to help with that."

* * * * *

Forty minutes later, a brief flurry of weapons fire was exchanged between the ISF fleet and the newly arrived Marauder-controlled Nietzschean vessels as they passed within a hundred thousand kilometers of one another.

Then the two Marauder ships split off and made an outsystem burn, while the six Nietzschean vessels made a short dark layer hop, disappearing from scan.

Rachel did her best not to pace during the twelve minutes that passed before Marauder-controlled Nietzschean vessels appeared on scan once more, just over an AU further insystem.

<*It's a good fiction,*> Priscilla said. <*It should fool the Niets further insystem into thinking Rika's ships jumped to escape us, and lost their hold on the captured Marauder ships.*>

The *I2*'s captain chewed on her lip, wishing she could feel as confident as Bob and Priscilla, but not wanting to ask why they were so sure of success. <*Well, at least we have control of the outer relays, and have blocked their transmissions insystem. Otherwise those Marauder IFFs they started out with would have ended this charade before it started.*>

<*Rule number one. Control the information,*> Priscilla replied.

<*Oh yeah? What's rule number two?*>

<*Send in the big guns.*>

Rachel chuckled as she watched the mech ships—which were already moving at 0.6*c* from their dark layer transition—continue insystem.

"Helm," she said, staring out into the starfield ahead of the ship. "Take us insystem. Let's give a good chase."

The FTN coordination officer relayed the order across the fleet, and the ISF First Fleet surged forward, appearing to chase the five Nietzschean ships racing ahead of them.

Good luck, Rika of the Marauders.

REINFORCEMENTS

STELLAR DATE: 08.24.8949 (Adjusted Years)
LOCATION: MSS *Fury Lance*, Bridge
REGION: Edge of the Albany System, Thebes, Septhian Alliance

Captain Rika glanced at Lieutenant Heather, who sat at the *Fury Lance*'s weapons console. "Didn't hurt them too much, did you, Smalls?"

Heather shook her head in amazement. "No…our weapons didn't do *a thing* to their ships. I can't even detect their shields. It's like they don't have any."

"Didn't you ever hear about the Battle of Five Fleets at Bollam's World?" Barne asked from where he leaned against the scan station.

Heather frowned at the first sergeant. "I don't think that's a real place, Top."

Barne snorted. "You wouldn't, Smalls."

"Whoa!" Rika stopped them short. "Barne. How come Smalls gets to call you 'Top', but I don't?"

Barne shrugged. "Dunno. Guess I like her more."

Rika wagged a finger at him. "Don't make me tell people about that time at Cheri's villa."

"Oh?" Heather asked.

"Captain…" Barne rumbled.

Heather turned to Rika. "Is it juicy?"

"Not particularly, but it bugs Barne for some reason, so it's useful leverage."

"Can we focus on the mission?" Barne asked.

Heather rose from her station and stretched. "What's to focus on? Biggest thing we have to worry about right now is avoiding the thousands of ships that are fleeing the system."

"For the time being," Barne replied.

"Well, we sent the message to Nietzschean Command telling them that Iapetus is secured and that we came to render assistance. Commander Kiers' codes turned out to be useful once again. We'll see what the Niets order us to do. At the least, they're going to want to have access to our close-range scan logs to see if we learned anything about that massive ship."

"Did you see some of those ship registries, though?" Heather asked. "I've never heard of the ISF or the Transcend. I mean, everyone knows of Scipio, and I've seen Silstrand on charts. Thing is, they're a year's travel from here. How does some weird-assed fleet with registries from all over show up right now?"

Barne laughed. "Not only that, but at *Albany*. Is this place some sort of crazy lightning rod?"

"Beats me," Rika shrugged.

No one spoke for a minute, then Heather shook her head at the holotank and let out a long sigh. "One thing's for sure. Those are a lot of ships out there. I've never seen so many."

"I have," Barne grunted. "Early in the war, some of the fleet engagements were this big. As many as a hundred thousand—counting both sides. That was back when both we and the Niets thought we could blitzkrieg our way past the other."

Rika rose from her chair and paced across the bridge, tracing her fingertips along one of the bent consoles. "Well, no blitzkrieging, here. Just get in, nab the General and Admiral, and get out."

"So long as our orders from Niet command allow for that," Barne replied.

"Just has to be something that gets us close enough to land dropships," Chase said as he entered the bridge. "Can you believe we're going to pound dirt on Pyra again? Jersey City, of all places."

Rika turned to Chase and leant against the back of her chair. "Not everyone is going down. It's going to be a small strike team," Rika said, looking from face to face. "SMI-2s only. We need to move fast and hit hard. Get in, grab them, get out."

"Well, I'm flying your ship down there," Chase said.

"You better than Ferris, or Mad Dog?" Heather asked skeptically.

Chase flexed his prosthetic arm. It wasn't smooth and natural-looking like Barne's, but the limb of an RR-3. "I've got some advantages."

"I'll think on it," Rika replied. "I doubt anyone's going to be sitting idle. I think we should consider some diversions, as well—but not ones that paint too big a target on anyone's back."

"What do you have in mind?" Barne asked.

"Well, we're going to need supplies, right?"

"Yeah," Barne grunted. "Would be standard for us to fuel up with a battle looming—fleet that large, they've jumped in supply ships for sure."

"I wonder if maybe we can make one of those go boom," Rika mused.

<*Our guests have arrived,*> Leslie called up to the bridge. <*Should I bring them up?*>

<*Bring them to the barracks we assigned, I'll meet them there.*>

"Stars," Heather muttered. "I can't detect their ship, and it's *inside* our freakin' landing bay. I wonder if that motley fleet is a lot larger than we saw?"

"That would be nice," Rika said as she straightened and walked past Chase, kissing him on the cheek.

"Rika," Chase called back as she left.

"What?"

"You're supposed to say who has the conn after you leave."

Rika laughed. "I'll never get the hang of all this crap. Uhhh, Lieutenant Heather, you have the conn."

"Aye, Captain. I have the conn," Heather said as she rose from her console and tool the command chair. "Sergeant Chase. You think you're so good at flying, take the helm station."

Chase shot Rika a dirty look, then laughed as he sat at the helm. "I'm gonna do loop-de-loops, Heather—show you what this bird can really do."

"Sergeant! You crazy idiot!"

Rika walked off the bridge, smiling to herself. She wondered about that. Here they were, flying toward one of the biggest Niet fleets they'd ever seen, with just five ships.

*We're **all** certifiably crazy.*

But then again, she was a mech, and those were Niets out there. What was her life about, if not killing them at every available opportunity?

<*I can think of a few things,*> Niki replied.

"I thought you couldn't read my mind." Rika frowned.

<*I can if your mind makes your lips whisper things aloud.*>

"Oh," Rika laughed. "I guess there's that."

<*Just, please. No suicide runs. I'm too young to die.*>

"Don't worry, Niki-mine, there are a lot of Niets to kill. I plan to survive this so I can keep on wiping them out."

<*That's…uh…a very healthy mental state.*>

"Liar."

Niki didn't reply, and Rika's mind began to wander as she traversed the passageways to the barracks decks.

<*Niki, do you believe in a god?*>

<*What a strange question to ask an AI. What's got you on this train of thought?*>

<*Well, I got talking to Lieutenant Carson about the Temple of Jesus thing—you know, after he explained what baptism is. It was interesting, and I didn't think much of it…but lately we've had a lot*

of crazy coincidences. What really got me thinking about this is that you came to me with no small amount of serendipity. I know for sure that I would have **not** *been able to rescue Silva and Amy—let alone overthrow the Politica—without you.*>

Niki sent an affirmative feeling. <*Agreed. I saved the day. Carry on.*>

<*And then we capture these Nietzschean ships, which are just what we need to sneak insystem to rescue the General. On top of that, you told me about the Intrepid just a few weeks ago, and we just encountered the Intrepid Space Force!*>

<*Not to mention, that ship* ***was*** *the* Intrepid, *they've just modified it since Bollam's World.*>

Rika nodded, she had suspected as much.

<*So what does this have to do with a god?*> Niki asked.

<*Not sure…just seems like a lot of coincidence, that's all.*>

<*Well, let's hope none of us die and get confirmation just yet, OK?*>

Rika laughed. That was one way to look at it.

A moment later, she rounded a corner and saw a white woman walking beside Leslie, a column of soldiers behind them.

The woman was quite the sight. Surrounded by the grey corridor—not to mention contrasted against Leslie and her jet-black skin—the white woman all but gleamed.

Upon closer inspection, it was apparent that the woman was not wearing any clothing, and that her 'skin' was a thick, semi-flexible polymer of sorts.

Her long, black hair reminded Rika of braids, but as the mysterious woman drew near, Rika realized that her hair consisted of thick, black cords that seemed to move of their own accord. Almost as though they were drifting through water rather than air.

Despite all that, it was the woman's completely black eyes that were most striking. They reflected no light, and, set against the pure-white skin, they looked like holes which had been bored through the woman's face and into space beyond.

She was speaking with Leslie, gesturing emphatically as she strode down the corridor. A moment later, her gaze turned to Rika, and a warm smile graced her lips—though it was difficult to make out her expression.

"Captain Rika," the woman extended her hand, showing no hesitation to shake Rika's left, nor at the robotic, three-fingered hand that reached out to clasp hers. "I'm Priscilla."

Rika noted the lack of title, military or otherwise. Neither was there any insignia on her…skin.

"Hello, very nice to meet you, Priscilla."

<*Stop staring at her,*> Leslie chided Rika privately.

<*They're all staring at me. I think it's OK to have a mutual stare-fest.*>

Priscilla turned and gestured at the soldier at the head of the column. "This is Colonel Smith, he'll be joining our ground team with his Marines."

Rika extended her hand and shook the colonel's, noting that he too did not seem at all perturbed by her mechanized body—that's not to say that he didn't look her over. But it was not in disdain or sexual interest. Instead, she got the distinct impression that he was evaluating her combat effectiveness.

She found herself doing the same. The colonel appeared to be completely organic, as did the group of men and women behind him. Even stranger, they wore no armor, and the packs they carried were not large enough to contain any meaningful protection.

Their bodies were covered in tight-fitting matte grey outfits, even their hands and feet. They bore insignia on their chests and ranks on their collars—which meant that these were uniforms of some sort.

"Very nice to meet you, Colonel. But I'm not sure unarmored humans are the right things to drop on the battlefield. We need strength, speed, and stealth, something my mechs excel at."

"I imagine you do," the colonel said with a nod. "I understand there are less than four hundred of you, yet you captured all these ships intact. Very impressive."

"Thank you, colonel, surely you—"

The colonel held up a hand. "Captain Rika, we *will* be going groundside. Don't let the packaging fool you."

A moment later, the colonel's body turned invisible. Not a simple light-bending that was visible at the edges; from the neck down, the colonel was *gone*. There was no IR signature, and Rika's EM wave mapping showed signals passing directly through the space where his body was. She half wondered if she could reach out and put her hand right though him.

"Shit," was all she managed to say, while Leslie nodded emphatically.

"This is what we call 'flow armor', Captain. Perhaps not quite as tough as what you're made of, but sufficient to carry out the task. And we may look fragile, but you just might contain more organics than we do."

The colonel shifted back into visibility, but now he was holding two pistols. She hadn't seen his pack move at all, and there were no holsters on his body.

"How—?" Leslie gaped.

Colonel Smith twirled the sidearms and then slid them into his thighs. Thighs which had the IR profile of an organic human.

"As you can see, we're not what the enemy will expect. We're an asset you can ill-afford to ignore."

"Ignore?" Leslie asked. "If I didn't think you would just disappear, I'd jump you and steal that stuff you're wearing."

Colonel Smith turned and nodded to a sergeant behind him. The sergeant swung his pack around and pulled out a canister. He checked it over, and then tossed it to Leslie.

"Figured you might have some non-mechs that want to come along. We brought a dozen of these."

"How do I use it?" Leslie asked, turning the canister over.

"Get naked, touch it to your chest, put your finger on the trigger plate, and hold it for a second."

"And then it just flows over me?" Leslie asked, staring incredulously at the canister in her hands. "I mean…you said it was flow armor, right? Do I have to wear a helmet still?"

Colonel Smith shook his head. "Flow armor doesn't have any ablative properties, so you may want to wear a helmet, but you don't have to."

As the man spoke, the matte grey covering flowed up over his head, somehow encompassing his hair without getting tangled or stuck in it. Then it flowed back down.

"See?" he asked.

"I've been standing for the last sixty-two days," Priscilla interrupted. "Are we going to find some place to sit down and talk?"

"Uh, sorry. Of course." Rika nodded and gestured for the group to follow her.

The entrance to the barracks wasn't far, and they reached it in under a minute. It consisted of a common area, a small galley, and shared sleeping halls.

"Will this do?" Rika asked.

"Very nicely," Colonel Smith replied. "Though I suspect her majesty, here, won't want to sleep with us plebes."

Priscilla swatted the colonel on the arm. "I'll sleep wherever. But I am starved. Haven't eaten in weeks."

"You don't sit, you don't eat…what do you do, over on your ship?" Rika asked.

Priscilla smiled again, the expression no less strange than it had been the last time. "I'm one of the ship's avatars."

"You're a what?" Leslie frowned.

"We'll, not the ship, exactly. The ship's AI. Bob is very complex, and his human avatars help him interface with people better."

<*BOB!*> Niki cried out. <*Bob is on that warship?*>

"*Thought* you had an AI," Priscilla winked at Rika—again, a bit creepy. "Though she's not neurally interfaced like normal. Curious."

<*I can't believe I was so close to Bob, and didn't get to speak with him!*>

Rika imagined that if Niki had a body, she'd be jumping up and down.

"Easy, Niki. When we're done kicking the Niets' asses, we can all meet Bob."

"Absolutely," Priscilla replied. "However, before we get to the ass kicking, anyone going on this mission is going to need some upgrades."

Rika's eyes narrowed, and Leslie asked. "What kind of upgrades?"

Priscilla looked Leslie up and down. "Well, if you really want to use that flow armor, you're going to need better nano, for starters."

Leslie held out an arm, a huge grin plastered on her face. "Hit me, do whatever you have to do."

Rika snorted. "You're like a stealth junkie, Leslie."

"Hey, I can't take a rail shot and keep on keeping on like you can," Leslie replied. "Not being seen at *all* is my jam."

*****

Rika sat in the small officer's lounge near the bridge and watched as Leslie appeared and disappeared in different parts of the room.

She'd be standing on the deck, covered from head to toe in her new flow armor, tail and all, then she'd disappear, only to reappear a moment later on a counter, or on the far side of the room. Once, she was hanging from the overhead.

If it hadn't been for the constant giggling, she would have been completely undetectable.

"I wonder why Priscilla is here," Rika said after a few minutes.

Leslie reappeared, kneeling on the table right in front of Rika, about to grab her beer. She sat back and stroked her chin as her tail flicked back and forth behind her.

Rika had noticed that while initially Leslie had always been very conscious of her tail, it now seemed to have a mind of its own, and was an interesting indicator of the lieutenant's mood.

"I mean…what skill set does a human avatar have? Which is really weird, by the way. Does she even have her own mind, or is she somehow inhabited by this 'Bob' AI?"

<*She has her own mind,*> Niki said without elaboration.

When Niki didn't speak further, Leslie shrugged. "She must have some sort of special power or ability. Colonel Smith did say she has extensive combat training, and her skin is a very effective armor. Think she just moonlights as a spec-ops person sometimes?" Leslie's armor flowed away from her face, and she grabbed Rika's beer, downing half before sliding back off the table.

"Leslie! That one's yours now. Go get me another."

Leslie licked her lips and walked to the counter. "Say what you want about the Niets, but they make a mean brew. Maybe when we destroy their empire, we can keep their brewmasters."

"I'll take it under advisement," Rika replied.

Leslie brought Rika a fresh glass of beer and then took another sip of the one she'd stolen.

"With these enhanced senses Priscilla's nano gave me, I can taste notes in this I could never pick up before. And I can see in the dark; not just a little dark, *pitch black*. I can see UV, IR, pick up shadows on backscatter radiation. It's like my eyes are the best tactical helmet ever."

Rika nodded. "Yeah, I'm with you there. Carson was nearly beside himself when he saw what her nano can do. Bet he's glad now that he transferred over from the *Golden Lark,* back when we were boosting out of Iapetus."

"I guess that explains why everyone in the galaxy wants to get their hands on that ship," Leslie replied. "And just think, this is the tech they were willing to share freely. What else do you think they have?"

"Stars if I know," Rika replied. "I bet if they had anything that could help with this op, they'd provide it, though."

Leslie disappeared again, giggling once more. "What could be better than this?"

PYRA

STELLAR DATE: 08.26.8949 (Adjusted Years)
LOCATION: Edge of Jersey City, Pyra
REGION: Albany System, Thebes, Septhian Alliance

"Finally," Tanis breathed as she peeked around the corner, her eyes settling on the Nietzschean staging ground.

"I count a hundred dropships at least," Brandt said. "Good stuff."

A strong gust of wind blew past, and Tanis eased back around the corner, glancing over at Ayer and Johnny, who were stacked along the wall behind them. Both were looking worse for wear, but still resolute. Still determined to survive.

After ten days on the ground, struggling through the sewers, maintenance tunnels, and alleys of Jersey City, Tanis felt like she'd lived here half her life.

The first spaceport—the small civilian one north of the city—had been a bust. The Nietzscheans had blown it to bits. From there, they'd worked their way to the harbor, searching for a boat that could get them further north to Ventara, where scattered radio signals told of a strong resistance against the Niets.

Unfortunately, most of the boats in the harbor were gone by the time they arrived. The only ships left were fishing rigs under heavy guard by the Niets.

Captain Ayer had suggested they try to go inland to Huntsville, but when they got halfway, they encountered a refugee camp that told of the city's complete destruction.

Niet patrols had picked up at that point, and it had taken five days to get back to the edge of Jersey City.

Compared to the destruction they'd heard of in other places, be it from refugees or scattered communications from holdouts, it seemed like Jersey City and the surrounding areas were taking the least punishment from the Niets.

Tanis knew that meant one thing: they were looking for her, and believed she was in the vicinity.

She'd already harbored the suspicion. The fact that the turncoat Theban cruisers hadn't fired on them during their descent was the first clue. The building-to-building searches through Jersey City were another.

Which was why Tanis had no intention of going back into the city.

Luckily, this Nietzschean staging ground lay on southern edge of the metropolis. Even better, it was mostly unoccupied, at present. The dropships arrayed on the hard-packed dirt represented the only noteworthy group of ships within hundreds of kilometers.

<*We'll wait for full noon,*> she advised, watching a small dust-devil trace its way along the slope behind the shed. <*All those ships maneuvering in orbit are dumping EM garbage everywhere. The last two days, the planet's van allen belts dumped a lot of radiation around noon.*>

<*What I wouldn't give for a solar flare,*> Ayer added.

<*Me too,*> Tanis smiled.

Ayer had warmed up—a bit, at least—over the past few days. She hadn't spoken further of how they'd left General Mill behind, not after Tanis reminded her that the lives of everyone else who had died were worth just as much.

Despite her words, Tanis felt especially bad about the pilot's death. Maybe if the woman hadn't been knocked out, she would have survived.

Even though she was less grouchy about Mill and the situation in general, Ayer had been starting to make comments doubting the rescue Tanis was certain would come.

<*Can't say I blame her. Ten days is a long time down here.*>

<*You estimated it could be longer,*> Angela gave a mental shrug. <*No big surprise.*>

<*Still, our friends above have a way of weighing on a person. I don't blame her for feeling like we've been here forever.*>

Tanis looked up at the thousands of Nietzschean ships, clustered in bands encircling the planet—enough of them to be visible in broad daylight. The ships hadn't changed formations in any meaningful way over the past week, which meant that the ISF was not yet headed insystem.

<*Or they're not that close yet,*> Angela suggested.

<*They could also be coming in with stealthed ships.*>

<*Maybe,*> Angela allowed. <*But with so many enemy ships up there, stealth would be hard to maintain. Vectors would be limited.*>

Ayer caught Tanis looking at the sky and she shook her head. "Hard to believe so many warships could assemble in one place—I mean, it's not busier than normal insystem traffic, but these things…it's different."

Tanis nodded slowly, still staring at the sky. "I've seen larger formations a few times. But they were either on my side, or I had a way to take them out."

"You've been around, Admiral Richards."

"I have. Stars, what I wouldn't give for even one Terran Space Force carrier and its fighter complement right about now."

"Fighters?"

Tanis nodded. "Back before a-grav, fighters were a big deal. Couldn't pull *g*s like ships can now, but what would you do if a million single-pilot fighters armed with nukes came your way?"

Ayer laughed. "Probably surrender."

"That's how it worked," Tanis replied as she held up her left arm, signaling her armor to retract. Most of the flowmetal her left arm consisted of was gone. Only enough remained to form a single rod connecting to her hand—which was also skeletal. Within the cavity the flow armor had encapsulated lay a jumbled mass of small, articulated limbs.

<*Damn wind…can't believe we have to go low-tech like this.*>

<*Could be worse,*> Angela replied. <*You could be entirely out of flowmetal, and I'd have to make these bots out of grass.*>

<*Funny, Ang.*>

Tanis turned her arm upside down, dropping small bots to the ground. They skittered around the corner and headed toward the Nietzschean compound.

"OK, that's just gross-looking," Ayer shuddered, staring at Tanis's arm. "You're practically a mech."

"I reviewed your mech models on the way here," Tanis replied as her armor sealed back up around her arm, stretching across the support rod and lightwand within. "Well, the Genevian models, I should say—not 'yours'. You'd be interested to know that I think that most of them may actually be more organic than I am."

"I believe it," Ayer replied quietly. "Though it's a lot harder to spot with you."

"Better living through technology."

"That's not been my experience." Ayer shook her head and then closed her eyes. The mercenary leaned back against the shed and slid down to a seated position.

Tanis took it as a signal that the conversation was over. She saw that Johnny was asleep, and Brandt pointed at Tanis and placed her hands against her head, miming laying on a pillow.

"Yes, Mom," Tanis mouthed silently, and followed Ayer's example, leaning her head back and closing her eyes. A bit of shut-eye before the mission was just what the doctor—or commandant, in this case—ordered.

STEALING A RIDE

STELLAR DATE: 08.26.8949 (Adjusted Years)
LOCATION: Edge of Jersey City, Pyra
REGION: Albany System, Thebes, Septhian Alliance

<Tanis, wake up,> Angela said quietly. *<Almost noon, get ready to roll.>*

Tanis opened her eyes and stretched languidly, her vision overlaid with the readouts from nano sensors around their hiding place and the staging area at the bottom of the hill.

"EM's getting crazy in the sky again," Brandt commented. "Let's hope a belt snaps."

"Wind's picking up even more, too," Johnny said. "I wonder if the ships are what's affecting the weather."

"Maybe," Tanis shrugged.

<I control all the Nietzschean sensors down at the staging ground,> Angela informed Tanis on the combat net. *<Unless someone is looking right at us with the Mark 1 eyeball, we can walk right up to the ship of our choice.>*

"Unless the cruisers are running active scan on this whole region—which they could be," Ayer replied as she stood up and stretched.

<Could be, but it will still give us time. I've falsified orders as well; a lot of conflicting directives that should cause some chaos for anyone trying to chase us. Once we get airborne, I'll unleash the dogs of confusion.>

Tanis, Brandt, and Johnny activated their flow armor and disappeared. Ayer was still plainly visible in her lightly armored uniform, and the plan was to have her walk in the midst of the others. Angela would link the flow armor's stealth systems, bending light around all of them as much as possible, and shield the Marauder captain.

They eased around the corner of the shed and began their approach.

The Nietzschean staging ground was only a kilometer away, but the going was slow. Tall grass and brush covered the hillside, and they did their best to avoid bending stalks and branches as they went.

Fifteen minutes later, they were only a hundred meters from the base, and it was at that moment that one of the van allen belts above the planet snapped, dumping accumulated EM radiation down onto the planet's poles, which then cascaded through the atmosphere.

Tanis saw her armor's readouts jump as the air ionized around them.

<Bet there are great polar light shows on the night side,> Angela said to Tanis.

<Probably. Should we pass over them with our shuttle on the way out?>

<Well, I did want to pick up a souvenir from this quaint little island up there. Think it won't be too much trouble during our escape?>

Tanis only gave a mental snort in reply, feeling Angela navigating the enemy network, altering sensor readings, and making it appear as though no one was anywhere near the staging ground.

The Niets didn't have any perimeter patrols out, but she could see a group of mechanics working on a dropship, midway through the field, and another pair of guards patrolling amongst the dropships on the same side as Tanis's group.

<That one,> Angela highlighted a ship on Tanis's HUD, and they began creeping toward it.

The vessel was two rows in and was out of sight of the building the Niets were using as their main base of operations.

So long as the patrolling guards kept on their current route, they wouldn't pass by it, either.

Just as the group passed the first row of ships, the ramp lowered on one, and a Nietzschean soldier stepped out, stretching and squinting as he looked around in the noon light.

Tanis stopped. So long as they held still and obscured Ayer, they were invisible. But with the wind gusts, they couldn't use any sound dampening nano to mask their footfalls. It was best to wait for the man to pass.

Then someone in the group shifted slightly—Tanis didn't know who—and a rock popped out from under their boot, skipping across the ground.

The Niet turned his head their way, raising a hand to shield his eyes from the sunlight.

She glanced down and saw that the wind was blowing eddies of dust around their feet, creating a strange, clear space in the air. If the man spotted it, he'd come to investigate.

The Nietzschean continued to stare in their direction. He was only sixteen meters away, and Tanis considered just shooting him and moving on, but then another man came out of the dropship from behind him, grinning as he fastened his pants and buckled his belt.

Steady, Tanis thought, praying that the new arrival would do something to distract the other Nietzschean.

Finished with his belt, the second man turned to the first as a gust of wind picked up, blowing even more dirt and debris across the landing field.

Clearly outlining the stealthed figures.

"Hey!" the first man yelled, reaching for his sidearm, only to find that it wasn't there.

Thankfully back in the ship, along with his belt, Tanis suspected.

She didn't hesitate to fire a pulse blast at him, bowling him over and knocking his friend back.

"Move!" she yelled, as an audible siren sounded, echoing amongst the ships. They raced ahead as a shot struck a hull nearby, passing the second row of ships and reaching the designated dropship a few moments later.

<*It's no good,*> Ayer said as she turned and fired on the pair of soldiers who had taken up position at the back of a ship in the prior row. <*They're onto us now. We have to run.*>

<*Run where?*> Brandt asked. <*They'll get every ship in the fleet scanning for us.*>

<*We have to get aboard one of these dropships,*> Tanis said. <*Get some distance.*>

Ayer looked back at Tanis, sadness in her eyes. <*I'm a liability. If it wasn't for me, you'd be home free. General, too…he had been covering me…*>

Tanis was about to reply, when the Marauder captain dashed out of cover and ran to the left, moving around to the far side of the ship the Niets were hiding behind to flank them.

<*Ramp's open, get in!*> Angela ordered, and Tanis fired again at the Niets, watching as her shot took out one, followed by a blast from behind the ship taking out the other.

Ayer nodded in Tanis's direction as she ran past the gap between the ships. Then she waved for Tanis to go. "Get out of here!"

Tanis made out the words on her lips, though the wind whipped away any sound. Then the Marauder was gone.

Tanis backed into the ship as the ramp closed, and turned to see Brandt settling into the cockpit.

<*I'll fly, thank you very much,*> Angela said. <*You organics crash too often.*>

"Ayer's in that dropship the Niets were banging in. She's powering engines," Johnny said from one of the external monitors. "It's lifting off."

<*We need to go at the same time,*> Angela said. <*Confuse them as to which is the priority target.*>

Tanis watched on the holo as the other ship began to lift off, then Angela brought theirs into the air.

"Stars. Good luck, Ayer," Tanis whispered, as both ships poured on max thrust, boosting up into the air.

Ayer's ship veered to the north, while Angela wove through the small hills south of Jersey City, headed to the coast.

"Another dropship is lifting off, in pursuit of Ayer," Brandt called out. Tanis watched in silence as the two ships continued north, appearing and disappearing from scan as they dipped in and out of valleys.

Then a beam of light streaked down from the sky and hit Ayer's dropship as it crested a rise. One of the dropship's engines exploded, and the craft angled sharply toward the ground.

"Fuck!" Brandt cried out as Ayer's ship disappeared from view, its passage marked by a cloud of smoke.

Angela increased the randomness of her flight pattern, exceeding what the internal dampeners could manage, rocking the three passengers from side to side.

A bright light flared off their port bow, and then a peal of thunder shook the ship.

"Close!" Johnny cried out.

<*I have to go for the city,*> Angela said. <*We won't make it to the coast.*>

"Do it," Tanis said through clenched teeth.

The ship veered left, headed toward the edge of Jersey City, half of the buildings below nothing more than smoking ruins as they flashed below the dropship.

<*Going to set down—*> Angela began, and then another flash came, this time to their starboard, accompanied by an explosion that shook the ship.

<*Brace!*> Angela screamed.

The dropship dipped and plowed into the side of a high-rise and came out the other side, falling like a rock before slowing at the last minute, only to smash through the front of another building and stop in its lobby.

Tanis shook as she pulled herself upright, and saw Johnny do the same.

"Well, shit," Brandt muttered as she tore off her harness. "We're right back where we fucking started!"

MARAUDERS

STELLAR DATE: 08.27.8949 (Adjusted Years)
LOCATION: Pyra
REGION: Albany System, Thebes, Septhian Alliance

Four dropships slipped out of the *Fury Lance* and began their descent toward the planet below. Inside one of them sat Priscilla. She was on the bench in the troop bay, along with a dozen Marines and Colonel Smith.

One of the dropships contained another dozen ISF Marines under Lieutenant Sal, and the other two held Rika and her SMI-2 mechs.

Each of the four craft would set down in different parts of Jersey City, and begin combing the ruins for any signs of Tanis and the others.

So far as Priscilla was concerned, there was only one objective: find Tanis Richards. Even Brandt, a dear friend to be sure, was secondary. A sacrifice that would be made if they had to.

These were Bob's directives. She was to save Tanis, no matter the cost. Everyone else, including herself, was expendable.

The Marauders—General Mill and Captain Ayer—who Rika desperately sought to rescue were barely on Priscilla's radar. Nothing other than leads that could bring them closer to finding Tanis.

Priscilla turned her attention to the ship's feeds and saw that, outside the dropships, space was chaos: hundreds of thousands of civilian ships trying to get further outsystem, the ruins of Appalachia Station—in ever deteriorating orbits—and Nietzschea's own ship-to-ship, and ship-to-surface traffic.

The end result was that the four ships didn't even have to get permission from an STC to drop; no one questioned another four dropcraft headed to Pyra, when thousands had already made the journey.

Priscilla watched as they came down over one of Pyra's oceans on approach to Jersey City. From what they'd been able to tell from comm traffic, the Niets considered Jersey City to be one of the most likely places Tanis had landed. She didn't know if they'd picked up Angela's transmission, or if it was just a lucky guess.

Over fifty thousand Nietzschean soldiers combed the city and the surrounding countryside, searching for the admiral and her group.

"Putting her down at the southwestern corner…looking for a nice, open plaza," the pilot, a talkative man named Ferris, called back.

"Just not too close to any enemy activity," Colonel Smith called up.

As they lowered through the atmosphere, Priscilla made contact with terrestrial wireless networks. A few were automated systems that had managed to stay up during the attack, carrying some civilian chatter and service data—which mostly consisted of alerts that everything was out of service.

What she was more interested in was the Nietzschean comm channels, where messages about the search for Tanis Richards abounded. There was not, however, any mention of General Mill, and Priscilla suspected why.

The enemy was calling Tanis by name, which cemented Priscilla's belief that Oris had been in on this attack, and that it had been intended to catch Tanis.

A far more devious plan than Priscilla would have credited the Nietzscheans for, from what she knew of them, though it fit perfectly with what Greer or the Caretaker were capable of.

Then an alert caught her attention.

Two shuttles had taken off from a nearby staging ground. One had been shot down, and the passenger, a Marauder captain, was found dead inside.

The other had crashed in the city, and search parties were already on the ground, hunting for survivors.

<*We have a location,*> Priscilla called up to Ferris and the other pilots. <*Set down at these coordinates, we'll search from there.*> She also passed the information about the Marauder captain to Rika.

Captain Ayer…killed by a self-inflicted gunshot wound to the head.

The Nietzscheans were taking prisoners in this fight, so the fact that the captain had taken her own life was a clue. A clue that pointed to her hiding information from the enemy.

The other pilots returned affirmation of her orders, and Priscilla drew a deep breath as the ships passed over the outskirts of Jersey City.

GONE TO GROUND

STELLAR DATE: 08.27.8949 (Adjusted Years)
LOCATION: Jersey City, Pyra
REGION: Albany System, Thebes, Septhian Alliance

Tanis crept along the rubble-strewn street, trying to avoid the debris while staying to the shadows, as the winds continued to whip around them. The storm was picking up, and dark clouds were rolling in from the sea.

Brandt was ahead of her, and Johnny was to the rear, watching for Niets, ready to signal for the group to freeze.

Twice now, they'd seen Nietzschean patrols, and once a small child had raced past, ducking behind a pile of rubble and disappearing from view.

Tanis resisted the urge to go after the kid—a little girl, from the looks of her. She knew that the child was safer away from them than with.

<*This is why I hate fighting on planets,*> Tanis complained to Angela. <*Weather.*>

<*I'll admit, I feel blind without probes telling me what's around the next corner.*>

Brandt reached the next intersection and held a finger out, using nano on her glove to see around the corner of the building they were pressed against. Tanis stopped a few meters behind her, and Johnny stopped behind her.

No one moved; the city appeared still and dead. The only sound was the wind howling amongst the tall buildings. It sounded mournful, as though it feared that humans would never return to these shattered towers.

Then the howl changed, and Tanis wondered what the wind was blowing through to make that particular whistle, before realization struck her.

"*Incoming!*" she screamed.

She raced across the street, watching through her armor's three-sixty vision as Brandt and Johnny followed after, each a second behind.

A streak of light flashed by on her right, then the wall behind them exploded.

Tanis was flung into the air, carried bodily across the street by the force of the blast, and through the glass windows of the storefront on the other side.

Her armor became rigid around her torso, protecting her organs, but still allowing her to tumble loosely through the air.

It felt like she was tossed around for a minute, before coming to rest, half-draped across a table.

<*You OK?*> Tanis asked on the combat net as she rose and checked herself over.

<*I'm here,*> Brandt waved from a meter away.

<*I have no reading on Johnny,*> Angela said, sounding almost panicked.

Tanis staggered to the front of the building and saw Johnny's body a meter away.

His head was further back.

<*He's gone, Brandt,*> Tanis whispered.

Brandt limped to Tanis's side. <*Fucking dumbass kid. I told him to run!*>

<*Leg?*> Tanis asked.

<*Fractured…twice. Armor jammed in a stabilizer—not sure which hurts more.*>

Tanis looked at Brandt's dirt-and-blood-covered body, then down at her own. Their armor's stealth systems were on low power, and unable to compensate for the grime.

They found some cloth nearby and quickly wiped one another as clean as they could, their stealth systems registering as seventy percent effective.

<*You need to move,*> Angela warned.

Tanis tossed a thermite grenade they'd taken from the crashed dropship at Johnny's body, turning toward the rear of the story they were in so as not to watch the young man be burned to ash.

The two women exited the back of the store and worked their way down the alley, slowly moving behind the building where the rocket had likely been fired from.

Tanis debated going up and finding who had launched it at them—Brandt probably was, too, by the way the commandant kept glancing up at the high-rise.

They were almost at the end of the alley, when a squad of Niets raced by its mouth. The women tucked into the shadows, praying they hadn't been seen.

<*We can't keep going on while blind,*> Tanis said, and drew the blade from her left forearm. She slid it into the armor on her left thigh, flexing slightly to ensure it wouldn't shift and cut her open, before signaling her armor to flow back up her left arm.

<*More dropships circling,*> Brandt said.

Angela instructed the remaining flowmetal in Tanis's left arm to form six small, spider-like bots. The bots leapt from her arm onto the wall and skittered around the corner, climbing the building and watching the street and surrounding structures.

<*Much better. Though I'm not sure it was worth trading an arm for,*> Brandt sighed.

<*If we don't spot rocket fire that blows us to bits, I'll be missing more than just an arm.*>

Brandt nodded silently and slipped around the corner once the bots showed the road to be clear. They made their way west. They still had no better plan than to take another dropship.

Luckily, several had landed near the edge of the city only ten minutes before.

Tanis knew it was a shit plan, but maybe in the storm, they could lose any pursuers and get into space, where they could bluff their way onto some small ship and take it over.

<It's like the confluence of a shit plan and wishful thinking,> Angela commented on Tanis's thoughts.

<You got a better one?>

<No. I wish I did, but no.>

Ahead, a plascrete barrier lay across the sidewalk and part of the road. A dozen bodies were strewn around it—the local police force, by their uniforms.

Brandt reached it first and crouched low, looking over the weapons laying on the ground. She seemed to find something she liked, then tossed a pulse rifle to Tanis.

Like a pulse rifle is going to stop heavily armored soldiers.

<Better than nothing,> Brandt shrugged as the wind began to pick up further.

Tanis nodded and considered grabbing more weapons—like the flash grenades sitting in a case—but they'd just make her stand out more. Even the pulse rifle could be a giveaway, if she didn't keep it out of sight.

The spiderbots showed no enemy action on the street level, though it was impossible to see into the thousands of windows stretching high into the night sky.

They covered two more blocks. Brandt was five meters ahead of Tanis, checking around a corner, when the heavens finally opened up, and sheets of rain joined the wind.

Their stealth systems dropped to only fifteen percent effective.

Brandt pulled back from the corner, but it was too late. A rail shot pierced her abdomen, spraying blood and bone out behind her. Another shot streaked through the night and hit Tanis in the leg, blowing a hole through her armor before exiting the back of her thigh.

Both women fell to the ground, and Tanis reached for Brandt, dragging her backward.

Behind them was an open archway, and Tanis pulled Brandt in with her as the commandant's armor tried to seal the large hole and stop the bleeding.

"What…what I wouldn't give for a simple can of biofoam," Brandt wheezed, grinning at Tanis.

"Fuck!" Tanis screamed looking around for something, *anything,* to help her friend. If only she had some flowmetal left. That would seal Brandt's wound back up without a problem.

Tanis's own leg wound had been sealed by her flow armor, though instead of covering the hole, it flowed through it, sealing the wound, but leaving a clear view of the ground through her leg.

It felt surreal, and she said to Angela, *<That's not something you see every day.>*

<Brandt,> Angela cautioned. *<Your armor's failing. It's losing integrity from trying to seal your wound.>*

Brandt reached out, grasping Tanis's shoulder. "Give me the 'nades."

"What?" Tanis gasped. "Brandt. No. It won't end like this."

Brandt nodded. "Not for you, Admiral, not for you. I'll just slow you down. You always were a lone wolf, anyway."

Tanis pursed her lips and handed Brandt the grenades. "I'll come back."

"Don't, Tanis. Remember me like this. Tell my girls…tell them I'm proud of them, and that I'll always love them."

Tanis was glad her flow armor blocked tears, or they'd be clouding her vision.

"I will," Tanis said hoarsely.

"And you give 'em hell," Brandt coughed. "All of them. Fucking Niets, Trisilieds, Orion, you crush them to dust."

"I will," Tanis whispered. "The Niets are going to pay for this."

"They're coming," Brandt wheezed.

<We have to go!> Angela shouted in Tanis's mind, and Tanis took off without a second glance, smashing through the door behind them and racing through the building toward its rear exit. Before she made it through, she heard a scream followed by a muffled *thud* from behind her.

Tanis clenched her jaw and kept running.

It was just her and Angela now.

* * * * *

Rain sleeted off the sides of the buildings falling to the streets in solid sheets of water. As if that wasn't enough, the storm was increasing in intensity.

Rika had heard of these coastal storms before. On Pyra, they called them 'cyclones', atmospheric monsters that could cover half a continent and drop decimeters of rain in a matter of hours.

Already, the city's sewers were backing up, water pooling in the gutters.

<Pumps are probably out,> Niki said. *<Or the Niets killed them on purpose so the water would flood out any remaining citizens.>*

<That sounds more like them,> Rika replied as she signaled for the SMI-2 mech ahead of her—Keli, from the readout on Rika's HUD—to check the street to the right, while she and Kelly went left.

Breaking her teams up into groups of only three felt risky, but they had several square kilometers of dense urban sprawl to cover. They'd never find Admiral Richards and General Mill if they stayed grouped up.

It would also make them an easy target for the Niets. She wasn't sure if they'd drop starfire in the storm, but Rika didn't want to give them a big target to hit.

<*I heard something,*> Keli called back. <*Sounded like an explosion.*>

<*Sure it's not lightning?*> Kelly asked.

<*Yeah, that sounds like a crack, not a snap.*>

<*Lead on,*> Rika directed.

Keli led them for two blocks before they reached an arched entrance into a low building. Body parts were strewn all around the archway, rainwater running red as it rushed to the gutters.

Rika could make out Nietzschean armor, and then saw an arm covered with the matte grey flow armor the ISF Marines wore.

Rika pulled off a bit of flesh from the limb and stepped under the arch and into the building beyond. Out of the wind and rain, she slid the skin into a small slot on her arm and surveyed the building while the DNA test ran.

Keli came in a moment later, moving further back in the building while Kelly covered the entrance.

<*Only looks like enough for one non-Niet body out there.*> Kelly said, looking back at Rika for a moment.

<*DNA matches one of the records Pricilla gave us. Commandant Brandt.*>

<*Shit,*> Kelly swore. <*That's one of their uppity ups. Fresh, though, right?*>

<*Got a smashed door here,*> Keli called from the back of the building. <*Someone passed through.*>

Rika considered passing the details to Priscilla and Colonel Smith, but she didn't want to risk any broadcast comms until they knew who they were following.

<*OK, let's keep moving,*> Rika instructed.

DARKEST HOUR

STELLAR DATE: 08.27.8949 (Adjusted Years)
LOCATION: Jersey City, Pyra
REGION: Albany System, Thebes, Septhian Alliance

Tanis fired a pulse shot at another Niet before shifting back into cover behind the pile of rubble in the building's atrium. She could see that the shot knocked him off his feet, but didn't take him out.

A red light flashed on her rifle, and its small display read, 'no charge'.

<*Well, time to do this the old-fashioned way.*>

<*Give 'em hell, Tanis.*>

She rose from behind the rubble and tossed the rifle aside before sliding her lightwand out of her right thigh. She flicked her wrist, activating its new, meter-long, monofilament blade.

"Bring it, fuckers."

The Nietzschean soldier struggled to his feet, and Tanis summoned the remains of her strength, let out a scream, and charged the man.

He brought his rifle to bear and fired a kinetic round as she closed the gap.

The shot struck her in the right side of her chest, and Tanis shrugged off the impact, though a warning flashed on her HUD that her armor's kinetic resistance abilities were nearly dead. One more shot like that, and she'd be on heart number eight.

<*Nine, Tanis.*> Angela commented.

Then Tanis was upon the man and swung her glowing blue blade at his rifle, slicing it in half—along with his hand—and then cutting halfway through his neck.

Good enough, Tanis thought as he fell to the ground.

She saw movement from her left, and dove out of the way as a pulse blast rippled through the air where she'd stood. Her limbs leaden with fatigue, Tanis scrambled behind a pillar, waiting for the shooter to get closer.

With the meager few probes Tanis had left, she saw that it was a Nietzschean woman, tall and lithe. She moved into the atrium, advancing on Tanis's cover.

Tanis slowly sucked in a deep breath and blew it out quietly, then ducked out from behind the column when the woman was three meters away, rolled over a fallen beam, and sliced into the woman's left knee joint.

As the Nietzschean crashed to the ground, she fired a kinetic slug into the air, striking the windows at the far end of the atrium.

For a moment, Tanis thought the glass would hold; then the windows exploded inward, spraying fractured plates of glass across the atrium. Tanis turned her head as shards swept across her body, most bounding off, but some slicing into her where the flow armor had begun to fail.

One moment, the storm was outside, and then the next, its fury was all around her.

Tanis crashed to her knees, feeling the last of her energy ebb away, draining out of her through the hundred cuts across her body.

As she struggled to catch her breath, she realized that the storm sounded different, almost as though it was screaming at her. Tanis slowly raised her head and saw a dozen Nietzscheans surrounding her, their weapons drawn.

She opened her mouth to speak, but something felt wrong inside of her.

<Angela, I feel—>

It was Angela. Angela was gone, her centuries-long presence snuffed out.

<Angela! Where are you?> Tanis cried out in her mind, feeling dizzy and wondering if she'd suffered a head wound. She sat back on her shins, the Nietzscheans forgotten. She lifted her right hand to touch her head, but stopped, afraid that she'd find a part of her skull smashed in.

You said we'd be together, that if this was our end, it would be our end ***together****.*

A boot lashed out and kicked Tanis in the head, and she fell to the ground.

Her vision swam, and then everything went black.

I am Angela, she thought.

And I am Tanis.

No. I am new.

She hadn't opened her eyes, but she was staring at…at something. Was it the ground? It looked strange, it was so porous. Kilometers of transparent rock, and then beyond that, glowing, molten magma, caverns of hyper-dense carbon crystals, seething iron, falling chunks of crust, gently drifting to the planet's core like leaves, creating rising magma flows…and then the crust of the world again, followed by sky, and space, ships, and stars.

What is this? She wondered, and pressed her hand against the world, only to have it pass through the ground.

She felt a moment of pure terror, fearing that she'd fall through the world and out the other side, or worse, be trapped in its core forever.

This new being concentrated and pressed its hand against the planet, and this time they met, and the planet moved away. No. She moved up. But the planet *did* also move away, if only a very little.

Sounds began to come back to her. She heard the storm—winds raging, lightning cracking, thunder rumbling.

The being looked up at the sky and saw right through it, into space. She felt like she might fall up forever; maybe she could catch hold of a starship, if she did.

Then something moved, pushing toward her.

The being, *Tangel,* she decided for now—though a better name would have to come—realized it was a pulse wave, a concussive blast rippling through the air toward her.

It was curious. Such a small amount of energy. She let it pass through her body, changing the composition of her form to vibrate in a way that posed no obstacle to the wave.

She looked up to see the people. Nietzscheans. *Enemies.*

One was holding a weapon, looking down at it as though something was wrong.

Tangel peered at the weapon, too. She saw all its components, its molecules, atoms, electrons…smaller things, too. She supposed they were all the bits Earnest was always playing with. Wimps, mesons, quarks, and the like.

She stretched out her hand and changed them, turning the weapon into dust, shifting the energy from within the atomic and subatomic bonds into herself.

The world around her became clearer as strength returned. She could see through things, but she could see new things, too. So many more planes and angles. She saw that flat surfaces were made up of impossibly complex objects, all coursing with strange energy that seemed to both push things together and pull them apart.

Is this what Cary sees when she deep-Links with Faleena? Tangel wondered.

There was more yelling, and Tangel realized the Nietzscheans were still there. Half were afraid, the other half were angry.

I've been staring right through them…

The Nietzscheans advanced, and Tangel clenched her jaw. She still had a jaw.

"Stop," Tangel said, and the Nietzscheans all froze. Not because she'd removed their ability to move, but because of how loud her voice was. Tanis felt like she'd spoken on every frequency all at once.

This is going to take some practice.

She tapped into the energy she saw pushing and pulling at the foundations of reality and drew it toward her, wrapping it around herself like a cocoon. It would keep her safe. Safe from the storm and from these soldiers who wanted to hurt her.

One of them was raising his rifle, and Tangel did the same to it as she had done to the previous weapon, removing all the energy from within it, and drawing it into herself.

She reached out to gesture for the soldiers to move aside, and remembered that she only had one arm.

That won't do, Tangel thought with a laugh.

Matter rose from the ground, streamed from the weapons the soldiers held, even from their armor.

She stopped short of drawing matter from the soldiers' bodies. Something felt wrong about that. She considered removing the energy from their bodies—like she had done to the weapons—but that felt wrong, too.

The matter drew toward her, and then coalesced into a new arm. Tangel looked down at it and flexed her fingers, peering intently at her digits. Were they organic? No. They were not quite like the other organic parts of her body. But they weren't non-organic, either.

What have I made? she wondered.

Tangel spotted her lightwand laying on the ground, and a memory resonated through her mind.

'Pry it from my cold, dead hands.'

She pushed past the Nietzscheans. Well, half pushed, half walked through them, and reached for her lightwand. As she did, small bits of debris exploded around her, and Tangel realized the Nietzscheans were all firing on her.

With a sigh, she disassembled their weapons, and then their armor, leaving them naked in the storm. Some of them screamed and ran, some backed quietly into corners, a few fell where they were.

Tangel ignored them and walked out of the atrium and into the storm, summoning a sphere of energy around her, watching the water sluice off it to the ground.

She looked up and down the street. She still had to get to a dropship and fly out of here. For a moment, Tangel considered that she might be able to simply fall up as she feared. Could she fall up and fly into space?

A deep breath made her consider that her body may still require oxygen to survive. Best not to chance it right now.

Yelling came from her left, and Tangel saw more Niets. These ones had heavy armor and railguns, and they began to fire at her, the accelerated particles and kinetics striking the protective sphere around her and turning into nothing.

No, not 'nothing'; the sphere was turning the matter into energy, and that was going into her body.

***Too** much energy*, she realized. Though she seemed to exist beyond the physical realm she was used to, her body was still constructed of normal matter and could not store an infinite amount of energy.

She had to discharge it somehow, in some form.

Much of the energy she held was in the form of photons and highly excited electrons. She could drop the electrons into the ground, or she could send them back at the Nietzscheans who were attacking her.

Tangel chose the latter, and a blue-white blast of energy poured out of the sphere surrounding her, burning away the enemy, as well as the buildings around them.

She felt a sense of satisfaction to see the power they'd directed at her sent back to them, but then realized she couldn't stop the blast. It kept going, sucking away all her energy, leaving her weak.

The process she'd initiated began to convert matter to energy, consuming her flow armor, the energy holding its atoms together now coming apart and flowing out toward the enemy that was long since burned to ash.

"Stop!" she screamed, but it wouldn't stop. Then, just when she thought that her body might be consumed and turn to dust as well, the blast ceased, and the sphere around her disappeared.

In an instant, the storm slammed back into Tanis's naked body, and she fell to the ground, unconscious.

ISF FIRST FLEET

STELLAR DATE: 08.27.8949 (Adjusted Years)
LOCATION: ISS *I2*, Bridge
REGION: Inner Albany System, Thebes, Septhian Alliance

If it wasn't for the fact that she was worried sick about Tanis and Brandt—not to mention Priscilla, Colonel Smith, and the Marines—Rachel would have been reveling in the fact that she was in command of a fleet.

And not just the First Intrepid Fleet, with its few dozen ships, but a *real* fleet.

A thousand ships were arrayed around the *I2*, organized in sub-formations where ships with stasis shields could offer protection to those without.

Beyond the thousand visible ships, another two thousand stealthed cruisers advanced above and below the star system's equatorial plane. But the enemy had no knowledge of those ships.

To the Nietzscheans, it must have appeared as though the attackers were insane. A thousand ships against seventy thousand was unheard of. At least for them.

Rachel watched the Comm team shunt another segment of traffic off to the secondary team one deck down. With so many ships still fleeing the system, the ISF had turned into the de facto space traffic control for the outer Albany System.

Stations and planets had begun deferring to the inbound ISF fleet for vector confirmation a day ago, and now they were asking about everything from when it would be safe to send more ships out, to what they should do with inbound traffic that was low on fuel, and had to dock somewhere.

Someone had even asked if they could find their missing dog on Pyra.

The volume was running everyone ragged, and Rachel was considering leaving a ship in the outer system with a team of traffic and logistics specialists aboard, just to coordinate the locals.

Even so, she didn't blame the people of Albany. Until two weeks ago, they didn't know ships *could* jump deep inside a system. They had never seen a fleet the size of the one now occupying their space, and they'd *certainly* never seen a fleet outnumbered seventy-to-one advance and not retreat.

Granted, neither had Rachel.

Organizing the fleet had not been easy. The forces sent from far and wide came with their own command structure, some of whom outranked Rachel considerably. Amongst the assembled ships were an admiral, two generals, and a host of colonels.

Though her title was 'captain', Rachel's own actual rank was that of colonel. However, the honor of having one's butt in the *I2*'s command chair far outweighed any rank.

At one point, the admiral and two of the colonels had attempted to take control of the fleet's strategy away from Rachel. It had been a tense period, but Sera had sent directives over the QuanComm network that she was in charge, and that her orders were backed up by Admirals Evans and Greer—even Empress Diana.

Joe had included a private message, telling her that sitting in the command chair of the *I2* was a de facto promotion to admiral.

The compliment from Admiral Evans had made her all but glow with pride—and worry that he was probably nuts, to put so much on her.

Not your first time out, Rachel admonished herself. *Not your first time at the helm of* ***this*** *ship in a pitched fight, either.*

"We've crossed the first marker," Scan called out.

The first marker denoted passage into the sector where they were in range of relativistic missiles with no time for fleet-wide evasion. Granted, there could have been RMs lying in wait further back, but now they were also at risk of live fire.

The stealthed ships, broken into four groups, were already well beyond the first marker; by the time Rachel's main formation reached the second marker, they would be almost at Pyra.

When the *I2* passed the third marker, all hell would break loose.

"Fire control, instruct Fleet Group One to begin random fire, pattern alpha."

"Aye, ma'am."

A smattering of ships in the fleet—a selection of Scipian, Silstrand, and TSF vessels—fired railguns at the Nietzschean ships in orbit around Pyra.

No one expected the shots to hit, but it would cause the enemy to spread out and decrease their ability to bring concentrated firepower to bear on single targets.

After a few minutes, the random railgun fire ceased. It would still take thirty minutes for the shots to reach the enemy, but it would create, she hoped, an image of an undisciplined, ragtag force.

The next nineteen minutes were filled with nothing but waiting for the enemy's reaction to the incoming shots. Then they saw groups of Nietzschean vessels begin to shift further out from Pyra, until over half of them were beyond the orbits of Pyra's two moons.

"Cautious. Too bad." A voice said from Rachel's left, and she nearly jumped.

"Finaeus," she breathed as she glanced at the man. "Scared the crap out of me!"

"It's a talent, I won't lie. Sadly, there's not a lot of call for stealthy engineers."

Rachel couldn't help but smile. Finaeus was the very definition of 'unflappable'. Perhaps it was because he'd seen so much, lived through so much, that nothing fazed him anymore.

Still, she was surprised that he was able to be so calm while looking out over the enemy ships.

"What do you make of our odds?" she asked quietly.

Finaeus snorted. "One hundred percent. These dickheads don't stand a chance."

"Not worried at all?"

Finaeus leaned against a console—earning an annoyed look from Major Jessie, which he appeared to not even notice. "Did I ever tell you about Star City?"

"I heard Tanis say the name once, but that was about it."

"We're trying to keep the place hush-hush and not let remnants or ascended AIs know about it—if they don't already. Which I think they do. Anyway, we know the *I2* is clear of remnants, so I'll lay it on you. Star City is out in Orion Space, in the Perseus Arm. And it's old, over three thousand years."

"Really?" Rachel asked. "How—"

Finaeus held up his hand, cutting her off. "Story for another time. Anyway, Star City has sixteen bastions, which have the most amazing AIs ever—also a story for another time—protecting it. We were having a little visit, when Orion launched a *major* assault on the city. They threw over a hundred thousand ships at it."

Rachel whistled. "I had no idea."

"Yeah, well, neither did Orion. Guess how many ships Star City had?"

Rachel shrugged. "Ummm…two hundred thousand?"

"Zero."

"Zero?"

"Yeah. Am I doing that thing where I think words, but forget to say them? Zero."

She rolled her eyes at her chief engineer. "Ha ha, Finaeus. Get on with it."

"Well, see, the thing is Star City had a plan, tactics, and superior technology. They knew how to use it, and they won the day. Guess how many casualties they had?"

"Finaeus, I hate guessing games."

"C'mon."

"I don't know…zero."

"Right you are!" Finaeus crowed. "No one died. Jessica came close, but in the end, no one did. The Orion fleet was *utterly* destroyed. To the last ship."

"How in the stars did they do that?" Major Jessie asked, apparently having forgiven Finaeus for leaning against her console.

"Classified," Finaeus replied. "But fret not. Earnest and I are working on a way to miniaturize what they sorted out. And when we do…"

"Yes…?" Rachel prompted.

"Blammo!" Finaeus shouted. "Game over, bad guys."

"You have such a way with words."

Finaeus gave a mock bow. "I try."

"So you're not worried about this at all?" Rachel waved a hand at the forward display to indicate the enemy ships.

"*Nietzscheans?* Are you kidding? Those guys are as dumb as rocks. I mean, don't get me wrong, Nietzsche had some good ideas, but he was a nineteenth century philosopher. Trying to take his precepts and blanket apply them to the ninetieth century? Build a civilization around it? These guys must eat stupid for breakfast."

"And Tanis?" Rachel asked.

For an instant, Rachel thought she saw a look of concern flash across Finaeus's face, then it was gone. "I'm worried about what she'll do to the Niets."

Something about the way Finaeus said those words felt wrong to Rachel. She wondered if it had anything to do with the reason both Bob and Finaeus had insisted that they send Priscilla with Colonel Smith's strike team.

She was about to ask, when Scan called out, "A section of the enemy's fleet is breaking off. They're on a trajectory to flank us."

Rachel glanced at Finaeus. "Looks like they didn't eat too much stupid today. That's the tactic we rated as best for them and worst for us."

"Only if they commit a third of their force to—OK, they've committed a third. Must have been Stupid-Lite today."

<Fleet Group Three,> Rachel called out to the ships on the right flank. *<Fire rails, Sigma pattern.>*

<Sigma pattern, Aye,> Fleet Group Three's fire control responded. Their NSAI configured optimal patterns, which were then confirmed by humans and AIs alike.

Fleet Group Three fired their rails, and hundreds of five-ton slugs streaked out from the ships toward where the Nietzschean vessels moving to the ISF's right flank would be in ten minutes.

Tanis and the fleet tacticians believed that word of the ISF's use of grapeshot had spread amongst Orion's allies by now. While still brutally effective, it was likely that its tactical usefulness was diminished.

To counter this, the fleet engineers had come up with a new rail-fired weapon system that—hopefully—would take the enemy by surprise.

"This should be good," Finaeus said as they watched the slugs creep across the holotank's display toward the enemy ships.

Scan showed the Nietzschean vessels moving aside, creating gaps in their formation for the slugs to pass through.

"Poor Neaties. Not moving enough," Rachel said with a smile.

" 'Neaties'?" Finaeus asked, a brow raised.

Rachel shrugged. " 'Niets' makes me think of nits, which is gross. It also makes them sound all tidy. The dichotomy doesn't work in my head. Trying out a new name."

Major Jessie gave a soft laugh. "Try again."

Rachel glanced at her XO, and then turned back to the holos. One side of the main tank showed projections, while the other showed actuals.

The projection estimated that over five hundred enemy ships would take damage from the shots. A nice opening salvo.

The slugs were traveling at ten thousand kilometers per second, and when they passed within twenty-thousand klicks of the enemy fleet, they exploded.

Actuals tagged thousands of impacts on the Nietzschean ships, most being deflected by shields, but the ships closest to the shrapnel bore the brunt of the impact. Twenty-nine enemy vessels lost power, and three exploded seconds later.

When the shots hit, a soft cheer sounded on the bridge, and Rachel smiled. This crew knew what it was doing and was determined to see their mission through and rescue Tanis.

Fleet Group Three fired again, and this time, the enemy formation scattered wide, spreading out to avoid the shots entirely.

She almost felt bad for the Nietzscheans.

SAVING HER

STELLAR DATE: 08.27.8949 (Adjusted Years)
LOCATION: Jersey City, Pyra
REGION: Albany System, Thebes, Septhian Alliance

A brilliant light streamed out from around a corner ahead, lighting up the city like it was noon. No. Brighter than noon. It seemed to be shining away from them, and Rika signaled for Keli and Kelly to follow her.

She reached the corner, which was occupied by a store selling a selection of soft and colorful bedding supplies, and peered around to see a star resting in the middle of the street.

At least, that's what it looked like at first.

A beam of blue-white light that reminded Rika of an electron beam shot from the star down the street—in the other direction, thankfully—burning its way through Jersey City, and clear over to a large hill outside of town, where lightning streaked from the ground into the sky.

<*Shit, what is that?*> Kelly asked.

<*They'll be able to see it from space!*> Keli exclaimed.

<*Is that some sort of fusion reaction?*> Rika asked Niki, who did not reply.

Then the light went out, and the sphere disappeared. In its place stood a naked woman. Her body wobbled side to side, and then went limp, collapsing to the ground.

Rika didn't give a moment's thought to her own safety as she rushed across the street and knelt beside the woman.

She was curled up in a fetal position, and Rika tried to turn her over. At first, her hand slipped off the woman's shoulder—or maybe went through it—but then Rika managed to find purchase and roll her over.

<*It's Admiral Richards!*> Niki exclaimed. <*What the hell did she just do?*>

<Beats me,> Rika muttered, unable to make sense of what she saw. Admiral Richards appeared to be completely unharmed, yet moments ago, she had been standing in a ball of energy more powerful than a starship's beams.

"We have to get her out of here!" Rika yelled. "Kelly, break into that store we just passed and get something to wrap her in, she's freezing."

She knew she didn't have to speak aloud, but she just felt like yelling.

Kelly was back a moment later with a large comforter that was soft on one side and covered in a shiny polymer on the other.

"Should keep the rain off," Kelly said as they wrapped Tanis in it. Once she was cocooned, Rika slung the admiral over her shoulder.

<Priscilla, do you read me?>

<I do! Did you see that light?> Priscilla's voice sounded worried—very worried.

<See it? We watched it blow away half the city. Then we found Tanis Richards where the light was.>

<You've got her? Stars! We're close, we'll meet you. We need to get the ships to pick us up; the Niets are going to come fast.>

As if Priscilla's words were prescient, Kelly and Keli both began firing uranium sabot rounds at Niets who were advancing down the street behind them.

<You're telling me! Where are you?>

<A block to your east. The Marines are coming.>

Rika turned east while Keli and Kelly covered her back. Suddenly, dark shapes appeared all around her, a dozen kinetic slug throwers lobbing HE rounds at the Nietzscheans.

Rika felt Tanis slip out of her arms, even though she was held securely.

"What the—"

"Hold still," one of the figures said, and Rika saw flow armor pull away from a face, revealing Priscilla.

Rika stopped as Priscilla pulled down the blanket, exposing Tanis's face.

"Stars, she looks perfect," Priscilla said. "Totally unharmed."

"Yeah, but what was that? Did she do that? How?"

<*It was a controlled…I don't know, matter-energy stripping reaction,*> Niki supplied. <*That should have blown away the entire city.*>

Priscilla didn't respond, but touched Tanis's head. Rika saw something flow from her hand into Tanis, and a moment later, the admiral felt heavier, as though part of her that had not been present before, now was.

"What did you do?" Rika asked. "More importantly, what did *she* do?"

<*Rika,*> Priscilla spoke only into Rika's mind. <*You must forget what you saw, speak of it to no one.*>

<*What?*> Rika asked, and Niki added. <*We can't just unsee that!*>

<*You must!*> Priscilla said. <***No one*** *can know.*>

<*Why?*> Niki asked.

<*Because.*> Priscilla looked down and stroked Tanis's forehead. <*She's ascending.*>

COMING UP

STELLAR DATE: 08.28.8949 (Adjusted Years)
LOCATION: Jersey City, Pyra
REGION: Albany System, Thebes, Septhian Alliance

Rika hung out the back of the dropship and fired her electron beam at the closest pursuer, a vacuum fighter that was struggling through the heavy winds of the cyclone tearing its way across the coast.

Her shot dissipated in the thick rain, but enough of the energy struck his port engine—for the third time—to finally knock him out of the pursuit.

Not that Rika's dropships were doing much better. Ferris was fighting the controls, screaming at the wind, his heavy load, Nietzschean engineering, and anything else that came to mind.

As if on cue, he started up another rant. "Oh, more fucking red indicators. *I know* our rear grav drive is losing power, the holes in the hull were my first clue, you piece of shit! Your mother was a Nietzschean garbage dump!"

Rika glanced back to where Priscilla sat with Tanis. Both were strapped into their seats, and Priscilla's arm was wrapped around Tanis's shoulders, keeping her head tucked close against her body.

She tried not to think about Captain Ayer and General Mill. They didn't know exactly *what* had happened to the general, but Priscilla had gotten onto the Nietzschean networks where there were records of his body being found.

Rika stared down at Jersey City. She'd be back to retrieve his body and give it a proper burial in space.

The ship bucked again, and Rika tightened her grip on the hull ribbing, then breathed a sigh of relief as the rain suddenly stopped and the clouds began to thin. A moment later, the raging elements dropped away below them, gently lit by the engines of thousands of starships.

<OK…for something that was really intent on killing us a second ago, that storm sure looks beautiful,> Kelly said.

Below, two more dropships pulled out of the clouds, then a third.

Stars, we all made it, Rika thought a moment before a beam streaked out of the sky, burning away one of the dropships.

"Fuck!" Ferris screamed and banked hard to port, then starboard, bucking the dropship like it was a wild animal.

Rika was nearly thrown from the ship before she slammed her GNR into the emergency switch, and the ramp swung up, slamming closed centimeters from her face.

She turned toward the front of the ship and saw starfire streak through the night, directly ahead of the shuttle, and then Ferris dove again. Signaling for Kelly and Keli to join the Marines and take a seat, she pulled herself forward to stand behind Ferris.

"Just like old times, eh, Captain?" he called out over his shoulder. "Look at that! I used rank! Go me!"

"How far?" Rika asked.

"Fucked if I know…damn ship is *invisible*!"

Another beam of starfire streaked past, and Ferris pulled the dropship up. The beam followed them, about to make contact with their hull, and then suddenly it was gone, stopped by an invisible object.

The *Derringer.*

<This is Captain Mel of the ISS Derringer. *Your chariot has arrived!>*

A light appeared on the side of the ship, and Rika realized it was a bay door opening. Ferris made a beeline for it, and Rika saw from scan that the other two dropships were hot on their tail.

The craft hadn't even finished settling onto the cradle before Captain Mel called out again. <*Hold onto your hats, it's going to get bumpy! Oh, and Captain Rika, we've updated your ships with our outbound trajectory. We're going to meet up with them when we blast through the Nietzschean lines.*>

Rika still hadn't gotten control of her breathing. Ten seconds ago, she had been certain they were all going to die. Now they were safe behind an ISF stasis shield, about to break away from the Nietzscheans.

<*'Kay,*> was all she managed to send back.

Captain Mel replied with a laugh, but didn't reply further.

Behind them, the dropship's ramp lowered, and Rika turned to see one of the ISF Marines lift Admiral Richards out of her seat and carry her off the ship.

"Will she be OK?" Rika asked Priscilla.

Priscilla stared after the admiral's retreating form for a moment before replying. "Yes, she'll be fine."

At the bottom of the ship's ramp, a woman waited, looking at the mechs disembarking from the ships.

"Captain Rika?" she asked.

Rika pulled off her helmet and slid it onto the hasp at her hip.

"Here."

The woman's eyes locked on Rika's and she nodded. "Captain Mel's asked that you come to the bridge. You can observe and coordinate with your ships from there."

Rika turned and saw Leslie descend from one of the other shuttles, a look of pure joy and relief on her face.

<*Go do captain-y things. We've got this down here,*> Leslie said with a wide grin.

Rika gave her friend an equally wide grin, relieved beyond words that Leslie hadn't been on the ship that was destroyed. The thought made her even more glad that Chase hadn't come along. She'd managed to convince him at the last moment that he'd be needed, should the *Fury Lance* get boarded during the fighting.

Rika followed the woman—Ensign Harriet, by the tag on her chest—as she led the way through the ship and up a series of ladders, until they reached the bridge.

"I can't thank you enough for saving the admiral," Harriet said at one point. "I don't know.... It doesn't bear thinking about."

The vision of the sphere encapsulating Tanis, blasting raw energy into the night and tearing a hole through the city, was all that came to Rika's mind. "No, no it doesn't."

Half a minute later, they stepped onto the bridge, and Rika saw Captain Mel, a tall, lanky woman with fluorescent yellow hair tied up in a knot on the back of her head.

"Captain Rika!" Mel said as she approached and clasped Rika's hand. "You have no idea the debt of gratitude the ISF owes you. You are, without a doubt, a hero of our people."

Rika couldn't help but think of General Mill, dead somewhere in Jersey City. The fact that he'd died ten days ago—back when she was still in the Hercules System—didn't seem to help.

He'd been a good man, good to her. A strong mentor. And now he was gone; snuffed out in a coup launched by the very people the Marauders had bled to save just a year ago.

"Thank you," Rika said quietly.

"Right, that must have been harrowing," Captain Mel said, her voice softer. Then she pointed to the holotank. "Look there. The five highlighted ships are yours. They're in a low polar orbit, right where you left them."

Rika nodded as she approached. "The Niets didn't make any problems?"

"One of their traffic control ships was getting persnickety, but then Rachel's fleet started lobbing rail shots, and everyone's focus shifted to her."

"So what's our route out of here?" Rika asked.

A plotted course appeared on the holo. "With any luck, we'll slip past most of them. If we have to, we can take a few out, but I'd prefer not to get ten-thousand ships on our tail. Stasis shields are good, but they're not that good."

"Where's the rest of your fleet?" Rika asked.

Captain Mel expanded the view, and Rika saw a cluster of ships approaching the Nietzschean formation. They were still over a million miles away, but RMs were already flying between the ISF and Nietzschean vessels.

"Once we're clear, are they going to turn and head outsystem with us?" Rika asked.

Captain Mel cocked her head and looked at Rika as though she'd said something crazy.

"Uh, no, they're going to defeat the Nietzscheans. Then we'll carry on and crush their empire—at least we'd better."

Rika couldn't help but let out disbelieving laugh. "That's…confident of you."

Captain Mel just flashed a smile and turned back to the holo. "Scan, any sign of Orion ships, or zero-point energy fields?"

"None so far, Captain Mel."

"You spot a single OG hull tucked into this mess, you get on all-fleet, you hear?"

"Aye, ma'am."

"Orion…that's the enemy Priscilla said is beyond the Orion Nebula, right?" Rika asked as she looked over the fleet formations on the holo.

"Yeah, plus just beyond half of known space. Orion's big, stretches into the Perseus Arm."

"Seriously?" Rika asked, certain that the captain was messing with her.

Mel waved her hand. "Not important right now. What *is* important is that they have good stealth tech. Not as good as ours, but damn hard to pick up. I don't *think* they're out there, but if they are, I want to be ready."

"Why don't you think they're there?"

Mel turned and locked her eyes on Rika's. "The Admiral, Captain Rika. If the Orion Guard knew she was crashed on that planet, they would have done one of two things."

"Which are?"

"Completely blanket the planet's surface with troops to capture her…or destroy it. They would *not* have left it to the Niets."

Rika wondered if Captain Mel had an extreme case of hero worship. "They'd destroy an entire planet to capture or kill Admiral Richards?"

Mel nodded, and Rika saw that other members of the bridge crew did, as well.

"Why—" she began to ask, but Mel held up her hand.

"It's begun."

Rika saw the ISF fleet's forward elements move into range of the Nietzschean ships. She didn't understand what the ISF, which she assumed was under the command of Captain Rachel on the *I2*, had planned.

The leading edge of the Niet fleet was spread wide, and a second group—which was on the ISF's right flank—was also distributed over a huge volume of space.

Rika suspected that the enemy had dispersed to avoid long-range shots, but now they were coalescing into a half-sphere, wrapping around the ISF ships. In a minute, over thirty thousand Nietzschean vessels would be within firing range of the *I2*.

Rika wondered why Captain Mel looked expectant. She should be terrified.

Beams lanced out from the Nietzschean ships, all targeting the *I2*. In an instant, the massive ISF ship disappeared in a blazing ball of light, its glow dwarfing that of the Albany System's star.

For all her bluster, Rika saw Captain Mel suck in a breath.

"Coming up on the Nietzscheans' polar line," a bridge officer announced behind them.

Rika turned her attention to a secondary holotank.

"You have a tightbeam to your flagship, Captain Rika," the Comm officer said.

<*Chase, Heather, you there?*> Rika asked.

<*You bet, Rika. How'd it go down there?*> Chase asked.

Rika didn't want to get into the details at the moment, and only said, <*Well enough. We're boosting past you. They've passed the coordinates.*>

<*We'll follow after,*> Heather spoke up. <*But the Niets are already suspicious of us. They're going to think we're deserting.*>

<*OK, let me see what we can do,*> Rika replied.

"Captain Mel, my crew is worried that the enemy will fire on them if they break formation."

Mel stroked her chin for a moment. "Valid." She turned to an officer on her left. "Flicker the stealth for a second so that the enemy doesn't think Rika's ships are deserting."

"Aye, Captain."

<*See that?*> Rika asked.

<*Ballsy!*> Heather replied. <*Though not as much as the* I2 *out there.*>

<*OK, we're coming after you,*> Chase said. <*Stay safe.*>

<*You too,*> Rika replied.

During the conversation, Rika had kept one eye on the ball of light that was the *I2*. She did, however, remember to thank Captain Mel for making her ship visible—however briefly—to the enemy.

"Welcome," Mel nodded calmly in response.

"Aren't you worried?" Rika asked, gesturing to the *I2*. "Your flagship is being annihilated!"

"That ball of energy means that everything they're throwing at it is being shed off by the stasis shield. If the ball goes away, *then* it's bad."

"Bad because they blew up?" Rika asked.

Captain Mel shook her head. "No, bad because they tore a hole in space-time, and this entire star system will probably cease to exist."

Rika's mouth was hanging open again, and she looked around the bridge. "Who *are* you people?"

Mel snapped her fingers and pointed at the holo.

While the Niets were pouring all their weapons into the *I2,* the rest of the ISF fleet began to respond, firing on Nietzschean ships in successive waves, their high-powered beams cutting right through the enemy's shields and shredding their ships.

Even though they had little trouble destroying the enemy, the ISF fleet was small, and they were barely making a dent on the enemy forces.

A moment later, the barrage hitting the *I2* ceased, and the ship's shields glowed brightly for another few seconds before returning to their normal transparent state.

The *I2* was unscathed.

Cheers erupted around Rika, and she was at a total loss for words.

<*Now* ***that's*** *a new thing,*> Niki commented.

"And…here they are," Captain Mel said, turning to Rika with a look of triumph in her eyes.

Rika looked back at the holo and saw two things happen almost simultaneously.

The first was that two thousand ships appeared on the far side of Pyra, well behind the Nietzschean lines, and were accelerating toward the enemy. As Rika watched, the ships closed within weapons range, and their beams began tearing through shields and ships in rapid succession.

Rika felt a thrill in her chest at the sight of it, but there were still too many Nietzscheans, and they began to concentrate fire on the smaller ISF ships.

At a thousand to one, they could breach the ISF ships' shields, and they did so a dozen times within seconds. Rika began to worry that the tactic would fail.

But then the battlespace changed entirely.

At first, Rika thought that the holotank had suffered a failure, as it seemed to show that the number of Nietzschean ships had doubled.

"They're here!" Mel cried out, and the bridge erupted in cheers.

"Who?" Rika asked.

Mel gestured at the roughly forty thousand new ships interspersed amongst the Nietzscheans. "Just about everybody, from the looks of it."

With the Nietzscheans spread wide, no more than three to four ships could bring meaningful fire to bear on the newcomers—who were all protected by stasis shields, easily shrugging off the meager attacks.

Tears formed in the corners of Rika's eyes as she watched the new ships begin to tear into the enemy, their brilliant beams slicing through the Niets like they were made of foil.

"What's wrong?" Mel asked Rika.

Rika drew in a steadying breath and she gestured at the holotank. "All my life, this was the thing I feared most." Her voice came as a whisper, and she took another breath, speaking louder as she continued. "The vaunted Nietzschean Space Force. They were unstoppable. A fleet this size was the stuff of nightmares, yet here they are, falling by the thousands."

Rika gave a self-deprecating laugh and then shrugged off her concern over being so emotional before strangers. "It may be one of the most beautiful things I've ever seen."

Mel didn't even miss a beat as she barked a laugh and slapped Rika on the back. "Rika? You're my kinda woman."

FALLEN

STELLAR DATE: 08.28.8949 (Adjusted Years)
LOCATION: ISS *I2*, Bridge
REGION: Inner Albany System, Thebes, Septhian Alliance

Rachel felt sweat pouring down her head as the Nietzscheans continued to fire on the *I2*.

The great vessel was wrapped in a fire hotter than the corona of a B-class star. Protons, electrons, and neutrons ceased to exist as they stopped instantaneously, halted by the *I2*'s shields.

The energy shed from atomic particles' relativistic speeds' instant cessation tore them apart, reflecting degenerate matter and quantum particles in all directions.

The nearby ISF ships were protected by the deadly wave of ricocheting energy by their own stasis shields. But as the energy reflecting off the *I2* spread back out toward the Nietzschean ships, they would soon find that their shields were being weakened by *their* own weapons fire.

Or so Rachel hoped.

<*We're reaching critical thresholds on the CriEn system,*> Bob advised. <*I will have to shut them down in seventy-two seconds.*>

Rachel nodded. At that point, their only hope would be to drop into the dark layer. Current maps indicated that there *should* be a pocket right here, but no one kept detailed public maps of dark matter this deep in a star system. Normally, there was no need to.

It was a terrible gamble, but one they'd all gladly make to save Tanis.

<*Understood, Bob,*> Rachel replied.

No one spoke for another thirty seconds; all eyes were on the CriEn shutdown timer.

Then came the words they all craved hearing.

"Enemy fire has ceased!" Scan cried out, triggering sighs of relief around the bridge.

Rachel still couldn't see the battlespace, but that was expected. The shields—and the space around them—would take a moment to cool off and bleed away enough EM radiation to see through.

"We have imaging!" Scan called out again, and visuals from beyond the shield began to filter in through pinhole sensor openings. Widening the sensor holes any further would bathe the ship in radiation.

The imaging was weak, and tactical NSAIs worked to plot out where all the enemy ships were.

"Mostly unmoved," Finaeus observed.

"But where are the stealthed groups?" Rachel murmured.

Then scan detected them behind the Nietzscheans, as they opened fire on the enemy's rear. Rachel signaled the forward elements of the fleet to begin their full assault as well, but not to use any kinetics. The battlespace around the Nietzscheans needed to remain as clear as possible.

More ships began to appear in the midst of the Nietzschean fleet. Not directly amongst the enemy, but as close as fifty thousand kilometers above and below the Nietzschean formations.

"Today's precision jumping is brought to you by the QuanComm network," Finaeus said with a laugh.

"How many blades did we burn up doing all this?" Rachel asked her engineer.

"You don't want to know," Finaeus replied.

Rachel disagreed with his sentiment, but if it was a critical level, he wouldn't sound so cavalier. She glanced at the ancient terraformer. *Or maybe he would.*

<We disentangled the quantum coupling in seventeen percent of our blades,> Bob informed Rachel. *<An acceptable amount for this victory.>*

Rachel agreed. Honestly, she would have burned them all up, if it meant saving Tanis.

"Scan, anything from the *Derringer*?"

"No, ma'am. We'll not be able to see them with all the EM and crap out here." The Scan officer was about to say something else, but his eyes widened. "Yes! They're here!"

The holotank updated to show three massive ships in the battlespace. The *Carthage, Canaan's Sword,* and the *Starblade.* Three Intrepid Class battle platforms, all with the same shields and weapons as the *I2*. One above Pyra, and the other two close to the main Nietzschean formation.

"Release the fighters." Rachel ordered.

A hundred thousand fighters, though well over half were NSAI-controlled drones, swept out of the ISF ships and onto the battlespace.

But there was still no sign of the *Derringer.*

"Ma'am," Scan called out. "I don't see our ship, but the five Marauder-controlled vessels have broken off from the formation over Pyra. It looks like they're chasing something.

Rachel closed her eyes and felt Finaeus's hand on her shoulder.

"They have her," he said, and she could hear the smile in his voice.

Bob spoke across the entire shipnet. *<She is safe.>*

THE CARTHAGE

STELLAR DATE: 08.28.8949 (Adjusted Years)
LOCATION: ISS *Carthage*, Bridge
REGION: Near Roma, New Canaan System

<All ships, prepare for jump!> Joe called out from the bridge of the *Carthage* as they hung in space near the Roma jump gates in the New Canaan system.

Arrayed around the new—and mostly complete—Intrepid Class starship were thousands of ISF vessels. As with the last major battle they'd fought, many of the ships were commanded by AIs and human skeleton crews, but he was confident it would be enough to win the day. At least, he hoped he appeared confident to his command crew.

Ahead of the *Carthage,* the jump gate came to life, negative energy coalescing in its center.

The New Canaan System only had one jump gate large enough for an Intrepid Class ship, so the others had been moved to Scipio and Silstrand. There, they too would be preparing to jump through gates left behind by the *I2*.

If it wasn't for his sickening worry over Tanis, the maneuver they were about to perform would be filling him with glee.

Thanks to the QuanComm network, they were about to exercise the largest multi-point fleet jump in known history. Forty thousand ships leaping from a thousand jump gates spread across over a hundred stars were about to leap into a crowded battlespace around one world, thousands of light years away.

Someone had better write a song about this. A ballad; this is definitely epic ballad worthy.

Joe glanced at Cary and Saanvi, who were standing beside him, before giving the order. "Helm, take us in."

"Aye, Admiral Evans. Taking us in."

The *Carthage* eased forward, and its mirror touched the not-space, hurtling the ship across the light years.

Joe counted to three, and then the universe snapped back into place around them.

"Confirmed, Albany System!" Scan called out.

"Matching stellar galactic motion," Helm announced, while Weapons confirmed that the stasis shield was online.

The holotank in the center of the bridge began to populate ships, trajectories, zones of fire, safe areas, and a hundred other notes and details, as the picture around the *Carthage* filled in.

He spotted the *I2* drifting in a sea of radiation, and relief flooded him to see the great ship in one piece, though it must have weathered a brutal assault. Elements of Rachel's fleet were hitting the Nietzschean ships from the rear, and all around, more and more allied vessels were appearing amidst the enemy.

None of that mattered to Joe. Somewhere, there would be a ship, the *Derringer*, and—stars-willing—that ship would have Tanis aboard.

He resisted the urge to ask Scan if they had seen it—he knew they would call out if so much as a hint of a stealthed ship was picked up by sensors.

"We have five Nietzschean vessels breaking off!" Scan called out. "They match the Marauder ships."

Joe nodded silently. It was a good sign, but he wasn't going to take an easy breath until he saw Tanis's face.

"There!" one of the ensigns on scan yelled. "I registered it, for just a second, the *Derringer* was there."

"Open the starboard A1 Dock doors," Joe ordered, fighting to keep his voice steady. He glanced to his side and nodded to Cary and Saanvi. "Go."

His daughters didn't need to be told twice and ran off the bridge without a second glance. Joe wished he could go with them, but there was still work to be done.

Though much of the Nietzschean fleet was engaged with the ISF and allied forces, many of the enemy ships were still close to Pyra, boosting out of the planet's gravity well, directing their engine wash onto the world below.

As the enemy fled, they were burning the planet to a cinder.

Although the strength of the ISF and their allies nearly matched that of the Nietzscheans, only the *Carthage* was within range of the enemies boosting away from Pyra. It was on them to save the people below.

"Weapons, I want a full barrage, every beam we have. Take out the engines of as many Nietzschean ships as we can. Comm, broadcast to the people on the planet to get below ground if possible. S&R, I want orbital fire suppression ships deployed the minute approach vectors are clear. We're going to save this planet."

As the first plumes of plasma began to strike Pyra's atmosphere, burning away clouds and ionizing the skies, he wondered if saving what was left of this decimated world would be harder than defeating the Nietzscheans.

* * * * *

Rika watched in awe as the *Derringer* was swallowed up by the massive ship. She'd docked in smaller space stations. *Much* smaller space stations.

The warship slid past hundreds of smaller craft, all of which appeared to be ready to disembark, but she couldn't discern why. They didn't appear to be military vessels of any sort.

"Fire suppression," Captain Mel said, nodding to the ships Rika was scowling at.

"How do they lay down suppressive fire?" Rika asked, and Mel laughed.

"No. Woman, you say the strangest things. The Niets, they've made a mess of your world down there. Now they're burning it as they boost out. Those ships are going to put out the fires that their engines make before they sweep across the entire globe. With luck, we can shift much of the radiation away from the planet, too…or at least get it to fall in the oceans, and not on land."

Rika had never considered such an operation, and she was amazed to think that these people were going to risk their lives to save the Pyrans, while simultaneously fighting the Nietzscheans.

<*We've finally fallen in with the right people,* > Niki commented.

"You're going to save the planet? Back in the…." Rika shook her head, she had to stop that thought pattern. "When we fought the Nietzscheans, they frequently used scorched world tactics. We never saved anyplace."

"Well, you've got new allies, now," Mel smiled. "Ones who care about people…even if their leadership is dumb as rocks. Your leadership, that is—not ours. Ah, look, your ships made it into the dock, too. Looks like they just got a few holes here and there. Nothing we won't be able to patch up."

Rika nodded silently. "If all is well, then, I'm going to go and join my company. Get ready for the search and rescue."

Mel glanced at Rika, her cavalier attitude gone in an instant. "I understand. Good luck."

A few minutes later, Rika stood on the *Carthage*'s dock, watching Chase and Barne drive across its vast surface in a dockcar, weaving in and out of cradles, loading towers, and gantries.

"OK…is it unreal to be in a dock that looks more like a city?" Leslie asked from Rika's side.

"I don't know, Leslie," Rika said, then laughed for a moment. "I've totally lost all sense of scale."

Leslie nodded for a moment. "You know…we always talked about taking the fight to the Niets…pushing them back from Praesepe, and then out of Genevia…."

Rika nodded. "But it always just felt like talk."

"Yeah." Leslie laughed. "It was flights of fancy, and we knew it. But this…"

"This." Rika replied, as Chase and Barne leapt off the dockcar and ran toward them. "Unconditional victory sure feels nice."

*****

Cary and Saanvi raced down the *Carthage*'s dock, driving their dockcar toward the *Derringer* at break-neck speed. Cary half expected Saanvi to tell her to slow down, but when she slacked off the accelerator at one point, Saanvi pushed it all the way forward and held it there.

Ahead, they saw some of the mechs and humans, but Cary didn't see her mother in the group and swerved around them, skidding to a halt at the base of the *Derringer's* ramp.

"There!" Saanvi pointed, and Cary saw two pale figures appear at the airlock.

The first was easy to identify as Priscilla. The second was easy as well, but that didn't make the sight any less shocking.

"Mom?" Cary whispered.

<*She looks…younger,*> Faleena said.

Their mother's steps seemed sure as she walked down the long ramp, though Priscilla had a protective arm around her. Tanis was clothed in a simple white shipsuit, over which a blanket was draped, hiding her arms.

She was safe, she was right there in front of them.

Cary wanted to touch her mother over the Link, to demand confirmation that everything was OK, but something stopped her. Something about the indomitable Tanis Richards seemed wrong. There was a strange look in her eyes, as though she were unsure of what she saw around herself.

Priscilla and Tanis reached the bottom of the ramp and stopped before Cary and Saanvi.

Their mother's skin was alabaster white, as though it had never spent a day in the sun; perfect and unblemished, like she was fresh out of rejuv.

Tanis winked at Cary before turning to Saanvi, her perfect lips curling up in a smile as her right arm slipped from the blanket to pull Saanvi into a tight embrace.

Cary felt like every nerve in her body was vibrating and she wanted to ask her mother what was wrong, why she hadn't spoken. *Is she injured?*

Priscilla appeared calm, so Cary took a deep breath and waited for her turn. A moment later, their mother released Saanvi and turned to Cary. Her eyes narrowed for a moment, as though unsure of what she was looking at. Then Tanis reached out her other hand and stroked Cary's cheek.

Cary almost missed the fact that her mother's left arm was flesh and blood, though she completely forgot that observation when Tanis spoke to her.

"Faleena, my dear, you're so beautiful."

THE END

* * * * *

The war has spread over a hundred fronts, battles erupting across the stars. Tanis has become something more, and her most trusted ally may have been playing a far deeper game than she'd ever imagined.

Find out what happens next in the
War on a Thousand Fronts

THANK YOU

If you've enjoyed reading *Attack on Thebes*, a review on Amazon.com and/or goodreads.com would be greatly appreciated.

To get the latest news and access to free novellas and short stories, sign up on the Aeon 14 mailing list: www.aeon14.com/signup.

M. D. Cooper

THE BOOKS OF AEON 14

Keep up to date with what is releasing in Aeon 14 with the free Aeon 14 Reading Guide.

The Intrepid Saga
- Book 1: Outsystem
- Book 2: A Path in the Darkness
- Book 3: Building Victoria

- The Intrepid Saga Omnibus – *Also contains Destiny Lost, book 1 of the Orion War series*

- Destiny Rising – *Special Author's Extended Edition comprised of both Outsystem and A Path in the Darkness with over 100 pages of new content.*

The Orion War
- Book 1: Destiny Lost
- Book 2: New Canaan
- Book 3: Orion Rising
- Book 4: The Scipio Alliance
- Book 5: Attack on Thebes
- Book 6: The Thousand Front War (2018)
- Book 7: Fallen Empire (2018)
- Many more following

Tales of the Orion War
- Book 1: Set the Galaxy on Fire
- Book 2: Ignite the Stars (Feb 2018)
- Book 3: Burn the Galaxy to Ash (2018)

Perilous Alliance (Age of the Orion War - with Chris J. Pike)
- Book 1: Close Proximity
- Book 2: Strike Vector
- Book 3: Collision Course
- Book 4: Impact Imminent (April 2018)

Rika's Marauders (Age of the Orion War)
- Prequel: Rika Mechanized
- Book 1: Rika Outcast
- Book 2: Rika Redeemed
- Book 3: Rika Triumphant
- Book 4: Rika Commander (April 2018)
- Book 5: Rika Unleashed (2018)

Perseus Gate (Age of the Orion War)
Season 1: Orion Space
- Episode 1: The Gate at the Grey Wolf Star
- Episode 2: The World at the Edge of Space
- Episode 3: The Dance on the Moons of Serenity
- Episode 4: The Last Bastion of Star City
- Episode 5: The Toll Road Between the Stars
- Episode 6: The Final Stroll on Perseus's Arm
- Eps 1-3 Omnibus: The Trail Through the Stars
- Eps 4-6 Omnibus: The Path Amongst the Clouds

Season 2: The Inner Stars
- Episode 1: A Meeting of Bodies and Minds (Feb 2018)
- Episode 2: A Surreptitious Rescue of Friends and Foes (2018)
- More coming in 2018

The Warlord (Before the Age of the Orion War)
- Book 1: The Woman Without a World
- Book 2: The Woman Who Seized an Empire
- Book 3: The Woman Who Lost Everything (March 2018)

The Sentience Wars: Origins (With James S. Aaron)
- Book 1: Lyssa's Dream
- Book 2: Lyssa's Run
- Book 3: Lyssa's Flight
- Book 4: Lyssa's Call (2018)
- Book 5: Lyssa's Flame (2018)

Machete System Bounty Hunter (Age of the Orion War - with Zen DiPietro)
- Book 1: Hired Gun (Feb 2018)
- Book 2: Gunning for Trouble (2018)
- Book 3: With Guns Blazing (2018)

The Empire (Age of the Orion War)
- The Empress and the Ambassador (2018)
- Consort of the Scorpion Empress (2018)
- By the Empress's Command (2018)

Tanis Richards: Origins
- Prequel: Storming the Norse Wind (At the Helm Volume 3)
- Book 1: Shore Leave (June 2018)
- Book 2: The Command (June 2018)
- Book 3: Infiltrator (July 2018)

The Sol Dissolution
- The 242 - Venusian Uprising (The Expanding Universe 2 anthology)
- The 242 - Assault on Tarja (The Expanding Universe 3 anthology)

The Delta Team Chronicles (Expanded Orion War)
- A "Simple" Kidnapping (Pew! Pew! Volume 1)
- The Disknee World (Pew! Pew! Volume 2)
- It's Hard Being a Girl (Pew! Pew! Volume 4)
- A Fool's Gotta Feed (Pew! Pew! Volume 4)
- The Plot Thickens (Pew! Pew! Volume 5)

ABOUT THE AUTHOR

Michael Cooper likes to think of himself as a jack-of-all-trades (and hopes to become master of a few). When not writing, he can be found writing software, working in his shop at his latest carpentry project, or likely reading a book.

He shares his home with a precocious young girl, his wonderful wife (who also writes), two cats, a never-ending list of things he would like to build, and ideas…

Find out what's coming next at http://www.aeon14.com

CPSIA information can be obtained
at www.ICGtesting.com
Printed in the USA
LVOW11s2305060518
576247LV00001B/77/P